Engagement

GUN-BRITT SUNDSTRÖM

Engagement

Translated by Kathy Saranpa

PENGUIN BOOKS

PENGUIN CLASSICS

UK | USA | Canada | Ireland | Australia
India | New Zealand | South Africa

Penguin Classics is part of the Penguin Random House group of companies
whose addresses can be found at global.penguinrandomhouse.com.

Penguin Random House UK
One Embassy Gardens, 8 Viaduct Gardens, London SW11 7BW

penguin.co.uk

First published by Albert Bonniers Förlag, Stockholm, Sweden
First published in Great Britain by Penguin Classics 2025
Published in the English language by arrangement with Bonnier Rights,
Stockholm, Sweden
001

The cost of this translation was supported by a subsidy from the Swedish
Arts Council, gratefully acknowledged.

Set in 11.25/14pt Dante MT Std
Typeset by Jouve (UK), Milton Keynes
Printed and bound in Great Britain by Clays Ltd, Elcograf S.p.A.

The authorized representative in the EEA is Penguin Random House Ireland,
Morrison Chambers, 32 Nassau Street, Dublin D02 YH68

A CIP catalogue record for this book is available from the British Library

ISBN: 978-0-241-68812-0

Penguin Random House is committed to a sustainable future
for our business, our readers and our planet. This book is made from
Forest Stewardship Council® certified paper.

Translator's Note

Almost all of the action in this book takes place in Stockholm, the capital of Sweden. Sometimes called the 'Venice of the North', it's located on the Baltic Sea and spreads over countless islands, including the archipelago to the east.

Where I felt that something may not be understandable to English readers because of the Swedish cultural context, I've added a footnote. All footnotes are translator additions. All Bible quotes are taken from the King James Version.

Martina and her friend Cilla study English; they (and other characters) often use English phrases for effect in the middle of Swedish conversations. I have underlined these phrases to preserve this effect.

K.S.

Translator's Dedication

To Maija

Imagine the fright it would cause if, from time to time, people were to fall down dead or were gripped by convulsions without anyone being able to provide a reason for it. This is how love enters people's lives, with the difference that nobody becomes anxious, and the lovers themselves consider it to be the pinnacle of happiness. On the other hand, we laugh at it, because the comic and the tragic stand in unremitting correspondence to each other therein.

Marry and you will regret it; do not marry and you will regret that too; marry or do not marry, you will regret both; whether you marry or do not marry, you will regret both.

Søren Kierkegaard

I

There's a note on my desk: 'Gustav called'.

Gustav. Do I know any Gustavs? The note's on my desk, so I must be the one this Gustav called. I'll have to ask my landlady when she comes back if he said what he wanted. I hang my jacket on the back of my chair and start to sort through my books. Since it's Friday, the cleaning woman has been here to disorganize my belongings as usual. On the bottom of the pile, I finally locate *Pride and Prejudice*, but I find myself standing there with that note again. It's the way it's formulated that irritates me: as if I *ought* to know who this Gustav is. What a ridiculous name, by the way – Gustav!

I ransack my memory. Is this the fellow who chatted me up out at Blockhusudden yesterday? Did he say what his name was? In any event, I didn't say my name, so he can't possibly have my phone number. Gustav. Oh yes, the fellow who was sitting across the table from us at Café Valand after the most recent lecture – maybe his name was Gustav. I try to reconstruct the evening so I can guess what he wants. Cilla had gone to sit at Bengt's table since she knows him from high school, and I took a seat next to her. Then another fellow came and sat next to Bengt. I can't remember what he looked like – blond or dark, tall or short? I don't remember much of the conversation, either. Probably mostly about the lecture topic, as it usually is when you go out for a coffee afterwards. We stood there on Surbrunnsgatan and talked to Bengt for a bit, and then I walked off with Cilla, who was going to the subway. Where this Gustav went to, I really have no clue.

All right then, so that's who he is. But now he's looking for me. I wonder what's on his mind? Shameful intentions, I think to myself, satisfied, and spread out on the bed with Jane Austen. In that case, he's sure to call again.

When the telephone rings in the hall, I still haven't heard the landlady return, so I slip a pipe cleaner in the book to mark my place and go answer. 'Gustav Lindgren,' he introduces himself and wonders if I remember who he is. Of course I do. Have I seen *Godot* at the Dramatic Theatre? I haven't. Am I planning to see it? Certainly not – isn't Beckett boring? But I allow myself to be convinced otherwise when Gustav guarantees that it's the most amusing play I'll ever see.

In order to get our student discount, we'll both have to show up with our IDs at the ticket window. We agree to meet there at four o'clock. My bike has a flat, so I have to walk and have barely enough time for a war dance. So I take small war steps along the way instead. The linden trees on Strandvägen already look greener than when I passed by a couple of hours ago. It goes so fast that you can hardly keep up with it. I stop to admire them for a bit so I'll arrive no earlier than four.

He's sitting on a bench at the back of the lobby, reading a newspaper. He stands up when I arrive. Very tall and gangly, with short, light red hair, and that pale skin that redheads often have. He looks childlike, a beardless youth, but he dresses like an old man: hat and coat. He gives the general impression of a high school student from the 1950s. And now I remember that I've actually noticed him before, during a lecture earlier this spring, because his appearance irritated me: he looks superior, arrogant.

Now, I admonish myself quickly, don't judge a book by its

cover. He may well have something to be arrogant about. Maybe he's actually far better than the rest of the crowd. Or maybe nature just made his facial expressions and posture that way. And that's not his fault. The fact that he wants to go to the theatre with me must, all things considered, speak in his favour.

We decide on the Tuesday performance and pay for our tickets. I was planning to head to the library afterwards; he's going home and lives in that direction, so we take the No. 7 tram together. We make awkward conversation on the most logical topics – the post-seminar we attended, our studies in general. He's younger than I am – not twenty yet. He's majoring in philosophy, and he wonders why I'm going to the lectures just for fun.

'Cilla was the one who lured me along,' I explain. 'She's also auditing out of pure interest.'

'So you're classmates in English, correct?'

'That's what they say. You should probably call us skip-mates instead. We used to go to Café Ogo around the same time every week, and then we discovered that it was because we were skipping the same lectures. And that we had the same opinion of the professor.' I tell him about Cilla's childhood in the US and my own year in England. I add somewhat apologetically that we're simply fishing for easy credits and that's why we're studying such a boring subject.

'What were you doing in England? Were you an *au pair*?'

I shake my head. Me, an *au pair*? Never! (When I hear the word 'housekeeping', I bare my fangs.) 'I was studying English and sowing my wild oats.'

The tram bell clangs during the silence my comment has apparently caused.

'What will you be when you grow up, then?'

'I don't plan on growing any more than I already have,' I answer curtly. What does he have to do with my future? It's a subject I avoid with everyone, including myself. The tram clatters around the corner of Odengatan. He looks out the window. I sit looking at his hands. A man's hands. Men have such large hands.

*

Gustav calls on Tuesday morning and asks me what we should do now. What do you mean? A notice in the paper says that *Godot*'s been cancelled due to illness. Bother, I hadn't seen that. They're presenting something called *Anatol* instead, he enlightens me, 'an erotic comedy'. He places the decision in my hands, and I think it makes the most sense to go anyway since we already have the tickets.

It isn't until the performance is underway that I understand what a grave error I've committed: he must have got the impression that I was so eager to go to the theatre with him that I was ready to see anything at all just to have that chance. A strange development: the idea of going to the theatre was his, it was supposed to be his responsibility, and here I sit, the one who's embarrassed about the play! You never understand how you end up in such situations. I comfort myself with the thought that I've worn my ratty duffle coat, so at least he can't claim that I've primped for him.

Afterwards we stand at Nybro Square asking each other if we know a good pub. We don't. Well, what do you know: something we have in common. He suggests that I come to his place for tea and sandwiches instead. All of my collected wisdom tells me this is a fellow who means tea and sandwiches when he says tea and sandwiches, so we take the No. 7 again.

He lives on Bragevägen, a tiny street set back behind Jarlaplan – a neighbourhood I've never walked. It's apparently his childhood home, but none of his family members are in. I take the opportunity to sneak around a bit while he putters in the kitchen. There's some kind of icon hanging on the wall in the living room, and the library hints that they're religious. Is Gustav as well? That would explain why he looks so abnormally clean-cut. A large library, by the way – one complete wall of shelves. A sofa group and a piano with family photos on it. A young bridal couple – one of his siblings? – and Gustav in his student cap, of course.

The windows in his room face the interior courtyard, but he sets the table in the living room. And we drink tea and we eat sandwiches and we make conversation, torturously. I ask about the wedding photo. Yes, that's his brother Erik. He's an engineer and lives in Västerås now. Not because the question excites me, but mostly in order to say something, I ask him what he plans to be.

He answers hesitantly: 'I plan to study literary history after philosophy.'

'Oh, a teacher.'

'Not if I can avoid it, but I probably can't.'

'Not with those subjects. In order to avoid that fate, you have to come up with some completely impossible combination, like mine.'

'Are you studying something besides English?'

'First I studied Old Norse Culture for a while. I'd seen a film about the digs at Öland and thought it would be so pleasant to have a job where you can be outdoors.' He laughs as expected, and I add that I pretty quickly realized that that wasn't what archaeologists do. What they do is sit in small cubicles and catalogue things.

Then it becomes quiet for a long time until he says, 'You're so quiet.' I'm certainly not the only one in that case. I'm really trying my best to make conversation, and by the way, I could be using my time better.

'Would you like more tea?' he asks. I tell him thank you, it was lovely, but I really should . . .

Just as I'm making my departure, his parents come home, and Gustav introduces us in the hallway. They're friendly and their faces say 'Ah, so this is Martina!' I try to make a face that says 'Absolutely not, or rather, it's not the one you think if you actually think anything', but it's so hard to mould facial expressions into such complicated denials. It simply ends up as a rather dour-looking grimace.

He follows me home despite my protests – as if I needed an escort just because it's late! He follows me all the way to the door of my building. Of course, of course I would have screamed if he'd tried to kiss me. But to be honest, it's just as horrible that he's standing there with puppy-dog eyes, one metre away, and wants to do it but doesn't make a move. So I scream because of that instead, all the way up the four flights of stairs to my room.

*

'Did you say Gustav?' Cilla says.

I nod.

'Is that really his name?'

'Not only that. He *is* one, too,' I say gloomily, stealing one of Cilla's cigarettes. 'A real Gustav if I've ever seen one.'

She patiently hands me her lighter. 'Aha, then. <u>So the bell tolls for you</u>.'

'Who said that?' I exclaim. 'He's the one on that track, not me!'

'So what track are you on, then?'

'Why can't I go to the theatre with him now and again? Just to get together, I mean. It's not a bad idea to broaden one's circle of acquaintances from time to time.'

Cilla's face says she's heard this before, and she has. As recently as this autumn, she witnessed my difficulties 'breaking up' with someone I didn't even know I'd started a relationship with. It's something you glide into, stealthily and insidiously, and somehow you never find the right moment to make your position clear: 'Listen, you have to understand that I don't feel anything for you in that way, but we can be friends, can't we?'

It's only in those old-fashioned novels that they ever get an opportunity to make such declarations.

'Watch out, Martina. You know that boys only want one thing.'

'I know, but now that I know that *I* don't, I can be on my guard more effectively. I've come to this realization, you know: that you don't *have* to pair off. Maybe it's even better to live alone.'

Cilla doesn't say anything – but I can read her face. But I really mean it, even if the insight still surprises me. For such a long time you go around thinking that when you grow up, you'll get married and have children. So many long, difficult years when it's your wild, fervent, sole desire to find someone to do it with. And once you're finally old enough and such a person reports for duty, you discover that it isn't what you want after all. And first you believe that it's the wrong man you've got a hold of. But my most recent insight is this: the entire idea is wrong.

At the same time, men my age seem to have gone in the opposite direction. This is now the only thing they think about – getting married. In any case, that's how it's been in all the relationships I've seen around me. It's the man who's nagged and nagged until he got his engagement or wedding or moving-in-together. You could probably construct prolix theories about the socio-economic background of this phenomenon, if you had the time.

I have to go. I snag Cilla's last cigarette as I stand up. 'On my way to the seven o'clock at Bostock Theatre.'

'With your husband?' Cilla teases.

'With Gustav,' I say with dignity. 'We're just friends.'

'Him too?'

That, of course, is the sore point. I have to remember that and give him not so much as my little finger.

I arrive with plenty of time to spare, but Gustav is already there. We look at the posters outside. He's seen *Viridiana* before and giggles in recognition. I almost have to slap my hand over his mouth so that he doesn't give the whole film away. It's a small, pleasant cinema, with hard wooden benches and a break for a film-roll change in the middle of the performance. It's a strange movie, about the fiasco of self-sacrificing human love. I can't remember when I've been so captivated by a film. But Gustav mostly giggles.

Just when the audience heaves a sigh of relief after the drugged novice escapes being raped by her crazy uncle, I realize that Gustav is fumbling in my lap for my hand. What should I do? Put it behind my back? Slap him, laugh at him, begin an explanatory declaration: 'Dear Gustav, you must understand . . .' You don't have time to think that far. The only thing you have time for is your heart skipping a beat. And so we sit there holding hands. With a skipping heart.

Of course it doesn't help that I say goodbye quickly and bike off. One moment of weakness and the marital contract is as good as sealed. No, I say, no, I don't want it. We will have no more marriage. I never want to see him again.

*

As the semester progresses, the lectures in philosophy attract ever larger audiences. Many of the listeners are actually studying something else but are drawn in out of pure fascination – all kinds of people, from language students to future engineers.

One evening, when the topic is Kierkegaard and the 'leap of faith', I take a wrong turn on my bike and don't wake up until I'm on the Karlaplan Circle and don't know which way to go. No, such things don't happen after lectures in phonetics or material mechanics. Such a thing has never happened to me before.

Even so, there are few enough people that it retains the camaraderie of a small department. After the evening lectures, teachers and their disciples go out together. For the last post-seminar we go to Old Bowler, a completely unlikely pub that looks like the hall of a train station. I'm sitting there looking around and loving what I have before me: crazy idealists with beards and burning glances as far as the eye can see, pacifists, socialists, existentialists, vegetarians – at one end of the table they're talking about the starving millions in India, and at the other the topic is Luther's doctrine of reconciliation. Somewhere in the middle, Vietnam is on the agenda. Directly opposite me, the teacher is occupied with a question the fellow next to him has posed: if there's anything in the Western cultural inheritance that you cannot find elsewhere and which he thinks is worth preserving. He answers by talking about the concept of 'personality', the individual who is unique and something more than merely a part of the collective.

I love them, I find myself thinking – as I sit there, I realize I love all human beings. Such a thing has never happened to me before.

*

I don't believe people should use their summers for studying. That's when you should only read for pleasure. I toss my book on the history of the English language in a cardboard box which I leave in my landlady's closet, and in my suitcase I pack *Either/Or* and *Ethics and Language*. Since I don't intend to take any credits in philosophy, this is by definition reading for pleasure. You shouldn't destroy fun subjects by hunting credits for them. That's when crass utilitarian thinking comes into play and you find yourself counting pages and wondering what you'll need to remember.

Of course, I have to think about making a living, too. Cilla's going to work the lingerie counter at Tempo, but I think you should be outdoors during your summer holiday. I have a long-standing, good relationship with the cemetery maintenance association back home, and it's easier to take it up again than to find a new job in Stockholm.

I have my mail forwarded. One morning I find an envelope on the shelf above the phone, written in my hand. I assume it's notification of the book I ordered through interlibrary loan from Lund and make an irritated comment about 'oho, now you show up, now that I'm on holiday.' But in mid-complaint I realize that it's not a notice from the library at all, but a letter, and not written by me, but by Gustav Lindgren. He's in Paris and tells me he's finally seen the love of his life: Athena at Olympia, a metope relief from the Zeus Temple, now on display in the Louvre.

He's probably seen *Pimpernel Smith* too many times, I think, and hide the letter in a desk drawer. I don't harbour any superstitions regarding handwriting, and I don't plan on considering him my soulmate just because he has the cheek to possess a hand so like my own that it even fooled me.

But more mail from him arrives. A postcard, another letter, and the following week one more. They are cultivated, articulate letters, yes indeed; what I object to is their relationship to me. Every line shouts that the person writing them is imagining me as the recipient, the addressee, the object of the missive. True – how are you supposed to write letters otherwise? But what I mean is this: the letters are drafted with A Woman in mind and during the act of writing he was full of the thought of himself as Writing to A Woman. I admit that I don't read them free of vain delight, but I've decided that I have nothing to say in response to such discourse.

In the first letter, he added the address of the hotel where he's staying. I don't write. I devote myself actively and deliberately to not writing – all the more deliberately the more letters I receive. I try to time it so that I'm home when the postman comes so my family doesn't see too much of my mail and get curious. But once I start at the cemetery, my breaks don't work out that way. One afternoon, there's an envelope on the shelf above the phone again, with a French stamp, and the sender neatly indicated.

'A classmate,' I mutter when Mum makes enquiries.

*

After my letter campaign (my campaign of no letters), I assume that Gustav won't contact me again. *Au contraire*: as soon as he returns from abroad, he asks my landlady for my phone number, and one day during my lunch break, as I'm sitting with my yoghurt and the comics from the local paper, Gustav calls and asks, 'Why haven't you written to me?'

You can't tell someone that you've engaged in not-writing to get rid of them – you can't just stand there and say that. Even if you're ruthless enough to do so, you're at least too well behaved. So I say I've been too busy and had many other things to think about.

He snorts over the phone. 'What would you have had to think about?'

It's the worst thing I've ever heard. Like, 'What could you possibly have to worry your little curly head about?'

'I'm working, actually,' I say in my least polite voice.

He's at his family's summer cottage in the archipelago just now, and later he's going to go sailing, but on the weekend he's coming into the city and thinks I should meet him. I have no place to stay in Stockholm, I explain. I only rent the room on Grevgatan during the school year. Gustav thinks I can make a day trip in. I talk about 'train schedules', which I feel is a term that commands respect. I describe a trip into the city as a wildly inconvenient and demanding effort, something you don't undertake unless there's a dire need. I think he ought to understand that he does not constitute such a need. He doesn't give up until I suggest that I'll get in touch once I've moved back for the autumn term.

That's a fine solution; I hang up very satisfied. Now the ball is in my court. I can call if I want to, and I can also simply not. We'll see. Relieved, I return to raking the graves.

★

But men are inscrutable. Doesn't he understand anything or does he simply refuse to acknowledge it? I haven't been back in the city for a week when the landlady calls me to the telephone: 'Martina, there's a gentleman who wishes to speak to you.'

Gentleman – there's only one person in my circle of acquaintances who would be able to sound like a gentleman. I answer curtly and in a hurry, as if I've been torn away from something very important and can't wait to get back to it: 'Yes?'

'Hi, it's Gustav. I just wanted to hear if you got the programme I sent you for the teach-in next weekend.'

'Oh yes, it was nice of you to send it. Thanks.'

'Are you thinking of going?'

'I won't have time to be there for the entire event, but I'm sure I'll pop in.

'So we might see each other,' I add.

He understands that this is a way of saying goodbye. To be honest, I've read through the programme carefully and ticked what I want to go hear. However, I don't have to reveal to him my guiding principles. I tick the lectures and give myself breaks during the panel debates, which are the most boring thing I know. The participants only become polemic and aggressive and you don't leave any smarter than when you arrived. But the lectures are another thing. You can learn something from them, and my need to learn is boundless.

The most effective means of acquiring knowledge is, of course, to read, but from time to time it's nice to see people, too. There's a colourful crowd in Folkets Hus, coffee on offer and book sales and Vietnam bulletins outside the hall where the programme is in progress.

At this point, my relationship with Gustav has entered the

most pleasant phase possible: he's finally realized that there isn't any relationship, so now he's keeping his distance and there's just an interesting Tension between us.

'You must be a deviating minority,' Cilla says when I describe this state of affairs.

'Wouldn't you like to be the object of an infatuation at a distance? Flattering and utterly without obligation. It's certainly nothing abnormal to enjoy that there's someone in the room who notices when I come and go.'

'You must be noticing when he comes and goes too, since you're so well-informed about what he notices.'

Well, yes. There's that. I notice him particularly on Sunday morning when he arrives in jeans and a turtleneck and suddenly looks like a normal person. (A suit with pressed trousers makes me impotent, but jeans are attractive almost no matter who's wearing them.) And the more I notice, the more I wonder. He never makes comments during the general discussion, but he laughs a lot. I mean really laughs – at what's being said. During a party politics debate when a Social Democrat talks about aid to Third World countries and the one-percent goal, Gustav giggles and I become embarrassed and angry. Why? Do I have anything to do with the fact that he's sitting there grinning?

I leave the party panel to its fate, grab my jacket in the vestibule and am on my way down the stairs when Gustav approaches me. A few people are going out to have a bite to eat, he informs me, and asks if I would like to . . . Yes, I'd love to. I think going to dinner is a bourgeois notion, as if you have to be eating all the time, but I like going out. And, admittedly, the stubbornness of his courtship has begun to arouse my curiosity. He can't be so stupid that he doesn't understand that I'm trying to reject him – he seems rather sharp otherwise. The conclusion I draw is that he thinks I'm foolish in doing so, that he knows better. And if he can convince me of that – well, let's see!

We go to Old Bowler with Bengt and a couple of others from the philosophy department. We talk about the teach-in, and Gustav says basically what I was thinking: that the lectures were what counted. He imitates the speakers, rather skilfully, though I think it's a little inappropriate.

Wine is served with dinner, and by the time we start to go our own ways, my attitude towards the world is so benevolent and I'm so sleepily defenceless that I forget how nice it was to keep Gustav at a distance – that perfect tension-creating distance – and allow him to accompany me to the No. 4. When the tram comes, he gets on as well, and I think it's silly of course, since he doesn't live in my direction, but that's his affair.

After we alight at my stop, we walk slowly through empty streets. The night is clear, the August moon as full as an egg . . . I mean, as yellow as an egg and full, and the sky – what you can see of it between the roofs – is sprinkled with stars. I point out Orion with its belt, and Gustav says he knows nothing about stars. He lays his arm around my shoulders and I lean against him, hoping sleepily that he won't misunderstand: Just this time, <u>mind you</u>, I think to myself. (It's not something you can say aloud, although it would be good if you could.)

At my door, I let him hold my bag while I look in my pockets for my key. When I've found it and stretch out my hand to take my bag, he pulls me into his arms and we kiss. It's a good kiss. Above us there are stars. It's completely sparkly with stars. The bag is between us. I take it, unlock the door and say goodnight.

2

'Settling in' – what an odd phrase. It could apply to so many situations. Hell on earth is what it is. When Harriet proposed that we share a flat in a condemned building on Frejgatan – one she got through the student housing agency – I accepted without a moment's hesitation. It's only once I've settled in that I realize what a good situation I had in my rented room. Being property-less: freedom from property! Other people's furniture, paintings and rugs – nothing you had to care about.

Harriet's flat is unfurnished except for three beer crates someone left behind, so now we have to find beds and desks and bookcases, pack dishes and unpack them, measure for curtains and mount curtains and arrange the books in their shelves – how abruptly we've been tossed into the temporal world! We have to order electricity as well – I didn't know you had to subscribe to electricity and water, I just thought they were there – and a telephone and devise a system for splitting the bills, and bring home wood for the stove and kerosene for the heater . . . the tasks pile up without end.

But once the practical evils have been disposed with, I find that I've improved my lot after all. The location is better, near Vanadislunden: closer to the department and the library and the student union and everything. It makes me less dependent, of course. We don't intend to mix our households – both Harriet and I are naturally so concerned about our privacy that we'll probably see less of each other, now that we're living in close quarters, out of pure caution – which will be the least time we've spent together since we met in primary school. When we take a break from our interior decoration efforts to play a game of chess, we decide to sit in the kitchen – although this is probably less in order to avoid violating each other's personal space and more because it's the only room with a table and chairs.

I get up to find something to drink while Harriet considers her next move, when the doorbell rings – it's from the florist. For me? I take the package into my room, terrified, and unwrap the paper. I think, not a red rose, not a red rose, please, anything but a red rose, and unwrap a red rose. I dash into the kitchen and find something to put it in. When Harriet asks, I say it's for my name day, although she ought to know as well as I do that my name's not Justus.

Something must have happened to me, I think. Before, I wouldn't have snuck around like this, like a co-conspirator. I would have sounded a blood-curdling cry, jumped up and shouted, 'Can you imagine what Gustav's done now!' Maybe I've become old and mature and tolerant. Yes indeed, I'm trying to get used to the notion that someone is walking around thinking that red roses are lovely and a man is imagining himself as Giving a Rose to a Woman. Of course, you have to understand them, too. What I can't understand is why they are giving them to *me*. I don't know what to do with courtship. I don't know how to behave when you're a cult idol.

Once I relegate the flower to a beer bottle, I discover a card as well. At the top it says *Eccl. 7:26*. Well now. This is a more original form of wooing – using Bible verses. That's never happened to me before. I wonder what the verse says, but I don't have a Bible handy. Underneath, he asks me to come help him with ideas about the paper he's working on: 'Nobody I've asked so far has understood my draft. If you don't either, I'll have to write a new one. Can you drop by around seven?'

The words 'drop by' irritate me because they're overly familiar, but otherwise it's entirely too flattering to resist. He thinks *I* would have opinions about *his* philosophy paper! Which nobody else understands! We don't have a landline yet, so I go down to the tobacconist and call to say that I can come by at eight, possibly. It's only a couple blocks there, but I make a detour to the library so I can look up the verse in a reference Bible. Ecclesiastes, seven, twenty-seven:

And I find more bitter than death the woman, whose heart is snares and nets, and her hands as bands: whoso pleaseth God shall escape from her; but the sinner shall be taken by her.

It gives me something to ponder as I pedal off towards Bragevägen. Maybe I could most easily make my position clear by sending him an answer in the form of another appropriate quote. 'We will have no more marriage' – doesn't the Bible allude to this at some point? But I don't know where. And on the other hand, his own choice of quote shows that he knows what he's getting into and is doing so at his own peril.

Just as it begins to rain, I park my bicycle against the side of the building and dash into the entrance. Gustav opens the door himself and shows me into his room. As I step in, I have such a feeling of cosiness. Cosiness, or what should I say – peace? Heavy, old-fashioned furniture; no overhead fixture but warm, yellow light from a lamp on the desk. A small gramophone on the floor plays muted music, Bessie Smith (was he listening to it when I arrived or did he select it to create a mood?). It's so cosy, so yellow and cosy, and the window with the dark outside. I curl up among a dozen soft pillows on the large bed. He cranks the paper out of his typewriter, turns off the music, settles himself in the armchair next to the lamp and starts to read to me. He's writing about Aristotle's metamorphosis of Plato's doctrine of ideas, about form and material and about change as a transition from possibility to reality . . .

I'm trying to listen, I'm really making an effort to listen and understand, but I've always had a hard time following along when people read, and when the person reading keeps interjecting self-ironic comments about the presentation to boot, it's impossible. My attention is being diverted around the room in all directions. There's so much to see and take in: the tile oven with shining hatches. The yellow light of the lamp. A painting – a Chagall reproduction? The crucifix above the bookshelf. The raindrops against the windowsill. The bells from Engelbrekt Church – two, three, four – eight.

'Or what do you think?'

I make an effort to collect my thoughts, try to find the red thread, but it's too difficult. He's reading it as if the listener knows what it's about – it's not for the uninitiated.

Light-grey, buttoned-up shirt. Blue jeans. Belt. Boy, I think. 'Boy'. A boy's body inside.

'I think it would be better if I read it myself,' I say carefully. He hands me the paper and sits next to me on the bed. This doesn't make it easier for me to understand his paper, either.

I pace the floor back and forth in my new room, still in complete chaos after the move. Back and forth between the window and the bookcase. What on earth is this? Hormones? Urges, animal urges, me?

It's confusing. I've been in love just like everyone else, constantly, since I was twelve. I'm familiar with being in love in all of its forms except for one: the sexual. Sex was something that was a part of it all, something you had to accept – but wanting it yourself? That's something I've never experienced. Is it true, then, that it's something that comes with age? Or is it just because Gustav is the first one who's ever given me the opportunity to have the idea first without beating me to it? And why, in that case? Why isn't he seducing me? What does he want?

If it were really true that he wanted my opinion now, he apparently asked the wrong person. I borrowed his paper and took it home, and I've read it carefully two times and think I understand it quite well, but I don't have any opinions on it, and certainly no useful objections.

★

'Well, well,' says Cilla. 'So you've fallen in love.'

'Who said I was in love?' I exclaim. 'I'm in lust, which is something entirely different, and, in my case, much more interesting.'

'Is that so,' says Cilla.

'He's not a communist is he, this Gustav?' my father says. I make a gesture that says 'Is it any of my business what he is? Can't I come home on a weekend without being interrogated about my classmate's possible political affiliations?' I gnaw with deep concentration on my pork chop bone, but, to be honest, there's no meat left on it at all.

'What do you mean, communist?'

I don't say this just to dismiss the topic but rather because I'm not really sure what a communist is, but it sounded so brusque that I have to tidy things up a bit and say, 'I guess he's some kind of socialist.'

That's when my mother starts in too. Both my parents chime in with the usual song-and-dance about all of these 'intellectuals' who promote propaganda for socialism and the oppression of free speech until I give in: 'Please, social democracy is a form of socialism too, isn't it?' – and stop short, mad at myself for allowing myself to be drawn into this discussion. Imagine if someone heard me: sitting at the dinner table arguing politics with her old parents – a long-haired little girl hardly dry behind the ears who's been to the big city and heard some ideas – no, this is a situation I wouldn't want to be caught bare-handed in. Particularly since I'm so unsure about it all that I don't even have a clear sense of the concepts myself. Oppression of free speech? What? Gustav, a communist?

Not because it really has anything to do with me, but I need to untangle the concepts for myself.

★

When I come out the door at Odengatan after taking an exam, I see Gustav standing on the steps. Has he been waiting for me? I greet him reservedly. He doesn't think we have anything going on, does he? He says he had a test yesterday too and thinks we should celebrate. He suggests lunch in the old steamship docked near Skeppsbron.

'How are we supposed to get there?' I answer crossly – people always assume you're ready to abandon your bicycle whenever they want so you can stand at a stop with them, as if life isn't too precious to waste priceless minutes waiting for public transportation.

'How about Sveavägen, Hamngatan, Strömbron?' he suggests, putting his book bag in the bicycle basket next to mine.

'You mean you bike too?' My astonishment is as sincere as my joy.

He snorts 'Do I bike too?' and allows me to understand that he's done nothing else, long before I started riding in this city.

'Well in *that* case.' He throws a leg over the frame as you do on men's bicycles and darts out into the right lane; I have trouble keeping up with him.

We eat a buffet lunch on the decommissioned steamboat *Norrtelje* with a view through the window of Strömmen. We eat herring salad and talk about techniques for sexual intercourse. Or rather, the word 'technique'. In his study of Aristoteles,

Gustav has come to the realization that it's entirely wrong to talk about technique in this context.

' *"Techne"* is knowledge that applies to *poiesis*, activities that involve producing something, building a house for example. But activities that are a goal in and of themselves, *praxis*, are governed by *phronesis*. Playing the flute is Aristoteles' example of *phronesis*.'

'And sex is more like playing the flute then, is that what you mean?'

'Yes, isn't it?'

I think for a moment. 'But if you're trying to make a baby, then "technique" would be the correct word, wouldn't it?'

'If you like, but that's not usually the way it's used. As it's used in the evening papers and in spoken language, that activity seems to be less important than the goal of producing an orgasm. Thus it's a means to that end, not something that is meaningful otherwise. There's no word for *phronesis* in Swedish. Which is typical.'

I am deeply impressed.

'You're not going to tell me you're reading Aristotle in the original Greek, are you?'

'Well, in the Loeb edition with parallel text in English. It's called "prudence" there.'

I'm terribly impressed, and rather curious about what these unusual insights would look like in reality. In *praxis*, I mean.

*

At the evening seminar, a guest lecturer from Uppsala is speaking about a detail problem in logic formalization that doesn't succeed in capturing my interest. Gustav slides his notebook across the table to me asking if I want to go have a coffee afterwards. I write in response, 'OK. Are you as bored as I am?' The notebook comes back with an X in the middle of the page. Graph paper – how foresightful. With my gaze firmly fixed on the blackboard – as if copying the formula for equivalence – I draw a circle next to it.

Our third game of tic-tac-toe, after we've each won one, is undecided when the lecture ends. Several of us go off to Café Valand, but rather than sit with the others, we take a table for two further in, behind a planter box full of plastic flowers. We each order a vacuum cleaner, as the cheapest pastries are usually called (a green oblong with each end dipped in chocolate) and start to talk about the Kierkegaard lectures last term. We discuss the aesthetic personality who lives free of responsibility precisely the way he wishes, simply chasing 'experiences', and about the ethical one who Chooses and gives his life a moral meaning. And in this plastic café on Surbrunnsgatan, while the television natters in the corner, I discover that we can actually talk to each other. We speak the same language and we understand what we're saying. This amazes me: why hadn't I realized this before?

'It's because you're full of prejudices,' Gustav explains.

'How can you survive if you can't simplify your existence with a few protective prejudices? You'd be completely overwhelmed by the sheer diversity of life.'

'That may be, but you have the wrong prejudices. You have a whole mass of foolish complexes about what's "bourgeois", for example. You care about what people look like, as if clothes were at all significant.'

Maybe that's what's blinded me. Now, in any event, I'm setting aside my preconceived notions and beginning from the beginning. Gustav: who is he?

He's religious, but in terms of denomination completely promiscuous: he goes to any church he likes, seems to read the service announcements as you'd read cinema schedules and worships with the Catholics and the Quakers and at the Rosenius Church and I don't know what. If there was a mosque with a good speaker, he'd be certain to go there as well. I've never seen anything like it; when I was in high school, those who were 'religious' were members of a particular denomination. If you were a Baptist, that's all you were, and you had nothing to do with the high-church Lutheran club at school. That's not the only thing that's confusing. He maintains the same odd distance from his religion as he does from his politics, and he's happy to mock his own idols. He imitates his favourite preachers just as disrespectfully as he mimics his university teachers. He cites Dostoevsky with delighted guffaws.

He says he hasn't been interested in politics that long – only since he began studying philosophy, and Vietnam of course. His socialism basically seems to be the same idea as his Christianity – simply something to do with love. (Simply!) I explain that I've been looking for an ideology in this direction. I recently went to the library and borrowed *The History of Socialism* by someone named Beer which seems to inspire confidence – he doesn't seem to be a communist – but it's a new direction for me. The author I've read just as much as Gustav has read Dostoevsky is Sandemose, who's no paragon of brotherly love – quite the opposite. But when I slip into that attitude, when disdainful comments about ordinary people slip out of my mouth, Gustav chastises me, and I accept it – until I forget the next time.

Can you learn to love systematically?

We speak the same language, we understand what we're saying, but we don't always agree. When we approach the topic of the kind of love known as the great one, we're not in agreement. I talk about integrity and dignity and interaction between peers and of the necessity of maintaining one's independence. Gustav talks about self-sacrifice.

'"For whosoever will save his life shall lose it,"' he quotes, '"and whosoever will lose his life for my sake shall find it" – *psyche* is the word used, which is closer rather to "oneself".'

'The one who loses his life for his sake, yes, but it doesn't mean for the sake of other people, in any case not just for one person.'

'Why not?'

'Really? Well, fine.'

Oneself? Sacrifice yourself? No longer be simply and completely and finally Martina, but lose myself and be dissolved, change – is that possible?

'Well, that's all just metaphysics. Everything we call love, it's just an invention of sorts – metaphysical structures on top of the physical realities.'

'Of course they're structures,' Gustav answers calmly. 'How can you live without metaphysics if you can't even live without prejudices? Love is a metaphysical invention that you either choose or don't choose.'

He looks dreamily at me across the table with the empty coffee cups, and to my surprise, I don't feel the urge to run away, but rather that he's a mirror of my gaze.

That's when he asks abruptly: 'Why didn't you write me last summer?'

This time I have to answer, and this time it's possible, although difficult: 'Because I didn't want, you to think, that, we were, a couple.' I sigh deeply after I finally get it out, and add, in the most tender voice I can muster: '*If* I wanted to be with anyone, it would be with you.'

He doesn't ask why I don't want to be a couple, so I don't get the chance to explain myself – he simply laughs, and the café closes so we have to leave. But when we walk our bikes across Sveavägen – walk them so that we can hold hands – he begins to tease me: 'Aren't you afraid I'm going to think something now?' And when I've locked my bike and am waiting for him to kiss me in the doorway (with feigned worry): 'But think of the neighbours! They could get the idea . . .'

I groan – how many times am I going to have to eat this up?

He looks at me and shakes his head, expressing his amazement that he's fallen for me in particular.

'I mean, you're not particularly nice or anything.'

He says it in an easy tone, but without thinking about it. I get the feeling that it's a strange statement. It sounds so uniquely hopeful: 'You're not particularly nice.'

*

On Saturday night, I had planned on inviting some old acquaintances to my new home, but Gustav is going out to the archipelago and wonders if I want to come along. And it occurs to me that I'm actually quite tired of my old acquaintances. It's not appropriate for us to spend the night, of course, he says. I assume he's joking and say that I don't have to worry about anyone but myself. Since the connections this time of year are scheduled so far apart, we'd simply be going out and turning around to come back. Taking the bus from Jarlaplan on Saturday morning, back with the boat from Hummelmora on Sunday evening – that sounds good, I think, after studying his schedules.

Gustav's parents, however, don't think it sounds good at all. They won't let us go unless we have a chaperone along, he tells me on the phone on Friday, so now he's talked to his brother, too, and by the way, they wondered if I've told my parents about our plans.

I'm so shocked that I start to hiccough. My parents? Chaperone? Gustav's brother, who doesn't even live in Stockholm: does he have to make the whole trip just so . . . ? Am I the one who's crazy, or is it them? Have I lived in freak circles in which all the ideas about what's appropriate in bourgeois society have been turned on their heads so that I can no longer tell the difference? Or have I simply happened to fall into an enclave of residual nineteenth-century etiquette? What are they thinking?

I'm an adult and single and independent (on government loans, of course), I have a flat where we're free to wallow in lust and lechery for days on end if we wish – we don't have to travel out to the archipelago for that.

'Let's just forget about it,' I say. 'I'd rather not go if there's to be such a fuss about it.'

Gustav says, 'That's parents for you', as if there's nothing to it, and he doesn't understand how insulted I feel. It's as if I'm a hundred years old and seen it all but I've been posing as an innocent – I mean, this entire apparatus to protect the little family girl's virginity and good reputation when, as it happens, there isn't anything to protect. And if it's Gustav we're supposed to protect, it's even worse – as if my intention were to ravish him as soon as I got the chance.

'I feel like a bad girl. I *am* a bad girl if people think I am, because there's no other meaning. A bad girl is something one is thought to be.'

'In that case, I'm a bad boy,' he says cheerfully.

'You are most certainly not! You are such a horribly well-behaved boy that your parents are completely out of their minds and believe we can't go out to the country for the weekend without raping each other, and by the way, it's completely different because there are no boys who are so bad that they're as bad as a bad girl. You know that as well as I do. And by all means, don't let me drag you down in the mud.'

Gustav laughs; I emphasize that I see nothing amusing at all in the situation.

At the last moment, his brother is unable to accompany us. However, his parents clearly feel it's now too late to stop us. As far as I'm concerned, I've washed my hands of the whole affair and explained that I'll come along only if I'm left out of his family conflicts. He can manage those on his own.

Conflicts notwithstanding, I'm happy that we get to go. We

leave behind us a city disfigured by election propaganda, idiotic posters on every single wall. Even better that we aren't eligible to vote yet and can turn our backs on the city without feeling guilty. It takes over two hours to get to Gustav's island, in total: we take the bus and the ferry and then another bus, and the last couple of kilometres we walk.

There are few year-round residents left – only smallholders and retired people on government pensions. The rest of the farms have become vacation homes which are now closed up for the season. Clear, chilly air. Forest. Maples in their autumnal splendour and pines with lofty crowns. *Trees*. I become utterly awestruck walking under these trees.

The road becomes increasingly narrow, and finally it's simply a path. Then we've arrived. There are two buildings – one larger, insulated for winter, on the crest of the hill, and a smaller one below: a renovated boathouse. And then, the Sea. Gulls crying. ('Terns,' Gustav corrects, but I think 'gulls' sounds better.) We stand on the dock and witness the sun glittering on the water. We breathe.

But Gustav is hungry. He makes a fire in the stove up in the larger cottage and goes out to chop more wood, leaving me to put on the potatoes and fry the sausage. I ask myself why I can't be the one to chop wood, but stand there with my question left unanswered and have to find pots in the cupboards and food in the sacks.

When we've cleaned up after our meal, we go out to inspect the property. Gustav's ancestors were skerry farmers for generations, and he's spent all of his childhood summers here. He shows me good climbing trees and boulders perfect for look-outs and the cove where he built cities in the sand, and I try to see through his eyes although I know it's impossible: it's only by analogy that you can understand such things. It's only by analogy to the trees and the boulders from your own childhood.

At twilight when it gets colder, we go inside and build up a
fire, read for a while, drink tea and become drowsy in the warm
living room until we can no longer avoid the question that has
now towered into a colossal problem: where are we going to
sleep? I didn't want to approach the subject first lest I stumble
into new ridiculous difficulties, but now I'm so sleepy that I'll
do anything for a bed, anywhere, and when he asks my opinion,
I say it's probably most practical to sleep in this room, both of
us, where it's warm.

He raises no objections until we're already in bed, once we've
distributed the blankets and extinguished the kerosene lamp on
the tiny table between the beds and snuggled down into them
and the rustling of bedding has ceased. Then he sighs in the
darkness.

'This night will change my life. I will never again be the same.
I'll be grey-haired tomorrow morning, or perhaps rather green-
haired. Check my hair tomorrow and see if it isn't green.'

'What on earth. What do you mean?' I sit up, uneasy, because
the idea of changing someone's life doesn't appeal to me in the
least. He doesn't answer, and I tremble at the depths of my
error – can he actually be as bound by convention as his parents?

'Do you mean to say,' I ask, agitated, 'that you've never slept
in the same room as a girl before?'

He sighs.

'Well then, maybe it's time for you to have that experience
as well.'

'That's true, but I didn't expect there to be a flaming sword
between us on the day it happened.'

'A flaming sword? How did that get here? I'm not the one
who's brought it in any case.'

'Should I jump on top of you, then?'

'If you touch me, I'll scream!' I say and pull the blanket over
my head.

He stretches his arm across the space between us and lays his hand next to my cheek. I pop my head out again:

'I've slept in the same *bed* with men before, and nobody got green hair because of it.' For clarification's sake, I continue: 'I don't mean with my lovers. I mean I've slept in the same bed as men without "lying" with them and nobody got upset about it.'

'Not even the man lying in it?'

'Are you trying to be funny? In any event, we didn't need any flaming sword to keep us from throwing ourselves at each other.'

'You must have been keeping strange company.'

'You're the one who's strange. Why wouldn't you be able to sleep together in complete decency when you can do so many other things together in complete decency?'

He sighs again. I yawn irresistibly. 'Can't we table this discussion?'

'Go ahead and sleep,' he says, locking his hands behind his neck. 'Sleep if you can.'

I puff up my pillow and assume my sleeping position, arms wrapped around it. 'If you had something against this arrangement, you could have said so from the beginning,' I mumble into the covers.

I ask myself if it's possible that he expected me to seduce him, or if he thought that I thought he would, or if he's hurt that I didn't think anything at all, but I'm too ferociously sleepy to say anything more at all and fall brutally asleep, leaving him alone.

When I wake up, the room's empty. The sun is shining and I dress and walk down to the sea to take in the morning and shake off the previous evening's unpleasant mood. I'm as helpless as a child around these sexual dramatics. To discover that you're wandering around causing fateful events without intending to or even noticing – it makes me feel like some monstrous combination of *femme fatale* and *enfant terrible*, and I want to go home. My instincts tell me to escape from this as quickly as possible, escape home where I can just be me and nobody has anything to say about it.

He's bailing out a rowboat tied up at the end of the dock. There's sun on the water, the September-blue water, and I sit on a rock on the shore. He's moving around on the boat out there, coiling a rope, tossing the oars and floorboards on land – winter preparations. When he catches sight of me, he nods a good morning and gestures towards the house: 'Coffee's ready if you want some.'

Then he continues to work on the boat, turns his back on me and bails with the scoop. The water flies and glitters in the backlight.

I miss him. He turns his back on me and I miss him. I've hurt him, and I want to be comforted.

Later on, after lunch, I go for a walk in the light drizzle while Gustav takes a nap – he claims he didn't get a wink last night. But he's not getting any sleep now, either: when I return and open the door carefully, he moves over so that I'll come join him on the bed. So we simply lie there, not speaking, entangled in the warmth of each other's bodies, and I would rather not waste one more word on the ridiculous situation of the previous night. But that's not the way to solve any misunderstandings. I hesitantly bring up the matter again and ask if he had a sex-negative upbringing.

'On the contrary,' he answers, 'it's a vulgar notion that Christians are sex-negative. Secularization is what's degraded the erotic.'

I have my doubts about this version of history, but he means that it's people who have a normal Swedish upbringing who consider sex to be a sort of dirty source of pleasure: 'As for me, I was raised in the opposite spirit – that sexual intercourse is a way to praise the Creator.'

'So you mean when we lie here holding each other it's a kind of worship service?'

'A little home devotional on a Sunday afternoon – do you have anything against that?'

'I'm not really sure. You can't really claim that it seems sex-negative, but it doesn't exactly help to lessen the drama, either. It doesn't make our relationship less complicated to have an unknown third party mixed up in it, does it?'

We lie quietly for a while, but someone has to keep feeding the fire in the stove. He gets up awkwardly and puts on several more pieces of wood.

'Were you expecting me to seduce you yesterday?' he asks.

'No. Although it wouldn't exactly have surprised me, either.'

'Would you have allowed yourself to be seduced?'

'What kind of girl do you think I am?'

This seems to calm him but also to raise some new questions, so I explain: 'Not here and not now – we hardly know each other.' (But someday, in a thousand years or so I mean, once we've known each other for a thousand years.)

'Can't we get to know each other?'

'Isn't that what we're doing?'

He turns to me as he kneels before the fire and looks at me, doesn't say anything, simply squints because of the smoke. Or maybe he's laughing.

3

A new delivery from the florist: this time what I unwrap is an uncommonly ugly little cactus in the plainest of pots.

'Well look at that,' says Harriet. 'Now the gifts are becoming a bit more suitable.'

'They really are. Now we're getting somewhere. I told him what I think about red roses.'

Red roses – a flower so banal that it doesn't express anything. They're like a worn-out phrase, such as Iloveyou. This prickly cactus, which I place tenderly on the windowsill, is far more expressive. There's a card, too: *Matt. 5:36*, it says. I've brought my confirmation Bible from home since it's clear I'll be needing it if this is going to continue. I look up the verse:

Neither shalt thou swear by thy head, because thou canst not make one hair white or black.

There must be a verse for every single need and occasion in that book. I assume that this one implies a conciliatory mood after he discovered that he remained just as red-headed as before. This calms me down considerably: I don't want anyone to get green hair for my sake.

'So are you together now?' Harriet asks. I have to admit that it looks that way. We see each other more or less every day. We go to the cinema and the theatre and we go to each other's homes. We hold hands as we stroll along the paths in Haga Park and we talk about where we would go on our honeymoon, what our children's names would be and how we'd decorate our home – he talks about building a bed, a huge bed he says – it's practically the only thing we need, and I look up at him as though it were the most beautiful thing I'd ever heard.

Gustav decided long ago that I'm the one he's going to marry. I have to admit that it looks that way, that it seems to be the whole point. What keeps me from admitting that it's Gustav I'm going to marry is simply that I had just arrived at the serious conviction that I'm not going to marry at all.

It's probably true that the urge to form a family is a kind of natural survival mechanism in humans, one that the organism is equipped with for self-defence. It develops when you fall in love, since infatuation is an illness, an inflammation that disrupts your normal functioning. In order to heal and restore balance, it's followed by a feeling that says I-want-to-be-together-with-him-*always*. Once you've given in to it and adjusted accordingly, the infatuation disperses and you become normal. Ultimately, this all serves nature's call so that you reproduce (in the feeling of I-love-him-so-much-that-I-want-to-duplicate-him).

But you're equipped with a brain, too. And you can use it to figure out that even if it feels like I want to be together with him always and give him twenty children, this is simply how I feel now, and it's nothing to rely on. I know I want to be alone often, more than would be possible if we lived together (let alone if we had twenty children). However, if you use the brain you have, you don't have to go along with such transparent hormonal attacks on your independence. When I use my reason, I also can't understand why you have to live together. Why do you have to eat together and sleep together when there are so many other things you can do together that are much more fun?

However, I don't allow my reason to prevent me from playing

with the idea and, together with Gustav, to explore its possibilities as we, like everyone else, walk hand in hand on the paths along Brunnsviken. We talk about Kierkegaard and how to give life an ethical meaning: to *realisere det almene*, effectuate the universal. This is to do just as everyone else does: get married and find a job, support your family and be a good member of society.

'Will you effectuate the universal with me?' Gustav proposes.

This isn't exactly what I had in mind as the meaning of life. He asks what I had thought it was instead, and, of course, I'm not really sure. But certainly it had to do with achieving something much more significant, making a contribution somehow? Then I laugh when I remember what Sandemose had to say about that:

To hell with women – great and important women who don't want to waste their lives peeling potatoes. They want a mission, they want to make a contribution, they want to go out and help people. Once they've explained this to us in detail, they go to another man to peel his potatoes.

'No matter what happens, I promise I won't go to another man to peel his potatoes. I may be daft, but not that daft.'

But Gustav says that this precisely is the meaning of life. Peeling potatoes. It's the everyday tasks that are the meaning, the smallest and most mundane objects, the simplest and closest relationships. And then he demonstrates this by going straight home to my kitchen and making lunch. He's more experienced in such matters than I am – both of his parents work, and from the time he was small he's had to manage on his own. By the way, I've never seen a person eat so much: two hot meals a day, with appetizer and dessert – I usually just eat a sandwich when I happen to remember. Gustav rubs his hands together in glee thinking of how fat I'll get if he has his way.

'Is there something wrong with my figure the way it is?' I ask, and he says, 'Yes – your hip bones cut into me. The more of you, the better,' he says, and shows me with his hands how little there is of me to grab. And when he explains it this way, I have a hard time coming up with any objections.

'*Sleep with*' – I've always giggled at this English euphemism. I realize that the Swedish 'lie with' is just as equivocal (that is, ambiguous). That's all we do. We lie with each other for hours on end on the couch in my room, and the term starts to be not simply ambiguous but also vague. In the wordless border areas (there is no word you can use: only ugly ones like snogging or stupid ones like making out or clinical ones like petting), we're dissolving the definition of what it actually is to lie with each other, so that what's left is almost uninteresting. In comparison, I mean, with what we manage to permit ourselves to do outside of the definition and which in and of itself is already excessively odd.

I tell him how, when we were once on the No. 7, I had noticed his hands and wonder if that could have been prescient, although I was otherwise so clueless at that time. He's quite sure it was. And I tell him how confused I was the first time I felt lust for him – how I sat looking at his clothes while he read to me and thought about what they were shutting me out from. How this was a sequence of thoughts that no other man's clothing had ever led me down. This is a story he hears with unbridled enthusiasm. He smiles his biggest smile and says generously, 'It is yours.'

There are so many things I suddenly realize. All of a sudden, I understand the metaphysical poets, who have never particularly interested me before: *O my America, my new-found-land* and all of that – the excitement of discovery and the joy of conquest, the desire to plant flags. The pride of being the one permitted to move along private roads, closed to trespassers: something that is mine beneath his belt. *How blest am I in this discovering Thee* – truly there seems to be something to it: I become utterly awestruck.

It's not clear how long we'll refrain from crossing the final boundary. Gustav believes that you have to be married first, but it's also a question of definition. He isn't entirely opposed to the notion that you become married, in a Higher and more Real sense, precisely through the act of intercourse. As far as I'm concerned, all you need is to know each other first, and you have to have done everything in your power to avoid an unplanned pregnancy. Any day now I'll call the student gynae-cologist and make an appointment to get birth control pills.

'Is there a long queue?' asks Gustav.

'A thousand years, so it's just right.'

*

According to Cicero, *idem velle, idem nolle* is true friendship: wanting the same and not wanting the same. That, and admir-ing the same and despising the same – this is the basis for mutual affinity. At the cinema, for example: being moved and snorting at the same places. Watching a film with someone who snorts when you're sitting there appalled at the same thing is incredibly upsetting, both for the viewing experience and the friendship. It's even worse with someone who sits there trans-ported by something you consider complete doggerel.

Gustav and I have such similar tastes in films that we don't even need to communicate through glances or touches. We can hear by each other's breathing that we agree. 'Well,' says Gustav, 'you're embellishing history a bit there: you had no idea why I was laughing at *Viridiana*.' No, that was then. Now I know that it's his way of expressing appreciation. During *Virginia Woolf* I also laugh out of horrified enthusiasm: this is a film we remem-ber for a long time afterwards. When we see Bergman's *Persona*, about the Actress Who Stopped Speaking, we express our feelings by shrugging our shoulders. It's expressive enough – there's no more to say about that matter. I shrug my shoulders for so long in order to show how very little more there is to say about it that Gustav warns me: 'Don't become like the woman in the film' as a result, and of course I become like the woman in the film. I glide away in silence and say no more, and playing this game, we wander home from Eriksberg along dark evening streets.

'You look couply,' Cilla says. So this is what it's like when you look that way. I never believed I would experience this. Not a half, not as in the *Symposium*, where Aristophanes talks about how humans were originally round but then Zeus split them in half. It's only in love that the halves are reunited (I've always imagined them as a croquet ball – with a coloured stripe around the crack). Gustav is not my other half; he's my other whole. I just didn't know that there was another one. To me, single is the default in life, and yet, I feel now as if we belong together – simply and amazingly so: cohesive. Like siblings or playmates; that's the way it feels as we horse around all the way home.

Sometimes I feel a wave of panic that Gustav is something I've made up: isn't it too good to be true? There are further observations that point in that direction: we are *suspiciously* alike.

★

> How precious are the constellations.
> One star dream a week
> And poverty piles up
> even around the water carrier.
> How cheap are the sparrows.
> The sun shines and they live
> and know nothing else . . .

Gustav is reading to me on the phone. It's half seven in the morning. Harriet works at the post office now and disappears at the crack of dawn. I sleep all morning if nothing wakes me up and I told him that he's welcome to call early so I'll leave my bed at some point. Now he's got the idea of reading a few strophes of Vennberg* every time. That's his favourite poet and the most pleasant way he can think of to wake up. I don't understand a word of it and wonder if I'd have an easier time even if I were more awake.

But I appreciate the thought, of course, just as when he comes over to cook – another custom he's established. It surprises me that I feel so comfortable having him around. Usually I have a greater need for solitude. It must be a function of the fact that, more than with any other human I've met, not even excluding Harriet, I can be myself in his company. Since from the very beginning he's had no respect for me, I don't have to posture. I don't make myself more pleasant than I am. We can be quiet together or sit and read together, and it's not strained at all.

We spend as much time as we can away from home: When the weather is passable and we don't have a lecture that's too obligatory, we take our bikes and books and a thermos of coffee and a blanket to lie on and find ourselves islands and peninsulas with undisturbed grassy areas and a view of the sea – Skeppsholmen, Långholmen, Djurgården. For example, way out on Hundudden, you can park yourself out of the wind behind a small pilot house with chipped green paint. Nobody passes by on a weekday. Or you can sit on a park bench above the terrace at Riddarholmen and watch the boats on the water below and the traffic far away. When the lunch hour ends, the people around you pick up and leave, and you're constantly reminded of the incredible privilege of being a student and having the ability to go anywhere you like at any time of the day or night. A blessed state of suspension – how long can it last?

We also explore the unknown nooks of Kungsholmen and

---

* Karl Vennberg (1910–1995), a Swedish modernist poet.

ride our bikes as far as we can along the Hornsberg shore. We find a restaurant called Joy and go in for a cup of coffee because of the name: a sad plastic dive in a godforsaken industrial hinterland that becomes 'ours' because we've found it, according to the common principles of explorers, and, of course, because it's so perfect for making bad jokes.

Another afternoon we annex the promontory Lilla Skuggan. I rest my back against an oak and look out over Värtan and the Tranholmen Boat Club. Gustav is lying on the grass with his head in my lap, his ear against my stomach.

'What do you hear?'

'Your lunch.'

I nod. Cabbage stew – that's bound to make some noise.

'I love your peristalsis,' says Gustav.

No man has ever said such a thing to me, but I don't think it sounds any stranger than anything else: Why should he make an exception when he loves me otherwise?

We probably look perfectly idyllic. But the harmony is deceptive; in reality, I'm the only one who's harmonious and have accepted our relationship as it is. Gustav is building so many structures on top of it that it's shaking underneath them. If this is the one great love, what shall we do with it, what do we want to *do*? Aren't-things-fine-the-way-they-are, I say, can't-it-simply-be-the-way-it-is, but this doesn't give him any peace. He lies awake at night thinking about our relationship and gets complicated ideas and eventually doesn't know his way in or out. 'Look at me,' I say, 'sleeping like a log every night and never getting any ideas at all – much more peaceful and pleasant.' But my calm maddens him.

And he continues to come up with new variations. Today at Värtan he declares all of a sudden that he's decided to flush the metaphysical part of his love and simply be physical and bestial and egotistical. 'As you like, my love,' I say as I hand him his coffee mug. I can't detect any huge difference immediately except for the fact that he kisses me a bit more roughly than usual, but he himself finds it so unpleasant that he discards that solution as well towards the evening. When I'm on my way to bed, he calls and proclaims that he's discovered something new.

'Love shouldn't be based on any good qualities in the object of desire. Qualities are temporary and mutable, you know. No, this is it: I love you because *it's you*.'

'Well then you could love anyone at all,' I decide. 'I think it seems safer to love qualities, of course. Individuals are temporary but you can transfer your feeling about a quality onto another carrier. For example, if it's the red-headed philosopher I love in you, then it doesn't matter if you die before me. There's bound to be another one.'

'Loving someone isn't supposed to be safe.'

'In that case, I don't know what it is that's bothering you.'

'Your lack of good qualities, of course. Although I've come to the realization that you have at least one.'

'I do? What on earth could that be?'

'Your sense of humour. You're funny. That's unusual for a woman – I've only known two in my life, a schoolmate and you. Girls laugh when you tell jokes and such, but they are almost never funny themselves.'

'You haven't known many,' I say drily. (I say it drily to hide how flattered I am. Funny – I think that's a fantastic compliment. 'My darling, nobody is as funny as you are.' I can hardly imagine anything I would rather be. Except beautiful.)

The sun still provides some warmth, so we bike out to inspect what's left of Hagalund. We sit down to rest at an old water tower, view the autumn and ponder how remarkable it is to get to be a student.

'Do you know what today is?' I ask.

'What is it?'

'It's our two-month anniversary.'

'Oh, right. Of course. Two months since you kissed me the first time.'

'Since I—what kind of revisionist history is that? *You* were the one who kissed *me!*'

'Absolutely not. I hadn't even thought of kissing you at that particular moment.'

'You did it anyway. I should know.'

I go on, insisting: 'Anyone can see that it would be a physical impossibility for me to kiss you. You're at least a head taller than I am and I wouldn't have been able to reach that far.'

'But you were the one who started it. You lifted your face and puckered your lips.'

'Puckered my lips! I never! Hold on and I'll tell you how it was. I was looking for my keys in my purse, and probably looked up, and then you made your move.'

We bicker for a bit longer and then compromise by saying we kissed each other, though each of us makes a private notation in the minutes.

As I'm retrieving my tobacco from our carrier bag and tamping it in my pipe, another thought occurs to me.

'We're just like in a book. You know? In romance novels the girl always thinks the boy is so ugly and boring at first, and then her eyes are opened like a bolt of lightning from a clear sky, and she discovers that he has a heart of gold, and in fact he's not that ugly either, at least his eyes become beautiful when they shine full of love, and at the top of the last page, where they get married, he teases her about how foolish she was at the beginning.'

'Is this an argument against getting married? Are you against being like someone in a book?'

'Not actually, on the contrary. But what I object to is that it's such a bad book.'

The sun is boiling hot; I unbutton my jacket and stretch out on the ground next to him.

'Tell me about your past.'

'My past – you know it already. Born in the maternity ward at Stockholm General Hospital, graduated from Norra Latin School . . .'

'The women in your life,' I correct.

'Oh. Where shall I begin?'

'Start from the beginning. Kindergarten?'

'In Sunday school. Her name was Elisabeth, with an "s". I carved it in the wood desk I got when I started first grade. I'll show you next time you come over.'

He tells me about Elisabeth, his first love, and his crush on Sonja in elementary school, and his high-school infatuation, Ingrid, whom he used to take to the cinema – though never anything more – and about his Great Love, Eivor, whom he worshipped from a distance for two years and then finally got together with. He describes the feeling when she placed her small, gloved hand on his arm during a walk for the first time and the experience of being introduced to her family. They had a few ecstatic months until she unexpectedly broke things off, one week before he graduated from high school. 'Nicely timed, don't you think?' he asks. 'Brutal,' I nod.

Then there was Birgitta of course, the blonde summer girl in the cottage next door on the Island. And then Anna-Maria, who was studying philosophy at university – oh, and then Monika, whom he met on a trip abroad and began to exchange letters with . . . I listen, overwhelmed. I had no idea that Gustav had led such a rich life before me. Finally there are so many names and events that he summarizes, a bit apologetically: 'But it was really just Eivor and Birgitta. Well, and Anna-Maria and Ingrid, of course . . . Are you jealous?' he asks expectantly.

'I don't know. I don't think so. It seems so distant, as if it were another life.'

But as it turns out, Gustav is jealous. Apparently he's made a lot of exaggerated assumptions about my time in London. He seems to have misunderstood something I said about my 'lovers'.

'But Gustav, you can only ever speak of lovers in the plural – you can't really say it in the singular. But in my case, there was just one, in fact.'

And so I tell him about the one: Aron from Sweden, whom I met when we rented rooms in the same building, and who became my Fate. Although 'lover' is probably saying too much. We had sex a few times but without any lofty conceptual structure: he was extremely careful not to be considered my anything. And by the way, 'lover' is an impossible word. It's both literary and sophisticated, and I've never heard anyone use it seriously. In our group of girlfriends, we tend to talk about our 'husbands' and 'marriages', even when reviewing our most distant obsessions.

I do a quick résumé of these as well: my thousand-and-one unhappy crushes, and my two or three unhappy relationships (love never coincided with these relationships, thus the unhappiness). The greatest and unhappiest has similarities to Gustav's high-school love: I tell him how I wandered the streets near his home and all of that.

'Do girls do such things? I had no idea.'

'They do nothing else. I thought it was boys who never did that. The things you learn.'

He digests this information in silence for a little while. 'So why didn't it work out with Aron?'

I laugh. 'This is a question I've often asked myself. But I assume it's because I loved him too much. He was older, he had other women, and the fact that I was faithful to him only annoyed him. It was over before I even moved away.'

I add, 'Things can probably never "work out" with someone like Aron. He was completely impossible. That's why I loved him.'

'What did he do?'

'He was in England to study, like me. He wanted to make films, but I don't know if he ever did.'

'Is he still in London?'

'No idea. The last time I saw him was the 27th of May, a year and a half ago.'

'I see, you have the same good memory for all the dates in your life.'

'For fateful dates, yes. There aren't that many yet that I can't keep track of them all.'

Aron is what irritates him the most about my past. It's not only that I slept with him or that he's my most recent past – he seems to hate the type itself.

'Why do women fall for the worst cads – precisely the ones who treat them the worst?'

'It's nature's law,' I answer from the depths of my experience. 'Everyone has to fall for a cad at some point. You simply have to get through it. The Impossible One – he's so attractive.'

Gustav snorts. 'In a few years, he's sure to be the most bour-geois of all – wife, kids and a house in the suburbs . . .'

'You're the one who wants wife, kids and a house,' I hiss. Aron would never! 'You don't get it at all,' I say.

'Are you still in love with him?'

I think about it. 'In some way, yes. As I said, I love him as an impossibility. You, on the other hand, I love as a possibility. That's an entirely different matter.'

He seems minimally satisfied by my explanation. 'Because you can "have me" then – someone like me you can have and then lose again.'

'That's not what I said.'

We collect our things, shake the blanket and fold it, ending in an embrace as blanket-folders are wont to do.

'I need you,' he says, his mouth against my temple.

'For what?'

He lets me go and thinks for a moment, as if the question were unexpected. Then he answers:

'For meaning.'

'You need me to peel potatoes for?'

'Precisely. Just as you need me. Although you haven't understood it yet.'

To be each other's meaning – it seems too easy to me, too facile an answer. But perhaps it's not as bad as it sounds. Maybe, in fact, it's so difficult to be selfless that there's a crucial distinction between living for yourself and living for others, even if it's just for one other person?

4

When I take my duffle from the hook in the coat room after the seminar, I find a chocolate bar in the pocket that wasn't there before. I replace it quickly with a red face – moved and irritated. It's my favourite kind, too, and it speaks just as clear a language as the flowers he insists on sending: I know your objections to courtship, and I intend to disabuse you of them.

He knows the routes I take. There's a note in the basket on my bicycle, parked next to the department. A full piece of graph paper with a short message: 'Tea? x G'. He's on the phone when I arrive at Bragevägen, so I take a seat in his room and wait. I can't hear what he's saying out there, but I can tell by his voice that it must be a male friend he's talking to – his timbre is entirely different. It's dark under normal circumstances – I mean, when he's talking to me – but now there's a certain man-to-man quality about it. I wonder if men always sound different when they talk to each other. I know they interact differently. It would never occur to Gustav to slap me on the back, for example. I curl up on the bed with all those lovely soft pillows and look around his room. There's now a photograph of me on his desk, under frame and glass. I don't like it, and I ponder the reason why. It's not because it's a bad picture – it's extremely flattering. It's a madonna-sweet Martina that Gustav created himself (hair let down, light at an angle from a window above and lightly overexposed – there's no trick to looking madonna-sweet, then).

Is it the fact that he's pinned me like this – captured behind glass, fit within a frame, parked on my husband's desk? I don't know if it would be any different if he had tacked up an enlargement on the wall above his bed – I don't think so. I ought to be flattered, actually, that someone wants my mug in front of him while he works. Is this a primitive fear of effigies – am I afraid that he's stealing my soul? But that picture isn't me. No, I'm not sure what it is, but Gustav's room has changed character somehow.

'Did you put on Bessie Smith for me that first time you were waiting for me here?' I ask once he's off the phone. He admits it without beating around the bush. 'Of course. That was a touch I imagined ahead of time. The record player isn't mine – it's usually in the living room. How did you guess?'

'A simple analogy. I'm rather careful myself with the music and literature I allow people to find me engrossed in. I've also guessed that you were just on the phone with your bosom buddy. Am I right?'

Quite correct, though men don't call each other 'bosom buddies' (well, of course not – that's why I used it). Halldén is his name and he's doing his military service at A1 at the moment. By the way, he realized that he needed to borrow one of Gustav's books, so he's going to drop by. You don't need founts of intuition to guess why he needs to borrow a book just now, but I don't protest since I'm curious, too.

It isn't just Gustav's best friend I get to see – it's an entirely new side of Gustav himself, and my feelings of insecurity grow as we sit with our cups in our laps around the desk in his room and drink tea. They speak in masculine voices and call each other by their last names, even when addressing each other. 'Lindgren' – that must be someone other than Gustav. I can hear the difference, and it's a Gustav I don't know. They tell stories from their school years and talk about classmates and Gustav imitates their old teachers, but his imitations are impossible to appreciate

47

when you don't know the originals. I feel so left out that they might as well have been talking memories from their army days. But Gustav hasn't done his military service, and he won't unless he can perform it without weapons, but he's hoping to postpone because of his studies until he's excused from duty because of old age.

The conversations I have with Harriet are of course also full of allusions to events at our school, when I think about it. Does it sound the same way to an outsider? Is there an analogy here as well?

Cilla and Gustav have appreciated each other from the beginning. They quickly advanced from tense politeness to squabbling, and now they can tease each other like normal folks do. But he's more reserved with Harriet. Without thinking about it any further, I've ascribed it to envy – 'why can't she live with me instead of with her' – does this have to do with the fact that Harriet knows so many Martinas that he doesn't? He has no access, as she does, to Martina at ages ten through nineteen.

However, it doesn't help that I try to find analogies in order to understand. I feel so much the outsider nonetheless that they may as well be telling war stories. So abandoned.

*

Gustav's brother and sister-in-law are in town on a visit, and I'm invited to a family dinner. I don't really like the parallel: Gustav's brother and his wife, Gustav and me. But he really wants me to come. To be honest, it's nice of them to accept me as a part of the family, because I'm hardly a dream daughter-in-law – more like, in their nightmares: a girl who smokes a pipe and swears and dips her hair in the soup. Ah yes, the thing about the soup wasn't supposed to happen. What's supposed to happen is that I grow my hair long enough so I can sit on it, but it's not that long yet – it's at precisely soup-length, and a little hard to manage.

If there ever were a dream daughter-in-law, it's Erik's wife,

Anna-Karin. She's picked berries at the Island and grown veg-
etables there, too, and she's brought her bounty home. She's
made jam and juice and brought jars as a gift to her mother-in-
law with the most tidily printed labels, including the year. (As
for me, I've never even had the patience to pick enough berries
for a dessert.)

Erik's had the same upbringing as Gustav, and he's learned
to take care of himself, but according to Gustav, this went to
smash about two weeks after he got married: now he's *forgotten how to do it* when it comes to washing socks. Well. Who
wouldn't forget, given the opportunity?

He's significantly older than Gustav and not a bit like him
inside or out, as far as I can tell. Anna-Karin is a licensed nurse
but she believes she needs to stay home while the children are
small. They don't have any children yet, to be sure, but she is
apparently staying home waiting to become pregnant. During
dessert (Anna-Karin's canned plums), the conversation turns to
what the rest of us will be when we get older. I squirm my
way out of it saying that I have at least a couple of years left in
my education, and after that there'll be something. Father-in-
Law reminds us that Gustav had ideas of becoming an actor
when he was in high school and Mother-in-Law heaves a sigh of
relief – so fortunate that he didn't go down that path. There are
so many bad girls in that world.

I look down at my plate of plums, frightened. Not because I'm
a bad girl, not that anyone has claimed as much, but I feel like I
should be one, in solidarity with bad girls. But Gustav only laughs.

I try to help with the dishes afterwards, but he sends me out
of the kitchen, telling me to be social instead. Anna-Karin is
seated on the sofa with yarn and needle. I sneak a look to find
out what she's making. Am I seeing right? Oh yes. A tie. I can't
help that I get hives when I see that a girl is sitting crocheting a
tie. Something inside me gets hives.

I just want to go home, to my own little flat, where I'm home and there's nothing wrong with me.

I can't love the everyday, as Gustav does, for its banality. I can't see what's sacred about it. He thinks it's conventional to want to be unconventional. Maybe it is, but in that case it's no better to be conventional in an unconventional way, as he is: programmatically and subtly Kierkegaardian. But when I look at Anna-Karin, I can see that this is actually what he's wanted, in his innermost heart, all along: a little lass crocheting ties for him.

Why in the world does he want me, then? I'll have to ask someday, when I remember.

There's a chess set on the bookshelf. I ask if someone wants to play, and when Erik declines, apparently Father-in-Law thinks he must step up in order to be polite. My social failures continue when I beat him. He is so much worse than I am that I'm not sufficiently good to lose on purpose in a credible way, and losing against your father-in-law on purpose so that everyone notices would be even more ill-mannered, wouldn't it?

Gustav offers to walk me home. His mother comes out into the hallway and admonishes him not to be late. I rush down the stairs so I'm not dragged into the conversation. I heard that she made a scene when he came home at three-thirty the other night.

'Have you ever thought of moving out?' I ask when we're out in the open.

'No. Why?'

'Well, it's not really any of my business, but isn't it a bit of a strain for all involved if your mother can't sleep because you're away at night?'

'I'll move out when we get married,' he says happily.

'Look at the beautiful moon,' I say. It's an entirely ordinary waning half-moon and he doesn't allow himself to be distracted.

'She thinks we're going to get pregnant,' he explains.

'Yes, I believe all mothers are afraid of that.'

'Well, my mother thinks we're going to get pregnant with twins.'

'Why? Do twins run in your family?'

'No, not at all,' he laughs, 'but she's just more anxious than others.'

I shake my head: here we go again. He's not only delighted that his mother is anxious like all other mothers, he's delighted that his mother is twice as anxious as others!

I try to avoid getting involved in the complications that arise from Gustav's insistence on living at home, but it's not feasible. Once he's had dinner at my house a few times, his mother thinks that I have to go over there in return, and when this reaches my mum's ears, she says that we must come for dinner: social life has its laws.

When Gustav meets up at Central Station, he's dressed in a suit and tie. I look at him with distaste: 'You know what I think of that kind of get-up!' Yes, he knows, but this time it's not to irritate me but because he's just come from a demonstration and didn't have time to go home and change. I have to relent: it's more important not to look like a communist when you're demonstrating for Vietnam than to look like one when you're being introduced to your intended parents-in-law. I feel a bit nervous on the train home, but in a rather giggly way. In all honesty, I have nothing against playing social games once in a while, and I can't deny that there's a deep satisfaction in this: Oh yes, look and see, I too can bring home something presentable! I take his arm shamelessly, something that would never occur to me in Stockholm, and I lead him the long way past the baseball field and the school sweet shop so that as many acquaintances see us as possible.

Gustav is a bit disappointed when he realizes that my parents have moved since I lived here, but I assure him that their home is just like ours was, minus my room, but that, of course, was precisely what he wanted to see – my childhood bedroom.

My giddiness increases when we get home. I feel pleasantly like an observer at this confrontation, like an irresponsible and bouncy birthday girl, or maybe the winner of a contest, with all of this to-do for my sake. But I've already done my part, and I can lean back in my chair and watch as they exert themselves to be as pleasant as possible, for my sake.

The event goes well. Gustav is good at making conversation, and the disgusting suit makes a good impression, predictably. Although then, of course, he ruins the effect by explaining, in his usual candid way, why he's wearing it, leaving them to come to the conclusion that he looks like a communist without one and is just wearing it to fool people (like Martina, naturally) whose prejudices make them judge people by their clothing and believe that convictions are carried in the jeans.

'Was that bloody necessary?' I pant, heavy with dinner and dessert, as we race from my father's car across the car park to catch the train on time.

'Don't you think it's fun – shocking the bourgeoisie?'

'Not my parents.'

'They're not as easily shocked as you think.'

'I see,' I say, slamming the door behind us. 'You already know them better than I do, I suppose.'

'It's very possible.'

We find a compartment to ourselves and settle in, each with our own book. I haven't had the chance to read more than a few lines before his giggling interrupts me.

'What?'

'Have you considered what consequences social etiquette will demand of us now?'

I haven't. The immutable law of reciprocation requires that

Gustav must invite my parents over now, or rather his parents must invite them, who will then . . . Had I imagined that such a chain of consequences would be initiated, I'm not certain I would have ever let Gustav come over to make cabbage stew.

*

In the morning paper, I read an article about our relationship to Third World countries and I get so depressed that I'm depressed the entire morning – world-depressed. (This is the current variant of *Weltschmerz*.) I ask myself: Is there any possibility at all of being moral when you're in a situation that is fundamentally immoral and over which you don't have any influence?

I play hooky from my English conversation class and bike to the afternoon lecture in group ethics in the philosophy department. The speaker addresses the following problem: Is it possible to be moral when you're in a situation that is fundamentally immoral and over which you have no influence? One concrete example is our relationship to Third World countries.

It's no wonder that this university subject suddenly attracts such large groups of listeners that they have to move the lectures to larger premises on Kungstensgatan. No wonder, when there are lecturers who do something constructive with world depression and release you afterwards with your head chockfull of thoughts. I ride out to Djurgården to process them, have a cup of hot cocoa at the café at Blockhusudden, watch the waves and read a brochure dropped into my postbox about Vietnam, written by the local Social Democrats. I think about society. I've realized that I belong to one, and how exciting that is. Throughout my school years, I thought politics was something silly – something those self-satisfied and precocious boys on the student council occupied themselves with, and the party bickering in connection with general elections. To discover that politics can be something entirely different and connected to morals truly lends a new dimension to your life.

I'm not just talking on a global level – the large relationships where our role is so troublesome – it's also the small things, what you see here in the city and every single everyday element in your field of vision – buses and trams and the like. You can't simply take these things for granted. It's society that keeps them going, and it also makes it possible for those who don't ride a bike to get out to Djurgården. A university – one you can attend for free and even get money to do so – that's what our taxes do! And hospitals when you get sick. And theatres and museums – I've just never seen it this way!

At the Nordic Museum, I hop off my bike and go in to look at the Almqvist exhibit so that society hasn't done all of this for naught. I walk around and savour my cultural inheritance and the fantastic feeling of being at home here: a citizen and an heir.

'Gustav's been looking for you,' Harriet says. I've hardly got my jacket off when the phone rings again.

'Where have you been all day?'

'I've been out discovering society. Why?'

'You could have called me.'

'Am I supposed to call you every time I go out on a bike ride? Did you think I had found someone else and been unfaithful?'

'No, I just want to know where you are. I get so restless when I can't get in touch with you. I haven't got anything done all day because of it.'

'Well, I'm here now, so you can start doing what you wanted to get done now.'

'Now I want to see you.'

'Tomorrow,' I say. 'I'm planning to read this evening.'

'You can read with me sitting there.'

Gustav wants to get together, I want to be alone. How do you compromise with that? You meet 'for a little while'.

No, Gustav isn't something I've made up. He's not an eman-
ation of my own reflection: he's standing here, utterly real, with
his own difficult feelings. You don't have a very nice 'little while'
under such circumstances. I can't read, and I become irritated: why
is he crowding me? I'm tired of lying on the couch making out. It
seems like he says the same things he always says. I don't want
more food and I want to be alone. He wonders 'What's wrong',
and you can't answer something like that. You can't tell someone
who wants to be with you Always that he should be reasonable
and ration himself out a little – if I saw you half as often, I would
like you four times as much – no, you can't say that.

Maybe it would be better to live together after all. If you live
together, you can go into your room and close the door when
you feel like it. You can't do that when you've a guest sitting in
the only room you have.

Quite late that evening, in the hallway, when he's already put on
his coat and is ready to leave after our parting embrace, he suddenly sets down his gloves and wraps his arms around me again.

'Take care of yourself!'

This is a phrase almost devoid of meaning, but he doesn't say
it that way. So I ask him: What do you mean?

He laughs. 'It just occurred to me how happy I am that you
exist, and how important it is that you continue to do so.'

I nod. Don't worry – I'm invulnerable.

In some way. In some strange way. It bothers me to be loved.
Not that I would rather not be, of course not. But I still don't
know what to do with it. How do you receive it? To be loved:
to be the object of feelings. It's so much more interesting to
love, to have feelings. When what happens is happening inside
me: feeling these sudden strange motions, the way they spark
inside, the movements of the foundations of your soul. To study
them, ponder them, live with them, attempt to express them.

But what's happening to you – it's yours, your feelings, your hormones and your ideas. I have no part in it, and I feel left out.

★

I wake up in the morning more sober than I've been for months. I look at myself in the bathroom mirror and wonder coldly and angrily how he can possibly be so stupid as to want to marry me.

'If we lived together, I wouldn't have to wonder where you are,' he says. He'd know that I'd be home sooner or later. I see! And then I'd know that he was sitting there waiting for me! Sharing a flat with Harriet is another thing. We don't get involved in each other's affairs. If I was away for 24 hours, Harriet would calmly assume that I was with a lover. Would Gustav do the same?

No, it's not that kind of freedom I'm trying to protect. I have no illusions about polygamy being worthwhile. People who brag about how many conquests they've made are, of course, pitiable, and they're the first ones to complain in between their boasts. The fact that they keep searching, from one to the next, only means that they haven't found someone worth keeping. It's most often the case that mass seducers (of both sexes) are the most desperate of romantics and they drag the dream of The One with them into grey old age.

But gloating over life-long fidelity and marital bliss seems to be just as absurd. Finding the one you want, or convincing yourself that you have – what does this have to do with morals? It can be enviable, but it can't be *simultaneously* commendable.

That it's enviable, I can believe. Happy marriages are probably the happiest thing there is for those who can have them. I don't at all subscribe to the principle of the worthlessness of the core family. Nor have I ever doubted for one second that Gustav would be an ideal marital partner: wise and good-natured and brought up in such a way that no household task is strange to him. An idiot can see that Gustav is the right one – but I'm the one who's wrong!

We're like dogs and cats. As natural as it is to him to be loyal and faithful, that's how natural it is to me to go my own way and scratch anyone who tries to pet me when I'm not in the mood. In the delight I feel over our affinity in other respects, I seem to have forgotten this or repressed it, but now it's time for me to look the truth straight in the eyes: Being married to me is a fate I wouldn't wish on my worst enemy – how much more eagerly do I want to protect Gustav from it, someone I truly care about. And I realize, as I consider my reflection in the bathroom mirror, if he is so blinded that he can't see what's good for him, then it's my duty to protect him from himself, since I'm the more clear-sighted of us. I can't let his infatuation pull us both down into ruin. Or our lust. Both of them are poor reasons for entering into marriage: when the lust ebbs away, you stand there like a fool. And I seem to recall that there are examples in world history of infatuation ending after seduction.

If he weren't so eager . . . if he were a little less eager so that I could reason with him, then we could enter into a marriage of convenience, the only rational form of marriage. But it can't be right to enter into matrimony with a man who is out of his mind with passion.

If I'm going to marry Gustav, he must first have recovered from his infatuation enough so that he knows what he's doing. And then he won't do it.

5

Being depressed is something you can do without any particular reason or excuse. Usually I'm in a splendid mood in the morning – I'm eager to get working on whatever the day's tasks are as soon as I'm out of bed. I can't put my finger on any particular reason for being sad today, which makes me even more depressed. 'Waking up on the wrong side of the bed', that's something people say – it can't be anything more serious than that.

I have to go downtown to buy a new pair of boots. There are crowds of people on all sides and suddenly I feel agoraphobic, afraid of all these strange people swarming about and bumping into me. Inside the department store it's humid and sweaty, on the street November-cold and grey, and it must have escaped my notice until just now that life is hell.

I've promised to eat lunch with Gustav somewhere, but now I think I'd rather go home and hide until this depression has moved on. I don't want to dump my sorrows on him, that bloody saint, no of course I'm not worthy of him, no I'm not, take him away from me so I can wallow in peace without having to be *ashamed* to boot. Take him, just take him, then I'll say the I-told-you-so: just as I thought, it was too good to be true.

'You have to eat anyway,' Gustav says when I call from a phone booth.

'Do I have to? All right, if you can find a spot that's sufficiently dark and gloomy.'

He tells me to walk up Drottninggatan to Tegnérgatan and he meets me there, takes me by the hand and draws me into an undeniably dark and gloomy beer pub and orders hash. We eat in silence, because I can't explain anything. When he wants me to follow him home, I do it – I let him lead me. We walk down Drottninggatan. He looks at me. I don't want to meet his gaze. His eyes: blue and very big when he opens them wide.

These eyes look at me: questioning, troubled.

Nobody else is home, so I sit on the couch in the living room. The clock on the mantle is the only sound except for the distant traffic on Odengatan. I can't help but weep, although I can't explain why. Gustav doesn't ask me anything. He simply kisses me, kisses my face, so that I have to smile when I understand what it is he's doing: he's kissing away my tears. He kisses away my tears and my final attempts to find a reason for them: Why do I of all people have someone who comforts me? Why are my tears the ones that are being kissed away when there are so many others crying in the world? It's not fair.

I close my eyes and bury my face in his sweater, rest in his warmth. It's just the two of us here. Far, far away, life is bustling on Odengatan. When the clock chimes two, he has to leave to go to a lecture. We part on the street below, squinting in the sharp, grey daylight.

'Even more unhappy?' he asks, looking at me.

'Well, no.'

I watch as he unlocks his bicycle. I stand there looking at his face and add, after thinking for a moment:

'On the contrary, I mean.'

He takes me by the shoulders and gives me a little shake.

'Then you have to say so, you know!'

'I said it,' I say meekly.

'But I practically had to drag it out of you.'

I spend the afternoon with a book I've snatched from the shelf in Father-in-Law's library: Tillich, *The Courage to Be*. I learn that anxiety falls into three categories: neurotic anxiety, psychotic anxiety and a third kind which he calls 'existential'. It's always a relief to be able to name things, of course, and 'existential anxiety' sounds better than waking up on the wrong side of the bed. I'm unable to find any other positive aspect in the diagnosis: if this is what you're suffering from, it's incurable.

★

Polygamous. That is how Gustav said he felt this morning when he happened to run into his previous girlfriend, Eivor. He said it was such a strange feeling to see her again. I sit and think about it all the way on the No. 4 to Puck Theatre to see Buñuel's *The Exterminating Angel*, sit and really chew on it, and when we get off at Sibyllegatan, I ask him, 'What do you actually mean by "polygamous"?'

'I suppose it's a kind of epiphany, as you say – I came to the realization that it's possible for me to fall in love with other women. To be attracted to someone who isn't you.

'But,' he says and waits while we cross between the cars and step safely on the pavement in front of the cinema, 'but I'll stay faithful to you as long as you stay faithful to me.'

A promise? I didn't ask for it. But now he's placed the matter in my hands, and I'm holding it here – large and heavy. Happy and afraid. As long as I stay faithful to him. As long as.

★

Most of the lectures in the English department are scheduled during the day – it's only the seminars that are held in the evening. And here there's no question about socializing afterwards – there are far too many students. We pour out onto Odengatan and separate into two streams, one heading up to the underground, one down Sveavägen, and then split again at each intersection. Usually I ride my bike although it's so close, but on this particular evening I'm walking and after a while I find myself chatting with a fellow who lives in student housing uptown. He has an issue of *The Worker* in his jacket pocket and we talk about syndicalism, which I don't know much about but have great sympathy for, if you can say such a thing about politics. I'd like to know more about it.

When I stop at my door, he suggests that I go to his place for tea instead. All of my collected wisdom tells me that this is a fellow who means something else when he says tea, but there's no way he can know that, so I'm cheeky enough to take him at his word. His student room is very small, dominated by an impressive music system, a speaker in each corner. The seating options are the bed and an armchair, so I choose the armchair while he goes out into the corridor kitchen after putting on a classical LP. I see it's Mozart when I peek at the sleeve.

The first lesson I learned in dealing with the opposite sex was not to 'play with fire', and if you go to a strange man's house, you can blame yourself if you fall victim to murderous intent. But how are you supposed to learn anything about syndicalism otherwise, or to make any new acquaintances? Once we've drunk our tea and listened to Mozart and Handel and talked about the syndicalist workers' organization and he moves into seduction mode, I get up and explain politely that I'm going home. He doesn't make any effort to attack me. He simply says, 'Women' and shakes his head. I smile from the door, and he smiles back.

'That was an unusually noble way to take it,' Harriet says as she sits in the kitchen solving crossword puzzles when I come home.

'Wasn't it, though? I'm not sure I would have been as amenable if I'd been him.'

'What were you thinking of?'

'What do you mean?'

'Going home with him like that?'

I've thought about this on my way home. 'Maybe,' I say, 'maybe it was mostly to find out what it would feel like to be unfaithful to Gustav without actually doing anything.'

'I see. How did it feel, then?'

'Dreadful,' I say, and close the bathroom door to brush my teeth.

*

I'm not the one scanning the job vacancies – it's Harriet. But when she leaves the newspaper open near the phone, I can't avoid seeing them here and there. My eyes fall on an advert from a book publisher who would like to hire someone, 'preferably younger', to work primarily with their children's publications.

Just one glance tells me that this is the Dream Job. Then I read the advert four more times, carefully, but it's no use. It's still obvious that this is something that would fit me perfectly – a job that crops up once in a lifetime. I spend a sleepless night realizing that I don't want the Dream Job. I don't want a job at all. I want to go to school for the rest of my life. (School means free time, according to the dictionary: freedom from work, 'rest and entertainment in mental occupations'.)

Employment: being at a certain place at certain times doing certain things – day after day after day. Year after year. I wake up with dark circles under my eyes to call the company for further information. I hope to hear that I'm not qualified, but no, by all means, please send us an application.

I go to the library and take copies of my transcripts, cold with terror. The development proceeds slowly but surely, like sleepwalking: You get an apartment. You get a fiancé. You get a job. And then you're stuck. Now all I need is a television, I think, as I drop the documents in the postbox with a wild prayer that I won't be chosen.

I'm called for an interview.

I put on a skirt, tie up my hair into a bun so I won't look any 'younger' than I am, find an old briefcase in Harriet's closet to have something to hold on to, and bid my freedom adieu. The company boss seems nice and sensible. She says that they aren't that concerned about formal qualifications – the only thing that's important to them is that the one who gets the job is truly interested in literature and engaged in the work. I make a face that says 'Literature – that's the worst thing I can think of. And engagement? How phony.' I believe that if they want me, they'll have to take me as I am. I'm not going to make any accommodations. I tell them the truth: I can't know if I'll like it, because I've never tried anything like it before, and I can't immediately proclaim that it will be my life's mission.

They promise to let me know of their decision after the Christmas break. The workplace looks nice, too – bright, clean rooms with pleasant textiles. I close my eyes and run towards the exit in acute desperation.

I've probably succeeded in making myself impossible at this place, but what's the use of that. Sooner or later I'll have to grow up and earn my bread by the sweat of my brow, and now that I've avoided the dream job, the only jobs left are those that are worse.

I call Gustav to ask him two questions: a) Will you marry me? b) Do you promise to become a schoolteacher so you can support me? It's true – previously, I forced him to swear that he would never become a teacher, but anything so that I don't have to be employed. I'd rather be a parasite, a prostitute – even a teacher's wife.

'I planned on becoming a saint when I grow up,' he answers.

'You can't support a family on that.'

'I thought you were the one who was going to support us.'

'I've changed my mind. If you become a saint, I demand a prenuptial agreement.' Gustav comes over to console me, but this time I'm inconsolable.

★

We've agreed to seduce each other at Christmas. Yes, recipro-cally: we agree that we want to avoid accusations of rewriting history in the future. The date is mostly determined by the fact that we'll have the entire night and can fall asleep in each other's arms (no half-measures here!), and this makes the holi-day perfect – Harriet will be visiting her family so we can have my flat to ourselves. At the same time, Gustav's parents are going to the Island, so they won't notice if he's away from home for a couple of days.

The date is also determined by the fact that, after exactly two months in the queue, I finally have an appointment with the gynaecologist. I get the impression, listening to the nurse's phone conversations while I sit in the waiting room, that this doctor is picky about the Pill. I'm prepared for that. Harriet didn't get them the first time she tried – she was considered too young although she was nineteen already. And Cilla's report about her latest visit at the family clinic has whipped me into maximum alert: intimate questions about whether she had a fiancé, etc. ('Of course I said I did, good Lord, since they asked!')

I'm prepared to do whatever it takes, and after approximately one minute of conversation with the doctor, I claim I'm engaged before he's even asked. Right afterwards, when I've settled myself in the examination chair, he wants to know when we plan to get married. I'm about to burst forth 'Marry? We're not getting married!', but I remember in time that that's what people nor-mally assume when you say you're engaged – that a wedding is in your future – and I mumble something about having to wait a bit, to finish our studies and such – I think it sounds incred-ibly responsible and solid. Such conversations – and the dreadful examination to boot – are enough to make anyone lose their appetite for anything to do with sex for a lifetime.

In any event, he writes the prescription. I bounce out of the

clinic and rush across Odenplan in three jumps to Örnen Apoth-
ecary and carry home the little case of pills like well-earned
spoils of war.

★

On Christmas Eve, it snows. At least, with a little good will, you
could call it snow. Down on the street it melts immediately,
but if you're sitting indoors and look up through the window,
the air is grey with whirling flakes. It's just such a day I had
imagined. Quiet snowfall outside the window, warm and quiet
indoors – a warm, quiet space for just the two of us.

He comes in the afternoon with his pyjamas and a toothbrush, and a Christmas book in his bag. We carry in the
Christmas tree I've bought – a real tree although, to be honest,
it's too dry to smell of anything. But at least it smells of paraffin
from the twenty candles.

'The first Christmas in our own home,' I announce festively
when I light them. (Our home? My home. Where you're staying with me.) Before we eat dinner, we wrap our Christmas
books in gift paper, and when we've eaten, we exchange and
unwrap them. Gustav gives me Buber's anthology of Chassidic
anecdotes, and I've bought him Sandemose's *Felicia's Wedding* –
and then we borrow each other's.

We listen to some music on the radio while we drink our
evening tea, sitting on the couch looking out at the starless sky
and at the neighbour's shining windows full of tinsel.

Then we go to bed. Ceremonially: twenty candles to blow
out. One is permitted to burn on and shine some warmth on
us. Bach pours from the radio as Gustav removes my clothes,
and the mood is perfectly reverent. Nevertheless I notice that
I'm actually nervous, as if this were my first time. Although
we're already so intimate that it would seem more obscene not
to complete our intimacy, it almost feels embarrassing.

'I thought women let their hair down at night,' he protests

when I sit on the side of the bed and put my hair into a ponytail with a rubber band for the night.

'Where on earth did you get that idea? Art, film, literature perhaps?'

'Yes, isn't that a classical motif?'

'And they call that realism! In reality, you never wear your hair down except for purposes of vanity in a public context. Never at home, and least of all in bed. You don't want hair <u>all over the place</u>, right?'

'When we were on the Island, you didn't have it combed back that way anyway, in a little rat's tail.'

'That was when I was showing off in your company. The fact that I've stopped doing so is something I hope you're sensible enough to feel flattered by.'

'Yes indeed. I'm so happy to be initiated into the mysteries of the female sex. To get to know how it really is.'

I stick out my tongue in a friendly manner and snuggle down next to him. Mysteries or not, my heart is pounding.

'Are you afraid?' he asks when he pulls the blanket over us.

'A little.'

I don't know what I'm afraid of: not of anything tangible, such as that it's going to hurt or that he's going to be impotent or that lightning will strike us – not about anything in particular, but even so. He lies still with his head against my chest, and I wrap my arms around his shoulders. Is he afraid too?

'You remember, don't you, that it's a question of *phronesis* and not *techne*?'

He lifts his head and laughs. 'You mean I needn't have performance anxiety?'

'There's no rush,' I suggest. 'We have our whole lives ahead of us. If you want, we can wait a while.'

'A thousand more years?'

'No, not a thousand years!'
No more than about ten minutes.

'Sleep with' is a euphemism in several senses. We don't fall
asleep in each other's arms – we don't fall asleep at all. It gets
crowded and sweaty in my narrow single bed. After midnight
I get a headache and Gustav puts on his pyjamas and rolls himself up in a blanket in Harriet's room instead. Sleeping in each
other's arms is probably something they only do in films.

It's just as dark when I wake up, but it's morning. I've asked
him if he wants to go to early morning service at church, but
Gustav doesn't understand why you have to rush out in the
middle of the night to get into the Christmas spirit. He would
rather go to the usual high mass at eleven (and avoid the crowd, I
imagine). There are many hours until then. I hear him slamming
around with coffee cups, and soon he comes into the bedroom
with a breakfast tray. It would of course be much more comfortable to eat at the kitchen table, but for some reason, it's more
romantic to do it half-reclining with the tray on our knees and
our elbows in each other's stomachs.

'What's that smell?' he asks suddenly, wrinkling his nose.

'Toast?' I suggest. 'Or the candles?'

'Not that. It's you. Is it perfume?'

'Oh, that. No, it's just deodorant. I washed up a bit while you
were in the kitchen.'

'Do you want to get up already?'

'Who said anything about getting up?'

'Are you performing your morning ablutions just to get back
into bed again?'

'Do you like me smelling like sweat in your arms?'

He gestures so that he almost upsets the tray: 'I love when
you smell like sweat! The only thing I love more is when you
smell like sex!'

I lift the saucer and pour back the spilled coffee. 'And here I thought it was nice to be antiseptic in the nuptial bed.'

He wrinkles his nose and his forehead. 'Where on earth did you get that from?'

'I can only imagine.

'We seem to have a few more mysteries to get through,' I add as a question.

'Mmh,' Gustav says through his cheese sandwich.

*

At the end of the year, Harriet has returned and Gustav has moved back home with his pyjamas and toothbrush and *Felicia's Wedding*. We hadn't planned on celebrating New Year's Eve anyway – we agree on that. The fact that time goes on is nothing to make a big noise about. There are people who have holiday panic, feel like social outcasts if they sit home on a Saturday night, and they worry there's something wrong with them if they don't have a New Year's Eve invitation. It's my assumption that it's the others who have something wrong with them when they start to *carry on* just because the year changes numbers – make fools of themselves with paper streamers and crackers as though the year getting older – and we with it – is something to celebrate. I have social panic sometimes as well, but it has nothing to do with the almanac.

Harriet disappears with a beau, and I go to bed, pretending nothing is happening. I just want to sleep.

6

'It doesn't seem like nature wanted people to have a sex life, does it?' Harriet says thoughtfully when I tell her I've contracted a shameful illness.

'Apparently not. It happens every time,' I complain, 'every single time I take on a new lover! It's only in films that they fall asleep in each other's arms and awaken with their mascara in place and never suffer from hives or a bladder infection.'

So it's happened before, and I know what to expect: call the appointment line, ask for a time, get in line at the clinic, be examined and interrogated thoroughly about my private life, and the first time the doctor says neutrally that oh, it's something you get, it may have started as a cold. The next time it's another doctor who doesn't talk about colds at all but makes you understand that this is clearly the wages of sin, and if the world were fair, he would leave you to suffer. The third time it's a doctor who jovially barks about the 'honeymoon syndrome' and bacterial flora that have to take time to adapt to each other. No matter who the doctor is, the result is the same: you're sent home with ineffective medicines and a tiny gross tube of vaginal cream – 'Vaginal cream!' I yell at Harriet, 'They call it that just to further humiliate you!'

You may as well enter a convent right away, when nature apparently doesn't want you to do anything else.

I don't say anything to Gustav. Men can't stand to hear such things, and least of all him. We women, hardened by our bitter experiences, share them with each other, in the interests of enlightening our fellows. But Gustav would simply be crushed. No matter what I said, it wouldn't prevent him from shouldering the blame, and the details of what happened last time I had a lover are something I would rather spare him.

To be sure, I'm convinced that he would rather I tell him everything and share my worries with him. But precisely, therefore, I am not going to pitch my burdens onto him, no indeed. This is my private penalty for sinning, and I shall bear it myself.

It's no big deal to make heroic resolutions. The thing is to carry them out. In this case, it would require me to play it cool, but my powers don't stretch that far. Maybe it's my evil subconscious (which of course blames Gustav for everything) that sabotages and gives him hints behind my back; in any event, he's sensitive enough to notice immediately that something's up. He looks across the dinner table at Corso at me, his big blue eyes full of questions.

My unaccustomed exercises in heroism develop, with their logical mercilessness, towards the final fiasco: I am troubled. He wants to know why. I say nothing so that I don't bother him. He becomes sad because I say nothing. He nags. I become irritated, and then I glide irresistibly into the role of Wronged and begin to enjoy feeling misunderstood. In order to say something, in order to justify my depressed state, I talk about Cilla, whom I had seen that afternoon.

'She was feeling so down that it was contagious. She's thinking about breaking up with that fellow she's with. She's come to the conclusion that she is <u>mismated</u>.'

'It would be so nice if you could speak Swedish,' Gustav says, and smacks the ketchup bottle over his chips.

'I never use English for no reason! Why shouldn't I use words from other languages when they happen to be more exact or more expressive?'

He doesn't answer.

'You understand what I mean perfectly well. You can't translate it – "poorly matched", "badly married" – there *isn't* any word in Swedish. Ours is a meagre language.'

Gustav chews and chews.

'Because this phenomenon exists,' I add, looking out the window.

'It's called "mésalliance" in Swedish,' he suggests, but I refuse to crack a smile.

'That's only when you marry beneath your class. You can <u>mismate</u> in many more dimensions. Cilla has discovered that she and her fellow don't match, and that's a shame because she loves him.'

'It's amazing how your heart bleeds for so many other people. Do you think you could muster a bit of concern for my love woes instead?'

I turn white with rage. Or at least I wish I could. How dare he speak that way about my friends – as though it weren't reasonable and natural to concern myself with their problems! I not only get mad, I get mad because I'm getting mad, and utterly furious. I stand up and take my duffle coat – there's a philosophy seminar in fifteen minutes. I walk up the street without even bestowing a glance upon him.

The teacher hasn't arrived yet, so people are milling about in the hall. A classmate asks what we did the week before since she wasn't there, and I exchange a few words with her. Gustav stands next to me and once she moves on, he lowers his mouth to my ear: 'You look like you're going to bite when people talk to you.' He glances at me as if he expects me to smile at him. I turn away and walk into the lecture hall, pretending I don't know him. That *horrible* man. What a *dreadful pity* on me.

A study in heroism?

What makes me the angriest of all is that I can see what I'm doing but can't stop it anyway. I see how ridiculous I am but I can't resist, see how laughable I am but I don't feel like laughing. I've lost any ability to be self-ironic. I'm closed up and locked tight.

From experience, I know that the only thing that can release me is laughter from within – for example, if I think of something funny, I can't help but say it, and to laugh at how amusing I am, and then I can't keep up my martyr-pout any more. Slap her, they say about people who are hysterical and can't stop laughing. Get her to laugh – the cure for hysterical pouters isn't as simple a cure.

Fortunately the lecture is captivating, and it contains an anecdote I giggle at before I can catch myself (in other words, before I remember that I am a Sufferer). The lock is sprung and I become boringly normal again. But I don't have enough energy to go to the post-seminar afterwards.

'I'm going to go home and pull something old over myself,' I explain, 'liberate the world from my sight. I'll come back when I'm finished being depressed.'

'Can I come with you and pull something old over both of us?' Gustav asks.

And so that's what he does.

But the truth can't be hidden for long: in any case not as long as it takes to get an appointment with the doctor and a prescription. In the long run, Gustav isn't satisfied with my vague reasons for rejecting his advances – now there's only one possible explanation: You don't love me any more! That's when I give up and say what men can't stand to hear. Just as I thought: he becomes crazy with desperation, convinced that, as a result of his negligence, he has somehow done me irreparable harm which will make me sterile for the rest of my life. He tears his hair and swears that he will have himself castrated like Abélard and join a monastery.

'That's the most idiotic thing I've ever heard. Nobody's going to join a monastery. I'll just go to the doctor, and I'll be fine within the week.' In order to calm him down, I even say that it's happened before, and, by the way, it could be caused by the Pill.

'I still won't dare have sex with you ever again.'

Men. Isn't that what I said? They can't take anything.

'Then I'm going to have to ravish you,' I say firmly. 'I promise I will ravish you in the middle of Odenplan as soon as I have a clean bill of health.'

Not until that prospect does he cheer up a bit. But I also swear an oath to myself: never again will I attempt to make myself more heroic than I am.

*

A brown envelope arrives with a company address in the corner – it's from the book publisher. Inside I find, as expected, a friendly letter with unfortunately and many qualified applicants and selected another. I decide that it wasn't the dream job after all. If I wasn't The Right One for the job, the job cannot have been The Right One for me, correct? I decide that it wasn't my calling. So the question remains: what *is* my calling? It becomes more pressing with every day that goes by and every test I pass. Although I drag my feet as much as possible, I don't have the energy to fall behind in my studies. After the final course, there will be an unavoidable need for new initiatives. Gustav thinks I should study philosophy, but I still don't want to. My reasons are partly because it would be a pity to ruin such a fun subject, partly because I've already attended so many of the lectures that it would take too little time to finish a degree. Privately I add the reason that I don't know if I'm smart enough for it, and I prefer to leave that issue unexamined.

Maybe I should take a psychological aptitude test. I can take one on my own, actually. I sit down and think about it. What am I actually good at? I'm good at languages, particularly Swedish. I'm the most unilaterally gifted stylist I've ever met. What can you do with that, then? Something with books seems logical. Write books? No, I don't have enough imagination. Write about books? I don't have an interest in literature. Publish books? Doesn't require any particular gift. So what then? Simple, obvious, why haven't I thought of it before? Translate books!

I call the publisher and report this insight. The publisher answers that, at the moment, they don't need any more translators than they already have, but maybe another time. I call Swedish Radio – they must have some use for me in television. But there the response is that they need someone who knows Finnish or Serbo-Croatian – they're drowning in English translators. And when I point out that what they need is someone who knows Swedish, they ask reservedly if I have a degree in any other language. I don't, of course, and I don't want one, either – a university is not a good place to learn languages. I call Swedish Film and inform them that the subtitles on their foreign films are so bad that your skin crawls when you see them. The woman who answers is entirely unaware of this fact – no one else has complained.

I hang up and now I'm sitting here. I have more insight than before, but this is of little help. Can you have a calling for something that doesn't exist?

*

'You're so beautiful,' Gustav says.

This is how he tries to undermine my self-confidence. What he really means, of course, is how beautiful he, Gustav, thinks I am and what a proof of his love this is. In order to demonstrate this proof, he has to constantly point out how ugly I am: what a ridiculous upturned nose, what lousy hair, what comically stubby legs – he laughs his head off every time he sees them without trousers. Then his eyes go glassy with devotion and he holds forth about how he loves them.

Maybe I'm assigning him too much intent– maybe it's simply a combination of how the one in love vacillates between a warped view and intermittent sober-eyed vision (although my legs aren't *that* stubby). But it could also be tactical: first tear down my self-confidence in order to build it up anew – on him.

Even so, he gets nothing for it, because my self-confidence is iron-clad.

'How can it be,' I ask Harriet, 'that most people lack self-confidence? And how can it be that I have enough self-confidence for an entire army? Of course, I *am* beautiful and intelligent, at least intelligent, at least intelligent enough to consider myself pretty enough – but that doesn't usually help, does it?'

'I suppose you had a happy childhood,' Harriet proposes. 'Successful potty training – they say that's the crucial thing.'

'I like people who are self-confident,' I say (congratulating myself). 'You aren't so poorly equipped in that sense either, and it's lovely to know, because then I can tease you without a bad conscience.'

She's sitting with her elbows on the edge of the table, dividing her long, Swedish-blonde hair into three strands to braid them into a coil on her head before her evening ablutions.

'That's true. It's more of a problem with people you have to encourage by telling them how good they are – to remember to praise them the whole time. It's clear,' she adds, with the rubber band between her teeth, 'that it's easier for us to tease each other because we both know we like ourselves.'

'Gustav must have had successful potty training, if that's what it depends on. He has the most solid self-esteem I've ever seen.'

This is probably the most important thing we have in common, I muse: being convinced of our own excellence. I also remember now that he said at one time that I'm the only person he's ever felt completely equal to: neither superior nor inferior.

'I wouldn't be so sure,' she warns. 'Some people are easier to crack than they appear. And, by the way, he seems rather nervous when it comes to you, the way he calls and frets when you're not home.'

'That's true – but only when it comes to me. He's in love with me. It's that kind of insanity. But otherwise he's abnormally secure – you should have seen him at the seminar when he was defending his thesis. Afterwards, the opponent came up and apologized for being so hard on him. Gustav asked him what he meant. He hadn't considered it that hard. He's so convinced that it's good that he doesn't even notice when other people try to shoot him down. Pathological lack of suspicion, what's a good phrase for that?'

'Inverse paranoia?'

I clear the dishes from our evening tea. Harriet's already in her pyjamas and disappears into the loo. After some toothbrushing noises she says something I can't understand.

'What are you babbling on about?'

'I said: What does it mean, actually, that he's ree-lijis?'

'I ask myself that as well. He never talks about it. But sometimes I wonder if his security is somehow based on religion.'

I stand outside the loo with the teapot in my hands and explain to the half-open door: 'He has some idea that what happens in the world isn't all that important, or something like that. That may be what gives him the ability to take things as they come, to laugh and be serious at the same time.'

'A sanguinistic piety?'

'Or a pious sanguinism.'

'It would be nice,' Harriet says and spits in the sink, 'if religion made people that way.'

★

The morning paper says, *USA Ramps Up War: 'Right Way to Bring Hanoi to the Table'*. I read it with the usual combination of fear and a kind of horrible satisfaction: They're making fools of themselves! They're making bigger and bigger fools of themselves! Gustav comes up to return a book he borrowed from Harriet and we leave together – I'm going to the dry cleaner and he to the library. A completely normal day in our lives, a day when it's good the way it is and can stay that way – the kind of day I love. There's an autumnal chill in the air and he has a black rain cape that looks like it belongs to someone from an opera – Don Giovanni or Charles the XII, I can't decide. It flaps in a fantastic way when he stops at the corner to wave.

I go on my errand and then I plan to continue on to the department, but I take the long way by Odenplan thinking that we may run into each other again, and we do, at the corner of Hagagatan.

'*Seldom meeting, swiftly leaving . . .*'* he declaims.

'Leaving swiftly,' I correct. 'It's supposed to have an internal rhyme.'

He has an exam in poetics in the afternoon. I think about it while I nod off through my grammar lecture (this fluorescent tube lighting in these airless caves they call lecture halls!). I think about how, if it had been '*swiftly leaving*' it wouldn't have been that rhetorical figure, what's it called? A chiasmus. I should have pointed that out to him in case he gets a question on it.

Cilla is leafing through a bookstore catalogue – the sale's just begun and I promised to go with her to the shop afterwards. When we come out, it's begun to snow – small, sharp grains that sting our eyes. Even so, it's a balm after the painful light and heat indoors. She follows me home after our bookstore visit to have coffee. She's realized that her 'husband' wasn't

* A line from a poem by Erik Axel Karlfeldt, 'Intet är som väntanstider'.

worth having, anyway. Cilla says that you should do something with your life instead – join a study group, for example. I tell her I started to attend one about developing countries, but I soon found it more efficient to read on my own.

We're sitting in the fading afternoon light and talking about men and what we're doing with our lives. It's a completely normal day. Just as I've started to make dinner and put a pan of rice on the hob for myself (new eating habits), the phone rings. It's Gustav, just returned from his exam.

'Can you love a man who doesn't know what a ballad strophe is?'

'I love you just as you are. Do you have class tonight?'

'Yes, but I'm skipping it. Besides, it's a snow day.'

'Harriet's off to a concert. So if you want, you can stand under my window at eight. Don't forget to pull your cape up over your face, though.'

It's not that often that we have the opportunity to meet undisturbed, or without disturbing others. To be sure, Harriet and I have never forbidden each other men in our rooms, but our sense of delicacy prevents us from copulating right under each other's noses: the walls are so thin you can hear the slightest cough, and who enjoys listening to other people in the throes of passion? Neither of us, in any event. So Harriet has season symphony tickets and I have a Film Club subscription.

When she comes home around eleven, Gustav and I are once again engaged in virtuous conversation about freedom of will and the substantial self. About equality and performance prejudices and believing that you're someone. I've realized that no person is anything. Gustav has realized that all persons are something. The question is whether we actually believe the same thing.

'I don't think I'm anything,' I say, 'but since nobody else is anything, then I have just as much value as everyone else.'

'I don't know if I *am* anything, but maybe I could become something. If we put together the two of us who aren't anything, maybe we can be something together.'

'What, for example?'

'Hmm, a happy marriage, for example.'

'That would at least be original,' I admit. 'It would satisfy my search for originality. You so seldom see a happy marriage.'

'Erik's been married for five years now,' he says, thinking. It's unclear what this has to do with the subject we're discussing, but I don't ask about whether Erik is happy or not. Instead I ask, 'In five years – do you think we'll be around then? Do you think the world will still exist?' (*USA Ramps Up War: 'Right Way to Bring Hanoi to the Table'*.)

'I suppose so.'

'In ten years, then?'

'Maybe the world, maybe not humans.'

'I mean humans. This world.'

'No, I don't think this world will exist in ten years.'

Then he laughs – as if he knows something about it – and throws on his cloak to wade through the slush.

'*Seldom meeting, leaving swiftly*,' I say, 'is a chiasmus.'

'No it's not. It's a living hell,' Gustav says, and wraps me in his arms once again with a fantastic flapping of his rain cape.

7

'Want to go have a coffee?' Bengt asks as we troop out of class and a group assembles. I can't think of anything I'd rather do, because sitting with a group over coffee and being an amateur philosopher is the best thing I know. But Gustav and I had made plans to spend the evening at my place, so I realize I have to rephrase the question and ask Gustav: 'Do we want to go have a coffee?'

No, we don't. We prefer to go home. He doesn't ask what I want to do. And I say nothing, no, I say nothing at all if I'm not asked. I walk along next to him and say nothing all the way home.

Why does it always happen this way? When we're alone, it's so good to be together. We speak our own language and are completely wrapped up in each other. But as soon as we're out and about with others – as soon as I feel a tug in another direction – then I realize that Gustav is there *too*. I can't do what I want, because I'm not just 'me' any more. I'm just a part of 'we'. Because there are two of us.

I wonder if I can ever get used to this.

The whole way home I pout, not because I enjoy pouting – although it probably seems that way. I've simply got caught in it again. I don't answer when he tries to discuss the lecture with me. I walk up the stairs without looking at him – as if it didn't interest me in the least whether or not he followed along.

But once I open the door, I see that the flat is full of people: Cilla and a friend of hers are sitting drinking coffee with Harriet.

At the sight of them, I'm immediately restored. I join their company happily and talkatively in Harriet's room (without asking what Gustav wants). He goes home as soon as he's finished his coffee and Cilla stays to dinner.

Later on that evening, regret catches up to me. I leave my books and go outside to walk off my mood in the winter storm. It's stinging cold and I'm already on my way back when I see a familiar figure disappear in the neighbouring doorway on Frejgatan – is that Gustav, sneaking around on my block?

He told me that he did such things when he was younger. And, besides, I was hardly any better myself, as I've said – I spent my teenage years lurking in people's neighbourhoods and remember what it was like: sometimes it was just a game, wandering around in a daze, excited at the thought of running into the one you worshipped. But sometimes it was something you did because you couldn't do anything else – you were out of your mind with unhappiness and just wanted to be in his *vicinity*. That's why you wandered the streets at night: it was the least unbearable thing you could do. Does Gustav have it that bad?

When he sees me coming towards the door where he's hidden himself, he emerges and follows me upstairs although it's already quite late. I want to apologize for the afternoon, but I don't know how to start. I don't know how such situations can ever be avoided, and asking forgiveness if you know you're going to do it again is dishonest.

'Tea?' I offer, but he shakes his head. I sit down next to him on the couch.

'This can't go on.'

'What can't go on?' I ask, hiding my fear by pretending I don't understand.

'I never get any closer to you. There's too great a distance between us.'

(As far as I'm concerned, I think the distance is just right.)

'I can't take it any more,' he says. 'I've tried, but you never change in the least.'

(Why should I change? This is the way I was when you chose me, and you knew that I wasn't particularly nice.)

'You never do anything for me. I'm sure that if you really loved someone, you'd do anything for him.'

(So I never do anything for you? Well, if you say so.)

These are not complaints that you can respond to. I close up completely. Offended to my very core (Why don't you believe in my love? Why don't you acknowledge my way of loving? Why don't you give me the right to be the person I am?) – and feeling guilty (It's true: I don't love him the way he loves me, and I should, naturally).

Offended and feeling guilty, oh yes.

'You're with me only because you can have me, just because you can. You're just looking for some kind of guarantee of security, the safe type that sits in his armchair with his pipe and his tweed jacket . . .'

'Tweed jacket!' This is too much for me. 'Security! If there's anything I don't need, it's security. I've always been secure enough in myself.'

'Then what do you want me for?'

'Well, you can't expect that I'm looking for an adventure in you.'

'You can look for me in me, that's what you're not doing.'

Maybe so. I just don't understand why there has to be such searching and rummaging and arguing all the time. Why can't it *stay the way it is*? Aren't we *happy together*?

He sits with his head in his hands, silent. Unhappiness incarnate. I can't think of anything to say. After he sits there in silence for a long time, he gets up and leaves. He simply leaves.

I sit on the couch crying because everything is so awful, but there's also a cold irritation in my anxiety: What use is it? Why does he make such scenes and pretend to leave when he knows as well as I do that he'll be back soon?

And just so – I haven't had a chance to do more than wash my face when I hear him coming up the stairs again, and I go out and open the door before he's had a chance to ring and wake up Harriet. Hopefully, she's sleeping.

★

So Gustav's love didn't disappear after we seduced each other. But where did my lust go?

I don't want to be that banal figure who loses interest as soon as the 'conquest' has been made, I certainly don't, but I can't help it that the bed-side of love isn't as enjoyable any more. Well, sometimes. But not as often as Gustav finds it enjoyable, because he always wants to do it, and I mean *always*.

To be honest, it's my good fortune that we don't have the chance to indulge more often than we do. Otherwise, I'm the last person to claim that there's any advantage to a clandestine love affair. It's not romantic at all to have to whisper and sneak around. What it is, is nervous and ridiculous: to 'grab the chance' when others happen to be out, brief and hurried moments of intimacy with your ear cocked: Was that a key in the lock? Did you close the door properly? What time is it? Not very intimate at all, and very little room for worship.

The only advantage to having the chance so infrequently is that the fact that I'm so seldom in the mood escapes more notice. My hormonal make-up must be sub-dimensional – it disappears completely next to Gustav's, and I would claim that his is not extreme for a twenty-year-old man with his male virility unspilt (at least previously unspilt on women). He says his urges are much like tigers on a leash. And I assume that's normal.

My hormones seem to be of a more mental nature. I am mentally attracted to him – I don't mean a union of the souls, but rather a mental lust for physical union. I like *thinking* about having sex with him. I like thinking about it more than I like doing it. It works rather well now, but if we were married and had unlimited opportunities, it would be a chronic source of conflict. Because I don't think it's fun more than about once or twice a week, but Gustav says he would rather spend his entire life in one uninterrupted coitus.

How fortunate that we're not married, when you think about it.

*

During Easter vacation, we go to the Island – without a chaperone, but accompanied by admonitions to 'take care of each other'. I make a grimace when I hear them – the usual nagging about not getting each other pregnant with twins of course – although I know it can have another meaning as well, larger and more difficult, and more relevant.

We're the only ones that disembark at the intersection. The bus scrambles off around the corner. I stand for a moment and simply listen. The soughing of trees! The powerful rushing in the treetops of the pines on the hill, up through the forest – oh, when did I last hear the soughing of trees? Probably the last time I was here: the same treetops.

I'm happy to return so we can layer new memories over the awkward ones from my last visit. The place looks completely different this time of year. You can see so far when the deciduous trees have dropped their leaves – you have a view of the entire world. Easter is early this year – there's sunshine but a wintry wind. Our breath steams white, even indoors. The first thing we do is to drag the damp bedclothes outside into the sunshine to warm them. And we chop wood for the stove and the heater. Gustav lets me handle the saw and I toil until the sweat drips. Is there anything that makes you happier than physical labour? Splitting wood is even better: an unparalleled way to let out your aggressions. It takes less time, obviously, if Gustav does it, but I have to practise. I refuse to let go of the axe and tell him to put on the potatoes if he needs something to do.

Towards evening, the temperature in the living room is satisfactory. We're staying in the larger cottage, which has embroidered aphorisms on all of the walls (Grandmother stitched them, Gustav explains): 'There's no place like home', 'Praise not the day before evening has come', 'The fear of the Lord is the beginning of wisdom'. We sleep under 'The fear of the Lord'.

When the trees are bare, you can see the neighbouring cottage, otherwise hidden by vegetation. A little old lady lives there all year round. She's about 100 years old and she's always been there. Gustav usually helps her to carry in wood and water. How she manages when nobody else is around is a mystery – it must be the elves. I look through the window one morning and see that he's stopped for a chat with her on his way back from the well. When he comes in carrying the pails, I ask, curious, what they were talking about. He laughs.

'She'd seen that I had a lass along with me, and said, "Well, well, you have to have a good time when you're young . . ."'

'What do you mean "have a good time"? How silly.'

'Isn't that the definition of a good time? Living in a little cottage in the country with a little lass?'

'I'm not a little lass.'

'Aren't you? You look like one anyway.'

'That may be. But it's not a *good time* to live in a little cottage with me, you can tell her that.'

There's only one bicycle in the shed, but Gustav saw that there was one in the little old lady's woodshed, and it appears she's willing to lend it. It looks rather shaky at first – it must be decades since it was last used. But with the help of a tyre pump and an oil can, we're able to tinker it into shape. 'How well-made things were back then!' I shout and wobble out onto the road on the high, strange vehicle.

We ride down to the fishing harbour and look at boats, and up to the country grocer to get provisions for the weekend. Then I chop more wood – not because we need it, but for future needs: I assume you can let out aggressions preventively?

On Good Friday, an icy north wind blows tiny grains of snow. Gustav calls the church to find out if there's a shuttle. The churchwarden is speechless – summer guests with no car who want to come to High Mass – there's no precedent for that. Eventually he mumbles that there's a church shuttle, but it's intended for members of the congregation only. The church of our fathers cannot take on such a case as ours.

This is a challenge we can't resist, so we put on everything we have and head off on our bicycles. It's more than five miles to the church and it feels like fifteen with the head wind. We don't arrive until the sermon has started. And it's hardly an adequate reward for our efforts. Not at all. Why must members of the clergy be so officious? I have nothing against psalms and ceremony, but these platitudes they call preaching? Gustav giggles when the vicar explains to the congregation that they don't have to be sad that it's Good Friday. I poke him angrily in the side and tell him that he can giggle silently if he has to.

The trip home goes twice as fast. We're hungry now, too, and we devour our pancakes with lingonberry jam. I mean, we have to cook them first before we can devour them. We take turns flipping them – not because of some sort of passion for equality, but because we're too hungry to wait, and we eat them as soon as they're ready.

Otherwise, we actually apply strict equality and share the cooking and dishwashing evenly. Gustav expresses such delight that I'm insulted: 'What do you mean, did you think I was going to let you take care of all the household duties?'

'You never know. You see what happened to Erik. And I've never noticed any domestic tendencies in you before.'

'No, that's true. If you want something delicious, you'll have to make it yourself. But even I can open cans and packages.'

When I discover that he's bought lamb cutlets for Easter Eve, I decide he can take care of that himself. He reads the cookbooks and fiddles at the hob for a long time while I lie on the sofa with a bag of liquorice strings and say, 'What a fuss.'

Of course, it's delicious once it's ready, I can't argue with that. But is it worth the trouble? I mean, when you can live on canned food and liquorice strings.

There are two boats that need scraping and painting – both the rowboat and the wooden sailboat. They require many days of work. But the weather doesn't allow for much time outdoors. Mostly we sit in our wicker armchairs in the warm kitchen with books and our feet near the wood stove. Gustav is reading the *Iliad*, required for his course on literary history, and I'm reading *Crime and Punishment* since he said that you can't associate with people who haven't read Dostoyevsky. Domestic bliss. A stove with crackling wood, a warm room at dusk, the wind keening around the corners, Gustav and me. And our respective selections from world literature.

Our domestic bliss is complete until the rest of the world announces its existence again. It does so in the form of Gustav's parents, who are to arrive on Easter morning. He begins to talk about setting an alarm clock so that he wakes up in time, in the interests of decency, to move his bed out into the kitchen. I groan. Here we go again. Decency – what is that? Is it more decent to be dishonest than to be unchaste?

'Do you really think they're going to believe that? Don't you think they're aware that we're having sex?'

'Maybe so, but there's a difference when you display it so obviously. If we do, they may feel they have to intervene.'

'Do as you like. I refuse to get involved in such nonsense.'

It's not that easy. After our evening tea, he wants to cuddle. I retreat, but he won't leave me alone.

'What's wrong with you? Why are you so inaccessible?'

'What do you mean, inaccessible?' I hiss. 'I'm just the way I always am.'

'True, when you're at your worst.'

'You can't keep copulating constantly. Didn't we do it yesterday, and the day before, and last Wednesday, twice – I don't have a limitless supply of hormones.'

'It's not just "hormones",' Gustav says, 'and not just "copulating".' (Why can't he use my words without quotation marks?) 'I can't reach you in any way at all.'

'I hate double standards,' I mumble. (To be sure, I don't want to discuss that topic either, but I'd rather talk about that than about my general inaccessibility.) 'First you make me a bad girl, then you want to appear to be a good boy for your family. I feel repudiated. Is that so hard to understand?'

'I've offered you marriage, haven't I? That's what you don't want.'

'They can't be aware of that,' I say curtly, and his eyes grow wide at this sudden shift in logic.

'I don't want to hurt them unnecessarily,' he explains. 'They see things from such a different point of view. Would you hesitate to do the same thing for your own parents?'

'As it happens, we're not talking about my parents. This is your problem. But I think you're a hypocrite, that's all I'm saying.'

Then I think about what it would be like if it were my parents, and I shudder at the prospect. 'If it were mine,' I say, 'I would admit what I was doing if I truly had a clear conscience, and otherwise I wouldn't do it.'

After I think about it a little more, I add: 'I would at least move the bed out the evening before and sleep there for one night so that it was true in any case – not move it in the *morning*.'

'Jesuitical reasoning!' he laughs. 'It's just a subtler form of hypocrisy. Just enough so that you fool yourself, too.'

We get no further – no further than that we find each other hypocritical or Jesuitical. So we have to sleep together as an act of reconciliation. But I have no desire at that point. I can't share his physical joy. Seeing it simply makes me more distraught. His face above me: so child-like, so soft and naked and completely exposed. He's such a child – 'take care of each other' – I collapse under the weight of this responsibility and burst into tears.

Gustav strokes my hair, worried, and tries to talk to me. I can't say anything more. He pulls on his robe and crouches next to the bed with his head next to mine. 'Sleep,' I whisper. 'Please just let me sleep.'

He ends up leaving me, moving his bed out and spending what remains of the night in the kitchen. And so it stands there in all of its false decency when Father-in-Law and Mother-in-Law make their entrance the next morning.

I take a walk in the forest.

*

Although we don't have the opportunity to have sex more often than we do, the situation comes up again and again: Gustav wants to, I don't want to. What do you do? How do you compromise on something like this?

For the most part, he can get me into the mood even if I'm not at first. But it requires endless patience and engagement. Gustav has both this endless patience and this engagement, but I don't. Sometimes I have no desire to feel desire. I'm not even in the mood to place myself at his disposal. So I say no. Then he gets so sad and upset and convinced that I don't love him that, every time, I end up having to go to bed with him anyway.

And that's how prostitution is born – I invent it anew just as it's been invented throughout the ages. It's a bit of an exaggeration to call it that, according to Gustav: we're not even married. But what is it otherwise? If you don't sleep with someone because you want to, you must be doing it for some other reason, and the nature of prostitution is the same whether it's for money or civil status or whatever else you receive in exchange.

'Grit your teeth and think about something else': this ancient advice to women. But with Gustav, that doesn't work, because he doesn't enjoy it if I'm not in as well; he doesn't think it's any fun if I'm not having fun, too.

To be honest, it's not such a high price for what I get in return: security, of course, and companionship. Sexual security as well: sleeping with him when I'm not in the mood means I'll have someone to sleep with when I am. But I never get the chance to save up for spontaneous lust any more when I'm always 'satisfied' in advance. I also doubt that it's psychologically possible to grit your teeth at certain times and think about something else, and other times to participate fully and think it's fun: doing it against your will is so traumatic that it must colour the entire experience and imbues the act of sexual intercourse itself with a feeling of aversion. Every one of his advances feels like a threat, and each caress mobilizes my resistance. We become stuck in our roles and can't get out of them: the yes-sayer and the no-sayer, or rather the no-sayer and the oh-yes-sayer, the shirker and the nagger.

'You cannot imagine how humiliating it is to be used,' I complain.

'You cannot imagine how humiliating it is to be rejected,' he answers.

'Oh yes I can. I can imagine that I'm the one who's randy and you're the one who withdraws – it must be absolute hell. I'm quite aware of that.'

'In that case, I suppose I can imagine what it's like to not be in the mood, too.'

'You cannot, in any case, imagine what it would be like to have sex with me under such circumstances, because it's a physical impossibility.'

He admits that I could have a point there. 'Although it's not that much more difficult a thought exercise to imagine that I'm being used than that I'm not randy.'

'No, both of those are equally alien. That's what I'm saying. Why are we so different in precisely *this* area?'

He wonders, too.

8

All that's left for me to do in English, strictly speaking, is to cobble together a senior essay. A bagatelle of a few pages, nothing to speak of. It's just that I can't decide on a topic, so that means I have to ask Gustav.

'I'm sure there are people in your department who've been through this before,' he answers. 'Just pick an area, and they'll have a long list of topics.'

'I can make long lists myself. The problem, you see, is that all topics seem just as meaningful.'

But since Gustav doesn't suggest one, I look up the administrative assistant's office hours in the catalogue to get some advice. However, he isn't in the room when I arrive – just another teacher who's giving a test. He tells me to go to my adviser.

'Oh, I see,' I say, as if it were an entirely fresh idea.

It's an old idea, of course: back when he gave me my test for the literature course, I asked him about a senior essay topic, and he looked like essays were the worst thing he could think of and said I may as well choose some book from the course to discuss.

However, unfortunately, my adviser's room is directly adjacent on the corridor, and since his door is ajar, he may have heard our conversation. I decide I have no choice and enter.

I try to strike a casual tone:

'I'm just looking for a senior essay topic.'

He looks up from his papers and removes his glasses.

'I see. Did you think you'd find one here?'

My eyes wander around the room. An armchair for visitors, the desk, the unwashed coffee cup, the box of Corn Flakes on the bookshelf, the papers he's working on.

'Well,' I breathe and smile apologetically, as if it should have been obvious to me that the English department is the last place in the city where you ought to look for a topic for a senior essay in English and English professors the least likely of all people whom you could imagine being able to advise you in such a matter.

'What area, then?'

'Modern literature, I think. Everything's probably been said about Shakespeare and such, I suppose?'

Of course nobody has ever believed that you could say something new in a senior essay of fifteen pages, but not even such an outrageous comment elicits any reaction.

'I see. Well, you can take something from your coursework. Orwell, Hemingway.'

I don't say a word.

'Lawrence,' he adds after a look that clearly registers my gender.

'Yes,' I say, 'one of those, for example.'

'So you'll have it ready for your exam later, too.'

Of course, I should have known. He doesn't even remember that he himself was the one who gave me my test in modern literature one month ago.

'Alright, then,' I say to end the conversation, 'I'll have a look at Shaw.'

He doesn't seem to notice that I've mentioned a different name than the ones he listed, or maybe he doesn't hear what I mumble. I retreat backwards and he returns to his papers before I've even shut the door.

Shaw is all well and fine – I know him inside out. But what

I'm going to do *with* him is what I have to figure out. I decide to hell with him. I bike home and lie down to read Naess instead, *Empirical Semantics*, which I've borrowed from Gustav.

*

'Do you love me?' Gustav asks.

'What do you mean by "love"?'

He sighs.

'I don't think,' I explain, 'that you can ask that question. The phrase "I love you" lacks any truth value – it only has emotive meaning. In the way the nihilists describe moral statements: it's like saying "ough" or "hurray", nothing more.

'It might qualify as a performative utterance, such as saying "I promise", which is performed at the moment it's said, and whose meaning is contained by the saying alone. But it couldn't be a statement, no; it only seems to be one. It doesn't correspond to any verifiable relationship in reality, such as "person P performs action A in situation S." It's something you can exclaim when you need to ease your inner pressure: "Oh how I love you." But you can't ask about it. As a question, it's meaningless.'

And thus ends my lecture.

'You know what I mean,' Gustav says.

'You're right, I know. I do love you. Sometimes. When the wind blows from the north-north-west.'

'Loving is an act of will. It's something you decide to do.'

'Oh no it's not. It's not something you have any control over. It comes and it goes, and nobody knows, but you can decide to ignore it.'

I've decided to ignore feelings and their transience: you can't build your life on passion. Being newly in love all the time can't possibly be something desirable, and it doesn't bother me that my feelings for Gustav are different now than they were six months ago.

But it bothers him. Day and night.

'You're not staking anything on me,' he complains.

'What do you mean, staking? This isn't a bloody game of roulette, is it?'

'You don't care about me, you just accept me like a home décor detail, a household item – like a pot or something, which you fetch from its place.'

Yes, and why not? This is my ideal relationship: a tidy and shining row on your pan rack, which stays where you've put it until you take something down as needed. Knowing where you have each other, taking it for granted and otherwise being able to use your energy on more significant things. But this incessant analysing of ourselves and our relationship and manipulating it – like a disobedient pot that constantly hops down from its rack and runs amok around the entire room to remind you of its existence – what am I supposed to do with that?

He leaves without saying goodbye. I'm tired of it, I'm weary and humiliated from finding myself preoccupied with something as idiotic as domestic quarrels.

Love, love, love. I suppose I do, but why talk about it? To me it seems like love for your country – just as unnecessary and risky as a concept. Of course I love this land above all others on earth, and I would die if I didn't get to live here. I love it because it's home, and I would probably do so even if it wasn't in fact one of the best countries there is to live in. But that doesn't mean I'm prepared to stand up and sing national anthems or wave Swedish flags: Love of country is only tolerable if it can be tacit.

That's how I'd like it to be with Gustav: to just be home with him without having to babble on about it.

I go to bed and sleep, and when I wake up I'm less angry but more unhappy.

'Some people are from birth unsuited to marriage,' Gustav quoted. Well, there you have it. Why doesn't he give up trying to transform me, then? Clearly, from all points of view, it would be best if we split up so that he can start all over again and get his happy marriage with some less unsuitable person, and I can grow old gracefully.

It becomes so obvious to me while I make my coffee that I set aside my cup without drinking it so I can lie down and cry instead. He rings my door bell at just the right moment for me to cry in his arms.

'Can't we stop arguing about it?' I beg. 'Can't we stop talking about how we want things to be and just be?'

'The weather is nice – we can go for a bike ride.'

And that's what we do. We take our bicycles and pedal straight through town. Here the streets are dry and dusty in the spring wind and at Tegelbacken we see a truck full of park benches on their way out of winter storage. The sun is shining and you can sit on the deck of the *af Chapman* and drink coffee, but we continue out to Kastellholmen, biking hand in hand with puddles between us on the road.

I've forgotten my cap and my hair is one huge knot after our ride. I don't have a comb, either, so I borrow Gustav's once we've sat down on the slope below the castle. He frowns as he watches me work on my hair, which I do in my usual way: when the comb gets stuck, I yank, and tufts of hair waft down into the grass. 'Let me do it,' he cajoles. 'You can't,' I say, but he insists: 'You can at least let me try.'

All right, then. I sit between his knees and he combs my hair. It feels nice to have your hair combed, that's true, but when he claims he's finished, I take the comb from him and try it myself, incredulous – where did all the tangles go?

'I untangled them. There's not much to it.'

I return his comb, once again baffled. Where on earth does he get his patience, I wonder to myself.

*

By this time I'm so furious that nobody will tell me how to write a senior essay that I set to work out of pure rage, and I simply write what flows from my pen, applying all the knowledge I've acquired about literary terminology and academic jargon. Soon I'm intoxicated with the joy of articulation, and the content suffers somewhat. Gustav says that you have to determine what the essay is going to be about before you start to write, but I just write; what it's about is something I'll leave to the reader to decide.

After sixteen pages, I cap my pen. I don't know if it's finished; since I don't know how you construct an essay, I can't know if it's finished. In any event, I'm tired of it, so I put it in a bag and go out to Gustav, who's on the Island to take care of his boats.

He says it's the best essay he's ever read on the topic 'What I think of Shaw's *Candida*'. Then it's good enough; I post it to my adviser.

Gustav is scraping his boats. I take a walk in the forest. Blankets of windflowers beneath the trees, now and again a rain shower, as light as a whisper; 'All kinds of weather must be beautiful in the country,' I say dreamily. For our lunch, we pick small home-grown nettles at the corner of the house and cook an exquisite soup.

But without any work to do, my existential anxiety haunts me. What will I do with my life? To start with, what will I do this summer? I'm not that fond of travel, but I like having travelled: memories from foreign countries once the difficulties are overcome. Last summer I did nothing, and it felt empty afterwards. I plough through several stacks of travel brochures and course offerings, and I sign up for a month on a kibbutz in Israel.

'Why Israel of all places?' Gustav asks when I return to the city to apply for a passport and he follows me to the steamboat dock.

'Because you can work and do something of meaning while

you're there. A round trip through Jordan and Lebanon is included as well, but that's just the touristy part. Israel is the main attraction.'

'Pay attention to the refugee camps, then, while you're travelling around.'

Refugee camps? Oh right, Palestinian.

'I'll pay attention to everything,' I assure him, and it would surprise me if I came home a Zionist.

I don't know if his disapproval is truly politically motivated or if it's mostly a justification of a private issue. He was in Israel himself on a holiday trip with his family a couple of years ago, so I think he ought to be happy that I'll get to see the country, too.

'Why can't you be on the Island?' he asks. 'Don't you think it's paradise on earth?'

'I just don't think I've earned paradise yet. And it's not my island. I want to do something on my own first, then we can be in paradise for the rest of the summer.'

'When are we going to go sailing, then?'

'Won't we have time to do that when I get back? I don't intend to emigrate.'

'Do you love me?' he asks me on the dock.

'What do you mean by "love"?'

'Take it in any sense you want.'

'In that case,' I say gaily (one foot on the deck of the boat), 'there's always some sense in which I love you.'

9

'Do you think you could at least stop snapping at me in public?'
Gustav says hesitantly. 'When we're alone, I guess I can take it,
but when we're around other people it's a bit embarrassing.'

You can't sink into the earth even if you'd like to – the only
thing you can do with your shame is to withdraw. I withdraw
and feel so ashamed I could die.

I try to figure out which occasion he's thinking about, and I
recall, with increasing distress, an entire series of them. Maybe
the other day when we were having dinner with his family
and Father-in-Law asked what my senior essay was about, and
Gustav laughed and said 'Martina's leaving it up to the reader',
and I explained icily that it was an attempt to analyse Ber-
nard Shaw's *Candida*, emphasizing 'attempt' as if Gustav were
responsible for its methodological flaws by not having written
it for me.

Or maybe, when I had found out that the trip to Israel
was cancelled because of the imminent threat of war, Gustav
explained to Harriet that Martina believes it's her fault: just
because she planned to travel, a war broke out in the Middle
East – and I hissed something about *schadenfreude* and that the
war had more likely been caused by his fervent prayers.

Or the weekend when we were on the Island with the family
and it rained and rained, and I went daft from being in the same
room with Anna-Karin all day and took my raincoat to go out in

the worst downpour, and Gustav said, 'Martina thinks all weather is beautiful in the countryside' and I slammed the door
behind me so that the window panes rattled . . .

Yes, he teases me, but he teases me good-naturedly and in
the way that's always been our natural tone of discourse – not
to make fun of me in front of others, but rather the other way
around: to establish a kind of common understanding with
me by alluding to things we've talked about before. I can see it
afterwards, but in the moment I can't see anything at all – his
attempts to connect with me just make me itch. I break away,
kick him in the metaphorical shin, snap at him and leave –
and it's not until then that those around us become aware
of what's happening and everyone feels sorry for Gustav, of
course.

I can't handle being around other people with him. I don't
like being 'with' anyone in company, I mean being in a larger
group of people with someone who belongs to me, who represents me in some manner and whom I represent – for example,
I detest being responsible for bad jokes that Gustav tells; even
if the others laugh, I sit there, cold. Most of all I detest his
intervention in something I'm saying to someone else, through
explaining or commenting, in the capacity of someone who
knows more about me. I've had the same thing with Harriet
at times. I remember parties where I've been annoyed by her
presence, since she knows me so well that I can't behave like a
different Martina if I want to – oh yes, there are many occasions
I can remember, and my conclusion is simply that this is the
way I am.

This is no excuse. Not at all: there's no excuse for snapping
at the person you belong to in the presence of others. You must
have enough loyalty that you can keep it inside until you're face
to face. I don't excuse myself, either; I say that I'm so ashamed
that I don't know what to do. I sit down to write a letter to him;

at the moment he's in town, of course, but this is a topic that's easier in writing.

> *I know that I'm insufferable – you don't have to inform me of that. I understand that it can seem small comfort as long as I don't do anything about it, but it means in any case that I'm aware that I'm in your debt because you put up with me.*
>
> *It's so hard to belong to someone. When I'm alone, it doesn't matter what mood I'm in. I can do something else and not think about it. But when I'm with you, it suddenly becomes so meaningful. You notice my mood swings before I do myself and they're enlarged through you, and then it feels like it's your fault. I notice that I act as if it were your fault that I can't write an essay, that I didn't get to travel to Israel, that it was raining at the Island. I don't know why, but it's as if you invite me to lay the blame for everything on you and to take my bad mood out on you.*
>
> *I won't get any better. Don't believe it: I'll get worse. I'll snap and carp and be irritated at you because it rains and repulse your advances and delay our marriage, and once we're married I'll be worst of all and snap at you in front of the entire world and travel and cheat on you and put glass shards in the sugar. But I'll stand by you. Because you're the one I belong to.*
>
> *No matter who I shared my life with, I would be irritated at him and blame him for the rain, but anyone who wants to put up with me will probably have to aspire to sainthood.*
>
> *Do you want me?*

I read through what I've written and don't feel it's quite the confession of sins that I had intended. It sounds downright unrepentant; the conviction of my inability to change seems to have slipped in and prevented me from making any promises I can't keep. I pick up my pen again and improve it:

> *PS: I mean, forgive me?*

I try to tidy it up with a Bible reference as well. I scratch 'Prov. 27:15' in the corner. (*A continual dripping on a very rainy day and a contentious woman are alike.*)

I run out to the postbox to catch the final collection and prevent a new round of break-up/reconciliation scenes.

OK, Gustav says, this time he supposes he can forgive me. But what about later? How will it be later – will it be this way our entire life? He talks about our life, our future. I sigh. We're lying in the grass at Haga, with our bicycles companionably leaned against each other by a giant oak tree. Brunnsviken is glittering in the sun, the lilacs are blooming above us, and we're arguing about our future.

He wants us to get engaged.

'That would just be involving our families,' I say impatiently, 'it wouldn't change anything between us.'

'Our families are already involved.'

'I'm not the one who's involved them!'

'It would be so nice to have a ring,' he says then, uninhibitedly naïve.

Of course it would, I do not say. Who doesn't think it would be nice to have a ring – who isn't naïve enough for that! Going about waving your left hand with a shiny gold ring on it – it's obvious that it's everyone's innermost longing and the reason why most engagements take place. But I thought mature people could refrain from such things. The only point of an engagement that I can see is declaring that one intends to marry; an engagement-instead-of-marriage is the silliest triumph of convention.

'They think it looks odd,' Gustav says, 'since you're at the Island and everything. The longer it drags out the odder they think it looks.'

I groan.

'First you invite me out there, then you say that your family thinks it looks so odd that I'm there, so now we have to at least get engaged. That's what I call blackmail. You make it look as if I've committed the crime of breaking marriage vows. I beg to emphasize that this is, in fact, not the state of affairs.'

'What are we going to do, then – aren't we ever going to get married?'

'I thought we already were.'

'Well, yes,' he admits, 'of course we are, before God and each other of course, I know. But in the eyes of the world . . .'

'A subterfuge! You wouldn't use that as an argument if it weren't for the fact that you want it yourself – but how can you want it? You know what I'm like. You have to realize that everything would just get worse, don't you?'

This is what he doesn't understand. He believes I'm going to change. Learn to adapt and to be considerate, to make an effort.

If only he hadn't said precisely 'make an effort'. To adapt and be considerate, I can accept that, but make an effort – that's the limit. He sounds just like an older schoolteacher or a parent, like a moral guardian preaching a lesson. No, I can't stand it. I cannot accept that someone is telling me to make an effort.

'No, that's enough,' I say and stand up. 'I want you, but I don't want to marry you in the name of the law.'

We ride home and part ways at my front door without any more discussion. I lock my bike and look at him.

'Don't you want me, then?' I ask, and since 'then' refers to what I said ten minutes ago, he answers no. We stand on the pavement looking at each other and try to determine whether we're serious, that this is the end. I start to giggle.

'Are you laughing?'

'Should I cry?'

He throws his leg over his bike and turns around:

'That book you borrowed, Naess – you can send it by mail, then.'

I start to giggle harder, hysterically and angrily: 'This is about our lives, and you start talking about Naess!'

He takes off. I go inside. Are we really serious? I push the thought aside, can't bear thinking about us any more today. I pick up *Saint Joan*, which I had planned to read in Haga Park, and lie down on the couch.

The sun shines the next morning as it did the day before. But my phone is silent. I drink my coffee and don't know what to do afterwards. I put 'Et maintenant' on the record player, a dreadfully sentimental old song.

What am I supposed to do with all this time, my life? How I abhor being confronted with 'my life'. If only it were simply a normal Tuesday morning. But it isn't. I can't bike out to Haga Park and lie down under a blooming lilac alone – how will I ever be able to lie under a lilac again? How can I be anywhere at all?

I pack a suitcase and leave. Away, anywhere, in any event I can't be here, with that song on the record player and a telephone that just sits there, silent. I take the subway to Vårberg and hitchhike southwards – maybe I can visit Cilla, who's at her family's summer cottage. I know approximately where it is.

After ten minutes I get a ride with a tiresome man who wants to talk. He asks where I'm going and I say Småland. That sounds so vague that he may start to believe that I'm hitchhiking just to be picked up, but he can't really complain, because he's just as mysterious about his own business. He claims his job is to drive around and check the surface of the roads. Because it's convenient, I assume that people are speaking the truth until the opposite is proven. I pay him no attention, and I sink into my own musings.

Just before Södertälje he suddenly turns off at the exit for Rönninge, and I don't understand a thing. I still don't understand anything when the police car that was standing at the crossroad catches up to us and pulls the car over. I'm just annoyed with the cops, and when they want to do a breathalyser test I even get embarrassed for their sake. I've never seen one of those devices before, but the package that one of the officers brings over to the car looks just as awkward and ridiculous as a package of condoms, a topic for stories on the same level.

Not until the officer explains that the test is positive and that we have to follow along to the station in Södertälje do I comprehend anything. The man denies having drunk anything and blames his unsafe driving on exhaustion, insomnia – he's in the midst of a divorce, he explains pitifully, can't you understand how that feels?

It doesn't help, of course. And by the way, anyone else could tell from miles away that the man reeks of alcohol, and the empty vodka bottle that the police retrieve from the floor has probably been lying there in full view – I'm the only one who's so idiotically oblivious.

The driver is taken away in the patrol car, and I have to stay in his car, which the other officer drives. I wonder if it was true, what he said about a divorce. Why not? One person takes to the bottle, the other to the road. Escape routes. Where do they lead to?

At the station, I have to convince them that I don't know the man, and that I was simple-minded enough not to have noticed that he was intoxicated. I happen to have my student ID on me and can at least prove that I am me, whatever that's supposed to prove, but I'm stumped when they ask what parish I was born in. Was I born in a parish? I was born in the maternity ward but have no idea what parish it belongs to – or do they mean where my parents lived, the parish I moved to after the hospital? Giving the address of my employer is also an issue, especially when a police officer is sitting behind the typewriter taking down my answers. Holländargatan? – no, that's just the student

association. Odengatan? Kungstensgatan, Drottninggatan? I'm
probably doing a great job of convincing them I'm a simpleton.

I'm released, but they don't take me back to where they
picked me up, even though that would have been a reasonable
request. Making my way back to E-4 by foot from here would
take for ever, and I'm on a motorway to boot. It's already afternoon. I won't make it to Cilla's before dark, and besides, I've lost
interest completely. The situation looks like a finger pointing in
the sky, it does. And it says: go back.

Since I'm already here, I call my mother anyway and ask to
spend the night so that my little trip doesn't feel quite as disap-
pointing as it is.

As I walk up my stairs, I wonder if Gustav has noticed my
disappearance. Oh yes, Harriet informs me that he's been there,
but she doesn't know anything else.

I call Bragevägen and Father-in-Law tells me that Gustav has
gone out to the Island. I'm confused:

'Didn't he have a test tomorrow?'

'Apparently that's not going to happen now.'

His voice is austere – as if I'm the one who should explain
why he cancelled his test – what has Gustav told them, I wonder?
I finish the call in as business-like a fashion as possible and call
the Island.

Gustav isn't austere – he's utterly beside himself.

'Don't you understand that you're hurting me?'

'It wasn't my intention.'

'Wasn't it?'

'I left because I was hurt myself. I thought that we had
broken up!'

'You did?'

Oh, these matters of conscience.

'I thought that you thought so.'

He complains that he didn't sleep all night and wasn't able

to get anything done all day, and finally he had to leave for the Island. Is that my fault, then? Is it my fault that he loves me so terribly? Have I done anything to fan the flames, have I?

Well, he makes it sound that way. He makes it sound like a terrible accusation when he says 'I love you.' I have to promise to take the first boat out. He's been able to postpone his test for a week and wants to see me right away.

That night, I'm the one who can't sleep. I'm afraid. How will this end? 'I can't be without you,' Gustav says. I can, but I don't want to. It looks like that must mean that he's more dependent, more vulnerable. But strangely enough, it's odd, I have a feeling that he's the one who's the stronger of the two of us. I'm harder, but he's soft-strong. He has a gift for happiness, but I don't. Well, maybe, but not for that kind of happiness.

By the time I get there, he's calmed down. I find him on the beach with a book. He's got enough sleep and thinks it's only fair that I've had to taste a night of insomnia. We say no more about it – apparently we've both succeeded in reaching the bottom of resignation where there isn't anything more to add. We're together, and that's enough. June is here and the sun has started to get warm; he takes my hand and we walk into the forest and make love on the ground, in the moss, with summer over us and under us. We're together and if we don't want, or can't manage, to do anything else, then it's fine the way it is. No, it's not fine, but it's the way it can be, and the June sun warms our pale bellies as we lie side by side in the moss and look up at the summery blue beyond the crowns of the pine trees.

It's the way it is.

★

In order to compensate for my cancelled trip abroad, Gustav comes up with the idea of taking a trip to Helsinki for a couple of days. He has neither the money nor the time for anything more elaborate since he's going sailing with Erik later on in the summer.

It's not really what I had in mind, but for lack of a better option, it's all right. Helsinki is a fine city, like and unlike Stockholm in a unique combination: the same kind of light, the same air, and then these wildly exotic features at the same time. A completely foreign language, for example. It's so foreign that we aren't able to explain to the hotel staff that we wanted a double room – a cheap little hotel we found on a back street, worn and smutty: it's not propriety at all that makes them give us each our own room, it's just to squeeze more money out of us, and I get angry with Gustav, who's too shy to argue about it.

Why don't I do it myself, then? I don't know. I become so paralysed when I'm 'with' someone. I somehow forget that I can do things myself and I let him manage everything. I'm used to travelling alone, not because I like it but because I've never had anyone to travel with, but now that I do, for some reason, I'm transformed into a helpless parcel. As we walk through the city, it's Gustav who reads the map and keeps track of where we are, and I simply follow along, blind and deaf and dumb. Four eyes see more than two, they say, but I don't notice. I think I only see Gustav, who's looking at me no matter where I look. He's in the way.

I have a headache after the long trip, and once we've eaten dinner, I want to go to bed. Gustav goes out to explore on his own. I sleep for a couple of hours, wake up at 10:00 and sneak carefully across the corridor and knock on his door, but he's not there. Where did he go? What if he doesn't come back – abandoned in this filthy hotel where nobody understands what I'm saying! Abandoned and exhausted and on the point of tears, I return to my room and get undressed.

I leave the door unlocked, and an hour or so later he comes in. I debate whether to pull the blanket up to my chin in offence or to open it up invitingly, and in the end I combine the two: I open up the corner of the blanket and say, offended: 'Where have you been all this time?'

'At the cinema,' he answers and accepts my invitation after kicking off his shoes. '*The Pink Panther*.'

'Cinema,' I snort, 'you don't really have to go abroad to do that, do you?'

'Nor to lie in a bed and sleep, either,' he replies, alert.

'But to lie in a bed *together* without anyone sticking their nose in,' I continue in my offended tone of voice and pull the blanket up to my chin, over his head.

'Hmm. Have you thought about how if this hotel is smutty, it's because people like us stay in it?'

'We who have separate rooms,' I giggle. 'Speaking of smut, what do you think about removing your clothes?'

The next morning, it's raining. We stroll through a bookstore and look at ceramics in the gift shops. Then Gustav wants to go see the Uspenski Cathedral. I'm satisfied to admire its domes from a distance and would rather walk around the harbour, so we split up for a couple of hours.

I take a deep breath and sharpen my senses so I don't get lost or run over. I wander along the docks and enjoy the foreign scents, notice how I walk around and register all my impressions as carefully as if I were going to report them. I walk around and formulate them in order to tell him everything later. I walk and write letters to him in my thoughts.

Two eyes see more than four, I write in my mind-letter. When we rejoin each other for dinner I get to see the cathedral too, through his.

*

While Gustav is out sailing, I visit my parents. We've never been apart this long until now, and when I pace back and forth in the hall waiting for the postman, as I did last summer with a different kind of urgency, I understand that this is how sin punishes itself: the repetition, the make-up homework.

Of course, he would have rather had me along, but the boat is hopelessly small for three people to live on board, and sailing with Erik is a kind of tradition. They are at sea for two weeks and return with their faces and hands red from the sun but elsewhere white from the collar and sleeves: it's cold out on the water. I have a considerably more all-over tan to show off, acquired on a blanket in Stadsparken.

I thought that Gustav would have had enough sailing by now, but he can't sit still in his island paradise and gives me no peace until he's convinced me to go along on a tour. As soon as there's a morning with the right wind, he'll plan a day trip.

Right wind, he says: if this is right, what's too much wind? I ask myself. It looks lovely to sail, I've always felt that way, and it's delightful close up as well, by all means: white sails stretched taut by the wind and sizzling foam off the bowsprit, and all that. But if it can look a bit terrifying and dangerous from a distance, when the ship leans so that the deck dips under the waves, it's nothing compared to what it feels like on board.

I feel more or less that sailboats are something I'd rather study from the dock or veranda. If you needs must be at sea, I prefer the modest little rowboat with its outboard motor sputtering half-heartedly in the back.

Gustav's parents are spending their vacation at the Island. They're living in the large cottage, so he's forced to sleep in the kitchen with them and I get the seaside cottage to myself. When we're face to face, I don't refrain from pointing out the ridiculous hypocrisy in this; when alone, I think it's nice. Being left to myself at night, at least. (Why have the custodians of morality throughout the ages not understood, or pretended not to realize, that fornication can occur in daylight?)

I read a letter to the advice column in the paper from a woman who writes about the Pill: it's no wonder they're an effective birth-control method since you become so mean and tired that you don't want to even look at your husband. Could that be my problem, my birth-control pills? Something is wrong in any event. My hormones are gone with the wind – I have fewer and fewer of them, and Gustav more and more. The first time we see each other again, it's fun to have sex with him, and the second time, too, but by the third time I think it gets tedious.

I cannot claim that the fault lies with him, since he's not at all one of those primitive brutes who only seeks his own pleasure.

'Why aren't you,' I nag. 'Why can't you be like all those Swedish men they write about in the advice columns: a quickie on Saturday evening and that's it.'

'Wouldn't you complain in that case?'

'You bet I would. I'd finally have a reason to.'

You never hear about people complaining about a selfless man who wants his partner to respond all the time and insists that she enjoy herself too. One that is constantly soliciting applause and reviews – you barely have time to catch your breath before he sticks the questionnaire under your nose: Was I good? Did it feel good? Five stars? Yes, yes and yes, I sigh, you're the world's best lover, I've told you that – why are you nagging me about it? Can't we have a game of chess now or go fishing?

These ought to be idyllic days, sunshine and swimming and boat trips, but if this is paradise, then I'm more like the snake in it than anything else. He makes me feel so mean, so bad.

I wouldn't mind a Saturday quickie now and again – if that were enough, if it were limited to an honest Swedish lay from time to time. I could deal with that. But his constant need for affection. His need to kiss me at every possible moment, his arms that catch me wherever I go – I can't walk by him in a doorway without his taking advantage of the opportunity to fold me in his arms, and if we go somewhere, he has to hold my hand. On our bicycles I have less to complain about; at least it feels a little daring (imminent risk of wobbling into each other's front wheels), but when we take our evening walk through the forest and he wants to put his arm around me – a wandering family idyll! – that's when I tear myself away. <u>Fathers and teachers, I ponder: the suffering of being unable to love</u> – isn't that Hell itself?

Our existence is tolerable as long as we're dealing with practicalities. When the weather gets worse, we start to repair the seaside cottage, and Gustav fixes the roof that's leaking. We also put up a new, lighter wallpaper in the room. We choose the pattern together from among the wallpaper samples – in questions of taste, we're uncommonly harmonious, and it's like playing at moving in together – or a surrogate for the real thing. He's still dreaming of a wedding, incurably romantic, incorrigible. For me, that possibility has glided out of sight. Some people are unsuited from birth, and it's best that they realize it.

A muggy evening. The thunder has been growling over the mainland all day, and now you can hear heavy drops in the leaves above. I'm sitting at the window, waiting to see the lightning start in the sky over the fjord. It's bound to be spectacular.

Gustav comes in with a basket of firewood, closes the door and hangs his rain-splotched jacket on the hook. He sits on the bed and looks at me.

'It's just my island you love,' he blurts out. 'You're just using me.'

'Aren't you satisfied, then? That's your system of ethics, that you're supposed to sacrifice yourself for others. How am I supposed to avoid stepping on someone who intentionally places himself at my feet like a doormat?'

'You can always place yourself at each other's feet,' he suggests, laughing at the visual image it conjures – 'that way it's not just one person who gets stepped on.'

'I think that seems uncomfortable. And not much of a sacrificial system if you demand a quid pro quo.'

'I'm not demanding a quid pro quo. But I think you could at least accept what I'm trying to give you.'

'That would be precisely what I'm saying, exploiting you. If you believe that the meaning of life is to peel potatoes, then you will have to do that, but you can't demand that I eat up everything you serve me when I, in fact, don't share your moral philosophy.'

'Why don't you? Haven't you realized that potato-peeling is a value in and of itself yet?'

'I admit, that metaphysical moral philosophy has purely aesthetic advantages. You can use it as a decoration, it's pleasant to look at and interesting to think about. But it's too impractical to act on.'

'So you mean you can hang my moral philosophy on the wall as an art object, but when it comes to action, you need another one?'

'Yes, then you probably have to pull out the usual old utilitarian prudential principles, no matter how flat and lacklustre they may be.'

The grumble of thunder comes from further away, and the lightning never materializes, but now the rain is spattering against the panes. He stands up and inspects the newly repaired part of the ceiling where the moisture stains used to appear: if it can hold up under this, then it was good work.

'The world's best roof repairman,' I flatter him and start to fold up the spread to get ready for bed.

'You don't love me,' he says, more sadly.

'Yes, I do,' I say, more angrily.

I do! In my way. Gustav thinks it's a poor way. I'm starting to wonder if he's right.

Next Saturday is our one-year anniversary – a year since we started to be together. 'How will we celebrate?' I ask, and Gustav answers, without hesitation: 'In sackcloth and ashes.'

10

Queues you would only see at the liquor store the last hour before a long holiday are filling the corridors of the department: new students are here to register. But such matters are handled by the administrative assistant; I'm here to ask my adviser if he's possibly had the chance to glance at the essay I sent him before summer started.

There's nobody in his office, but the announcement board says it's his office hours, so I sit down to wait. I hear his voice somewhere nearby – it sounds like some of the teachers are sitting around chatting. After half an hour he shows up, wonders in surprise if he's the one I was looking for, and in that case, what I want to talk about.

'An essay.'

He can't recall any. He looks among the papers on his desk but can't find it.

'That's not a problem,' I say generously, 'it's probably no big loss – I can write another.' (Yes please: then I'll have something to do, and it was quite fun once I got started.) But he assumes that he has it at home and asks if I can come to his next office hour instead.

'Of course,' I say politely.

By then he's had a week and he's actually found and read it, and says that it wasn't bad, really. This apparently means that I'm to pull out my exam book and have him enter my grade.

I still need two terms for my degree, but what are you supposed to do with a degree when the surplus of academics is
growing at ten per second, or whatever it is? Better to try to
find a job while there are still some out there. If there are any,
you probably won't find them through the employment office.
I assume it's the same situation as at the housing office: if you
want a flat, you have to go around telling everyone you know
until you find someone who knows someone who has an extra
one; that's the only way I've seen people find flats. So I spend
a few weeks telling everyone I know that I'm looking for a job.
Just when I'm about to give up that method and go to the Post
Office to ask if I can sit sorting letters (if Harriet could, then
why not I?), I'm contacted by a former classmate who's happened to hear about a substitute teaching position in Swedish
and English for the rest of the term, and I may have a chance at
it if I contact the school right away.

'Where is it?' I ask grudgingly – we swore to each other
when we graduated from high school that we'd never set foot
behind a lectern, and even though most of us have violated this
oath out of bitter necessity at this point, I had planned to be
the last conscientious lectern-objector. I expect her to answer
'Mörby' or 'Kärrtorp' or some other dreadful suburb, but she
says 'Härnösand'. Härnösand, in the far north? It's so beyond
my wildest imaginings that it's irresistible.

I call the principal, who wants me if I can come right away.
I'll come right away.

Of course there are several good reasons not to set one's foot
behind a lectern besides having sworn to your classmates that
you wouldn't, namely that you'll probably die of fright. But the
alternative is to die of starvation. Or existential anxiety.

Gustav causes no difficulties. He realizes that a letter-writing
Martina is more pleasant than one with existential anxiety sobbing about how nobody wants her. He promises to come up

and visit me sometime, helps me with my suitcase to Central Station and waves goodbye.

It's October, but I'm travelling towards winter. In Hälsingland, the trees are already bare. Then comes Medelpad, and then Ångermanland (I've read up).

It wasn't hard to arrange for a place to live – in this school town with so many pupils boarding, it seems that every other person has a room to let. The principal himself recommended an address belonging to a relative of his. I walk past a few blocks that are quite entrancing with their quaint old wooden houses, but the address itself is an entirely common block of flats, two flights up with a window on a quiet little street. The room is chock-full of furniture and decorative items. All I do is leave my suitcase and go out to take a closer look at the town.

You can't say it's big, exactly. On the contrary. A nineteenth-century church and a modern city library, and then schools – that seems to be it. I find a bulletin board on a street corner and study it attentively, but the only flyers feature a lecture at the IOGT Hall on 13 March and a movie poster: *Desperadoes of the West* on Friday at 7:30 p.m. It's Tuesday.

Let's not panic now. I walk into a café, empty save for a group of youths at one table. I order coffee and a sandwich and look at the local paper lying on the counter: 'Bear Population On the Rise'.

I sneak a peek at the other table: What if they're my pupils? How old can they be? No idea. I don't know how youth today look at that age. Youth today is what I know the least about.

But let's not panic. The worst thing that can happen is that I'll die.

When I walk back to my room, it feels like people are turning around on the street to look at me, and in two places, I notice very clearly that someone is observing me from behind the lace curtains in the window.

On the wall above my bed there are two small ceramic tablets with sayings: *Love never faileth* and *Have you prayed about it?* I write a letter to Gustav and send up a prayer that I'll survive the following day.

To be honest, when I unlock the classroom door with my new key ring and let 'the children' pour in, I realize that it's less a question of holding panic at bay than holding back the laughter. To sit here and pretend I'm a teacher – it's enough to make anyone point and roll on the floor. But 'the children' keep a straight face, and as long as they do, I guess I can, too. 'The children', as they say in the faculty break room, are large in stature and look much older than we did when we were seventeen (than I do at twenty-one as well for that matter), but whether this reflects an inner maturity as well, the jury is out. In any event, they're definitely nicer than children from Stockholm. Obedient: they do what I tell them, to my increasing surprise, and jot down with almost embarrassing orderliness every word that comes from my lips. When the bell rings, a few stay on to talk. They think it's remarkable to be from Stockholm. Well, if I can impress them with so little, so be it.

I use the afternoon to visit the sick teacher I'm replacing and get more information about what they're doing in different classes. I borrow his lesson plans, notes and test questions, and I decide that the teaching will cause me minimal trouble. The problem will be avoiding mental death during my spare time.

Desperadoes of the West, Friday at 7:30 p.m. It's Wednesday. There are other cinemas of course, but they're basically all showing the same film.

The weather is cloudy, hazy and mild. Beyond the city is the Forest. Through it, E-4 runs northwards towards Haparanda and southwards towards Stockholm.

It's Wednesday and dusk is falling.

E-4 runs southwards, and I promise myself I'll hitchhike

home on Saturday morning. Not one weekend in this place –
that's too much to ask.

The fog lies heavy over the region when the day comes and the
roads are wet and slippery – accident weather. But a promise is
a promise, and how can you trust yourself in the future if you
don't keep what you've promised yourself?

When I walk up Norrtullsgatan, Saturday-empty, where the
autumn leaves blow across the pavement, I nevertheless feel a
bit out of sorts. It feels like – what does it feel like? – ah yes, like
cheating. Slipping out of the way, not facing the music. There's
nothing to living in a backwater in the autumnal dark of the
north if you escape home to Stockholm as soon as the weekend
comes – definitely cheating.

I don't let anyone besides Gustav know that I'm home. His
parents are at the Island, so I can spend the night with him.
I entertain him with anecdotes about school and my mentally incapacitating spare time. As for him, he's not had a free
moment since I left: he's working with the Vietnam bulletin
and his paper on Tito Colliander when he doesn't have to take
care of Halldén, who's unhappily in love, and stretching his student loans by working as a clerk at the Sergel Book Store – his
anecdotes from that store exceed most of what I can provide
in terms of entertainment value. The annual Christmas story
collection is the only volume the owner seems to bother to
market, and the clerk's task is simply to hear if the customer
wants it autographed and gift-wrapped. If this is what it means
to work for a living, Gustav says, then he's starting to admit
that I'm right in saying it's better to remain a student your
entire life.

We have a lot to talk about, and we have a worthwhile night
in every way before I have to get to the E-4 by Haga at dawn.
It seems to be an excellent solution to our intimacy problems.

(Intimacy problems, what a detestable expression: sounds like some horrible disease.)

Between Hudiksvall and Sundsvall, what I've feared most of all happens: I get a ride with two bearded boys who are pupils of mine. It's pure luck that I recognize them at all – I have a total of over 100 in different classes – but if the face of someone in that age group seems familiar to me here in the north, it's not so difficult to guess where I know them from.

As for the boys, they don't seem to have recognized me before they've already stopped – their surprise is unequivocal. And rumours of the incident have surely spread across the school as soon as the next day. I just wonder whether I've now gained more respect or, on the contrary, undermined my authority; what do I know about youth today.

*

Teaching isn't quite as simple as it seemed, not at all. Every morning I feel full of confidence, every afternoon dull and confused. I'm aware of my responsibilities, and prepared to the smallest detail when I walk into the classroom. I have the tasks ready and know exactly what I'm going to say. But as soon as the pupils are there, everything gets so messy. Letting them do group work on their own seems to be a convenient method, but it's already a huge ordeal to get them to divide into groups – this one wants to be with that one and that one doesn't want to be with this one and doesn't want to do the task at all. Democracy? Hah. The choice is between chaos and dictatorship.

And it's true, they take down everything I say as if it interests them, but do they remember it? No. I naïvely believed that they would remember things that I had properly said once. Soon, very soon, I notice that if I write it on the board, distribute dittos about it, and remind them verbally a couple of times, there are prospects of its being retained by fifty per cent so that they remember it the following week.

My colleagues laugh indulgently at my beginner's optimism. I notice that they've developed a professional cynicism, a jargon about the pupils' stupidity and general hopelessness, and I understand that it functions as a defence mechanism. It's surprisingly easy to slip into it, even if you've been a pupil as recently as I have myself.

One of my discoveries is that the teachers in the break room gossip just as much about their students as the students do about the teachers. This surprised me at first, since I believed that teachers would have higher interests in life – that pupils, in their oppressed position, don't have them is more natural. But this, too, is a defence mechanism: you have to check your experiences against those of others to convince yourself that you're not mistaken, that you're not crazy or a more incompetent teacher than the rest. You just have to compare classes and individuals. That's gossip.

It creates prejudices, of course. I had already heard that 8c was an unusually difficult class from several sources before I even met them, and since I expect it, they naturally live up to my expectations. White mice do, so why not schoolchildren?

*

I can't keep up the schedule of going home on the weekend, but Gustav has been in such a splendid mood ever since the day I travelled over 400 miles just to see him that, for the first time in our history, he's started to believe in our relationship – to believe that it is a relationship, just as it is and without external legalization.

Given this turn of events, you would think we could simply relax, but I find more fuel for conflicts. 'You're actually more interested in our relationship than in me,' I write accusingly. 'Your love stands between us. I wish we could simply have each other, like you have a pot on the shelf without calling it something special. You're cheating on me with our relationship.'

Admittedly, there are worse kinds of betrayal. But no matter how far-fetched it may seem, I really mean something in talking this way. I'm jealous of his pure zeal, I envy his great passion. And I'm afraid of it, because it creates an image of me that I do not match. That's why I try to construct a view of love so nominalist that there's only room for Gustav and Martina in it, not for any relationship between the two.

I Corinthians 7:29–30 is what Gustav sends in response:

Thus it remaineth, that both they that have wives be as though they had none; and they that weep, as though they wept not; and they that rejoice, as though they rejoiced not; and they that buy, as though they possessed not.

Well, yes, maybe what I'm saying is something like that. Having each other as if one didn't have each other. Loving each other distractedly, whistling and looking the other way – maybe that's the only form of love that wouldn't give me claustrophobia.

But when our correspondence has drawn out this long, we're already in the second half of the semester, and the long separation has even got me to resort to self-satisfaction and to comfort myself with our relationship – to place his photo on my nightstand in my solitary camp, to defend my virtue at faculty parties by saying I have a Fiancé in Stockholm, to attach my daily happiness to the letters and phone calls from him. I haven't got to know any of my colleagues very well – almost all of them are married and uninterested in socializing outside of parties, where they expect you to be prepared to go abruptly from no relationship whatsoever to an intimate one.

Finally there's a weekend when Gustav can come up and visit me. I send a telegram, 'Prov 7:18', which I've been saving just for this occasion, and the woman at the office has no idea what she's promoting: *Come, let us take our fill of love until the morning: let us solace ourselves with love.*

I refrain from including verses 16 and 17 as well, even though they sound even more tempting (*I have covered my bed with coloured linens from Egypt; I have perfumed my bed with myrrh, aloe and cinnamon, come . . .*) – partly because the Telegraph Company charges per word, and partly because I am so incorruptibly truthful: I haven't perfumed my bed with aloe and cinnamon, I've simply reserved a room at Lilla Hotellet.

The evening before, I'm lying in my rented room having a vision. I see the train from Stockholm roll in at the platform, how Gustav descends from the train with his suitcase, how I rush forwards and throw myself in his arms and cover him with kisses.

But, I think, you don't treat a pot like that, do you? It's not a household object, identical to others, a utilitarian object for practical comfort? Such longing, such a vision of the bliss of reunion – it must be something utterly special after all.

The train from Stockholm rolls in on Saturday afternoon, Gustav descends to the platform and I walk over to meet him. Is that what he looks like. Was that the shade of red. Was this the way it feels to embrace him, with my nose at the same level as his FNL lapel pin.*

And after we've gone sightseeing in the town and taken a walk through the harbour and eaten dinner at the railroad station restaurant and had a night at Lilla Hotellet without aloe or cinnamon or linens from Egypt, and we walk out to the train to Stockholm waiting at the platform again – it's then I understand that I've allowed myself to be deceived. I've allowed myself to be tricked into waving flags and singing hymns although I knew that that was what I shouldn't do. I've had just one month to nurture my love, to wrap myself up in all the notions of what Love is, and the confrontation with its object is already a disappointment.

* FNL = National Front for the Liberation of South Vietnam.

After our previous encounter, it occurred to me that I would make an excellent seaman's wife: the occasional impassioned meeting with many months in between. That was a mistake as well. In my case it would be the wife of a seaman who never returned to shore.

'You once said you were thinking of applying for a scholarship to America,' I say through the compartment window once he's found his seat, 'are you serious about it?'

'Will you come along if I get it?'

'The US is the last place on earth I want to visit. No, I thought if you were there, I'd probably never love you more.'

'If I were dead, you probably would.'

'Oh yes, of course, if you were dead!'

Immediately a vision of the young widow in black – alas, all too young to be a widow, but inviolably true to the deceased, every day a walk to the cemetery with fresh flowers . . . That would finally resolve our intimacy problems.

*

The darkness swells and devours the day, every free piece of the day. The first morning lessons take place by the flickering light of fluorescent tubes, so anaesthetizing that you can barely keep yourself awake, never mind the pupils. When I wander home through the streets to my room at 3:30 p.m., it's night once again, the electric lights on the Christmas tree at the market square illuminated.

It's only during the free period sometimes that can I run out and breathe in what light there is. Sun and snow, on the mountains in the distance sun and snow, it pulls at my chest: out, oh out into the *world*. Or is it the other way around, homesickness? I'm always longing, it's constitutional. I can leaf through a calendar and start at the word 'April' as if it were the name of bliss, simply because we happen to be in December. And the other way around. I long for spring in the autumn, for autumn in the spring and for Gustav when he's not with me, away when I'm home and home when I'm away, and just now, I long for everything at once – away since I'm here, and home since away is home.

Otherwise, I do think it's amusing to live at such a latitude. It's so ridiculous, so obviously not meant for humans to exist in a region the sun doesn't reach, where you have to stay indoors almost round the clock in order to survive. It's so clearly unsuited to humans that it's amusing. When I crawl out of bed in the black of night at 7:00, I simply need to consider this global perspective to burst out laughing.

On one of the last days of the term, the principal comes to offer me a substitute position for the spring as well, for a different teacher. It pleases me that they're so satisfied with my performance that they've considered it, but I decline without thinking it over much – it's not *that* amusing.

All that's left is a night of soul-searching about grades (Tomas Nilsson, who on earth is that – did I have a pupil by that name?) and a night at a staff party that resembles a mid-winter sacrifice ritual where I have ample opportunity to defend my virtue. I've protected myself ahead of time by wearing a pair of thermal underwear under my elegant trousers, and their appearance guarantees that nothing on earth could compel me to show myself to anyone other than Gustav in them (three-quarter legs and jailhouse stripes – I could possibly slip out of them hidden in my trousers, but not get them on again).

These precautionary measures prove to be unnecessary. Not because nobody tries to seduce me, but because there are so many who do, in such an indiscriminate fashion that it's more insulting than flattering and least of all seductive: you paw at the person who happens to land within touching distance, and if it doesn't produce results, you casually paw at the next, not wasting time on talking so that you stand there without a partner for the last dance. But if people aren't interested in me when they're sober, they can't possibly expect me to be delighted that they are when they're lacking in judgement after too much alcohol, can they?

The head of the Swedish department wastes quite a bit of time dancing with me and tries to convince me to take him home for the night, verbally as well and in all possible keys:

(Enticing): 'Wouldn't it feel good? Hmm . . . ?'

(Challenging): 'You're not a convent maiden, are you?'

(Frivolous): 'It doesn't have to mean anything, does it? I know you have someone else, so do I . . .'

That's the worst invitation I've ever heard. (Don't take it personally, but I think we should go have it off.)

'If it doesn't mean anything, we can just as easily go home separately and masturbate, can't we?'

He doesn't ask me to dance again. An hour or so later, I see him stumble out holding the music teacher's hand.

Libations and mating rituals in the midwinter darkness. I sit on a windowsill and drink my juice in pure contempt for the human race: chaste as a convent maiden, solitary as a stylite.

★

I celebrate Christmas with Gustav in prayer and fasting. This isn't a further development of that idea about sackcloth and ashes, remembering the previous Christmas, but simply because we're participating in a Third World country campaign against commercialization, excess and Christmas hysteria. It started gradually as a Christian action last year, and now the movement has grown. There are events in several different places in town. We're sitting in a poorly heated space near Medborgarplatsen, with entertainment from the stage by journalist Barbro Alving, Communist leader C. H. Hermansson and a few others in between.

After two days of fasting, I'm so weak that Gustav has to

help me home. He apparently believes that he's proven something with this, that the need for food isn't simply a bourgeois prejudice or something like that, but I'm too dizzy to express an opinion on his argument just now and too weak to take up the challenge.

II

I've had enough of gainful employment, also in the sense that I've saved enough money these past months that I can live on it for an indefinite period of time. In any event for just as many months again, and that's about as far as I'm able to envision.

And what is a retiree to do if not pursue studies for pleasure? One day I discover that the fairy-tale building opposite the Nordiska Museum, which we've ridden past many times, is a university department, where anyone can simply walk in and register for a first-year course. It's irresistible: a fairy-tale castle in the middle of the city, a small knight's fortress with pinnacles and towers and balconies, and in the lecture halls there are tile ovens and golden-leather wallpaper – I've never seen golden-leather wallpaper before, but now I understand that it's precisely the thing I've been missing in the fluorescent-tube modules in Vasastan. The fact that ethnology is the course that's taught in the fairy-tale castle is something I'll just have to live with.

'Not everyone can be as earth-bound and goal-oriented as you,' I explain to Gustav, who has now resigned himself to the fact that the teaching profession is the only future there is and who's finishing the final details of a master's thesis in order to apply to the teacher-training college.

It's clear that I could become a teacher as well. But not a good one. Not worse than most, either, but that's no excuse: after so many years as a student, I believe that it's a teacher's duty to be good. Otherwise they have no right to take up people's time.

There are good teachers – I've met a couple in my life. After trying it out myself, I've observed that I am not one of them. I know when I'm standing in front of a class that what I say is intelligent and true, but nevertheless, I lack the ability to say it with the kind of authority that makes it stick. I believe authority is what you have to have to be a teacher. Some of that comes from knowing what you're talking about, but another part probably has to be inborn. A commanding presence. Can people in the featherweight class have a commanding presence?

Besides, more than other people, I lack interest in pedagogy, and that's probably also something foundational in this context. It isn't enough to be interested in your subjects and to like talking about them with others. You have to be involved in the learning process itself. I become impatient with pupils who struggle to find words when they're trying to say something in English, and I can't resist interrupting them with the correct phrases. Or when I give them a fun topic to write an essay about, I would much rather write it myself because I would do it so much better . . .

Quite clearly, I lack the aptitude for this activity. It's with unadulterated joy that I step away from the lectern and return to the student's desk.

Even the address of this department is appropriate: Villa Lusthusporten, Gazebo Gateway. Soon I discover that the castle also has a fairy-tale prince. No, not a prince – he has nothing kingly or aristocratic about him. But fairy-tale. Black-haired and black-eyed, small in stature but not stocky: a diminutive fantasy character. He always wears the same clothes, brown corduroy trousers and a blue-striped bricklayer's shirt. He and his pets have an attic apartment in Gamla Stan, the old part of the city, with a ceiling so low that even a person of his size can hardly stand upright. He lives there with his aquarium of fish, a small monkey and two cats; all that keeps him from having a seal in the bathtub is probably that he doesn't have a bathtub.

He plays the flute. He writes poems that he doesn't try to get published and he lets his guests read them if they ask, but he doesn't encourage anyone to do that.

To be sure, it all seems suffocatingly affected – when I tell Gustav about him, I realize how suffocatingly affected it seems. The miracle is that there's no suggestion of theatrics or affectation about him at all: he *is* that way. He's so uninterested in how he looks that he doesn't see that it's precisely this that's taken for affectation, and he doesn't understand that he's the one the flock of children on the street are snickering at. He has pets because he likes them. He wears a bricklayer's shirt because it's practical. (This proletarian piece of clothing is like a caricature – I have one myself that I wear at home, but as a student, I would never dare to wear it in public.) He plays and writes because he likes to. And he's studying ethnology because he's interested in people. (As opposed to me, who's only interested in the wallpaper.)

He's very accessible, helpful and considerate – the best example of a Friend I've ever met. Flirting with him would be like flirting with Snufkin* (I explain to Gustav): an absurd thought. He's a mythical creature, above such determinants as those related to gender.

Snufkin is probably the best description I can think of. He's an outdoor being, one that comes and goes as he likes and nobody holds him back, attached to his friends but not to the point that it binds him.

---

* Snufkin and the Hattifatteners are characters from Tove Jansson's *Moomintroll* books.

Integrity is the word. Mikael has that rare kind of integrity, an inner inaccessibility, that makes you go crazy with the desire to get inside. The friend incarnate, with whom you fall instantaneously in love.

★

At the beginner's level, there's quite a bit of class time, a blessedly large amount of class time, so almost every day of the week I have to go to the castle. Almost every day, a few of us join up afterwards to go have coffee or take a walk in Djurgården, to go to a museum or Skansen. I love small excursions; why don't Gustav and I take them any more, the way we did at the beginning?

Most of all, I enjoy the walks in Skansen. It's snowy and quiet, with no people in sight and hardly any animals either, except for the seals in their pools. I always stay longest with Mikael. We can sit talking about this and that for hours at the railing near the seals in the snowy dusk, until the guards come and tell us they're closing.

One of his supernatural qualities is that he doesn't sleep. I've never considered the need for sleep to be a bourgeois prejudice, since I'm a slave to nine hours a night, but Mikael never seems to get sleepy. He can hang out at a public place all night long – not a pub, because he's a teetotaller and, besides, he's poor as a church mouse (no students loans because, of course, he's exceeded the statutory period of study by a long way), but at a coffee house: at Autobar or Röda Rummet, I leave him when nature calls, the nature to which I must submit.

Late one evening he calls from a newsstand. He's been sitting in the department library reading and now he thinks it's time to explore the Kaknäs Tower. I was just brushing my teeth before going to bed, but if Mikael wants my company at the tower, my bed will have to wait. I give a fleeting thought to how I wouldn't be able to do things like this if I lived with

Gustav. I give a fleeting thought to how good it is that I don't live with Gustav.

Mikael is waiting at the bus stop, sitting on an ice-crusted couch and smoking a corncob pipe, looking as if it were the best thing you could be doing on a January night. We take the elevator as high as it goes in the tower, then the stairs, and then a forbidden stairway even higher up, and then a door out into the dark; it's not that many metres above the viewing floor, but it's forbidden, and just as exciting as it was to explore the fairy-tale castle's secret passages. The wind blows up here. It's entirely dark and he takes my hand so I won't fall. We stand at the railing and the city lies at our feet, a pattern of lights as far as you can see, and in the other direction the sea, the ice.

The wind is cold and strong, and it's hard to breathe when it gusts the strongest. Once we're completely chilled through, we tiptoe back down the stairs and thaw our hands on a cup of hot chocolate from the vending machine on the viewing platform.

'Travel,' Mikael says. 'It would be good to travel somewhere.'

I nod eagerly: 'Just what I was thinking. That's the best thing about travel: the views and the landscape. Otherwise you learn more about foreign countries by reading books.'

'But the sense of a landscape,' he agrees, 'you can't even reproduce that on film.'

On the bus back into town, we talk about trips we've taken. He comes home with me and we sit on the floor next to the tile oven and warm ourselves, and Mikael talks about the time he hitchhiked through Finland, all the way from Treriks-röset, where the three countries meet, to Helsinki. I stretch my toes towards the fire and think something blurry about campfires at Kilpisjärvi. Of course those are the kinds of trips you should make.

I wake up and realize that I've been sleeping. Mikael is gone, but there are traces of him in the room: there's a pipe on the rug that isn't mine, a sheath knife next to the wood basket that he pulled out to split kindling (pulled it out of his shoulder bag like anyone else would pull out a ballpoint pen or a cigarette lighter when needed). He's always forgetting things, I've noticed, or leaving them. You could call it sloppiness, if you didn't prefer to call it transcending the material world, his way of not considering possessions to be part of himself.

I bring them with me to the lecture in the afternoon and hear that he walked all the way home since the night bus was no longer running. 'I could have given you money for a taxi,' I say. It's a completely unnecessary thing to say: he likes to walk.

*

Gustav doesn't ask me how I'm spending my nights – he's used to me sleeping. But he's starting to wonder what I'm up to all day. Tonight he comes by without advance notice.

'Where've you been?'

'I had a lecture.'

'That was over at four. I went there and thought we could go out and eat, but they said you'd gone home. I called and there was no answer. Where were you?'

'At Skansen. Do you want some coffee?'

He shrugs his shoulders. I put the water on the boil.

Being met, I think, being fetched. If I'd run into Gustav on the street as I was on my way to the seals with Mikael? He could have come along, right? Of course, but it wouldn't have been the same. He wouldn't like Mikael. He'd be jealous. So ridiculous, so ugly, so wrong: Fairy tales aren't supposed to have any jealous husbands!

I serve the coffee. We drink the coffee. He suggests movies, the theatre, something. I'm too sleepy. Besides, I have to do a little studying sometime, too. Gustav snorts: he doesn't respect my studies since they've taken this turn. Gustav, the one whose course of study runs so straight that you could have drawn it with a ruler.

Once we've drunk our coffee and he doesn't say anything more, I pull out my course book. Gustav picks up a newspaper. I'm entirely too sleepy, can't read, stare at the book blindly and think that this isn't working at all. It's just going to get ever more ridiculous, ugly and wrong. When I observe myself I can see that what I'm striving for with respect to Gustav is to have as little to do with him as possible without being completely without him. Constant excuses, half-truths, subterfuge.

'You don't love me' is his standing explanation. I've never believed that you could base a marriage on being in love – it has nothing to do with love, but rather affinity, comradeship, solidarity. But how am I supposed to feel any solidarity with him if I'm in love with someone else?

He's not reading either, although he's holding the paper. He folds it up and stands to leave. Then he sits down again.

'What is it?' he asks. 'Something has come between us.'

'No, on the contrary,' I say.

That's always a good thing to say – distracting and confusing. So confusing, in fact, that even I don't know what I mean, if I'm admitting that something between us has disappeared or if it's that I'm complaining that there isn't 'something' that's come between us, that Mikael hasn't.

But Gustav is familiar with this conversational technique and doesn't allow himself to be distracted. 'What shall we do about it, then?'

I'm silent – what use is it to talk about it?

'If there isn't anything between us, it's probably best that we split up,' Gustav says.

'We can give it a try. See how it goes. A trial divorce, like they suggest in the advice columns?'

It's going to be difficult; as entangled as we are in each other's worlds it'll be difficult until we've disentangled ourselves. It's not just one or two books we have at each other's places now, it's a lot of things. And our families, of course – first and worst of all, a divorce has to be announced to our families. But others have managed, so why wouldn't we? Certainly you just have to decide to do it and it'll work.

'We can still be friends, can't we?' I say, although I know it's the stupidest and harshest line in the world. I say it nevertheless, for my own sake, because I cannot bear the thought of losing him entirely.

But he doesn't stay to discuss the conditions of this experiment. He takes his coat and leaves.

★

Two days later, a book arrives by parcel post, one of the ones Gustav borrowed from me. Not a line, not a word. How am I to understand this?

I have to call and find out how I'm supposed to understand it.

'Lindgren,' he answers in his usual voice, a happy and attentive tone, as if he expected a phone call to be about pleasant things.

'Hi,' I say carefully.

He's retreated miles away, into a fort of icy 'what do you want', when he answers:

'Hi.'

'I just wanted to hear how you are. How are you feeling?'

'Thanks, splendid,' he answers, and he describes eloquently how he's begun to sleep well at night and to gain a little weight – we both laugh at that, and the horrible tone in his voice is already gone again.

'What did your parents say?' I ask.

'They say that it's probably for the best.'

'And Halldén?'

'That we probably weren't suited anyway. And what about yours?'

'I haven't notified them yet,' I murmur, 'we don't see each other as often.'

'Will you marry me?'

'I want us to be friends. Can't we? Seriously?'

The answer is a categorical no: that is precisely what we cannot be. Not for a long time, in any case – not for a long time yet.

Weekends are when I usually go home and see my family. On Friday evening, my mother calls and asks if we're coming soon. I play it out for a while, don't really know . . .

'Maybe you're going out to the Island?'

'Nnnooo, no, I guess I can come home.'

'Does Gustav still have a cold?'

'No, no, not because of that, but— I'm going to come alone anyway.'

'You're not breaking up, are you?'

Deep breath:

'It seems to be going in that direction.'

'That would be too bad,' Gustav's intended mother-in-law says. 'He's a fine young man.'

'Of course he is, but that's not enough.' (Quickly.)

'No, you have to have common interests too, but you do, don't you?'

'Of course we do, but that's not enough.' (Defiantly.)

'Did something happen?'

'No, just the opposite.' (Mysteriously.)

<u>Lousy sex life</u> is what I could also say – we don't fit together sexually and we don't fit together in terms of our ethical world view; our theoretical values are utterly incompatible – but that sounds so lofty. 'No, quite the opposite,' I say instead. 'It's nothing in particular, it's everything.'

I don't understand why everyone immediately assumes that I'm the one responsible for the break-up, but they do:

'Have you met someone else?'

'Not at all.' (Pouty.)

'What if he finds someone else now? What'll you say if that happens?'

'How nice for him.' (Aggressively.) 'He wants to get married, I don't want to get married, my life is fine the way it is.'

'That's what you say now, but imagine when . . .'

'When-I-get-old-and-ugly-and-nobody-wants-me!' (Chirping.)

'Finding someone who cares about you doesn't happen that often, you know, someone who doesn't simply want to exploit you.'

I sigh. When she says that, I hear it so clearly: I need him for security in my old age, like a pension plan, and if someone is exploiting someone, I know who it is.

'Well now, think about it,' my mother says (with generations of experience in her voice), 'think about it before you run away from a boy like Gustav.'

I shudder. I truly do not dare to think about it. Think about what I'm running away from. Running, by the way, what does that mean? As though I needed to get to a safe place, as if he were pursuing me. He's not doing that.

That is what he's not doing.

*

'It's probably just as well,' Cilla says. 'You two weren't really suited to each other anyway.'

'No two people have ever suited each other as well as we did.'

'But you're not in love with him any longer, are you?'

'Love, love, love.' (Irritated.) You can't stay in love for ever, either.'

'No, of course not, but what did you need him for, then?'

'To be married to, of course. We were so happily married, *basically.*'

137

'You mean you were the one who was happily married, basically.'

'Yes, that's right. He was the only one putting up a fuss and insisting on being unhappy all the time.'

'You can marry somebody else, you know.'

'That's precisely what I can't do. If I couldn't be married to Gustav, I can't be married to anyone.'

'What about, what's his name, Mikael, then?'

'You're daft. He's just a crush; you can't marry someone like that.'

'The fact is,' Cilla says, 'that I remember as if it were yesterday that you declared you had a great insight that you didn't need to pair off at all, that you'd got over all of that.'

'That was then. Now I've become used to it. And it's his fault – it's completely and utterly his fault!'

'I'm sure you'll manage to become un-used to it again.'

Stupid Cilla. She doesn't understand anything. Nobody understands me. Nobody besides Gustav has ever understood me.

And that thought makes me laugh, and all the stones fall from my heart as if that were the only thing necessary: We belong together. How could I forget that? Split up? What nonsense. We're the ones that belong together.

Happily forgetful of the fact that it was Gustav, in fact, who had taken the initiative to break up, I go and post an invitation to reunite: Eccl. 3:7.

Gustav calls and says we can meet and have dinner sometime. Today, for example, I say, I can make dinner. But he won't agree to that: it has to be a restaurant, <u>neutral territory</u>. There have to be a few wrinkles before we can declare that, after sixteen days, our experiment is a failure.

We meet outside of Drabanten at Odenplan, sit across the table from each other, sit across from each other and giggle. At the comedy of not touching each other, the comedy of pretending that we're divorced.

To my undisguised surprise, it turns out that he's actually already started to become acquainted with someone else. And, to my even greater astonishment, that he's prepared to drop her.

'That is,' Gustav says, referring to Ecclesiastes, 'if you mean that we should stitch the mess back together again?'

'I thought about writing "3:5" actually, but it seemed so forward. If maybe you didn't think it was time for that.'

'Time for that, yes indeed, it's definitely time.'

'Although I stopped taking the Pill,' I warn him.

This delights him: that I stopped having a sex life when we separated.

'In fact,' he says, 'I've always wondered what it's like to eat candy with the wrapper on.'

I nod.

'There's a vending machine on Frejgatan.'

We come up with the required sum in one-crown coins.

12

Perhaps there are reasons to become engaged after all. Having a ring could be practical, to signal that you're not fair game, and to bear it in mind yourself.

And to mark Gustav – if it's true that Other Women are after him.

It's probably the fact that he was a virgin when I got to know him that's given me the impression that he wouldn't be successful with women. But it was just that he hadn't been enterprising enough. When I take a look, I realize that he's not at all repulsive: since he's let his hair grow, he doesn't look as high-schoolish any longer, and assuming that it would be difficult for him to find someone else to peel potatoes for is apparently a foolish delusion.

I present my thoughts to him, but Gustav – who for years has dragged me to the window of every jewellery store we've passed by – is no longer as enthusiastic. He points out matter-of-factly that the first of April would be an appropriate date.

'So you can break it off on the second, saying it was a joke.'

Well, we'll cross that bridge when we come to it. For all contingencies, we apply for the housing queue together – the student queue for renovation flats with a wait of six months to a year. (But it must have at least have three rooms, I insist – I don't intend to share a flat with fewer than three rooms: one for you and one for me and one to be together in.)

Harriet's started to talk about moving in with her man, so I may get to have our flat to myself, but I can't take over her contract. And besides, Gustav needs a flat for himself even if we don't move in together – he can't live with his parents for ever. It would be too difficult to keep declaring divorces and presenting new wives all the time, he explains.

I can understand this. I feel rather silly myself on the day of the new opening of the family performance 'Dinner at Brage-vägen'. His parents are just as friendly and welcoming as before, but the question is how many rounds of this it'll take before they can no longer convince themselves that what's happening is all for the best.

I make thorough enquiries about how far things had actually advanced with that other woman. As it turns out, he had only gone out with her a couple of times – it was a classmate from Nordic Languages – they went to see *Ulysses* together. I go see the film with Mikael to even the score, and then I go home to discuss it with Gustav.

When Mikael proposes that we go out for a coffee after the evening lecture but I've promised to see Gustav, I suggest that he come home with me instead – I haven't told him about Gustav before – and introduce them to each other. That is, what I'm doing seems more like introducing Mikael to Gustav than the other way around, whatever that means. I suppose it means that I identify more with Gustav, that Mikael is the one who's foreign, an *objet trouvé* I'm bringing home to display.

Although, afterwards, Gustav says that he was rather boring, and, as far as he was concerned, he didn't see anything special about him. Well of course not – he's blind.

*

Harriet moves out. I'll stay on for the time being, until someone starts to quarrel about the contract. That can happen at any time, so there's no point in Gustav moving in with me, if he's going to have to move later on anyway. That's what I tell him.

He's in agreement with this, but what he's not in agreement with is that we're not going to copulate morning, noon and night now that we have our privacy.

'To everything there's a season,' I lecture. 'Studying folk tales has its time, and writing essays has its time, making dinner and washing hair and seeing Cilla – everything has its time.'

'And refraining from embracing. And when did you think it might be time for that again?'

'When did I "think"? I don't mark sexual intercourse in my calendar. Do you?'

'We've actually only done it twice this past month. Twice!'

'I see. You're keeping a tally.'

'You don't get it.'

'No, I don't. I don't get how it can be pleasurable for you to have sex with me if I'm not in the mood.'

'Pleasurable, pleasurable. It's no pleasure to have tigers roaring from starvation, either.'

'It was fine before you had me.'

'There's a difference. Can't you see? It doesn't help if I jerk off four times a day when you're the one I'm longing for.'

'Four times a day – I really don't have time for that,' I snort, superbly illogical (nothing makes you as superb during an argument as illogic). 'And I don't understand your tigers – do you have a special kind that can only be satisfied by me? I don't believe that. It's no sexual emergency if it isn't just as good to jerk off. It's something psychological, then, some kind of need to manifest ownership.'

'Ownership! It's something I want to *give* you!'

'That's precisely what I don't understand: you want to give me something I don't want just then, and then you're the one complaining about unmet needs?'

'Unmet needs to give, yes. Don't you ever have them?'

'In any event, they don't express themselves as roaring tigers.'

He sighs and puts out his hand: 'Come along now.'

I hesitate for a moment – better to get it over with this time, easiest actually. But now that we've already argued about it, it would be completely wasted.

The main thing is that you can talk to each other – that's what all the sex experts say – if you can only talk about it, things will always work out. We talk and talk until we're blue in the face and there isn't one corner of our sexual lives that isn't penetrated and analysed to its core, but the conclusion remains nothing other than that our needs are incompatible. And after talking about sexualia for two hours, there's nothing, and I mean nothing, that I would rather do less than have sex with him.

'We were going to go see *Ubu* at the theatre sometime; I saw in the paper that it's running this evening. Can't you get your tigers to sit nicely, just until then?'

He growls.

*

It's Easter again. As soon as we've trudged up to the cottage and carried in our fifteen paper bags with the most necessary items for our survival, I ask him how he'd thought we'd arrange our sleeping quarters this year.

'Tell me right away and I'll simply obey your orders. If any sensitive family members are coming then I can sleep in the woodshed, all right?'

Only Erik and his wife are expected to come out at some point, but if they're offended, he's prepared to deal with that.

'I suppose the tigers will have to live in the seaside cottage,' he says sorrowfully.

'My darling, the tigers can live here as long as they behave.

There's plenty of space under the bed – we can stick the chamber pot in the cupboard.'

'Under the bed, I see. Will it never be time to release them?'

'At some point,' I say generously, 'at some point I can see us doing that. Shall we say Thursday and Sunday?'

'Wednesday,' Gustav says and pulls me down under 'Fear of the Lord'.

'But the bedclothes,' I say.

'They're damp,' I say.

'We'll get bladder infections,' I say.

'And we have to put the ground beef in the cellar,' I say.

'And the bread in the box and the stove has to be lit and the wood has to be chopped and the fence fixed and the boat needs to be put in the water, but to everything there is a season,' Gustav says, 'and now I plan to take you by force.'

'You mean give me by force,' I correct him.

*

The paint in the seaside cottage looks shabby since we put up the new wallpaper. Gustav is fully occupied with his boats, but I bike to the country grocer and buy paint to freshen up the white on the windowsills and door panels, and since there's paint left over, some of the furniture gets a coat too from sheer momentum.

It's pleasant to paint – you get so *affectionate* from doing so, from the sheer intimacy with what you're painting: seeing all of its small defects, touching its surfaces – oh yes, there's definitely something erotic about painting. (Although I won't tell Gustav that – he'd just say something crude about sublimation.)

He praises my industriousness and has no shame about boasting that he's brought such a competent wife into the family. But the next second he can admit a sense of loss, a feeling that in this whitewashed home, he doesn't recognize the shabby little shack where the brothers spent summer nights during their childhood.

I don't do anything without permission. Formally it's his parents who own the place, but if I've been encouraged to paint, nobody can complain, can they? As for me, I'm pleased with my handiwork: I leave my tracks and paint myself into his life.

On Easter Eve, Erik and Anna-Karin arrive in their new car (a manor-house Saab: with space for all the children, I note cattily out of earshot). We've just got the rowboat in the water and are taking a maiden voyage. Erik and Gustav share sailing memories with each other. Anna-Karin has also been along for a longer sail, and I feel left out; why haven't I?

This summer, I think. This summer we'll sail.

It's April and the sun is glittering on the water, and this summer I will, in fact, learn to sail.

There's something about Gustav's relationship with the sea that makes me jealous. Maybe that's what I sensed that first morning when I sat here on the shore and watched him working with oars and floorboards – he turned his back on me and looked out over the sea as if it were something that meant more.

It's his relationship with these people too – they have a fellowship that I'm not part of. Even this irrelevant Anna-Karin knew Gustav before I did, and Erik has known him his entire life, all the years before I knew that he existed. I'm jealous of his childhood.

A dark lust moves within me, a dark lust to manifest ownership.

The others don't spend the night. In the dusk we follow them down to the paved road and walk quietly back through the forest. It's Gustav's turn to cook dinner. He starts to scramble with buckets and cram wood into the stove. I'm sitting at the kitchen table looking at a newspaper, no, I'm looking at his feet moving across the timbered floor. He's wearing tennis shoes on his feet, those blue tennis shoes people wore in school way back in the past. They've lain here under the kitchen sofa since way back in the past.

Within me, a dark lust to seduce him is moving, right now on the spot.

Strictly speaking, I don't know what to do. I've never seduced anyone before. How do you start? Wrap your arms around his waist as he stands there at the stove?

If he says 'What are you doing', if he drops the pots so they *rattle* and says, 'What *now*, are *you* taking the initiative?' Or 'Oh, I see, when you want it, I have to comply' – if he says that, well then, forget it.

I set aside the newspaper, hide myself in my hair and say:

'Do you have to cook dinner right away?'

He turns around, I get up and wrap my arms around his waist. He doesn't say anything – for once, he's wise enough to say nothing.

Until afterwards – that's when it comes, of course.

'What came over you just now?'

'I got so randy looking at your feet,' I explain.

*

Gustav is studying for his final examination and I keep dabbling with my ethnological studies, but I can't claim that it's more than a way to pass the time, and I'll soon be forced to find something else. There's something called career counselling at the university, and of course it's a bit late to go now, but I do it more to have confirmed what I already know: that with my combination of subjects, I've managed to make myself impossible not only for a teaching career but also for every honest type of work that exists. The only place where a liberal arts degree can be useful no matter what it consists of is when you apply to library school, the career counsellor explains.

Library school, I think with frost around my heart. Am I supposed to sit in a *library* the rest of my life?

Through a relative of Cilla's, I succeed in grabbing a temporary translation commission, and thus that illusion is also dispatched. (That this would be my calling.) I discover that it's impossible to translate. Not only difficult and in some details impracticable, but in principle and generally: impossible. Languages are not interchangeable.

Maybe I ought to have realized this before, but I've never seriously attempted to convey a longer text that's intended to function in real life. Maybe this exercise has succeeded in revealing to me the translator's secret, something that they all knew this whole time but have put up a good front about.

It's painful not knowing what you're supposed to be doing. I'm causing more and more pain to those around me as well. It's worst for Gustav, since he's closest.

I comfort myself by being unhappy in love. This must have become a vice of mine, a bad habit formed during my childhood that I can't quit although I ought to have grown up by now.

THE STRANGER: *Since every man who loves you is ridiculous, how can you love him back?*

THE WOMAN: *We don't! We tolerate him – and look for another man who doesn't love us!**

Gustav comes up in the morning before I've left for the day and we make love. Then I bike to the department humming

* From Strindberg's play *To Damascus III*.

with pleasure that I'm going to meet Mikael. It's perverse, and it's completely unsustainable. I know this but I repress it; changing anything is beyond me.

So I tolerate him. I tolerate the marital rights that he sometimes demands – I pay it as the price of security and instalments on my pension. But my joy, my daily excitement, is something I seek in a man who doesn't love me.

Gustav has never been convinced that Mikael is as sexless as a troll, and unfortunately I have to admit that I've romanticized him. The truth is that his girlfriend's attending a folk high school somewhere in Lapland; it's just that he's so faithful to her that it seems like he lacks any interest in women. I don't tell Gustav, although it would probably mollify him, but I won't grant him that satisfaction. I don't grant him the ability to say 'Look, there are people who are faithful.'

I feel like a bad person, and it's a terrible feeling, but I am the way I am, and every time I try to be something else, it only makes things worse.

Of course I understand that there's something wrong with people who prefer to get involved in a hopeless crush. Some kind of immaturity or inability to deal with the realities of life, with a fellow human who demands something concrete of you. But it's far more interesting to be unhappily in love than happily! And it's so much more aesthetic to be unhappily in love than to be unhappily married!

*

'You're not expecting me to congratulate you, are you?' I say curtly when Harriet informs me she's getting married on Saturday.

'Not at all. But you can come and congratulate Jonas.'

'That wouldn't be honest, either. I wouldn't want to be married to you. Almost as much as I wouldn't want to be married to me, in fact.'

'No, but you know how men are.'

'Will it be in the church and everything?'

'Not in the church itself,' Harriet emphasizes, 'not at the high altar, just the little chapel next door at Gustav Vasa. And you don't have to come for my sake,' she also points out, 'but the family will think it's nice if a few people are there.'

The whole spectacle seems to have been planned mostly to please the family, but why not, if you can make them happy with so little and you yourself don't care. I've never really understood the people who assert that marriage as an institution is utterly meaningless and in the same breath say they'd never get married. If it doesn't matter, it doesn't matter.

On the contrary, I think it's odd that Harriet doesn't want to do it all up with a bridal gown and everything since they're putting on a spectacle anyway. Why have a church wedding if you're not going to take advantage of the pleasure of dressing up? Gustav agrees with me (with dreams of tuxedos in his eyes), but for him a church wedding would never be an option – he's a believer.

And I'm inclined to agree with him when I hear that ritual. I've never thought about it before, but who actually cobbled it together? 'The greatest happiness on earth'! 'For the well-being of society'! 'Prepare the welfare of your descendants through careful upbringing'! What has Harriet got herself into? It's even worse when the pastor says a few words off script. I peer uncomfortably at Gustav, but he succeeds in muffling his giggles this time.

As for me, I thought I was going to sob, and so I do. Not because I feel moved about society's well-being, but out of pure sadness: that horrible Jonas, who's a lawyer and is dragging Harriet out to the countryside where he's going to be serving in the district court – things can never be the same between us.

The dinner afterwards is just for the families, and they go off in their cars; I stand in the gravel driveway and wave meaninglessly at Harriet's blonde nape in the back window.

'Is it a marriage of convenience?' Gustav asks when we return to our bicycles down on Västmannagatan.

'Very much so. A marriage of resignation. She'd given up on getting the one she wanted, so she was able to marry anyone at all.'

'It doesn't sound very sustainable.'

'Resignation is probably the most sustainable force in the world. Do you think for one moment that marriages of inclination last any longer?'

And so we're there again.

*

'I cut myself on you,' Gustav says.

That's probably a way of expressing our distribution of guilt. It's my fault that the way I am means that he hurts himself on me. But he's the one hurting himself. He has the freedom to stop doing it.

I'm using him, he allows himself to be used: our guilt is shared.

He takes on his share of the responsibility, yes he does; in his ideology, you decide with whom you want to fall in love, and since he's decided on me, he stands by it, whether it be the death of him or not, I believe.

He shoulders his share, but mine is heavy enough.

On his final examination, he gets the highest grade, which is a relief – a relief that I didn't make him incapable of studying, too (in addition to sleepless and emaciated). My classes are also finished and I don't know if I'll see Mikael any more. The last few weeks I haven't seen much of him – he's been busy with subversion. The universities are brewing it, inspired by the student riots abroad; the opposition to the university reforms is starting to develop into a real revolt. We've added our names to lists and participated in demonstrations, but in our own departments there hasn't been any particularly subversive vitality, and since nothing else is keeping us in the city, we want to go out sailing as soon as possible, before the archipelago becomes clogged with vacationing tourists.

Erik has already been out for a sail and he brings the boat in to dock at Värmdö, appropriate for a change of crew. We set our course over Kanholmsfjärden towards Möja, then maybe we'll continue up to Blidö – I would love to see Strindberg's Fagervik and Skamsund.

But if you're not happily married when you set foot in a boat, you're probably not going to become so on board, either. Sitting as a passive passenger can't be anything but monotonous, so I try to understand something of the principles of sailing. I'm really trying, but there turns out to be a blind spot in my mental equipment precisely there. I can't learn the difference between 'gybe' and 'tack', I don't understand how you're supposed to figure out the direction of wind when the pennant at the top of the mast indicates *motion wind*, and I have no idea why he can't tell me to pull the tiller to the right or to the left instead. He just shouts 'gybe!' and gets mad when I pull in the wrong direction. He even insists on saying 'starboard' and 'port', just to make it all seem more special.

I've never seen Gustav as uncontrolled as he is at sea – it's probably because he's nervous, and that's not hard to understand. What I don't understand is why he himself loves this existence, one that transforms him into a braying Mr Hyde.

As long as the wind is with us, I mean we're sailing downwind, it's rather enjoyable, in fact. Then, at least, it doesn't blow so your teeth are chattering – you can even take off one or two of your sweaters and lie on the deck and sun yourself if the sail isn't in the way. But when you tack, when the boat tilts, I know it's not going to capsize, I take him at his word when he says that the boat is practically uncapsizable, with detailed explanations of the weight of the keel and the wind that won't catch the sails if they're too low. I comprehend this rationally, in the same way as I can comprehend that a roller coaster at Gröna Lund is constructed in such a manner that you won't fall out of it, that you're simply supposed to feel as if you will.

But the fact that it feels this way is not something I can get used to, and much less find enjoyment in. I grip the edge and curl my toes and try not to watch the deck ploughing under the surface of the water, but I obsessively sit calculating how far it is to swim to the closest shore and how many degrees the water can have warmed up to – twelve? Fourteen?

He takes care of the sail himself, but I have to relieve him at the tiller now and again. 'You sail really well,' he says suddenly, encouragingly. I have no clue at all as to what's good since I still don't comprehend anything, and I take care not to ask so I don't ruin the effect. But what's good one moment isn't at all good the next. 'Gybe just a bit now,' he commands, and I tentatively pull the tiller towards me – 'NO, I said GYBE!'

The worst part is coming into docks and leaving them again without demolishing other people's boats or entangling yourself in their anchor lines. My participation is required then, when you have to hop on land with the ropes and 'steer off' and all sorts of things, and Gustav gets nervous and screams. 'Steer off on the starboard side! STARBOARD, I said!'

I'm not just cowardly – I'm stupid as well.

Some people are simply unsuited from birth to be mates. If I could only cook and make myself useful doing household tasks. But I'm just in the way wherever I am, and most of all when the vessel is transformed into our quarters. There's no room for a cabin with stable bunks or other comforts in a simple StarBoat.

Everything has to be packed carefully each morning – sleeping bags and mattresses and food sacks and garbage bags and dishes and gas stove – and be unpacked every evening. By then I'm half dead of hunger after only being able to tease out one or two pieces of hard-bread from my pack during our sail.

When the weather is nice, we spread out our dinner in the cockpit. The wind dies down towards evening and the sea can be as flat as a mirror, and even I can't see much wrong with life. But when it rains. When it rains so that everything you set on the floor gets wet, everything dry you pull out of their plastic bags gets wet, gradually everything gets wet and the mess on board indescribable. Then, I say, then you would need a love of utterly supernatural dimensions.

Once we get as far as Furusund, it becomes so windy that even Gustav feels it's too much although we've reefed the main-sail twice. He decides we'll anchor in a protected bay and wait for better weather.

I have nothing against that either: lying on the deck in the sun and reading in Janhem's *Guide* about other pleasant bays you can anchor in, while the waves slap against the side of the boat and you can go ashore if you need to pee or stretch your legs. Untouched archipelago islands, the entire world smells of early summer, and under the trees it's so quiet that all you hear are bumblebees humming and birds chirping, although it seemed like a full storm out on the open sea.

By next morning, the wind has tapered off, but there are several days of constant rain, and we change our course. It's a relief when our home harbour comes into view and we finally, after a couple of failed attempts, succeed in taking the buoy and Gustav manages to pull down those wildly flapping sheets of fabric one last time. The peace afterwards is possibly worth all of the horror.

Gun-Britt Sundström

On the Island, we turn on the radio to find out how the revolution in Stockholm turned out – the last we heard, the student liberation army was going to occupy the Opera House. But nothing is said about it in the news, so the revolution apparently petered out into the summer holiday.

13

We plan to celebrate our second anniversary by breaking up. Not as before, abruptly and in temporary disagreement – that's sure to fail. We'll do it in mutual agreement and after a proper period of preparation. The 26th of August will be just right. Besides, it's practical to collect all of our noteworthy dates into one and the same day so there won't be that many to keep track of.

We want to have each other, but we can't agree on the forms of this having. We want to have different 'each others'. The only way out is to break up once and for all, we agree on that – there's nothing we agree about more. In token of this agreement, we spend the summer together, as a token of a surrender that makes our lives together mild and peaceful. At the beginning of August we go out to the Island one last time – this is about the fifth time I'm going out to the Island one last time, but this will be the last time I'll be going to the Island one last time.

The stage is set for quiet solemnity and melancholy maturity. The autumnal mood, the cold and wind – the trees already dropping their yellow leaves. The well has run dry and we have to fetch water in drums from a neighbour who's deep-drilled. We pick blueberries in the forest and bake rye bread in the wood stove. Existing occupies us completely.

Autumn and maturity and solemn resignation: a death in

beauty. Mature and resigned, we make love and each time is the next to the last. I don't reject his advances since every time is the next to the last.

Naturally, we fall into such a conciliatory mood as a result of all this that when the day arrives for us to part ways, it'll be impossible for us to see any reason to do so, but if one of us starts to suggest anything in that direction, the other one quickly hushes the other. Not again! You know exactly what will happen!

We do.

*

'I've realized what's wrong with you,' Gustav says. 'You don't have a soul. I've never before doubted that women have souls, but you've made me change my mind.'

'If you mean having ideas and such, that's true. I've never pretended otherwise.'

I'm not an ideas person. It's not just that I don't think up any myself – those who do are in the vast minority – but I don't go around thinking about ideas either, working with them, as Gustav does. I thought I did for a while when I was attending philosophy lectures, but that slipped away. Ideas only interest me aesthetically, as constructions, or psychologically, as people's attributes (not because I'm interested in people, least of all that, but in human attributes). What I lack is the ability to work up interest in ideas intellectually, to embrace them.

If this is typically feminine, I can only lament it. If a womanly trait has snuck its way into my character, it's my character all the same.

'So that's why you have a vampire nature,' he observes. 'You need fresh, new blood all the time. Because of a lack of an independent inner life, you have to feed off that of others.'

'It's true, your ability to ruminate is something I haven't been endowed with. I have social needs – I need new stimuli.'

'We're such a shitty match.'

'That's why we're going to break up,' I remind him. 'Although I still intend to see you, just so you know.'

'What are you going to do with your sex life?'

'Oh, that. I'm planning on abandoning it. Putting it out in the forest. By the way, we can still sleep together now and again if you want.'

'Then there won't be any change in our relationship!'

'No practical change, of course. Purely metaphysical.'

'Darling, that's something I do appreciate about you: your sense for metaphysics.' He laughs. 'You don't have a soul, but you do have a sense for metaphysics.'

Suddenly the heat returns for a few improbably beautiful and sunny late summer days. The sailboat needs to be taken up but we make one last trip. Erik also comes along, so I don't have to work as a mate. The lightest of summer breezes is blowing and I'm lying on the foredeck in the sun with a novel, slow reach, the water glittering as it glides by, my back glowing from the heat. 'This is life,' I think. I become aware of what I'm thinking and correct myself quickly, pull myself together out of my euphoria and correct myself: '*One* kind of life.' I can't let myself be fooled now, can't believe that life is supposed to be like this – there are other forms of existence. There must be others.

We undertake a deep clean of the seaside cottage so that it can be shut up for the year afterwards. I sweep under the beds with care: no summer memories will be allowed to stay hidden behind – pine needles and tobacco crumbs encapsulated in dust bunnies like small organisms in lime from eons past. The worst thing is all the strands of hair – both Gustav and I seem to shed hair like cats and the rugs are covered in them. If you pinch one between your fingers, an entire skein follows suit, his red-blond and my brown ones intertwined into a dirty extra carpet on top of the striped rag rug his grandmother wove.

At lunch, our last meal together, Gustav lets slip something about a girl he's set his sights on. Maybe he isn't saying it in a conscious attempt to inspire jealousy in me, maybe he simply can't refrain from blabbing about everything – but just now he really ought to think before he speaks, if he's in agreement about executing this separation cleanly and cooperatively.

I am both hurt and angry, and glad that I am: it's an indication that my self-esteem is still intact. I mobilize a sense of aggression: I walk around the Island collecting my possessions and feel the aggression I need streaming up from the deepest recesses of my soul. (This place is theirs; I've never really been welcome here, of course – I don't belong here. I belong somewhere else. I've painted this cottage, but I can be generous. That blue rowboat bobbing in the water at the dock – it has nothing to do with me. Crappy boat, by the way – always difficult to steer.) My aggression streams and I'm happy that I'm built to be functional.

I pack up my belongings – I even take the hammock Gustav bought me. I have no real use for it in the city, but it's mine, and no other woman is going to be lying in it. I take a solitary walk along the beach, stride in the evening breeze and feel fascistic. Strong and healthy, and proud of being strong and healthy: fascistic.

And then we rattle home to the city on the bus, sitting in one last traffic jam together.

On the 26th, we meet to break up. We've chosen a café for this formality, an outdoor locale at Norr Mälarstrand. Afternoon sun, wind through the withering reeds. The usual exchange of borrowed books, and then there's not much left to say. There's just one uncertainty that remains now: the possibility that I'm pregnant.

Since I stopped taking the Pill, he's barely been allowed to touch me before I call for candy wrappers – I'm a virtual germophobe in this regard, convinced that it's more contagious than the worst cold (don't you read everywhere about people who get pregnant simply from taking a bath in the same tub?). I do realize that it isn't particularly probable this time, and my period is only a week late. But Gustav is worried. He doesn't long for a child any more than I do, which is to say not at all.

'It could have purely theoretical interest, of course,' he suggests, 'to see what the kid would be like.'

'The actual experience of becoming a parent would probably not be uninteresting either, I mean as <u>consciousness expanding</u>.'

However, we're both clear that such an interest is not sufficient for *having* a baby. If you're interested in taking care of a child, you can just as well adopt. It's a good test of character for your attitude towards this issue: it wouldn't occur to us to adopt.

'Less suitable parents have never existed,' Gustav notes.

And I have to admit that it would be an inglorious end to such a promising divorce.

'But if it's twins, we can each take one, so we wouldn't have to get married after all.'

'It will probably only be one,' he imagines. 'An evil little girl the spitting image of you.'

'Well, in that case, you can take her. If there's a shoebox in your stairway at some point in May, you'll know what it is.'

He looks seriously worried, and I promise:

'I'll inform you as soon as my monthlies arrive.'

We monitor each other for nostalgia, but we don't succumb. We've prepared this so thoroughly and become so used to the

Gun-Britt Sundström

thought that we've eliminated the shock effect and the impulse to fall into each other's arms again out of pure emotion.

Now all we have to do is go our separate ways. We unlock our bicycles; I take St Eriksgatan home, Gustav rides off towards Tegelbacken.

The flat has felt large and desolate since I took it over alone. I walk back and forth between the rooms and contemplate moving my bed to Harriet's old room, but decide that I may as well keep things as before. If it's a cold winter, I can manage by heating just one room. I'm going to get a new phone socket so I can lie in bed and talk.

I eat dinner, straighten up, look at the clock. Am I waiting for him to show up after all? I sit in my reading chair and do nothing, hearing the clock tick.

The way things used to be, he would have come around this time.

*

With muffled loathing for the task, I've finished that translation job – muffling my loathing for participating in a pretence that something is possible that, in fact, is not.

Nothing else comes along. I find a course for TV producers in the paper and send in an application. I'm called to an aptitude test and go through the first one, but lose interest before the second one – what use is there for stylistic giftedness on television?

The university catalogue is still full of subjects I haven't studied, but I don't have the energy to take up something new. Apathetically, I start to take an advanced course in English and sign student loan papers.

There aren't many lectures, and mostly I sit at home – it's so quiet. I hear from Mikael now and again, but now that I'm free to see him as much as I want, I don't want to as much. His girlfriend has left him and he's depressed – I'm afraid he'll fall in love with me. Mikael is, in fact, a bit boring in the long term.

Harriet has moved away from Stockholm. Cilla is also engrossed in a man.

Why don't I know more people? Why haven't I made any friends in the past few years? It's more difficult than making babies, I think, not knowing why I'm comparing: it's probably just a linguistic association. <u>Make love not war. Make love not babies. Make friends not love.</u>

My period is a long time coming, so long that I start to see small children around me, I mean I start to notice small children, observe mothers on the subway as they haul prams and bags, and think *what if*. And I think no, no children, not me, no!

Eleven days late, I finally wake up one morning with an unmistakable pain in my belly. I could let Gustav live in uncertainty for a while longer, but I keep my word and send a letter immediately: 'The twins send their greetings and deny their existence.' I consider adding an appropriate Bible verse – I think there's something about it being better to remain childless, but I don't dare to start skimming through that book and risk stumbling across old memories.

Week after week the same quiet life. Every Saturday I think I ought to Find Something to Do, leaf through the evening paper's entertainment ads, go out at random, end up at Odenplan and buy a hot dog, go home and read through the entertainment ads once again. I go to bed. Every Saturday.

An inner life – it would be nice to have an inner life. Entertaining.

The summer heat is definitely at an end, it's windy outside and it's cold in my condemned building. I'm too stingy to heat as much as I ought to – both wood and kerosene are expensive, and I rationalize my decision by attributing it to my life philosophy:

try everything, even going around being cold for once in your life. That's what it was like in the olden days. Sitting and reading with gloves on your hands and a blanket over your knees. Also an experience to collect.

*

In the middle of September, Gustav calls me to let me know we've got that apartment we applied for: the student housing agency is offering us a two-room flat on Högbergsgatan.

'Do you need it?' he asks.

'Not as far as I know.'

'Then I'll move into it myself.'

'I think you should.'

Pause.

'If we're certain we don't want it together?' I say.

He's absolutely certain we don't.

*

I read. I look for work. I eat and I sleep.

Doesn't it get more fun than this? Life, I mean.

I see a poster in the department about folk dancing at the student union building. We learned folk dance in PE at school: I remember the times when I was able to pull myself out of my apathy and get into it – what a pervasive joy it was to skip around to music.

I pull myself together and go to the student union building with the thought that I'll get to dance the schottische with a dewy-eyed student from the countryside. Instead I'm bought a beer by a balding defector from East Germany who makes conversation about the parliamentary elections and wants to know how the hell you can vote for the Socialists.

I wander home in the cold autumn night after realizing that neither my German nor my schottische is what it once was.

I feel washed up.

*

After a lecture, I run into Gustav outside of the library. We walk down the street together. He tells me about the flat he's moving into at the end of the month and says I should stop by sometime.

We part at the corner.

He looked at me the way you'd look at anybody. As if I hadn't been his wife, as if I hadn't been the love of his life.

I think about how he looked at me before, once when we were walking up Drottninggatan and I was sad and he looked at me with his big eyes, eyes that asked me if there was anything in the world he could do for me and said that if there were, he would do it.

Sentimental idiocy. Senile sentimental dementia.

I shove my bike into the stand and kick the front door open.

And the whole thing, after all, was his idea from the beginning, I think dimly.

*

But I lived a life before Gustav, didn't I? What did I spend my days on then? I dig out my old diary from the depths of my dresser drawer in a desperate attempt to rediscover an identity from my pre-Gustavian existence. The results are quite disheartening. Unhappy crushes down one page and up the next. From my school years there's the occasional outburst about a teacher and from my time in England, a few terse notices about other experiences, but for the most part it's all about crushes, ardent crushes on objects identified as 'E' and 'K' whose names I can hardly recall now. An inner life? Not the faintest whiff of an inner life in this quasi-erotic rot.

Two years ago, my notes stopped abruptly. On the last written page there's a newspaper clipping with a quote from Ebbe Linde – where did I find it? – that says this: 'The diary age begins at sexual maturity and ends as soon as a lasting sexual connection has been established.'

Is it to be understood thusly that it's normal for diarists to devote themselves mainly to their sex lives, or their lack thereof? Or is the point that a lasting sexual connection means a confidant who replaces outpourings on paper?

Fortunately I'm rescued from my brooding when I suddenly get notice that a job application has borne fruit. It's a publisher – a different one from last time, smaller and apparently more boring – which produces nonfiction and textbooks. And a boss who seems decidedly dyspeptic. But the girl who trod on the dream job must take what she can get. I'll start on the first of the month with two weeks of training provided by the fellow I'm to replace.

During those weeks, I hate it there intensely, but that's not so strange: to sit like an idiot at the edge of someone else's desk, not getting to do anything sensible yourself, to be shuffled around to look at incomprehensible printing processes and to be given the task of paginating manuscripts.

Once my predecessor finally leaves, it's considerably better. Having my own desk in my own office at a real Job! A phone connected to an exchange. Letterhead with the company logo.

And then I get a book manuscript for editing, and at last! A task for a stylistic talent. My contribution is truly needed here. After three pages I begin to wonder if the author is even Swedish – he hasn't put together a single sentence that I can allow to pass as it is. I cross out and reposition and punctuate and have such a good time that I work through the coffee break. I go to the supply room and ask for more red pens, and soon become known at the company for my voracious consumption of them.

*

Gustav invites me over for dinner so I can admire his new flat. Now, it's not much to admire, really: a building in its last stages, worse than my own. No regular tenants left, only evictable students while the owners wait for the demolition permit. Window facing the back courtyard, rather dark, although a picturesque southern exposure. He's painted one of the rooms, rolling the walls in white; the other is only half-finished. A few pieces of furniture from home, some purchased at discount furniture shops. A lovely old rocking chair, almost completely whole. He's built the bed himself out of particle board.

'Roomy,' I remark. (I mean: typical double bed.)

'It's a requirement if all my tigers are to have enough room,' he answers.

I refrain from delving any deeper into that topic – I refrain resolutely from asking anything whatsoever about his relationship to sex.

He's cooked pork tenderloin with sautéed mushrooms and pours red wine, and we sit at the table in the white-rolled room and exchange information. The teacher-training college will have to wait since he's no longer been able to postpone his service to the motherland: now he's at the government's development cooperation agency, Sida, doing his alternative service during office hours among papers about Third World countries and foreign aid. He's enjoying it so much that he's glowing, and I have to admit that it seems like an unusually sensible way to defend the motherland. And as an uncommonly meaningful way to use one's time besides – my red-inking doesn't seem like an equally important task any longer.

'But it won't last that long – it's just a temporary job,' he reminds me.

'Yes, of course. On the other hand, I'm gainfully Employed and have a Monthly Salary!'

Then I make sure to ask Gustav how you can vote for the Socialists.

'Who else would you vote for?'

'I'd never voted before and hadn't realized that you could possibly not do it, so I did it, of course.'

'So who says you can't?'

'A balding East German.'

It was probably because the conversation was in German that I had a hard time explaining my reasoning. But I became confused – such a relief to hear Gustav, a wise person, tease out the concepts.

Once we've done the dishes after dinner, he takes out a bundle of newly developed photos to show me – a roll from last summer which had been lying around until now. Pictures from the Island and from sailing: we comment on the exposure and exchange opinions on camera angles and cutting as if the motifs didn't have anything to do with us more than the illustrations in the *Photography Handbook*.

Yes, well, time for me to go home, then. Bye in the stairwell, bye.

We part as friends do.

It's a long way home from the southern part of the city – Gustav has moved so far away. There's a cold wind blowing along Skeppsbron and this city is entirely too littered with memories. There's not one place where we haven't been together. During the time we were together.

I force myself against the wind, pedal stroke by pedal stroke, cursing in impotent rage at being such a hostage to my moods – have I truly forgotten how it was? No, I haven't forgotten, I remember it all too well: being married is a disaster. But being divorced is so tragic!

It's the fact that an intimacy that existed is simply left to wither and die. It's horrible to have no contact at all, but it's just as horrible to have such a formal relationship as this. How are we ever supposed to act naturally around each other? I don't want to be married or single or divorced, but there's no civil status called zero, and what's been done cannot be undone. So we'll have to spend our entire lives walking around like this, being no-longer-together. Each other's divorced partner. Each other's exes – what a bloody awful relationship to have.

14

Sitting at your own desk at a real job feels meaningful, to be sure, but the novelty wears off at a frightening speed, I have to say. To be forced to sit there every single day – this is what I object to. My colleagues are few and monumentally boring, with their nose in the middle of their face.

This is the kind of thing Gustav tried to wean me away from saying about people – there are no average people, he said. All people are unique and interesting. This is easy to believe in theory. However, upon closer observation, it becomes apparent that most people *do* have their nose in the middle of their face. Previously this was my working hypothesis; now that he's weaned me off it, I assume that all people are original and exciting and only discover gradually, case by case, that they are not. It's much more tiring.

No matter how many times I look at the gents at work, there isn't a single one that I can fall the least bit in love with, and that means the situation is quite dire, because I truly need very little to hang a crush on someone. In school, at the university, no matter what subject you were studying, there was always someone you could rest your eyes on. But middle-aged businessmen in nylon shirts who talk about capital gains! Could you sleep with a right-winger? It's a question I read in a book by Jan Myrdal, one posed by his wife. The answer as I understand it is no.

The only one I might be able to work up a crush on is one of the girls, but she's married. I don't mean anything like That, I just mean that since Maria has a family, she dashes off home to them every day at five o'clock like the others do, and then you can't socialize. A little small talk during breaks – you never get any closer to each other. Never as you do with school and university friends, never a question of hanging around at a café and going to the movies or sleeping over on each other's floors.

I still attend a seminar or two, but finding enough time for more regular studies is impossible. Sometimes I bike down to Café Marx and sit there to read, just so I can see other people around me, or in the hope that something will turn up. Suddenly someone does turn up – a boy with glorious curls asks if I want to follow him to Ängelholm this evening. He doesn't mean That, on the contrary: it has to do with the trial of a demonstrator from Scania, and I would love to come with him if I didn't have to be at work tomorrow.

I've almost lost contact with Harriet. We started to play correspondence chess when she moved, but it doesn't seem as if she's really engaged in it, and say what you will about chess – it's not much for a vampire nature to exist on. Cilla has also moved in together with her fellow, which didn't come unexpectedly, but nevertheless the news felt like an icy breeze: Now I'm the only one left!

What do you mean, left, you could ask. Left, you say, I can't be 'left over' if it's my choice, can I? The World can't know that, you could answer. And left in solitude is just what I am: I understand what old people feel when they scan the obituaries in the paper and see one after another of their peers disappear – I'm at that age now, although for me it's wedding announcements.

If they were just getting married, but it's a question of *marrying off* – away, out of the picture, and then you never see them again.

It isn't the same, anyway. Cilla never stops by for a cup of coffee on her way somewhere else any more, and even if she invites me home after work on the odd evening, I hesitate – I could be coming at a bad time and maybe her husband thinks there's too much coming and going. I can't even call Cilla any longer knowing that it's Cilla I'll get to talk to.

There isn't anyone at all who 'comes by' for a chat like before. What I've understood is that you're supposed to have outgrown that sort of socialising. At my age, you're supposed to be mature enough to form your own family: the only affirmation of maturity and manliness that exists in our society. Perhaps instead I'm actually the one representing a higher form of maturity – perhaps I've skipped over one developmental stage of civilization and represent a non-family-building type of human which in a few generations will be widespread?

Well, yes, I can amuse myself with that in my loneliness.

★

That idea of putting my sexuality out in the forest wasn't quite as simple as I believed. It returned stealthily on some back road.

Not without embarrassment, I remember what I said to Gustav on some occasion about urges and self-gratification. It's clear that there's a special kind of urge to embrace, hug hormones. The belly demands its due. One front side longs for another front side – perhaps it's like in the *Symposium* after all: the cut surface making itself felt.

'Is it pleasant being married?' I asked Harriet when she called. 'It's pleasant having company,' she replied. It sounded crass, and that's probably the point: you can't get more romantic than that if you've married out of resignation.

Until now, I've avoided going with men I'm not in love with, but perhaps that's a principle whose days are numbered. The need for a little human closeness is starting to get so out of hand that I'm afraid I'm going to end up in bed with just about anyone because of it, right-winger or not. I don't want that. I don't want to start copulating with the hoi polloi simply out of a need for closeness – intercourse to socialize.

I remind myself of an occasion at the beginning of my acquaintance with Cilla. We were sitting at Ogo gossiping about our classmates. It started when we exchanged opinions on which of the boys in the class were 'womanizers' and which weren't and whether you could tell by looking at them. Otherwise we were in complete agreement that the ones who weren't were the interesting ones – it's a strange notion that notorious Don Juans are attractive, men whom everyone has had. What's challenging is the possibility of making a conquest no one else has succeeded with. 'The sexiest man I can think of is a monk,' Cilla said.

Naturally, we then moved on to the Don Juanettes (analogue meaning: those who are very interested in and / or have had many affairs with the opposite sex). The archetype, we immediately agreed, was the *femme fatale* Miss Björk – the teacher addressed us by our last names, we distanced ourselves from the others by doing the same – a woman of the type who gets up one hour earlier in the morning to tend to her appearance before she shows herself to the world, and who seems to change personality as soon as a male enters a room where you're sitting and talking, wriggling and starting to coo somehow, and in fact addressing the male even if she is talking to you.

At the other end of the scale I wanted to place a tidy girl with a tartan skirt and glasses, but Cilla wasn't so sure – such appearances could be misleading.

Of course I was burning with curiosity about where Cilla would put me but didn't want to ask, and she pre-empted me by asking where I would place her. I said I would put her somewhere in the middle, although probably more in the direction of Miss Björk – I modified it out of politeness, although I had already realized that Cilla was advanced in that area.

Then I had free rein to ask her about me. She thought for a good while before she said: You don't belong on that scale.

Her answer pleased me immoderately. It would annoy me just as much to be perceived as a spinster, prude and asexual as to appear man-crazy, unchaste and fast, or as some kind of mediocre normal case. I wanted to be a case entirely to myself, one that demands tailor-made scales and cannot be measured by the yardsticks of others. That is my pride.

But not having anything to do with men other than those you truly like is a luxury you can allow yourself only as long as there *are* any men you like. Am I going to have to go to the student union and pick up East Germans to have someone I can be belly-to-belly with for a while?

No, in that case, I'd rather ask Gustav. That might seem to be the one thing my pride ought to forbid me above all, but, for some reason, pride has never forbidden me anything at all when it comes to Gustav. And having sex now and again although we're only friends is something I mentioned to him as a possibility before we separated.

Shamelessly I call and ask him to come over. I tell him precisely how things are, and he's so delighted that he's the one I'm calling that he doesn't need any persuading, his sense of pride doesn't protest. He says precisely what he's feeling and comes over.

But things get no better after that. In fact, this is the moment that it gets truly bad. For, before he leaves, he takes the time to inform me that he's about to remarry. And not with just anyone this time: he's seen the Summer Girl again, blonde Birgitta of his childhood from the architect's home on the Island. During the winter, the family lived in the north somewhere, but now she's moved to Stockholm. She's studying to become a kindergarten teacher and has rented a room with a relative in posh

Östermalm, not far from Bragevägen. That's where they ran into each other one day and exchanged phone numbers.

'A summer romance,' I say, 'a moonlit walk or two, nothing can ever come of that.'

'The summer romance of all time,' he corrects me, 'year after year!'

This implies miles of moonlit walks altogether. Oh yes, I remember, he told me. It all ended when she rejected him for another, I recall, some attractive and simple youth who was the son of the Island's country grocer.

'Surely you understand what a joy it is to have my revenge on that?'

'Yes, doubtless. But if you're supposed to have your revenge on everyone who's rejected you for someone else, you'd never have time for anything else.'

'Do you think all other people's relationships are a rejection of you?'

'All of them. I'm jealous of the entire world.'

'That's fine, then. Then one more or less makes no difference, right?'

But it does. It's a difference like night and day to be rejected by Gustav or not to be. I thought it would be usefully de-dramatizing to go have sex with him in a business-like and prestige-free spirit, but, the day after, I'm completely out of balance. More nostalgic than ever – mushy is the word – in all of the nuances of its etymology: soft, dissolved in sensitiveness and out of my mind. When a delivery from the florist comes and I unwrap a bouquet of yellow chrysanthemums, I'm entirely capable of watering them with my tears. Chrysanthemums: the flowers of autumn. Alas the memory of my mad youth, when I didn't have the sense to be grateful for a red rose.

The problem, of course, is that I don't have a soul. I can't embrace an ideology that provides me with behavioural norms to follow consistently. In my confused mind there are only rudiments of a heap of different ideologies that float to the surface and indicate opposite results on different occasions. Every argument can therefore be used both as a pro and as a con in the relationship between Gustav and me, and I cannot succeed in arranging them on the same side no matter how much I move them around.

Gustav suffers the most when we're together; I suffer most when we're apart. If it's an ethical rule that another person's suffering is more important than one's own, then it's his duty to tolerate me and mine to leave him. If, on the other hand, you also have to take your own suffering into account and every person takes responsibility for his or her individual suffering, then Gustav should have left me a long time ago, and I have the right to cling to him as tightly as I can.

Applying one ethical standard to myself and one to him can never be right. The only thing that remains then is to assume a primitive, utilitarian stance and say that it's the sum total of all the suffering in the world that has meaning, not its distribution – and then succeed in solving the question of which one of us is suffering the most.

It's not easy to create a formula for this – it's not just the quantity but also the quality that must be measurable: has the unhappiness been deeper and greater than the happiness, perhaps? Or, on the contrary, can medium-sized happiness compensate for a great deal of unhappiness?

Before I've got to this point, I tire of being utilitarian and become some kind of aestheticizing deontologist again. One that says that our relationship has an intrinsic value, such as in realizing our destinies, and if it could also be proved to a degree bordering on probability that we would eventually live in eternal unhappiness, that's immaterial. Or the other way around: perhaps it would be Happiness, but what says that you're supposed to be happy? Perhaps the meaning of life is something else entirely.

How am I supposed to be able to see through my own obscure motives and determine whether my desire to have him is a correctly perceived sense of belonging or an unsustainable romanticizing of potato-peeling, whether the desire to be alone is egotistical indolence or healthy independence, and whether the fact that, at this particular moment, I don't think I can live without him is simply a function of the fact that, just now, he seems to be doing splendidly without me?

You choose, Gustav says. It 'isn't' at all – you yourself have to determine how to interpret reality. As if it were that simple! I can't choose until I have an ideology – but first I have to choose one.

He complains that I can never make up my mind. At least it would be easier if he'd make up his own first.

'She was better suited to one great sorrow than many small cares,' I remember reading in one of the horrible novels from my youth, some tragic story about a complicated woman's marriage with a man too simple and good for her – that this disgusting little aphorism has stuck in my memory must be because, as a perceptive young girl, I already felt spoken to.

I'm probably best suited to the great sorrow, and I don't want to stand in the way of his happiness if he's now finally met a suitable woman for crocheting ties. This much is clear to me: I don't want him to sacrifice himself for me, accept me as a burden to carry. This much is clear enough to me to tell him in a letter: 'Of course,' I write, 'you have no obligations with respect to me. Don't be ashamed to step over my corpse. That small pleasure, at my own nobleness, you must grant me in return.'

I'm awakened by the phone. I hope it's Gustav, and it is. I pull the receiver into the warmth under the blanket and complain weakly, for the sake of tradition, that he woke me up, and then suggest quickly that we meet that evening. No, he's busy. He's just calling to ask what that letter meant, that I can't decide before he does:

'You mean that if I want you then you don't and vice versa?'

'That's an excellent summary. Just tell me if you get married to someone else so that I know what I'm dealing with. By the way, you promised to report how things were progressing with Birgitta.'

'Yes indeed, things are going in the right direction.'

'Held hands? Kissed her? Seduced her?'

'Yes; yes; no,' Gustav answers.

I can't think of anything to add.

'Are you sad?'

Don't be ashamed to step over my corpse, you must grant me the small pleasure at my nobleness . . . That's not much pleasure! That's entirely too little pleasure!

I sit silent and simply sigh.

'But what do you want, then? To continue as before? We both know that didn't work.'

I present my thoughts about this, and issues of ethics always interest him, so we keep talking for an hour. We reason hither and thither but naturally don't get anywhere – because where would we be able to get?

He ends the call by saying we can start to see each other gradually, spend time together and be friends. 'Keep in touch,' he says.

And then we hang up.

It's half ten. I was supposed to get up, clean, do my errands. I pull the blanket over my head and try to fall asleep again, but in vain – I've already slept ten hours.

I shove my feet over the edge of the bed, shuffle into the kitchen and start the coffee. I think: He's coming over. No, he's not coming over. Before, he would have done. After those kinds of conversations, he always came over so we could fall into each other's arms.

Not now. He's thinking that it has to pass, and it's best if he leaves me alone. Besides, he has 'Birgitta' to think about. It's Saturday – of course he's seeing her tonight.

I drink my coffee and skim through the morning paper without seeing it. I turn on the radio – sentimental Swedish top-ten songs about happiness in love, as always. 'Who cares about another / now that we have each other . . .' I turn it off again, can't stand to listen (so defenceless, and defenceless in the face of something like the Swedish top-ten – what humiliation).

I glare at his flowers on the table: what's he giving me flowers for, if he loves another? They're hardly drooping yet but I stuff them in the rubbish bin just the same.

November: the floor icy cold under my feet. I leave for the post office but instead I start to wander towards Norrtull, my hands stuffed deep in my duffle-coat pockets. Small, deserted streets. The ground frozen, the trees naked. A Siberia: a neighbourhood for the marginalized, poverty and cold.

As a reflex, a contrasting thought: with her warmth, in her newly renovated nest with a wealthy relative on Floragatan, wall-to-wall carpeting and softly pattering slippers, central heating and body warmth . . .

The thought is unbearable. Warmth between them, closeness.

I wander in this proletarian quarter where I make my home – just now without considering the fact that a salary of 2,000 crowns a month from the publisher means I'm probably better off than preschool-teacher Birgitta: she has wealthy parents of course, she lives in Östermalm, the neighbourhood of the secure upper class. For a moment I see in black and white and only know that she is everything I am not, and that everything I am is wrong if she is right.

She's blonde and voluptuous, I'm dark and delicate, and that's wrong. She's feminine and soft, I'm intellectual and difficult, and that's doomed. She was born to be a wife and mother, I was born to be a comrade and a hetaera, and if he makes her a wife and mother, he will have need for neither comrade nor hetaera for the foreseeable future.

The demons of jealousy dance their chain dance, dance my common sense and reason away: I observe, my fascination mixed with horror, their strange twists and turns – this bizarre performance has a certain undeniable entertainment value. Perhaps it's true that I'm happiest when I'm unhappily in love. But being like that with Gustav – I had never imagined it.

I return to my poor condemned flat. The kerosene is almost gone – best to save it for the night.

The night?

Be noble, I remind myself. Generous: let him have this. I search myself: can I?

I want her to hurt him really badly. I want him to return to me cheated on, disappointed, rejected and humiliated. Then I'll toss my curls and laugh my tinkling laugh, and say, 'But of course we can see each other and spend time together at some point, and have sex too, I don't mind, but nothing else. It's too late,' I'll say, 'now it's too late, I shall never more be your woman!'

Noble, oh, noble as an angel am I. In actual fact, a classic psychopath: maudlin and brutal, sentimental and sadistic.

I call Cilla and tell her to come and hear my latest insight, but Cilla is having her in-laws over for dinner and doesn't have time for insights.

I start a fire in the tile oven, lie on my back on the floor and watch the demons dance.

The phone rings. It's Mikael – he needs the address for one of his teachers but has lost his university catalogue. I find the address for him and can't find anything else to say. Mikael doesn't like talking on the phone and finishes the conversation quickly: 'So nice to hear you're alive – please continue. Bye!'

On the other side of the wall, my neighbour's hall clock chimes crisply five times. I get up and turn on the light in the kitchen, look in the cupboards. Dinner will probably be coffee, but maybe a sandwich, too. I'm starting to get tired of gorging on my unhappiness and open the unread morning paper.

When I've got to Names & News and my second sandwich, the doorbell rings. If it had been back then. But it's not, right? If it's Gustav, then it *is* like it was back then anyway.

It's Gustav, in his black rain cape.

'I just wanted to give you this,' he says and hands me a bag of liquorice.

'Why?' I say, retiring into the darkness of the flat, not taking the gift. He sets it on the hat shelf.

'I was just riding past, have to keep going.'

'To your new wife,' I say (my countenance glowing with noble generosity).

'What do you mean,' Gustav says, astonished. 'I'm going to the FNL office to make flyers.'

We stand in my hall and look at each other, laughing in confusion. He's at a loss, doesn't know what to do – oh, he's not as hard as I am, not as easily hardened – he can't hurt anyone. He looks at me and his eyes scrunch up in laughter, as they usually do when everything is muddled up to the point of perplexity, desperation and comedy.

'You look so skinny and sad.'

I hold back my laughter, smile tragically and try to look even skinnier.

'I shouldn't have come,' he mumbles. 'Now I feel polygamous again.'

'So you're married to her now?'

'No, I seem to have ruined things with her as well. She asked if I had decided and I said "um, well" . . .'

'What do you mean, decided?'

'I told her how difficult it was for you and me to decide how things would be between us.'

He said 'um, well'! He *hasn't* decided! He's just as wishy-washy as I am!

I stand up straight; my self-esteem extends once again into its full height.

'What about her? Does she know what she wants?'

'I don't know. She's so shy. I bet Halldén twenty-five crowns that I'd get her in bed, but it looks like he'll be the winner.'

I laugh: he would never talk to her about me that way. You only talk that way to confidants, with male friends and hetaeras – and you're closer to the one you talk to than to the one you talk about!

'I don't think I should get involved in that bet, but do keep me informed as things develop. It's so lovely to have these small confidences.'

'We're more like each other, you and I,' he says matter-of-factly.

There goes the last demon tail; I'm fully recovered, fresh and healthy and standing straight: what do I care that he prefers her as long as he admits that I'm the one who's his type!

He quickly embraces me, my cheek against his slick rain cape. A few seconds – in a few seconds he's going to go, but in this one he's mine, I love him, and not only because I know he's going to go in a few seconds, right?

*

Meanwhile, the student flat association has discovered that Harriet stopped studying; I can't live on her contract past the new year. I tell everyone I know about my emergency in the hopes that someone will happen to know of a free apartment, and indeed, just a couple of days after I complain during the coffee break, Maria comes up to me to say that she's talked to her brother, who has a studio flat on Alströmergatan that he wants to be rid of. It's stood unlet for a couple of months, but if I can pay the accumulated rent for that period, he's ready to turn the contract over to me.

I get the key and ride off immediately to have a look, suspicious at first – because there has to be something wrong with a flat in the middle of the city that's been standing unlet. But Maria's brother may not have made much of an attempt to get rid of it before – in any event, after a quick inspection, I can't see anything wrong. True, it's dark, on the first floor, and without a tile oven. And not as quiet as I'm used to, right next to the noisy intersection of St Eriksgatan. But there's nothing seriously wrong with it.

Although – the wallpaper. Three of the walls are a kind of municipal grey and the fourth a gigantic floral print to contrast. I can't live with it. I go to the wallpaper store and browse through samples, and I quickly begin to despair. I can't possibly select wallpaper on my own. If only I could ask Gustav for advice. He has the same taste I do but he's more confident in his judgement: if he were to choose it, it would be one that I would still like after two months – I can only tell what I like here and now, and in the size of a sample.

I ask Gustav for his help, and this wallpaper is our undoing. It starts with the wallpaper and becomes an entire interior decoration project, because then, of course, I need help putting up Venetian blinds and light fixtures. Obviously I can do such things as well, but it's so much easier for him since he's much taller and has the advantage of a male upbringing – he's acquainted with screwdrivers, caulking and the innards of electrical outlets – and there are limits to my sense of principle. (The limit is two metres forty. I can't reach any further than that even on a chair. And the ceiling is three metres high.)

And then, of course, I have to invite him to dinner to thank him for his help, and why shouldn't we go and see a film afterwards that we had both wanted to see anyway, and then as a return favour he wants me to look through an article he's written – about a support project in Tanzania which isn't so hard that I can't understand it even though he's sitting next to me wearing jeans and a belt, but the memory of essay reading from the past is close at hand nonetheless, and so we seduce each other again. And then there's not much left of that divorce any longer.

On Monday, I run down to the shop on the corner on my lunch break and send him a red rose by floral telegram, to his workplace to really harass him, writing 'Prov. 26:11' on the card that goes with it (*As a dog returneth to his vomit, so a fool returneth to his folly*).

He continues to see Birgitta, but as long as I know that I'm the one who's closest to him, he can see whomever else he wants to. (As long as he's not directly cheating on me, of course.) In addition, he reveals to me now, to my unbounded *schadenfreude*, that she is 'actually' with someone else as well – there's clearly not much conviction in that relationship either, but of course she's not going to let it go for a Gustav who only says 'wellll . . .'.

And so we drift together again, without any appreciable celebration or large-scale resolve. On the contrary: we are more resigned than ever. It's like giving up smoking: you start by making grand resolutions, but then your character is too weak and you fall down, new resolutions, new relapses, and then you don't even bother to make resolutions any longer. You've lost your belief that you can follow through with them, and the issue takes its course. The longer the break, the greater the fall, and the deeper the despair.

After this truly honest attempt – one that didn't end up lasting longer than three months – we give up trying to get away from each other. Gustav says that it would require a Herculean effort to find a different way out, and that the strength he could possibly muster for it is something he needs for other things. He, too, seals his capitulation by sending me a Bible verse – I. Cor. 7:5: *Defraud ye not one the other, except it be with consent for a time, that ye may give yourselves to fasting and prayer; and come together again, that Satan tempt you not for your incontinency.*

Asthenic individuals lacking in both character and Herculean power should never be allowed to marry each other. There should be a law against it, like the ones for siblings and epileptics. A mistake cannot be repaired in such a case, and then they're stuck: they'll never be rid of each other.

15

Gustav vouched for the wallpaper; when I looked at the sample, it seemed too dark and the pattern too chaotic. But once the painter's been and I return from work and get to see the room papered in this pattern for the first time, it feels like coming home – so obviously that it makes me start to believe in reincarnation: I must have lived in a room with this dark-green Jugendstil pattern on the walls in a previous life. There's no other explanation for the fact that I get such an intense feeling of recognition.

After two days, I don't see it at all any more – it's so self-evident.

'That wasn't the point, was it?' Gustav protests. 'What do you want it for, then?'

'If it wasn't there, I'd miss it,' I explain, 'but I don't want to have to see it – you certainly can't sit there being distracted by your walls the whole time. It should harmonize with my soul and otherwise blend in with the view without my having to think about it.'

'I see. And I'm supposed to blend in with the wallpaper, is that it?'

'Isn't that how I've always described my ideal relationship? When you're not here, I'm unhappy, but when you're here, I want you to be quiet and inconspicuous and as self-evident as the wallpaper itself.'

Gustav frowns at the green-patterned wall. This is still not his version of an ideal relationship.

So here I sit, after all: with a flat and with a job and with a boyfriend. A new insight I've acquired is that it's not just a common development but also a necessary one: in any event, a job requires a boyfriend. When you've been working for five days a week, you never have the time to meet any other people, and you obviously want to. You want to have a social life, but who's supposed to serve that purpose if you don't have a family? I don't socialize with my workmates, as I've said, and my old friends have all married off. Who's left to socialize with if you don't keep your own man around? You're forced to borrow the ones that belong to others, an existence that seems to me more humiliating than the worst possible marriage. I may be able to live without men, but not without friends, at least not without at least one real friend, and the only way to ensure you'll have a friend that won't get married off is apparently to marry one yourself.

'Don't think I'm keeping you for lack of better,' I add so that Gustav doesn't misunderstand my reasoning. 'You are the best man I know, the likest.'

Likest: it's a dialect word for 'best', but it also means 'most like', which is probably because the one who's most like you is the one you like the best – that is, if you, like us, basically don't have anything against yourself.

We don't just share the same taste in wallpaper and films. In politics, Gustav is the only person I know who can fulfil the conditions of being both leftist and wise. At work, they're so bourgeois that all I want to do is throw bombs around, there's an almost ritual complaining about taxes during the coffee breaks, when they're not talking about food or yesterday's television programmes or behind the backs of those who aren't there. On the other hand, when I find myself among young social revolutionaries, I only feel like crawling behind a *Svenska Dagbladet.** At the university, the leftist crazies are blossoming as never before. There's not a single seminar where you don't see someone popping up and saying something programmatically revolutionary. If they would only say something interesting, but it's simply contradiction for the sake of contradiction, an escape valve for aggressions and the need to assert themselves. To be sure, our courses and instruction need to be radicalized, and the Marxist groups in the departments are beginning to accomplish something in that direction, but it's accompanied by so much hot air and infighting and unnecessary harassment of teachers. There are endless meetings and assemblies with students who see it as their mission to 'expose' reactionaries.

Downy-chinned youths with dirt under their nails saying that Stalin was misjudged is something that I find more unappealing, if that's possible, than publishing managers in nylon shirts whining about taxes. It's only when I'm with Gustav that I don't have to feel like a social fascist or a bomb-revolutionary by contrast, because he stands at the same point on the political scale: the just-right left. As far as I can see, this is our country's smallest faction. Gustav claims that there are a few more at *Aftonbladet†* – I don't know; maybe I'm reading it too carelessly.

Extremism has also swallowed up the anti-Christmas movement this year, which has become a gigantic trend with anti-presents, anti-Advent calendars and anti-everything. It's too much – it's protest for protest's sake, and we decide to celebrate a traditional Christmas quietly in the bosoms of our respective families.

'My parents will be sad if I don't come home,' I explain to a

* The more conservative-leaning major daily newspaper in Sweden.
† A Swedish evening paper with a large circulation.

person passing out flyers outside the Domus department store who's trying to enlist us for some anti-event. 'After everything that's been said in the papers this year, they'll think I don't want to celebrate with them because I despise them.'

'The bourgeoisie should be despised,' the flyer distributor sneers.

'No, they should be re-educated,' Gustav says.

'And I don't think you're going to accomplish that by making your old mum sad,' I say.

The boy turns towards someone else on the pavement – *his* old mum, that wasn't what this was about – and we move away with the flyers in our pockets.

'Where are you going to contribute your Christmas money,' Gustav asks, 'FNL?'

'I'll give fifty crowns to FNL for you if you give fifty to Amnesty for me. Then we can go home and eat some Christmas ham without it being anyone else's business.'

He thinks that sounds reasonable.

'We're not celebrating immoderately in any event.'

'No,' I say resolutely, 'no orgies this year.'

*

I register as an English student for the spring term as well, but I never have the time to study. Without studies, my soul withers. I'm envious of Gustav, who has an occupation that he finds meaningful. It's not that my work tasks are directly soul-killing – it's this sitting in a chair at a desk that I can't stand. As long as I can take work home, I'm happy to work twice as many hours with the same thing. For example, I take home the proofs for a travel guide with illustrations that need to be set into the text. It's a huge puzzle of a job that I spread out on the floor and crawl around full of such a zest for work that I don't take time to eat. But permission to take work home only happens as an exception. And at work, I can't crawl around on the floor – the module is too small and the Boss doesn't like it, either. (I've tried, but he thinks it looks bad if visitors come.) Not being able to do a job in the most efficient way – this is the kind of thing that irritates me to the point of ulcers.

And so I sit in my chair at my desk and look at the clock every five minutes to see whether it isn't time to go to the break room /out for lunch/home. And that's how life slips away, that's how the days slip away while you wait yourself to death.

It undermines my company loyalty so seriously that I resort to playing hooky. I 'call in sick' although it's nothing worse than a headache that can be cured with an aspirin and lie in bed half the day reading and smoking, get up in the afternoon to sneak out for a walk or to a seminar or ride off with Gustav to look at the boat show.

Playing hooky doesn't give me a guilty conscience – it's wearing out my life in an office chair that gives me a guilty conscience. Every reminder of those lives I'm not living gives me anxiety: the lives I could have chosen but for which it is now too late – now or soon, very soon.

All I need is to see a book review by ethnology professor Daun to start wondering why I didn't take ethnology seriously. That was a meaningful subject in any event. Or an article about the digs at Helgö – then it's time for anxiety about archaeology: why did I drop that before I had even reached the point where I got to try my hand at a dig? I call the institution and ask if there's any field work you can participate in during the summer, but it's already fully booked, and attending courses isn't an option for those working full time since they're only held during the day.

Cilla has started one of those TV producer courses that I dropped out of. Mikael is going to be a Third World development worker and Gustav is going to be a teacher. Harriet writes that she's going to be a mother, and not even that fails to give me the existential shivers. If Harriet can, why can't I? Maybe after all that's the most remarkable of everything I'm missing out on, and soon, oh soon I'll be too old!

Everyone is becoming something – everyone except me. You've become a publishing administrator, Gustav says, but I haven't. That's just the way it looks.

'Why don't you become an academic, then, since you love to go to school?'

'You mean get my doctorate? But that's a calling. And a calling is precisely what I can never decide on.'

'It's not any more than a five-year plan these days,' he says and shows me a newspaper article about the new doctoral degree: they call it a mail-order doctorate to show how easy it is to get one.

Gustav, of course, thinks it's excellent that I have a job and can support him when he's graduated and unemployed, but he declares himself prepared to do without that for the pleasure of being mentioned in the foreword to my doctoral dissertation, with one of those disgusting little phrases ('last but not least . . .') which authors usually bestow upon their wives with thanks for their having kept themselves and the children out of the way while the dissertation was being written.

I'll think about it, I promise him.

Mail-order doctor – what a title for the phone book!

*

A job requires marriage; on the other hand, it poisons that marriage. When I come home after an arduously spent day, I'm seized by a boundless desire for entertainment: out on the town, out into life, whatever, simply out! And then Gustav comes with his hormones, Gustav, who only has a boundless desire for me. It becomes a new standard formula for rebuffing him: Darling, I've been at work and want to have fun. Useful five days out of seven.

Why did we stop taking small excursions? I ask. Why is it only people who are newly in love who have the sense to take advantage of life? I drag him out on the town instead, to the movies, to a café, on a walk in a snowstorm or spring chill, the worse the weather the better.

One Sunday I go with him to a church service where the sermon happens to discuss wasted opportunities and grace periods; in a humane spirit, the pastor gives it an application outside of eternal punishment. 'That's the last time I go to church with you,' I argue on our way home. 'Here you think you're going to get a little spiritual comfort and edification, and then you get something like that thrown in your face. Wasted opportunities!'

And the days grow longer and a touch of melancholy twilight lingers when I'm released from my workplace; if I ride straight out into nature instead of home, I can catch a glimpse of the setting sun. One evening after a wasted sunny day in March, I dash out to Lilljans Forest, and when I get to see the white-trunked birches I burst into tears, I actually burst into tears at the sight and have to go touch the closest one to convince myself that it's real, that white-trunked birches are something that exist.

What are we doing with our lives?

When I come home after dusk, Gustav calls and wonders where I've been. 'Hugging birch trees,' I answer. 'That's what I've always suspected,' he says: 'you're a deviant minority', and that's something I've never denied.

I don't get an Easter holiday – you don't get one when you work. Just a few measly days off, hardly enough to get out to the Island, and queues and crowding with everyone else who's going out at the same time. The little country grocer is literally bulging from everyone who wants to do their holiday food shopping at the same time as we do.

The Island: yes, that's a disgrace. I was never supposed to return again. But I put up with it, because now I'll do anything at all to have an orgy with nature for a few days. I lie on the dock and listen to the ice breaking up. Out in the fjord there's already open water, but there's ice in the bay, and between the two is a layer of moving floes that rock with the waves and rub against each other with a mournful sound, not unlike the cries of sea birds – if you close your eyes, you can almost believe you're hearing gulls (or terns, then, if one must be so accurate). Closer in there are other sounds: a quiet soughing from the floes melting in the sun.

I lie on the dock and hear the ice melting. This is the only thing that helps with existential anxiety.

*

'Well, it's absolutely your soul,' Cilla says when she comes to visit and inspects my newly wallpapered home. Drily noting it – it's certainly not her soul (hers prefers IKEA), but she sees at one glance that it's the wallpaper I've always wanted.

Otherwise, my flat is furnished roughly the way I had it before. She laughs at my bed:

'You're sticking with your spartan single bed?'

'Well of course, I'm only one person.'

'Yes, I know. But it's all the rage for singles to have quadratic beds these days. You, of course, would think it looks too hungry.'

'I think I have too little space to let the bed take half the room. My lovers can provide the bed space themselves.'

'Yes, well, you have a couch, too.'

'Any new insights?' I ask and pour coffee from a thermos (brewed in advance so as not to lose any of Cilla's precious minutes).

'That gynaecologists are crazy.'

'That's an old one, isn't it? One of my oldest in any case.'

'I just don't understand why they think the right moment to <u>strike up a conversation</u> is when they're in the middle of carving cell samples out of you.'

'That's probably so you'll relax and think of something else. Like dentists – they always ask for your opinion on Delblanc's latest novel or the situation in the Middle East while they're stuffing instruments in your mouth. It's part of the profession.'

'Is it part of the gynaecological profession that they're anti-sex as well?' Cilla wonders. 'I asked as carefully as I could if it was true that the Pill can cause discharge, because that's what I had read, and he somehow made it sound like on the one hand that was wrong, and on the other hand that it would serve you right if you're so loose that you need the Pill.'

'But we're so used to that by now. These days, I think the other kind is more shocking. I asked about discharge the last time I was there, if it's true that everyone has it and that there's nothing you can do about it, because that's what I read. And he said that it's completely according to nature's plan, but it's just that some people have more and others less, just like with other kinds of secretions, and that I should see it as a kind of talent.'

'A talent?'

'Precisely what he said. A Talent that Makes Life Richer, just as with other talents, musicality and the like, although we're talking about hormones here.'

'He meant you should consider yourself a hormonal talent?'

'Yes! Me, the hormonal idiot!'

'And you got your laugh of the year, didn't you?'

'Not just then – I'm never really in the mood for laughing in the gynaecological stirrups. But I noted it as a good story to tell afterwards.'

I told it to Gustav afterwards, for example; he got his laugh of the century.

For <u>woman-to-woman</u> conversations, there seems to be no more beloved subject than the Pill and fallopian tube infections. When Harriet comes to town on a quick visit one weekend with her new-born daughter in a buggy, new contributions are made to our common font of genital experience. I thought I knew what it was like to have a baby, approximately, but Harriet's picture reveals that my image of everything is highly euphemized. Not that she's negative in any way – she's almost sickeningly happy about her kid and hardly lets anyone else touch it, but she doesn't sidestep detailed realism and explains without sentimentality how sloppy it is to give birth. She can tell me about 'lochia' for example – I've never heard of it. About leaking breast milk, about stuffing sanitary napkins like sponges in your bra to suck up the worst of it.

Goddamn. No wonder women scare men to death. I'd be scared too if I wasn't one.

*

When I fully realize that you don't get the summer off, either, when you work for a living, I quit. One month's notice and then I walk directly to the Royal Library and borrow an armload of books. Now I'm going to become a mail-order doctor.

What I'm going to get my doctorate in, I don't know, but I suppose it'll be in the literary strand of English, not the linguistic one. There's got to be something within the field of English literature that you can devote your life to for four to five years. First however I have to finish those last three terms. Meanwhile I borrow an armload of fun books to see if I can find any ideas.

Gustav puts the boat into the water as soon as he's finished his service with Sida, and I sail with him on a day trip now and again, but I still can't appreciate it: being scared and hungry remains for me the epitome of sailing. He gives up trying to make a serviceable ship's mate of me and lets me stay ashore on the Island, and so I lie on the beach and read books about sailing instead – that's much more pleasant. And then we can exchange experiences when he returns: Gustav tells me about a trip to Nassa and I tell him about a trip on the Nile, although it was Göran Schildt who took it.

But when it's become our custom and he stops asking me if I want to come along, I come along just because of that, simply because he doesn't ask.

Now I can no longer blame my job for poisoning our marriage; all that remains is to declare marriage a poison in and of itself.

I become completely unreasonable when I live with him. I long to be left alone, but when he rides off to the country grocer and is gone half an hour longer than usual, all I do is contemplate where he's gone off to. He's probably met an acquaintance and is sitting drinking coffee in someone's arbour and talking to pleasant people, I think, neglected and bitter.

When we sit on the bus, he pulls a book out of his pocket, and it hurts me that he'd rather read than talk to me – even though I have a book in my own pocket. It's a mere coincidence that he's pulled his out first, and if I had done so and he had tried to talk to me, I would have been irritated that I couldn't read in peace.

There's no reason to it, no sense, and it tortures me, some-one who's usually such a sensible person. It's not Gustav I can't stand – it's me-together-with-Gustav.

He just thinks I'm capricious and difficult, but it's not a ques-tion of caprices. My reactions are iron-clad bound by a rule: the steadfast principle of Opposite. When he wants to copulate, I want to talk; when he wants to talk, I want to sleep. If there was ever an occasion when he didn't want to copulate, I'd want that as well. The fact is that I fantasize about seducing him – I can create truly arousing visions of it for myself, but I never get a chance to turn them into reality since I'm always beaten to the punch.

Morning, afternoon, evening. In the morning he has the most lust and I have the least – as soon as I open my eyes, I want to get out into the sunshine, up to the tasks of the day, take a morning dip and put on the coffee. Sometimes I can get up before he's awake, but usually he comes over to my bed and I pull away and then he clams up, wronged, for several hours.

In the middle of the day, it's easiest to defend myself: some-one might come in! In the evening – well, if we ever do it, it's in the evening, because then I'm too tired to assert any will. I'm half-asleep and let him do as he wants and he complains that he feels like a necrophiliac.

An infernal interior? Oh, I'm sure there are marriages unhap-pier than ours, in any event more monotonous. The Opposite principle naturally means that every time he turns away from me, I discover that he's the one I want.

'Is my back more attractive?' he asks bitterly. But it's simply his clinging to me that I can't find appealing. When he loves me with that self-effacing, self-consuming love, there's nothing left of him for me to be in love with. All that's needed is a little apathy, a little stimulating apathy. *But you must know*, I quote from *The Tragedy of Love* in cheery-sounding Norwegian, *that the more one loves, the more the other's love dwindles.*'*

Then of course there's simply the fact that he, for his part, works in the opposite way – that's what forces us into a vicious circle. Like this: He wants me – I don't want him – he doesn't want me – I want him – he wants me – etc.

In this constant turning towards and away, there are regular instances in which we are turned towards each other, situations

---

* From Gunnar Heiberg's *Kjaerlighedens Tragedie*, 1904.

of mutual wanting-to-have. More or less momentary, of course, but of such a quality that I don't want to be without them.

In any case, nobody can claim otherwise than that we match. We complement each other perfectly, our inclinations mesh and our relationship becomes a true *perpetuum mobile*, a perfect *circulus vitiosus*.

*

In July, Gustav's brother comes to the Island too, and I get to hear Anna-Karin nag at Erik for a change instead of hearing myself nag at Gustav.

'Do you *really* not have anything nicer than that shirt? I just washed your yellow one.' 'You're going fishing *now*? We're going to eat in a half hour!' 'Well, yes, it's nice, but I'm the one that's going to have to clean it. And we bought pork chops for dinner!'

Nagging seems to have become her natural conversational tone with him. He can't appear in front of her without her commenting on something, not open his mouth without her contradicting him. 'Nineteen-hundred and sixty-*six*, are you daft? It was the autumn of sixty-eight, I ought to know!' 'It wasn't a nice flat at all, it was utterly dreadful, and it was on Skånegatan by the way, where did you get Bondegatan?'

She's usually wrong, but this only increases her persistence, and when she's proven wrong, she moves on, unfazed, to correcting him on some other point that's just as immaterial. My sympathies stream irresistibly to poor Erik, who has to live with this, although it's not so hard to 'understand' Anna-Karin. Her case is painfully obvious, I think (the little home psychologist): contradicting Erik is her only way to assert herself since she has nothing of her own, nothing to build her self-esteem on. They haven't succeeded in getting pregnant, and so instead she cloaks her role as a housewife in the glow of martyrdom. To be sure, she herself is to blame for the situation: she didn't have to stop working simply because Erik took on the duty of supporting her. But the way things are now, her irritability cannot be considered all that difficult to understand. I mean, I have an easier time understanding it than understanding my own.

With her frightening example before my eyes, I try to pull myself together in my dealings with Gustav. Besides, we always change our conversational tone when we're around the family – they would be so confused by our cheerfully raw jargon, our standing jokes about his horniness and my aversion.

Erik brought a couple of bottles of wine from the city to celebrate his holidays. We eat dinner together on the veranda, and when I've got a few glasses of rosé into me, I become so kind that my own husband barely recognizes me. The night is cloudy and dark, we hold on to each other tightly so we don't trip on the path down to the seaside cottage, we consider a midnight dip but agree that we prefer our beds, and whether it's thanks to the rosé wine or Anna-Karin, we have a nicer time there than in living memory.

Gustav takes the Vaxholm boat to go to the library, I retreat from the family and enjoy the solitude as long as it lasts and as well as it can be enjoyed with deep-seated guilt feelings (this is his place and I have no right to be here without him and enjoy it).

The next evening he's back, and he wobbles on his bike from the steamboat dock with sacks full of books and food hanging from the handlebars. But when he sets a bag from the state liquor store on the kitchen table with a sly look in my direction, I leave the room.

Oh no you don't.

★

Take a psalm, and bring hither the timbrel, the pleasant harp with the psaltery. Blow up the trumpet in the new moon, in the time appointed, on our solemn feast day. (Ps. 81:2–3)

This is Gustav's florist greeting on our third anniversary. Up to now there's been no mention of celebrating the occasion with trumpets and psalms; if this isn't simply ghastly irony, it's probably his intention to evoke nostalgic reflection by means of contrast.

16

Mikael's completed a course of study on humanitarian aid activities and is going to Colombia as a development worker in the autumn, heaping burning coals on my head. Of course I realize that this is the kind of thing one ought to do, that this is precisely the way to stake one's life on something meaningful.

Placing yourself at the service of the revolution. (I mean the upheaval, the necessary upheaval, however it's supposed to take place.) This is what one ought to do. I try to wriggle my way out by referring to the idea that each person should do something for which he or she is equipped, and with my equipment, I would do so little good in Colombia. But what am I doing instead, then? All I'm equipped with is a small stylistic gift, a little ear for language, and I don't know what to do to place it at the service of the revolution.

Incidentally, I don't know if there's much to that stylistic thing either, when it comes right down to it. Dissertation topics are like wives, the professor says: you should choose them yourself and not take advice from others. I've transposed these words of wisdom to suit my gender with the result that I have to sit and wait until I'm chosen by a dissertation topic. I'm still waiting. Day after day, I wait for a dissertation topic to come to me and say, '*You* are the one I want to research me!'

But now I'm starting to despair. If I get too old and calcified, there won't even be a dissertation topic that wants me. I try to take some initiative and borrow old dissertations, looking for a little side theme that can be developed. I no longer count on meeting one that can be exciting, passionate – I simply hope quietly I'll find one I can stand to live with for a few years.

*

On a normal Wednesday morning, I wake up confused by a dream. What was it about? Who? It was a male, a completely unknown male I usually see in the reading room at the Royal Library and have never thought such thoughts about before – but it was a dream of the type that leaves behind sensory memories.

I awaken and look around me, and all the men I see are, all of a sudden, men. With bodies, necks and hair and hands, and legs and I don't know what else.

What's this? Hormones? Well, that would be a happy reunion. And at the Royal Library of all places.

For a long time, Gustav has been looking forward to my reaching an age at which, according to science, a woman's urges awaken. As for me, I believe it's temporary – I don't trust my hormones one inch. They've always been haunted by Wanderlust. I think of them like Hattifatteners from the Moomins: electrical, unpredictable to the point of danger, shy and constantly on the move.

'What do you think a psychologist would say about your habit of depicting your sex life in fairy-tale terms?' Gustav wonders; I can only imagine. As for him, he talks about tigers, but he's not the one who's come up with that, but Lord Peter Wimsey.

In reality, he suspects that I go around sublimating the whole time: he can't get it into his head that there are people who have as little need for the erotic as I do. This dreaming simply confirms his suspicions, and he doesn't understand why I can't go home and satisfy those lusts that have been awakened by other men with my spouse. But what drives my Hattifattener hormones is precisely this curiosity – they want to go on excursions, make new discoveries, and yes: new conquests.

Of course this isn't the first time I've been made aware of the fact that men are something exciting. But that first time it hit me and I looked around and realized how many there are, and my mind was boggled thinking about how many more there are whom I will never even get to meet, and at the insight that I would most of all like to have relationships with all the men in the world – already at that point I came to the conclusion that, since over an entire lifetime there would only be time for a small, crappy and hardly representative selection, it would be just as well to settle on something else. If all the relationships I've never had made me just as worried as all the careers I haven't chosen, I wouldn't be able to stick my nose out the door without being throttled by panic.

In any case, Gustav certainly prefers that I look at others with lust (at least as long as it limits itself to looking) to my being frigid. He does it himself, by the way, looks at women I mean – looks unchastely at women. If looking with lust is to commit adultery in your heart, then surely nobody is innocent. Faithfulness is an imprecise concept, of course – you're forced to agree on some ad-hoc definition, somewhere between not being aware of the existence of others and, for example, sleeping with anyone you want but being metaphysically monogamous In Your Heart.

As long as you stay faithful to me . . . that's what he promised in the beginning. It's a promise that expired long ago, and since then we haven't technically made any pledges regarding our relationship; it's simply understood that we're not actually 'cheating on' each other. After Gustav's dealings with Birgitta, and after all of these norm-dissolving and concept-confusing divorces, I no longer feel guilty if I make out a little with others.

Regarding parties – the kind that his classmates at the teacher-training college and mine at the department arrange and where partners are generally not included – making out is otherwise almost unavoidable. It's a sliding scale between dancing and friendly groping to necking – you don't really know where the boundary is drawn, and you don't want to seem wishy-washy, but once you've started necking, you continue to slide, and it's not easy to know where to draw the line. Instinctively, and since a natural dividing line seems to be offered by the belt, that's where I draw it: promiscuous above the waist, the rest is reserved.

Maintaining this line has never caused me any difficulties – my hormones have never had that much power over me. However, I experience insurmountable difficulties in keeping myself from falling in love. It's been a long time since such an infatuation has been of such proportions that it's been worth mentioning to Gustav, but I'm probably going to have to tell him about Torsten.

He's a member of the English Club in our department, an energetic and active lefty, somewhat aggressive in appearance but sharper than most of them. We've had our eyes on each other since the beginning of term – I don't mean any kind of flirtatiousness, much more business-like: we've noted each other as someone we'd like to take a closer look at. I have no illusions about him being some kind of soulmate, and he's not a character in a class with Mikael either, but your standards clearly sink over time when you're starving for acquaintances.

We don't have any classes together but we see each other at the student union evenings and in the department. In addition, we belong to an elective group that gathers under the direction of a teacher for play-reading at each other's homes once or twice a month – a unique and unusually cultured type of get-together. On such an evening when we're working with *Man and Superman*, we happen to be given the roles of Tanner and Ann.

It's not just that funny tensions develop when you sit playing a pair of lovers with each other; the most attractive thing about him is his pronunciation – he sounds almost exactly like Leslie Howard. Fellows who can speak English without an accent from Dalarna or Gothenburg are a rare attraction, even among the subject teachers. The element of surprise is even stronger since he doesn't look like he could: big and blond and coarse-limbed, with a Mao pin on his Icelandic sweater. He also uses snus.*

We're at Kungsholmen, and since Torsten is heading for the subway and I live in that direction, it's only natural that we walk together, and when we're at my door, it's only natural that we embrace each other, and since I know what would only be natural next, I have to say no when he wants to come upstairs although it kills me.

I let Gustav know: not to praise my own steadfastness, but to complain. It's your fault, I complain, that I can't develop my contacts.

I think it would be so nice to be able to take a man home now and again – it's the only way to get to know new people: <u>making friends via making love</u>. As far as I can see in my circle of acquaintances, friends are recruited from among one's lovers. And that way is blocked to me! Yes, there are hormones, but I have social needs, too.

Besides, I'm the type of person who becomes obsessed with nothing more than with the men I've rejected – I can go and think about them for decades afterwards. I don't know what

---

* 'Snus' is a kind of tobacco used in the Nordic countries, rolled into a clump and placed under the upper lip.

causes this, exorbitant empathy perhaps, based on my own exorbitant self-esteem, imagining what they're missing? That's what happens, anyway.

'You know what I'm like,' I plead. 'If I wasn't forced to reject Torsten, my infatuation would subside much more quickly.'

'You mean that the best tactic for me would be repressive tolerance?'

'Precisely. Would it really be so important to you if I cheated on you now and again? Would you really object that much?'

He would. As a matter of fact, Gustav wants me to be reserved from the top of my head to the soles of my feet, apparently, and he doesn't want to hear anything about social needs.

I see. Well then.

Cheating on him in secret is not something I'll sink to. So I'm 'faithful' then, bitterly and grimly. I'm faithful to him and I let it bite him in the ass.

*

'The journal's literary criticism was accused of being guided by political values,' I read in a book at the Royal Library. It sounds familiar, but it's not referring to Marxists in today's Swedish newspapers, but about the *Edinburgh Review* and Whig liberalism in the nineteenth century. I order a couple of years' worth to see what the journal looks like, leaf through the pages randomly, read a little here and there, wonder how on earth you define which criteria you use and how they can be systematized, read more articles and am already filling in an order blank to get a few more years before it occurs to me that what I've started on is a dissertation.

This discovery makes my hands so shaky with eagerness that I have to take a walk in Humlegården Park outside the library to calm myself down. Can this actually be something? Analysing criticism during a certain period of time, scrutinizing the basis for assessment and the methods? In any event, there seems to be plenty of material – the library has 250 volumes of collected issues of the periodical up until its last year in 1929; the problem, in fact, will be to limit the selection in some sensible way.

Best of all would be to work with a topic with which it was possible to take books home, but you can only do that with items printed during the past century, and such a limitation would probably be difficult to justify objectively. Besides, the journal was significant at the beginning of the nineteenth century, so concentrating on that period of time is probably unavoidable, even if it forces me to spend my time at the Royal Library.

The next few days I devote to skimming through more texts, and it seems to me that the idea could be feasible. My fingers are itching to get started with a thorough basic analysis of argumentation, and my scalp prickles with delight when I start to perceive patterns and think up classifications . . .

Autumn is at its loveliest, but that doesn't bother me. I'm not even troubled by the glowing coals on my head. I shut myself in one of the small cubbyholes at the library to make excerpts on a typewriter – a cubbyhole not even one-fourth of the size of the publisher's office that felt like a prison. The difference is that I do what I like here. I go into the cubbyhole when I want and take my coffee break when it suits me: behold all I demand of freedom. Nobody gives me any orders, except I myself, and from that direction I accept a discipline of steel.

My oral exam goes handily, but the professor doesn't give me the highest grade when he notes it in my book, which puts me off my stride and I simply say thanks and goodbye instead of talking to him about doctoral studies as I had planned.

Am I actually too stupid to be an academic? Or is it simply his petty revenge for my having read *Aftonbladet* under my desk during his seminars?

After weeping for a little while, I decide to be angry instead. Oh no, they won't be rid of me that easily. I go to see the professor

during his office hours and inform him that I plan to pursue doctoral studies. By no means does he clasp me to his bosom and say
that it was precisely what he had hoped, but, on the other hand,
he doesn't laugh at me either. All he does is find an application
form for me to fill out.

In time, I receive a dittoed note in my postbox that informs
me that I've been accepted into the research programme. The
fact that the professor didn't give me the highest grade on my
exam was probably a result of distraction.

In the first doctoral seminar I attend, we discuss research
methods and it's truly exciting. There are no more than fifteen students there, and the surplus of women is suddenly
transformed into a surplus of men. All seem terribly well-read
and conversant, and I have the sense I've ascended to a higher
sphere: the feeling that this, of course, is how academic studies
should be. A circle of knowledgeable people sitting around a
table and talking about things they know something about – it's
enriching. You feel as though you start to grow as you sit there
drinking it in.

For the next meeting, I'm assigned the task of presenting a
report on a chapter from Wellek's *Concepts of Criticism* as a point
of departure for our discussion. Proud and happy, I set to work
and fall down rudely from the higher sphere when I fail at the
basic task of getting a hold of the book. It's loaned out at the
Royal Library, the city library doesn't have it, the Humanities
Library's reference copy was taken home by a teacher who has
since emigrated. I call all the bookstores in the city but nobody
has it in stock, and placing an order abroad takes weeks or
months. I'm finally reduced to ignominiously asking to borrow
the professor's own copy.

This, of course, is simply a foretaste. It soon becomes clear
to me that in the four-year study period normally stipulated,
they've not included the years it takes to track down books.

Truly there would be no trick to getting your doctorate if you'd inherited an adequate personal library.

*

It's so hard to draw boundaries, I complain to Gustav. In my socializing with the male sex, there are situations that develop with an interior logic such that a natural opportunity to say 'no' never arises. 'Then you should avoid putting yourself in such situations,' he responds.

But he can't mean that I'm supposed to avoid the department party on Friday because Torsten will probably be there, can he? This puts it automatically into the category of such a situation, but I don't ask permission to attend. After having caught no more than a glimpse of Torsten at a distance in the halls for a month, I'm so bursting with frustrated hormones that you could charge batteries with me. And I don't wear the prison-stripe thermal underwear under my trousers when I get dressed for the evening.

It's the usual kind of event with tuna salad and wine and baguettes and political discussions and taped pop music and eventually dancing. Torsten doesn't show up for the first few hours, and I start to become desperate at the prospect of not having the opportunity to reject him. But then there he is, standing in the doorway after all. I see that he notes my presence before he fetches a paper plate with salad, and a while later he comes over to my corner. We dance one dance and then two, and then I say thank you but he's not listening to me. We dance another one and then yet another. Then I'm too tired to go on, but he doesn't let me go, and so we sink into the closest empty armchair. And when you end up sitting in an armchair in a half-dark room with your arms around each other, it's not such a big step to kiss each other a little, too – on the contrary, it would seem odd not to do so.

Or wouldn't it? After all, the room is only half-dark, full of people too, and snogging in public is something I've always been an opponent of. He notices that I'm not focused and tugs my hair playfully:

'Where are you, anyway? There's such a distance between us.'

It might seem an odd thing to say when you're sitting in the same armchair, but it does bear witness to a certain sensitivity.

'It's because I despise crowds,' I explain. 'Can't we go somewhere else?'

He thinks we certainly can. We search for our overcoats, leave the pop-booming barracks that were rented for the occasion and walk at random down Drottninggatan. We end up at Wallonen, go in and get beers, and then we sit opposite each other to begin the task of getting to know each other.

He tells me about his life, and my image of him changes: he grows. I've classified him as more or less crazy-left by default, but here, face to face, he suddenly seems much more mature. And more experienced than I had guessed: he was at sea for a couple of years and has a broken marriage behind him as well as a small child somewhere in another city. He tells me about growing up in a wealthy doctor's family, about his overly emotional youth and about his political awakening as a recovery into rationality.

I look at him and feel the urge to touch him, but I'm too shy to reach my hand across the table. His hair – it's long, light and thick, reminding me of that kind of wool yarn you usually make rag doll's hair out of – I want to ask to feel the quality, but I don't really know how much to dare to challenge masculine feelings of self-esteem.

When I, in return, have told the most interesting things I can come up with about myself – Härnösand and the publisher don't seem like much to offer given Torsten's life as a sailor – we agree that it's almost bedtime. He follows me to the subway, and from the subway to my door, and as he's walked so far and spent his entire evening on me, I can't reject him there yet again. I let him follow me upstairs.

We lie on my couch – not my bed, not there – but that seems to be a slippery slope as well, and I don't say no until he reaches my belt. He quickly grasps the principle and scolds himself when he once again strays there:

'Shame on you, Torsten,' he says to himself.

'Good,' I mumble, 'you say it so I don't have to.'

It's nice that he takes it with humour, expresses himself in terms of boundaries:

'I'm sorry, did I violate your air space just now?'

But of course he wonders why I stop him just there, and I have to admit that it's random, a compromise and possibly a strange moral standard. Not a double one but a half-one: moral below the waist.

Of course it feels silly. What we're doing feels like the most natural thing in the world (and who can actually claim that it isn't), and it's unnatural not to continue – I've never before felt so much lust for a person I know so little and am both delighted and horrified to discover that it's possible. Of course it's nothing more than a desire for the new – a desire for the new simply because it's new: initial desire. But what if that's the only kind I'm capable of?

If it weren't for Gustav, I think.

Or is that simply an excuse? I really do want to have sex with Torsten, right now, but I don't know if I want to have slept with him, tomorrow and for ever after. It's so you can anticipate this issue better that I think you should know each other well beforehand. Otherwise, relationships can suddenly change in the most astonishing way: some men can't look you in the eyes afterwards and go circuitous routes to avoid you, others think that the seduction gives them a kind of right, yet others fall in love with you accidentally – I've learned not only from my own experiences, but I have the sense to take heed from what Cilla's told me about hers as well.

To be honest, I don't know how 'liberated' I want to be, and for the moment I don't have to decide, because Gustav exists. I explain this to Torsten, and he is neither indignant nor respectful – he accepts it without saying anything at all. It probably doesn't matter to him enough to waste any more effort on it.

So we lie there and doze in lazy lust – I nuzzle his chin in delight. He smells so foreign, excitingly foreign, uneasily and hilariously foreign. Then we fall asleep on the couch. My bed would be more comfortable, but that, too, is a demarcation line. Furniture morals.

Gustav fetches me at the Royal Library. I'm tired. Torsten and I went our separate ways at the bus in the morning, an abrupt bus-stop goodbye, and nothing indicates that I'll see him again under similar circumstances.

We walk through Humlegården Park, through the drifts of leaves on the paths – only the oak trees still have theirs – up to the Promenade and eat dinner.

Gustav is happy and buoyant, he's enjoying teacher-training college – he'd enjoy himself, I suspect, no matter where you put him – and he talks about how lovely it is that I'm sitting at the Royal Library doing research, how excellent it is to be married to a Researcher.

That he's never embarrassed to admit such feelings is part of what I appreciate about Gustav, but the occasion is poorly chosen. This line gives me the segue I need:

'Researcher, yes, but married?'

I ask him if he wants to be married to a woman who's done what I've done, for he must know what kind of woman he's going around with. I feel, in any event, that he has the right to know.

No, he doesn't want to, just as I suspected. So now we'll be divorced again. So we'll have a little autumn divorce this year, too.

It's shorter-lived than the previous one. That is, our standards and concepts are so confused that we can't even remember what we actually are: we see each other anyway, and we sleep with each other, and when I ask a week later what he thinks about the situation, he laughs and explains that he feels more married to me than ever before.

'I think it's so typical – that we're divorced again. It's so utterly typical for this marriage.'

'Well, all hope seems to have perished, then,' I note.

When you start to perceive that being divorced is one of the characteristics of your relationship, when it becomes something about which you amused-angered-lovingly say 'Well, well, it's so typical' – then all hope seems to have perished that you'll ever be able to get away from each other in earnest.

The fact is that you can live without defining yourselves anyway. We are Gustav and Martina, and if our relationship is of a kind that man has never before beheld, then it doesn't matter what you call it. Married or divorced? Neither nor. Both and.

The only place where the definition issue is important is with our families. We've given up keeping them informed and up-to-date with our breakups and reconciliations; now we consistently keep to the principle of non-involvement and avoid bringing each other to family events – something that's become possible now that he too has moved into his own flat.

Now and again he brings up the issue of moving in together, nowadays mostly using practical arguments: he's short on time since he started to teach regularly, and it's difficult that, every time we see each other, it's a special effort and involves complicated travel through the city – wouldn't it be so time-efficient if you lived in one and the same place and simply saw each other when you came home?

I still think it's good to come home to my own place when I come home and see Gustav when Gustav's the one I want to see. It doesn't take long to get between Fridhemsplan and Medborgarplatsen, and I still can't see why togetherness must be manifested by living in the same building, eating at the same table and sleeping in the same bed. By what right does anybody make the claim that a life together must look just like that in order to be seriously intended? I refer to Sartre and Simone de Beauvoir as a model: for decades they've been known as each other's 'constant companions' – they're not married, and they don't live together!

Being like Sartre and Simone de Beauvoir is naturally an idea that appeals to him, but he maintains that the term 'constant companion' is a bit cumbersome, hardly something you can use during introductions. 'My wife' would be simpler, he thinks. Why isn't introducing me as 'Martina' good enough?

In order to convince him that it's not the marriage formality I object to, I toss out the idea of getting married without moving in together, and that's also a suggestion he likes: just enough against the tide during a time when the opposite is the norm. We think seriously about this solution, so seriously that we start to research what marriage means in a legal and financial sense, and in doing so discover that, as a wife, I lose the right to student loans when he eventually gets a teaching position, and then we forget about it; it's not worth getting to call yourself 'wife' and waving your gold rings.

And if we needed further arguments against moving in together, I can also point out that we don't have a flat to move into. My studio cannot be considered, and his student accommodations are provisional. So we continue to live apart with one foot in our own flats and one in the other's. It feels undeniably a little rootless living in several places, but I try to claim that this feeling can only be good for us.

When I think about it, I realize that I have a toothbrush – this symbol of rootedness – at no fewer than four places in the world: one at home, one at Gustav's, one at my parent's home and one at the Island.

As for Gustav, he's bought a package of disposable tooth brushes. 'It may be a provident investment,' I admit. 'It's a symbol of our relationship,' Gustav says.

★

His second term at the teacher-training college is a practicum, located in Visby, which seems good considering my perverse preference for cultivating my love in peace without disruptive involvement by its object. It will be as it was when I was in Härnösand, but the other way around.

But the fact that it's the other way around is not something I like – it was much better to be the one going away than the one left at home. He sends letters about life in the small town, how it looks there and what the teachers do when they don't work (drink, that is). The whole thing sounds terribly small-townish and dreadful, and I'm terribly envious of him. I envy him precisely this: that he's somewhere else and has something to do there. Not specifically in Visby, and not specifically doing a teaching practicum, but even so – it's probably the old familiar schizoid idea that Reality is somewhere I'm not, wherever except just where I am – yes, even in Visby.

Sitting in a cubby at the Royal Library and rattling off excerpts on my typewriter seem for some reason to be much less real than living in a rented room in Visby with old sayings on the wall. Maybe simply because the latter is more picturesque, more like fiction: when something resembles what you read in a book, that's when you feel most real. I'm sure it's because I felt like someone in a book that I liked being in Härnösand. It was like being in an autobiographical novel about someone who's spending their youth toiling away in some impossible place.

But now I'm sitting at the Royal Library. And I come home to a lonely flat in the evening and discover the breadth of my dependence on Gustav. Materially and mentally: completely dependent. My drain is clogged and my bike light is broken – I can't take care of either of those things myself. My hair needs cutting, and to whom other than Gustav can I entrust that task? And how can I write a dissertation when I don't have anyone to discuss it with?

This means long, complicated letters and expensive phone calls. Yes, that's how it goes. You start with wallpaper and end up as a clinging vine.

*

The seminars aren't as fun as I found them in my beginner's exaltation at being raised to the position of 'doctoral student'. The first time, everyone seemed so knowledgeable and wise, and now I just think they say the same things they said the first time. At the meeting where I was to present my Wellek report, there was so much talking beforehand that there wasn't much time for me at the end. I was forced to shorten my exposé and then there was no time at all for discussion, and at the next meeting there was a dissertation chapter to debate – my task was thus, as usual, just an end in and of itself, something you have to have done to get a few credits recorded in your transcript at the office.

Afterwards, we go out and drink beer. The gents talk about books as if they knew everything about them, but nowadays I think it sounds suspicious: as if they're talking for the sole purpose of showing what they know. Otherwise, they differ from the pupils at lower levels not only in that they're older and there are more men than women, but also in that they're more conservative. I hadn't thought about that until an evening when we happen to talk about Tolkien, and the fellow next to me says that he's not actually a good writer, and the one across the table says 'Naw, but you like him anyway because of his political tendencies.'

'Political tendencies?' I say, astonished, and everyone laughs and won't answer such a stupid question, and I have chills down my spine when I realize what he means.

I'm so used to spending my time with left-leaning folks that I go completely mute when I realize that I'm the only one of my kind sitting here in a group of students who take their bourgeois politics for granted. Later on they talk about the experiments with student democracy and they make fun of the actions of the lefties in the department, and, it's true, I have a hard time identifying with the aggressive, immature persons who most usually represent radicalism in those contexts, but, even so, I feel like a traitor sitting there silent as they're defamed over the beer mugs.

Every so often, Gustav calls and asks if I've been unfaithful with Torsten. No, I answer, pouting, and he claims that it's probably just because I haven't had another opportunity. I don't think he needs to tease me about that. On the other hand, I get even by teasing him about Barbro: a classmate of his at the teacher-training college, who according to his description is a rather plump lady from the country, considerably older than he is. 'Cougar hunter,' I tease him. At the party they had before the group dispersed for their practicum term, she apparently laid it on thick for him in a shameless manner, and at Christmas she presented him with a jumper she knitted herself (which I allowed him to accept under the condition that he not use it against me and imagine that I'm going to start knitting in order to render my rivals harmless).

His letters consist mostly of morality tales, describing the boredom of the countryside and the drinking habits of the teachers, while mine consist of dissertation ideas and drafts for his perusal. Gustav shows a surprising interest in my research results – I don't know if it can actually be so interesting to him or if it's just that he's realized that the way to a woman's heart is through her dissertation.

After a couple of months he tells me that he's entered into a relationship with the local FNL group, where he meets reasonable people. (Why didn't I ever think of that in Härnösand? Perhaps one didn't exist there yet.) Otherwise, the rest of our correspondence is full of excerpts from our free-time reading, particularly on the theme of marriage.

Gustav quotes Gregory of Nyssa:

Wenn es möglich wäre, die Erfahrung der Eheleute zu haben, bevor man in die Ehe tritt, und wenn es ein Mittel gäbe, um mit einiger Sicherheit vorauszuvermuten, was sie einem bringen wird, dann wäre die Zahl derer riesengross, die statt der Ehe die Jungfräulichkeit erwählten.*

I answer with Nietzsche, in a ceremonious translation:

Not only onward shalt thou propagate thyself, but upward! For that purpose may the garden of marriage help thee! A higher body shalt thou create, a first movement, a spontaneously rolling wheel – a creating one shalt thou create. Marriage: so call I the will of the twain to create the one that is more than those who created it. The reverence for one another, as those exercising such a will, call I marriage. Let this be the significance and the truth of thy marriage. But that which the many-too-many call marriage, those superfluous ones – ah, what shall I call it? Ah, the poverty of soul in the twain! Ah, the filth of

---

* 'Were it possible to have the experience of a married couple before one enters into marriage, and were there a means to predict with some certainty what it would be like, then the number of people who would choose virginity over marriage would be colossal.'

soul in the twain! Ah, the pitiable self-complacency in the twain! Marriage they call it all; and they say their marriages are made in heaven.*

Gustav continues with Berdyaev:

Marriage constantly turns out to be a trap in which people are caught either by being forced into it, or through mercenary motives, or through thoughtlessness and passing infatuation.

But it's Kierkegaard who gets the last word:

Marry and you will regret it; do not marry and you will regret that too; marry or do not marry, you will regret both; whether you marry or do not marry, you will regret both.

---

* Translated by Thomas Common, https://www.logoslibrary.org/nietzsche/zarathustra/20.html

17

Torsten's on his way out for a coffee with a few classmates when we run into each other on the steps of the city library; I follow him to Ogo and there we sit talking politics while the day fades to night. Maybe I've outgrown this kind of socializing after all. I feel useless and uncomfortable and would actually much rather go to the Royal Library and continue to work, but I keep sitting there. It's clear that Torsten doesn't give a fig that I'm there, and I sit there waiting for him to start.

How ridiculous. I'm not even that charmed by him any more; just like the others, he shrinks again and becomes nothing more than your common pompous little left-leaning student (I'm referring to his mental growth; externally he's impressive enough, even if his upper lip sticking out over a recently placed wad of snus gives him an expression of uncommon idiocy).

Why am I sitting here, then? It's just that I want to conquer him. Precisely this: defeat and occupy in a traditional, imperialistic sense. And how are you supposed to disabuse a man of his notion that he's the one who's the conqueror if not by rejecting him when he tries to seduce you and seducing him when he has no thoughts in that direction?

That he's lost interest in me is understandable – he's sure to think he can use his life for something better than having a half-affair with me once every two months. But I'm acting as if there weren't anything more urgent in my life just now.

Per-Erik, a fellow with glasses who's recently become an administrative assistant, suggests a movie and we find a newspaper, and so we take the subway south and go to Göta Lejon and see a dreadful old western. The other girls have left but Torsten doesn't become any more interested in me when I'm the only female in the party. Afterwards he invites us home to hang out and so we do. We sit around his kitchen table guzzling beer and discussing political strategies. We talk about the crazy left and the wise left, and when Per-Erik says that he collects sensible people, I light up and ask him to name a few. He takes off his steel-rimmed glasses, looks at me and thinks for a while, and says: 'Armas Lappalainen, for example.' That's not what I mean by wise left – among the lunatics he's one of the more interesting, but that's something else.

Then we drink more beer and discuss the consequences of the government's recognition of North Vietnam, namely consequences for the Swedish FNL movement. That the reason for recognition was nothing other than to 'take the air out of the sails' of the movement, they take that for granted, but whether they've achieved any success in this evil business – there's no agreement here. Torsten believes that it's created confusion among the leadership, that some are no longer aware of the true imperialistic nature of the Palme regime. Per-Erik believes that his saying this reveals that he's greatly underestimating our comrades' awareness.

I say goodnight and finally leave.

I'm awakened by noise from the street, and a bad mood hangs like a cloud in the room, a grey fog that I awaken into. Tired. I'm tired because I've slept too little, tired of having spent the entire day yesterday in uselessness, tired and weary of being rejected by Torsten.

However, I don't understand how truly bad my mood is until Gustav calls. I hear myself answer in a voice that's low and querulous as if out of the depths of great suffering – I hear my own voice, as he must be hearing it, and realize aha, that's how bad my mood is.

As usual, it boils up in my conversation with Gustav. It boils up all over him, as if it were his fault that Torsten doesn't care about me. Well, it's his fault, of course, that I didn't have an affair with Torsten when the opportunity presented itself. And once I've started on this bad-mood tone, I can't change it.

I had planned to take a refreshing long walk but don't have the energy to do more than drag myself down the street to Metro to do my shopping. It feels a little better once I've eaten lunch, but then Gustav calls me again and it feels worse immediately.

'What's wrong with you?' he asks.

I insist that I'm in a bad mood, that I believe it's a human right to be in a bad mood and that the best thing he can do is to stay away.

'OK, until tomorrow, but tomorrow is Saturday and I'm coming home to Stockholm.'

'I know,' I say, in a tone that suggests all the world's suffering rests on my delicate shoulders and Gustav's return home is the straw that would break me.

I'm utterly disgusted with myself and head for the Royal Library.

*

I only feel truly useful, in such a way that my conscience is good enough to sleep on, those days I've spent many hours in my cubby and amassed a real pile of excerpts to take home. But you can't let yourself be fooled by this blissful feeling of performing your duty – you also have to think now and again, although it's much less pleasant. Stop and think about what it is you're doing.

On Saturday I stay home thinking all day, think so that my nails are bitten down to the quick when evening comes, but then

I also have a half-page of ideas, good and juicy ideas I think, and I get up from the floor pleased with myself. (Thinking is also an activity I do best on the floor.)

Pleased and conciliatory, I start to make dinner for Gustav. It proves to be a pleasant surprise for him – he had planned to take me out to eat but would rather come to my place even though I haven't managed to think of anything more tempting than fish sticks with rice. He praises the meal so much that I have to warn him not to <u>overdo it</u> (what on earth would he do if I actually *cooked* for him some time?). 'It's not me you should thank, it's Findus,' I point out, and I put on the coffee.

We sit drinking it and talking about the revolution and I complain as usual that there aren't more of us who are actually sane. Gustav talks about his sample lessons and his reactionary pupils and his almost-as-reactionary colleagues. At their parties, there's the same uninhibited drinking there was in Härnösand, which is odd: the teaching profession doesn't have that reputation, the way journalists and actors and similar professions do. This leads my thoughts to Barbro – she apparently called him a couple of times – but now it occurs to me that he hasn't said anything about her in his latest letters, so I ask him:

'And how's Barbro?'

'Pooh,' says Gustav.

'Has she given up?'

'Well, no, she hasn't given up – I think she's horribly in love with me.'

'But you're the steadfast tin soldier,' I tease him.

He starts to clear the dishes from the table and says, turned away, as if to himself:

'If you only knew.'

'What do you mean? Speak clearly, please.'

He looks so guilty that I've never seen anything like it – in fact, I don't know if I've ever seen a person look 'guilty' precisely, but this is the appearance that must be meant by the word. It's written all over his face that he's hiding something that he's ashamed of but wants to talk about anyway.

'Are you sure you want to know?'

'How am I supposed to be sure before you've said what it is? Tell me and then I'll tell you whether I want to know. Have you been unfaithful?'

He sighs.

'Yes, I slept with Barbro.'

'WITH BARBRO?' I say, but what I mean of course is SLEPT WITH?

At first I don't believe it, 'it can't be true', I would have never thought . . . Not that it ought to be a surprise, given what our relationship has looked like. But I hadn't expected this.

'When?'

'At Christmas. During the Christmas break.'

'Once? Several times?'

He fidgets in torture.

'Three, four, I don't remember exactly.'

Three you can remember distinctly, so it's four. Four times?

'Will you do it again?'

'No, I won't.'

'Was it nice?' I ask (not ironically, completely seriously – it's just one of the things I need to know: whether it was nice).

'It was pretty awful. Pretty embarrassing actually. There's no point when you're not in love.'

'Did you really have to ascertain this empirically?' I say (and now I'm undeniably a bit ironic, a bit acerbic is what I am). 'I could have told you. You could have read it in a book – it's all over the place, it's written on every wall.'

He doesn't deny it. That there's no point to sex without feelings, he doesn't claim that it's some esoteric secret that you have to experience yourself to be convinced of.

I actually have a hard time understanding him: with a woman he wasn't even attracted to?

'How did it happen?'

'What do you mean? As in, purely practically?'

'Yes, how did it start?'

'She groped me.'

'Where?'

'At that party we had at the school.'

'Where on your body, I mean.'

He laughs.

'You want to know how you do it? A little here and there – here for example, and here.'

'She's old enough to be your mother,' I say stupidly. (Yes, just that stupidly.)

'She's only thirty-six, actually.'

'OK, but you said it was embarrassing, wasn't it?'

'Not then, that was later. It was fun at the beginning. It was so fun to be with a woman who thought of me as a sex object.'

Oh yes, I understand that, of course. Who doesn't need to feel like one from time to time. And how long ago was it that I made him feel that way?

'Well,' he says when I don't ask anything else. 'Did you want to know?'

'Of course. You must understand that – it's so obvious that I've just never thought to point that out, that I want to know if you cheat on me.'

'Or rather, that's literally what "cheating" is.'

'Being dishonest.' I mean: his having slept with another woman upsets me at first less than the fact that he's kept quiet about it for two months and allowed me to live with a false perception of him. That he's continued to joke about this older woman afterwards, intentionally joked to hide the fact that something had happened.

'As recently as last week you wrote in a letter that no, there wasn't anything with Barbro.'

'That was true. There wasn't anything then. Any longer.'

'Jesuitical definition of truth! In function it was a lie. Deception, to be precise.'

'Isn't it the definition of truth that you yourself often use as needed?'

'Me, yes. But I didn't think you did it, not towards me.'

That's what makes me the most disappointed. It brings him down to my own moral level, and to that extent it's a relief. I don't have to have an inferiority complex any longer. But it makes the world worse.

Now, in any event, he's confessed voluntarily. He looks at me, worried, waiting to see how I'll react.

About his faithlessness, I don't know what to say. I'm the victim of conflicting emotions. Or rather of expectations about my feelings: should I dash out sobbing into the street, pulling my hair, ripping my clothes – I've been cheated on! Should I feel violated and enraged, shouting 'Go away and never again darken my doorstep'?

I'm caught off guard, unprepared. Of course I see that I should have predicted it. The way I've kept him on a starvation diet year after year. Of course I understand that this is my fault. I'm not too stupid to understand that it's my fault if Gustav cheats on me. So how am I supposed to find any justifiable indignation?

I ought to feel jealousy, according to the rules. No matter how I search in all the crannies of my soul, I find nothing like it. Imagining him with The Other is just strange, almost impossible – just as difficult as it always is to imagine other people copulating: actually, deep inside, you don't believe it happens.

It's not that I'm generally above such feelings – I only need remind myself of the time when he was seeing Birgitta, I can't imagine that there's a more classic jealousy than what I was feeling then. But it disappeared immediately as soon as he explained that I was the one who was closest to him. The affair with this woman is over, he wasn't the least bit in love with her and didn't get anything out of it – what's there to be jealous of?

No matter how I look at what I'm feeling, it doesn't look like envy – it looks more like sympathy. Yes it does: I feel sorry for him. That Gustav had to make do with something like that, a little leftover lust at a drinking party at work – such an exceedingly sad and banal story.

I even feel sorry for her, the unknown Barbro. Middle-aged and unattractive, one of those women who have to borrow other people's men. Rejected and unhappily in love – he's even worried about what she 'may do'. Rejected by Gustav: this is something I cannot envy anyone. It's something I can feel sympathy with, effortlessly. No, I don't know whether to feel more sorry for him or for her. There's no reason to feel sorry for me.

The most tangible feeling in my confused mind is the impulse to seduce him immediately on the spot, as a manifestation of our togetherness, that it's we two. But it would be too simple a solution, falling into each other's arms in general sentimentality. A sham solution: our relationship cannot continue on the basis of his regularly cheating on me in order to arouse my lust.

He'll have to go home tonight – I'm tired and just want to sleep now.

'But do you forgive me?' he asks, traditionally and inadequately.

'I can't see that I have anything to forgive. Well, yes: that you didn't tell me about it immediately – I'll forgive you that just this once, if it doesn't happen again.'

'If it doesn't happen again, I see. If I cheat on you again, then?'

'Are you going to?'

'It could happen. Yes, probably. If I meet someone I like better.

'I suppose you'll seek compensation,' he adds.

'It could happen. If I meet someone I like.

'The question,' I add, 'is simply what's left of our marriage, then.'

'I've had the feeling that it's been thinning out more and more anyway.'

'Of course.'

On the contrary, I ought to say. In my case, I've had the feeling recently that we were completely, utterly married. Just because our relationship is so rotten, just because it is so incredibly rotten and continues anyway – I saw that as proof there must be something metaphysical that unites us. An invisible, irrevocable bond: 'We were made for each other.'

In actuality, of course, it's nothing more metaphysical than Force of Habit.

I fall asleep as soon as he's gone but awaken near dawn without feeling rested, sadder than when I fell asleep.

I'm now less relieved than disappointed. And of course, one should feel sorry for me. Could anyone be more pitiable than I: not only have I been cheated on, it's also my fault! This seems more significant than I thought at first – not in and of itself, not as an event, but as a symptom. Something is definitely different now. It's a new era.

Once again I have to think about our first time together, about his eyes when they looked at me that autumn: his eyes full of me.

It was undeniably difficult to be the object of such a love. Now I no longer have to deal with that difficulty. I guess he still loves me, but not in that way, not 'inviolably', obliterating everything else. This is natural – who claims otherwise? It simply means that he's stopped being supernaturally saint-like and is starting to demand something for himself as well. And wanting to have a sex life is certainly no abnormality.

I wish he could have it with me – there's nothing I wish for more. But I don't understand how I'll ever be enough for his needs. How will we manage in the future? Can you practise polygamy? I doubt it, but it's supposed to exist. There are purportedly feelings of togetherness that are so strong that they can survive that, too. 'We'll have to see' is the only statement I can come up with.

I eat breakfast, call Gustav and tell him I'm going to the library (blessed reading room that's open on Sundays). I dig myself into a few old volumes of journals, dig myself deep, deep down into volumes from the nineteenth century, and Gustav leaves for Visby without our seeing each other again.

But what force can be greater than that of habit? Everything continues as before – I work on my research, Gustav on his lectures. He assures me in every letter that he hasn't cheated on me 'lately'. What does that refer to – the past two hours? 'Since the last time,' he explains when I ask. Oh yes, this is a vow of love worthy of our current relationship: Beloved, I haven't cheated on you since the last time. I pledge eternal fidelity to you until further notice.

For simplicity's sake, to avoid nagging and asking about this issue in every letter and phone call, he suggests that we pledge eternal fidelity to each other until Easter, for example. *Better is it that thou shouldest not vow, than that thou shouldest vow and not pay* (Eccl. 5:5) is my response. But by all means, let's say Easter.

Then he sends me Song of Solomon 6:9: *My dove, my undefiled is but one; she is the only one of her mother, she is the choice one of her that bare her. The daughters saw her, and blessed her; yea, the queens and the concubines, and they praised her.*

It's cold, very cold, with lots of snow, and all of a sudden, I long wildly for spring. For riding my bike. 'I want to ride out to

Djurgården and take the elevator to the top of the Kaknästor-
net and drink coffee with you,' I write, 'ride in the spring wind
on roads wet with snow melt.'

'What is it you long for most, actually?' he asks.

'Why must it be ranked? But if it has to be,' I answer, 'I long
most of all to ride my bike, then for you, then the rest, spring
and everything.' (Honesty above all.)

Once the mercury has reached ten below, I carry my bike
up from the cellar: a homeopathic conjuration. Indigenous cul-
tures have rain dances; I wish I knew a thaw dance.

By Easter the temperature has risen to zero, but there's more
snow. Easter Eve at the Island looks more like Christmas Eve,
new snow atop what was there before, Christmas-card-white
firs. We try to take a walk in the forest but the snow crust won't
bear us – we sink down to our knees. All that remains is to stick
to the ploughed road, and otherwise stay inside the four walls
of the cottage.

The little old lady that lived next door is dead and her house
is apparently for sale. I wish I had the money to buy it. Thus
I confirm Gustav's belief that it's his country place I love and
not him, and it doesn't help that I assure him that I would love
him much more at a distance of three hundred metres. I try to
clarify the distinction that it's not him I can't stand but rather
me-together-with-him, but that doesn't help either, since the
gist of it is still that I can't stand it.

The cottage is too cramped. And the marriage. The joy of
reunion lasts for two days, then everything is just the same. It's
not simply his constant gabbing about food and nagging about
sex; everything he does gets on my nerves. His way of slamming the door – why can't he do it like other people and use the
doorknob to close it? His false whistling as he walks down the
hill to the well, the sound he makes when he eats, his clomping
steps across the floorboards.

They're undeniably rather normal, small bad habits, strictly speaking a vitality that simply makes more noise than I'm used to in myself. I could just as easily say that what gets to me is the fact that he walks across the floor and he breathes: that he exists. This is something that doesn't just apply to Gustav, but it's only Gustav who's here. So close, so up close.

At lunch he turns on the radio. Granted, I think it's good that I don't have to hear his eating noises, but not that good that anything at all is better. Not high mass.

'I don't want hymns in my soup.'

'You could use the Word of the Lord too.'

'That's not what I object to – it's that human blather.'

That pitiful so-called singing of hymns. Are those supposed to be anthems? The congregation cheering about the resurrected one – it's the most inhibited cheering I've ever heard and it makes me lose my appetite.

Gustav makes no move to shut off the radio. I take my soup bowl and go sit in the main room. It hasn't been heated and smells like rat poison. Then he shuts it off, but now that I'm sitting here pouting anyway, I may as well stay.

When I come back to the kitchen, he's started to do the dishes – pointedly, of course, because it's my turn. I take the brush and tub from him:

'Stop playing the martyr.'

'Who's being the martyr here?'

'I am, and don't try to steal my role!'

We laugh, and it eases things for a while. He sits in the bedroom with a book. When I'm finished doing the dishes, I put on my jacket and stick in my head to tell him I'm going out for a walk.

'Can't I come along?'

Can and can. He can go wherever he likes. The question was poorly posed.

He's a wise person, Gustav, very wise and intelligent. But that's the limit of his perceptiveness. He doesn't perceive that I could want to be alone without having a reason for it. That certain questions shouldn't be asked because they can't be answered.

He looks for his boots, which he's kicked off somewhere, stuffs the stove full of wood so it won't go out while we're gone. The wood basket is empty now and I take it along to get more as he's putting on his winter gear.

The bike stands in the woodshed with cobwebs on the handlebars. I pat the saddle wistfully.

A sled is what you should have in this weather, or a kicksled: the roads are as if made for it – ploughed but not sanded, just hilly enough and almost free of traffic just now.

'A kicksled,' I say accusingly when he comes out on the stairs, 'why isn't there a kicksled here?'

'There's one in the outhouse, although I don't know if it's useable.'

'You have one, and you've never said anything!'

'I think it's broken, but we can look at it.'

It's broken – the backrest is loose and one runner doesn't have a foot plate to stand on, but it's definitely useable. Gustav wraps some string around the back sticks to secure them and once we've scraped the rust off the runners, it works the way it should.

The sparkly roads are just as idyllic as I thought they'd be and we whizz off so fast that it whistles around our ears. We take turns sitting and kicking and our feet remember what to do with the runners when you turn a kicksled downhill, and it's a bliss without compare – or a bliss only comparable to that of riding a bike.

We race around on the little forest roads in the afternoon dusk, push the sled uphill and whoosh downhill, manage the curves on one runner sometimes and sometimes tumble into the drifts. The handlebar breaks again and soon our hands start to remember what it feels like to wear mittens with ice lumps in the fuzz. We both walk behind on the last uphill stretch and he puts my closest hand in his pocket to warm it up.

'Are you happy again now?'

'Nice, do you mean? Oh yes, now I'm happy-and-nice. I could even tolerate you starting to gab about food again.'

'And if I start talking about fucking again?'

'Even that,' I sigh. 'After all, it's the last night.'

On Easter Monday, Gustav has to go back to his school, but since I'm a free student, I can stay out in the country until I need to go to the library.

I follow him to the bus stop and wave goodbye. The bus disappears around the bend, the motor's humming dies away and then there's silence. Complete silence. I walk back through the forest and it's so quiet that I flinch when a sheet of snow collapses off a fir bough. My own steps are the only thing you can hear – the last human on earth.

The cottage is just as quiet – the door squeaks when I push it open. I make a circuit of it and tidy up after Gustav, hanging up a jacket in the hallway, putting the dishes away in the cupboard. I pull his big sweater over my head – it's like a tent on me and it's a funny feeling to wear someone else's clothes, clothes you're used to seeing someone else in – a unique mixed experience of identity swap and embrace.

Dressed up like Gustav, or with his sweater arms around me, I spread my notes out on a table in the room. I discover that I don't like to sit staring at a wall when I work so I get up and move the table to the window so I have a forest view.

Strange to be alone here, rummaging about as if it were mine, sit here in the window and look out over the property. I feel like something Strindberg invented. The hideous woman who penetrates and devours all human life around her until she's enthroned in sole majesty – oh pooh, I don't suppose it's forbidden to enjoy solitude, either.

Or am I enjoying it?

Well, it's a little too quiet, of course. A little on the quiet side.

Outdoors it doesn't feel so strange – it's worse in here. As a matter of fact, it's a bit creepy. I didn't think I was afraid of the dark, especially not in full daylight, but I don't know what else to call it. I'm not scared of anything in particular, not of rats or wolves or rapists, just scared.

Rubbish – I'm supposed to be working. I read through my notes and try to start thinking, but it's like getting blood out of a stone in such a deafening silence, such an intrusive undisturbedness that incessantly demands my attention.

Is the fire burning in the stove? By the way, it's time for <u>a little something</u> so I put the kettle on the boil. I rearrange the kitchen and move the table to the window – I want an ocean view while I eat. The wood supply is getting low again, which gives me an errand to the woodshed, which in turn gives me reason to shovel snow. Not that it's necessary – we've trudged through before, but I find the shovel and clear a proper, wide path. Then I carry in wood. Load after load. I carry in enough wood to last until summer.

It takes so long that it's actually time for <u>a little something</u> in the kitchen again. I enter the room with the desk only to ensure that there's a good fire in the stove, and then leave quickly and return to the dining table.

That's when I discover the radio and thus my rescue: a human voice! The best thing ends up being a foreign station, a calm voice talking in a language I don't understand a word of – that's the best for working.

Although when I go see what's on Channel P1, I get stuck: what's on is namely an exceedingly educational popular science programme, a lecture on common superstitions and 'sounds in nature'. You can hear ghosts and mylings, the spirits of murdered newborns. Excellent: I'll be able to identify them later.

I call Visby to inform Gustav what a myling sounds like, but nobody answers.

Once darkness finally falls, it's less creepy – being afraid of the dark is less absurd then. I have to go to the outhouse and push open the squeaking door although I hardly dare to actually, but once I'm outside again it feels better: the night vast and open around me.

I leave the radio on through the evening worship and news and sea report. I slip down between the chilly sheets – the other bed is empty and there's nobody here who can disturb my sleep.

What's rustling is simply the firewood in the stove, collapsing into embers.

18

All shall remain as it is, but that's not how you want it, and anyone can suffer from eczema because of it. – The desire to have her is a breakwater outside a harbour, and his hatred of her is the surf that tries to crush the breakwater during a storm – thus an inner fight that strictly speaking only pertains to the person himself and which should be fought under the supervision of a neurologist.

'Divorce' in *Felicia's Wedding.*

OK, I'll go to a neurologist. The student association has a psychologist you can see almost for free. I make an appointment, and the queue is considerably shorter than for the gynaecologist. Going there feels approximately like going to such an examination, although for your soul. In other words, it's something I would only subject myself to because I'm prepared to do whatever has to be done if it can save my marriage to Gustav.

I seek help. Does this mean I'm admitting that I'm crazy? Well, I suppose you can be even if you aren't actually climbing the walls. There's something wrong, and by all accounts it's in me. I can also figure out that it isn't something physical that I should see a gynaecologist about even if it seems that way: it feels as if I've closed up, that's how much it hurts when he tries to enter me. But such things probably depend on something having deadlocked in one's soul, and as far as I understand, psychologists exist to help unlock people who've become deadlocked.

Although when I sit in the waiting room at the doctor's practice on Körsbärsvägen, I naturally feel completely raving sane and healthy. I don't know what to say to the psychologist. 'I'm not randy for my boyfriend' – are there drugs for that?

This is ridiculous. The fact that people both want to and don't want to be married to the person they're married to – this must be the most normal thing of all, the very gold standard. And you can read about the cure every day in the evening paper: a small glass of cognac with your coffee, you don't need anything more, Inge and Sten assure us. We've discovered this on our own, by the way – it's just that Gustav can never get me to drink that cognac because I get too angry when it's revealed that he's been such a calculating scoundrel and bought some.

And what can the psychologist say? It wouldn't surprise me, I think in the waiting room, if he believes that I have subconscious guilt feelings because we're living in sin and suggests that actually I would rather get married most of all – that I'm imagining the opposite can always be explained as one of those clever inversions of desire that the subconscious does. In that case I'll accuse him of collusion with Gustav and be diagnosed with paranoia.

What I really can't stand is the idea of marital rights. That Gustav would have any right to me at all – legal, moral, de facto or common law – this is what gives me eczema.

I want him, yes I do, I just don't want him to have me. I begrudge him me (except after a small glass of cognac when I can be generous towards everyone in the world), and how are you supposed to be able to 'give yourself' in stinginess? If this is the standard, then I'd like to know what patent solution people in general have for tolerating it.

And if the psychologist asks me to tell him about my dreams?

My dreams are so straightforward that I'd be embarrassed to share them. I've never understood Freud's patients who dream a bunch of strange things and don't understand that they're sexual symbols. When I dream about sex, I dream about sex. And those are pleasant dreams! Should I ask the psychologist if my dreams about phalluses could be snake symbols, revealing my oppressed fear of snakes?

I remember a nightmare which I've actually had several times, although it's been a while now – it was before Gustav. I dreamed I was about to get married, a big church wedding and many guests. The pastor is waiting at the altar and the procession is about to start. And I, the bride in white, am hiding in a corner, panic-stricken: I don't want to do this, I've changed my mind! It's too late – it would create a scandal if I didn't go in now, my family is swarming around me, upset, and I crouch in a corner, crying hysterically.

The details varied to some extent, but it was always the same church, the one back home where I was confirmed and where all of my childhood acquaintances who had become bourgeois enough to marry got married. Among the other things that were always the same was that there actually wasn't any groom there, no specific one I mean – when I would wake up, I wouldn't know whom I was about to marry. The central thing was the altar and the fact that I didn't want to go there, and anxiety of the same type as in a missing-the-train dream: it's too late too late too late.

I see. For heaven's sakes, I don't need any psychologist to interpret that. I'll have to make it a little subtler if he asks me to recount my dreams so there's something for him to do.

After twenty minutes of waiting, it's my turn. The psychologist is a she and she isn't wearing a white robe – she looks like an office secretary in a dress suit and bun. I explain my issue: that I no longer have any sexual desire and if there's something I can do besides become an alcoholic. She doesn't ask me to recount my dreams, but she asks about my childhood. Oh I see, that was obvious.

I talk about my childhood, and since I can't report any forbidden attraction to my father and can't remember having seen any horses mating and have always known that the stork doesn't bring babies, she doesn't seem to have anything to say. All she says is that it's enough for today and gives me a slip of paper with a new appointment in one week.

The sun is beaming down, the melt water is bubbling down the hill along Körsbärsvägen. I crouch on the pavement, fold a little boat out of the piece of paper and let it sail down the gutter until it runs aground at the sewer (*hommage à* Freud).

How can you be so stupid as to think that a stranger is going to be able to say something about you that you don't know better yourself? It's obvious that therapeutic conversations take a long time, but if it's going to take twenty-four years before she knows me as well as I do now, then I can use my time better. I won't go there again, not until they have to pull me off the wall.

I ride home to call Gustav and tell him the whole thing like a good story, giggling ahead of time at its laughable points. But Gustav never gets to hear this good story. When I come home, there's a letter from Visby lying on the floor in the hall, a letter informing me that he's entered into a new relationship.

Nothing has changed in my feelings for you, he writes, and once again cites the Song of Solomon 6:9, but this time including verse 8 – he didn't think of it last time, he claims, but there you see the danger of pulling out random Bible citations. They always have to be read in their context. And so here it is:

There are threescore queens, and fourscore concubines, and virgins without number. My dove, my undefiled is but one . . .

Fourscore – so eighty? No, only one concubine thus far, but one that he plans to continue with. Apparently it was pleasant this time.

I sit on my couch and read the brief letter and don't know how to answer it now. I just feel so tired it's as if I'll never be able to get up again, never be able to lift another finger.

It's an actress he met down there. Previously a model and then a member of the National Touring Theatre. All of my inherited and acquired prejudices rush to my assistance to visualize her. Model: elegant, provocative and worldly. Actress: exhibitionistic, capricious and lascivious. And at the National Touring Theatre: half-bad, of course, a second-class actress on tour in the boondocks . . .

How could he?

Cowardly of him to write, I think, that he didn't dare say it to me. Just then, the phone rings.

So, he wonders if his letter has arrived, and what I have to say about it.

'The document has been received and registered. At the moment, we have no comment.'

'No comment at all? Don't you have anything to say to me?'

'You'll have to wait for my next communiqué.'

'Are you upset?'

'Upset? Why? You must know that I'm the first to applaud your conquests in the provinces, I'm going to put up a map on the wall and mark it with pins . . .'

'Martina,' he cries, 'I love you, you're the one I love!'

'What good is that?'

'Should I break up with Eva?'

Eva. Her name is Eva. Figures.

'But why should you do that, if you're having such a nice time? No trouble on my account. Wouldn't you rather marry her?'

'She is married.'

'Is she really?'

'Legally in any case. Her husband lives in Stockholm, or some suburb wherever it was. She goes home on weekends so we usually go on the same boat.'

This blindsides me. A married woman – doesn't he have any morals any more?

'And you're the one I want. Do you want me? Shall we get married?'

'Not because of this,' I say. 'We're not going to get married because you're cheating on me when we haven't done it thus far.'

Then I get tired of this patter and don't say anything more, refuse to say anything at all. He'll have to wait and I'll write when I've recovered – that's all I say.

I give up trying to get any work done, get on my bike and ride over to Cilla, who happens to be home. Not to talk about this, not yet – I first have to decide what I think of it.

There are threescore queens, and fourscore concubines, and virgins without number.

'Do you have anything to drink?' I ask, but Cilla only has raspberry juice. So we drink raspberry juice and read *Aftonbladet* and talk about her TV job, which she hates, and, strictly speaking, you can't claim that the world is much different than it was a little while ago.

Cilla invites me to dinner, then I ride home and sleep. I dream about my dissertation, get an idea for systematization of the material which seems ingenious to me, but when I awaken, I find that it's the same idea I'm already working with.

I pull my chair up to my desk and the cover off my typewriter to begin my declaration. I read his letter once again.

'Dearest', it starts. (Relative superlative these days? Not the absolute: very dear, but relative to eighty concubines and countless virgins most dear?) 'Now it's happened again . . .'

I use this as my point of departure:

What do you mean, happened again? This has never happened before. It's new in all aspects, at least for me.

a) *Last time it was something that was over and which you didn't tell me about until afterwards, and your infidelity seemed less upsetting than your dishonesty. This time you had warned me that it could happen, and it's only just begun. I thus have no reason to be surprised, but to be far more upset.*

b) *Last time it was something you described as a crappy experience and I felt truly sorry, both for her and for you. This time, if I've understood you correctly, I can devote myself entirely to feeling sorry for myself.*

c) *That time there was a moment of relief in my reaction, because it's complex-producing to be married to a saint, and it was as if I had got on more equal footing with you. Now the balance is disturbed again, but in the other direction: now I'm seriously beginning to feel like the aggrieved wife aspiring to martyrdom.*

d) *At that time, no measures were required from my side since the issue was passé. Given the current situation, I can simply stand by silently and watch as things develop. I shall make an inventory of my alternatives for action:*

   (i) *Assume that I make an ultimatum: her or me. This will probably lead to you saying that you choose me but continuing to sow your wild oats in secret. The poorest solution I can imagine.*

   (ii) *If I say: OK, do what you want as long as you tell me about it, then I get to look forward to a chain of reports of this kind – fragmentary reports where I myself will have to supplement what you, out of consideration, leave out. It's possible to get used to it with time and become desensitized, but is such a desensitization desirable?*

   (iii) *It's not usually difficult to practise emotional blackmail on you – I could play on your feelings by talking about our past*

> *and your dreamy eyes one November afternoon on Drottning-*
> *gatan, I could quote from your old letters or, in my thoughts,*
> *lead you around the Island and remind you of moments of*
> *bliss (remember the time we played* From Here to Eternity
> *on the shore?) etc.; this would probably result in your running*
> *back, dripping with sentimentality, which would disgust me.*

I roll the paper out of the machine, light a pipe and start on
a new page:

> (iv) *I could mobilize the atavistic moral beliefs that are lying*
> *atrophying at the bottom of my soul and shout that I never*
> *want to see you again. But I want to, of course. (By the*
> *way, I have a new draft ready that you have to read.)*
>
> (v) *What you would most like to see, of course, is a personality*
> *change in me of such character that I would be sufficient*
> *for your sexual needs. I just don't know how that could be*
> *accomplished. To dissemble and pretend to like something*
> *I don't like – this is beyond my capabilities.*
>
> (vi) *In order to escape the humiliating role of betrayed wife, we*
> *could temporarily abandon our relationship and resume*
> *it during the breaks between your liaisons. But it doesn't*
> *seem as if there will be any appreciable breaks now that*
> *you've tasted blood.*
>
> (vii) *All that remains then is to restore the balance by doing the*
> *same – I'll have to get started and sow my wild oats as*
> *well. That would be a relief for the moment, but in the long*
> *run, it'll be a strange relationship if we're standing there*
> *jiggling our scales with the help of others.*
> *Do you have anything better to suggest?*

I refrain from Bible verses and end with Almqvist instead:
'Must I be betrayed? And betray?'

And they say that women aren't capable of logic and only react emotionally, I think as I stuff the letter into an envelope. I consider taking a copy and depositing it in the Royal Library's manuscript collection as scientific proof against the theory. But maybe it has to be historical first.

*

It's Saturday, but Gustav won't be home until next weekend. I look at my typewriter; most of all I want to sit down and get to work, and I have an unusually weak desire to go out and seduce someone. But this simply cannot continue. If I must be betrayed, that is.

I sit down and flip through my address book. I get irritated about how this has happened so inconveniently: I truly cannot think of anyone I feel like seeing. But surely, there must be at least someone I can go to the movies with. Torsten – ruled out. Aron – apparently it's time to get a new address book and remove all my old lovers; it's been years since Aron lived at that address. I wonder briefly where he is now, if he's alive, as I flip further. Per-Erik? He's not fun, but at least he's male. In any event, I care too little about him to worry about whether I'm going to fail.

I'm not unfeminine enough to be direct; I decide I need a handout from the department and call upon on him as the administrative assistant. It's true, I have to ring him at home since it's Saturday, but he has to be given the chance to perceive this as a non-business errand.

Per-Erik answers and sounds happily surprised that it's me. He promises to send the handout on Monday and looks for a pen to jot a reminder. While he's searching, we start a conversation that continues even after he's found it. About our studies and the teachers. About the weather and spring. About the music in the background – he tells me it's an album by Fria Proteatern that he's just bought and he suggests I come listen to it in person.

This is going too fast.

'So where do you live?' I ask, stalling for time.

'Jerum, on Lidingövägen.'

'The boondocks,' I say, 'that's too far to go for a record.'

He mumbles that that's the way it always is, it's no big deal to take a bus there but everyone thinks it sounds so far away. But after we've exchanged a few more opinions about the different advantages of one's home location, he admits:

'Where you live there are more cinemas, of course. What if I were to tempt you to go see a movie with me?'

I giggle a joyless giggle and congratulate myself on both finding a fellow to go to the movies with and to have made him believe that it was his idea. (I weigh the possibility that he on his end is congratulating himself that he has got me to believe that he believes that it was his idea, but dismiss it: Per-Erik can't outsmart me.)

Then I can work in peace for a couple of hours until I have to go. We meet outside Grand and see Pasolini's *Pigsty*, then we go to the pub across the street and Per-Erik explains to me what the film was about. If it had been Gustav, I would have simply done my ape imitation as a comment on it. Why isn't it Gustav? And what's the point of going out with others if you just sit there wishing the one you were out with was your husband?

We continue our conversation about the department and the teachers and the intrigues between radical and conservative phalanxes. I try to be witty but it seems to be wasted: he answers as if he understood the things I meant ironically as literal and argues against opinions I've never voiced. I nod and agree with him. It feels like – what does it feel like? – it feels like casting sun reflections on a gravel path, something that doesn't reflect back, that simply doesn't spark. Or like playing ping pong with someone who catches the ball with his hand when you serve it.

By all means, it's good that he doesn't reject my serve, but you can't make a game of it.

He has a car and drives me home. He drives jerkily, a little jolt every time he downshifts at intersections – it's like his abrupt and tense way of moving. I wonder if driving is always an extension of a person's deportment in general. I wonder if you can read anything about a person's abilities as a lover into it. I wonder how Gustav would drive a car, if he had one.

Per-Erik brings me to the door and pulls up the hand brake to kiss me goodnight but doesn't turn off the motor to come up with me before I've suggested it, and I don't suggest it, because all I want to do is sleep and can't see why I shouldn't get to do so just because my husband cheats on me.

'It was a nice evening,' he claims in any event. 'I'll call you again sometime . . .

'Oh wait, no,' he reminds himself and smiles, 'you were the one who called me.'

Walking up the stairs, I ponder whether if it would have been the final triumph of female wiles, the seal of success in the moth-eaten old gender role I've draped myself in, if he had actually remembered it as having called himself.

*

I meet Gustav at Central Station – down on Vasagatan, not at the bus at Klaraberg Viaduct so that I don't have to be confronted with Eva. But here he is now, direct from her arms.

During our continued correspondence, I've made it clear that our relationship can remain a *marriage blanc* until further notice, not as blackmail but for my own sake: atavistic or not, it goes too much against my instincts to accept bigamy. Commingling. I don't want to be mixed together with something of which I know nothing.

A mild April evening, still a hint of dusk above the rooftops to the west. We walk home.

He immediately begins to assure me of his love again, that I'm the one he's married to. And that Eva understands it – she doesn't want to contest my rank.

'She calls herself my concubine – she was actually the one who thought of it. I hadn't said anything about the Song of Solomon to her.'

'I see. Does she sing my praises as well?'

'Your praises?'

'Wasn't that what their job was, those concubines?'

'I'm the one who sings your praises – I never do anything else. That's what we have in common, Eva and I: our unhappy love for our spouses. Her husband is a jerk of the type you claim is so irresistible. A jazz musician.'

'Does he cheat on her?'

'Incessantly. There's some chick who lives with him during the weeks she's in Visby. Eva loves him like crazy and makes herself as beautiful as she can when she goes home.'

I pull up the hood of my duffle coat.

'I can't stand hearing that. Don't think I'm going to take any hints.'

'No, I don't think that kind of effort seems enviable in a marriage, either. In any event, she worships him as much as I do you. My wife is the only one who understands me, I usually say.'

'And so you practise singing praises in harmony? How incredibly creepy. Can't you keep me out of that?'

'How am I supposed to do that?'

We pass Tegelbacken and the white boats at the City Hall quay; a happy troupe disembarks from an excursion to Drottningholm.

'An actress,' I say.

It's a question.

'School theatre,' he specifies.

'Didn't you write that she's with the National Touring Theatre?'

'That was before she came to Gotland. This is some kind of

free group that's settled there. They've been at my school too, although I missed the performance.'

I see, that kind of theatre. The operetta costumes I had mentally clad her in will have to fall – school theatre: something more social and unglamorous . . . At least it sounds more familiar.

'How did you meet?'

'She was helping to paint posters for a demonstration.'

'Do you see each other often?'

He hesitates. 'Do you want the details?'

'I want to know what I'm asking, nothing more.'

'They're on tour and at times away, but recently they've been playing in town. So this week it's been . . . well, every day if I think about it.'

'And night?'

'She lives pretty close, right next to the school actually . . .'

'Thanks so much, that's enough.'

But I can't help but conclude:

'So to be honest you *live* with her?'

'She has her own flat, and I can't have girls in my room.'

'Oh, I'm sure.'

We're quiet for a while.

'Are you jealous?' he suddenly asks, as if this were a possibility that didn't occur to him until now.

'I don't know. I'm confused. It's just that I don't understand you. I think I believe you when you say that I'm the one you want and all that, but I can't really understand why you need her, then.'

'It's just something entirely different. It's nothing you need to be envious of, because I'm giving her something you don't want.'

'You mean that for all intents and purposes, it's a pure unburdening that I ought to be grateful for?'

'I mean that my relationship with Eva has activated some part of me that wasn't used before, and which would never have

been used with you. It feels, in fact, like a personality transform-
ation, as if I've changed hair colour or however you want to say
it. But it doesn't change the person I am with you.'

'A new part of your personality,' I say darkly, 'I'm guessing
it's nothing other than <u>dear old</u> John Thomas.'

'He's an important part of my personality. That's what you
don't get. It's not so strange if I become a new person when I
don't have to go around feeling unsatisfied.

'Going around carrying a bunch of flattened hormones,' he
translates then when I don't say anything.

I remain silent and my silence makes him clarify – not to hurt
me, I don't think he has any need to do that – simply in a desperate attempt to make himself understood:

'She's a wonderful lover.'

We've made it a ways up Hantverkargatan and we're right in
front of the Rimondo Cinema when I burst into tears. Right
in front of the Rimondo Cinema on Hantverkargatan, smack in
the midst of Friday evening cinema-goers streaming out of the
theatre, I just stand there, crying.

He wraps his arms around me, he hides my head against his
leather-clad chest and presses my nose against his FNL lapel pin.

'I didn't think you cared that much about it,' he mumbles
helplessly in my hair.

'I'm trying not to,' I sob.

A decision not to have marital relations with Gustav grows
during a sleepless night into a decision not to see him at all,
which during a day of usual togetherness shrinks to its being as
it is, and a night of marital relations. No decisions – it's exactly
as unfeasible as always to switch to just-friends status: we eat
dinner in the kitchen and drink coffee on the couch and everything is just as usual, and 'commingling' seems like an overly
fraught word. I was serious when I said the thought goes against
my grain, but you can simply not think about it. When we're

together, the other stuff seems so distant, everything is less desperate and dramatic. Maybe you get used to it. Maybe you truly can get used to anything.

He places the decision in my hands: if you want, I won't see her again. I refuse to take responsibility for it. I wish it had never happened, but now that it has, I don't want him to have to break things off 'for my sake'. On the other hand, it's soothing to know that I have everything in my hands, that their relationship depends on my generosity.

It would be much simpler if I could convince myself that he no longer loves me. But it's not that simple. He goes back to a new work week and celebrates his reunion with Eva over dinner at Gutekällaren, but there's no reason to doubt him when he writes that he misses me both physically and emotionally, that midriff and mind are united in their longing for me.

As for me, I don't write anything, but I send Bible verses. I initiate a campaign of terror by letter with 'Prov. 7:26', 'Matt. 5:32' . . .

I only quote – I don't say a word about his having to break up with Eva, I simply send him a Bible verse every day to consider. If I've ever had that book at my fingertips it's now – I can go to practically any page and find useable passages.

Hast thou a wife after thy mind? forsake her not: but give not thyself over to a light woman. (Sirach 7:26)

But I say unto you, that whosoever shall put away his wife, saving for the cause of fornication, causeth her to commit adultery. (Matt. 5:32)

Sit not at all with another man's wife, nor sit down with her in thine arms, and spend not thy money with her at the wine; lest thine heart incline unto her, and so through thy desire thou fall into destruction. (Sirach 9:9)

Lust not after her beauty in thine heart; neither let her take thee with her eyelids. For by means of a whorish woman a man is brought to a piece of bread: and the adulteress will hunt for the precious life. (Prov. 6:25–26)

Men do not despise a thief, if he steal to satisfy his soul when he is hungry – But whoso committeth adultery with a woman lacketh understanding: he that doeth it destroyeth his own soul. (ibid. 6:30, 32)

Drink waters out of thine own cistern, and running waters out of thine own well. Let them be only thine own, and not strangers' with thee. – Let thy fountain be blessed: and rejoice with the wife of thy youth. – And why wilt thou, my son, be ravished with a strange woman, and embrace the bosom of a stranger? (Prov. 5:15 ff.)

I say nothing. I simply quote. He shall have a daily Bible verse in his postbox. That is, if he goes home to pick up his post.

It's probably a result less of the authority of the Word than of a natural development that Gustav, after another week, is suddenly gripped by remorse. He writes that he's come to the insight that he seems to be terribly monogamous by nature when it comes down to it. He says he doesn't think he's as in love with Eva as he first believed. But now she's fallen in love with him and is dependent on him: 'What shall I do? Can't you give me some advice? You're so wise.'

Signed 'Husband'. Salutation 'D. wife!'

My laugh tinkles like little silver bells, as they say in the novels. I call Visby so he can hear it.

19

The days continue in the same way, the cold persists, and the only thing that gives a feeling of time elapsed is the growing pile of papers on my desk. When I work at home, I almost never see anyone. I run errands to the Royal Library once in a while just to go down to the Sumlen Café and see an acquaintance, to verify that I can still speak Swedish.

What most often gets me outdoors are different kinds of demonstrations – it's become an occupation that can actually lay claim to all your free time. For expelled Roma, against the regional plan – there's always something going on. Above all, of course, Vietnam. There's a constant running to the American Embassy nowadays – you've barely made it home before it's time to go again. The US has by now made such a disgrace of itself that it's starting to be generally obvious, but what use is that if they don't realize that a disgrace is what they're making of themselves?

So we march off to Strandvägen to get them to understand it, time and time again. It's certainly not a political activity that costs much effort – if you're going to take a walk outside, you can just as well do it underneath a few inspiring posters. As a contribution, I suppose it's better than nothing, and I at least muffle my guilty conscience about my *flâneur* attitude towards life by strolling behind banners and getting checked off by those standing on the corner counting protestors.

Chanting slogans is something I've not yet been able to get myself to do, but now that it's time again, just a few days after 1 May, suddenly it's no longer a question of being able to get myself to do it but rather an actually compelling need. I find myself standing and screaming 'USA OUT OF CAMBODIA' with 10,000 others at the sleeping façade of the Embassy, fortified by a violent police presence.

It feels powerless, but what's more natural when you're feeling powerless than to scream?

*

This weekend, Gustav comes home with a new confession: he's contracted a shameful disease.

I don't let any little silver bells tinkle now – if there are bells chiming in my laugh, then it's clanging, thunderous iron: this is the funniest thing I've ever heard in my entire life! Sin punishes itself!

I laugh more heartily than Gustav did when my gynaecologist said that I was a hormonal talent. I laugh until I'm completely worn out.

As for him, he's shaken up by the little pamphlets about VD that he got at the clinic in Visby, little fire-red brochures about symptoms and treatment. The doctor apparently didn't think this was something venereal in the worst sense, but Gustav's basically prohibited from engaging in sexual activity until the tests have been analysed. So now I just clang the bell when he tries to get close: Not one step closer! Don't for one minute think I'm going to allow myself to be infected by my husband's lover's husband's promiscuous activities!

Even though he isn't able to share my glee, he can't help but tell me yet another tragicomic aspect: when he was in the waiting room at the clinic, he saw two of his pupils.

'Do you think it undermined your authority as their teacher or made them respect you?'

'Hard to tell, just about as hard as it was for you to know what to think when yours found you out hitchhiking. These kids mostly looked like they wanted to hide, too.'

'Such things happen in the best of families,' I giggle. 'It happens in the best of families that sin punishes itself.'

'The wages of sin is death,' Gustav mumbles and reads about brain softening caused by syphilis.

I give him a pat, feel like The Great Mother and tell him what the doctors usually say about bacterial flora and the honeymoon phenomenon.

It's with an unusually light heart that I follow him to Central Station on Sunday evening. What the Holy Word wasn't capable of doing, the Law of the Kingdom of Sweden must be able to bring about.

But I don't follow him out to the bus, as usual – Eva is waiting there.

'Why don't you want to meet her? She's nice,' he assures me.

I believe him. I no longer feel any aggression towards her, and I'm certain she's nice if Gustav says so.

'Does she want to meet me?'

'Oh yes, she really wants to know that you don't hate her. And she's curious about you, too.'

'After everything you've told her, of course. Well, we'll have to see.'

In the long run, it's probably unavoidable. We'll have to see if there's any long run – his stay in Visby is soon over.

*

I look for the professor, my supervisor, during his office hours to talk about what I'm working on; I was thinking he may be wondering.

I believe I caught a glimmer of recognition in his eyes, but it's probably just my imagination.

He approves of everything I say, without any objections, and without agreeing, as if he's saying 'is that something worth working on, very well, if you think so, I won't get involved'.

I've waited an hour to get in, I'm in his office for four minutes, and three phone calls interrupt us while I'm there. When I come out, six others are waiting although his office hour is over.

I've actually jumped the gun with my dissertation and don't have the right to any supervision yet, since according to the schedule you're supposed to complete most of the literature courses first. But first I want to know if I can write – otherwise there's no point in starting to take courses.

My first draft chapter is in its final stages – that is, the stage when I'm cutting and pasting; I've discovered that if I reorganize everything and build the argument backwards instead, it could function as an introductory chapter. This means papers spread out over any clear surface and a heavy scent of glue all over the place. In other words, it's the stage at which you can't carry the work out into Kronoberg Park.

But spring is at the stage when the birches are about to open their buds. I can't see anything from my window, just a building façade directly across. I have to run down the stairs and around the corner to see the birches. I run down the stairs and around the corner every other hour to see how far they've come. Up again and cut and paste.

Then I'll start on the reading courses, which are portable.

On Ascension Day weekend, Gustav is free and we get out to the Island as soon as we can. The ice is gone and the liverwort is sneaking its way up through the brown oak-leaf covering on the ground. Gustav has been declared healthy, it was nothing serious, and in the sun it's warm enough for us to dare to make love on the ground – it always adds an extra dimension to the act: you feel at one with nature. One with the Island, with the oak leaves and the liverwort, and with each other as a part of the great whole.

His parents come out on Saturday. Gustav and I stay in the seaside cottage that night too, and it passes without comment. In this fourth year of not being engaged, we're accepted as we are – they're clearly resigned to it.

But I'm also resigned to it. We may as well get engaged. Since we can't divorce anyway.

Although he's met the perfect lover, who's a nice person besides, and who may be prepared to abandon her vainly adored husband if Gustav so wished – despite this, I'm the one he wants. There's something supernatural about such a love; you have to capitulate to it.

Or is it actually because she's been a threat that I feel a new necessity to slap golden handcuffs on him? Because I can't stand the prospect of no longer having an island to come to when the ice thaws and the liverwort blooms?

At dusk we take our bikes and find our way down a small path along the shore, sit on a spit of land at sunset and talk about getting engaged. If it's to be done, it has to be maximally inconspicuous and painless, without the spectacle of family. I sketch out a strategy:

'Let's invite my family out for Midsummer when yours is here, too. Then everyone will believe it's time for an announcement – "Now! Finally!" they'll say to each other. And then nothing will happen. We'll just make them a Midsummer dinner and then we'll wave goodbye to them the next day and can rejoice in their long faces.'

'Really?' says Gustav. 'Am I supposed to stand there with a long face, too?'

'No, wait just a minute, I'm not finished. Then we'll exchange our shackles in all simplicity on a regular weekday right after that. Then they can't get the idea of throwing another family party if they've just had one! So we'll have cheated them of the family celebration and got yoked anyway.'

'Mean,' he says thoughtfully, 'mean bordering on perfidious. And why not until Midsummer by the way, why not Whitsuntide?'

'Whitsuntide? That's only a week away!'

He laughs. 'Exactly. That's your way of pushing the date ahead of you like a pram, with at least one month's safety margin, which means that we never get there. By the way, it's strange that your interest in legalization only crops up this time of year. Am I more attractive in May? Or is it the Island that is?'

'I have difficulties separating my feelings for the two of you, I admit it. It's possible that it's simply that winter's been too long and I don't want to miss out on the summer here.'

'Wouldn't you be able to love a man without an island?'

'I actually don't know. So it's better to wait and see if my feelings remain. November is probably a better month for engagements – more realistic.'

'When you're in your right mind, you mean, instead of rising sap and the like?'

'Speaking of which, I've forgotten to tell you that Harriet's left her husband.'

'Already? It was supposed to be one of those marriages of convenience that were so durable, I remember you saying when they entered into it.'

'Clearly it wasn't. It was probably desperation rather than resignation, and that's not durable at all. You have to despair in the right way.'

'Yes, I don't want to marry a desperado,' he says, getting up. 'And spring feelings or no, we'll freeze our bums off if we keep sitting on this rock.'

★

Gustav keeps nagging about introducing Eva and me, and I have to admit that my ostrich attitude is unworthy: since she exists, there's no sense in pretending that she doesn't. And besides, I'm naturally just as curious about her as she is about me. One of the last Fridays of the term, I go to meet them at Central Station.

At first it crosses my mind that I should improve my appearance as much as I can – my best corduroy suit and an elegant hairdo – but then I decide the opposite, that I should show how insignificant my appearance is (I who am loved by Gustav): some people don't have to dress in an eye-catching manner – some of us have soul. So I go as I am, in jeans and a sweater and my hair hanging down. I even knot my scarf under my chin, country-style, instead of in the more elegant manner at the nape of my neck.

They've taken the train from Nynäshamn this time. It's already on its way in before I've found the right track. I stop at a bench with a back to hold on to.

I see Gustav from far away – he's easy to pick out because he's so tall. Next to him must be the woman who's Eva. She catches sight of me at the same moment – recognizes me from the photos he's shown her? – and makes an attempt to disappear in the crowd, but he stops and say something to her. They continue forwards and he introduces us although it's obviously unnecessary:

'Eva – Martina.'

We smile at each other.

We stand on the platform and smile at each other, and it's utterly strange, as if it weren't strange at all – that's what's strange. To smile, and in this smile attempt to put in – well, everything we know about each other, that we know it and we ask each other's forgiveness and <u>no hard feelings</u> – to try, in a single little platform smile, to insert a credible denial of everything society and the whole goddamned world expects us to feel for each other: the betrayed and the mistress.

How childlike she looks! Much smaller than I had imagined, a little chubby and girlishly cute rather than model-beautiful – by far not as remarkable as I had imagined. Wearing an ordinary light-green poplin coat. And when she opens her mouth, she speaks *dialect*. Gustav has never mentioned this. She speaks some kind of dialect from the north, and God help me but it strengthens my feelings of superiority. (You can't be free of prejudice in all respects.)

What she's saying is something about train schedules – she's going on with the regional train to Sollentuna leaving in twenty minutes. We walk into the hall, Eva considerately by herself a bit in front of us. He's still carrying her suitcase and I get an importunate feeling of having taken her place. Next week I'm supposed to go to the graduation party at Gustav's school and I had planned to supply myself with a schedule. He nods when I mention this: 'That's fine, we'll go out to Eva's train.'

There's no line at the window and I'm given the schedule immediately. I stop at the newsstand to buy an evening paper. When I walk out to Track 2, I see only Eva there – I slow my steps for a second but it's too late to turn around. To encounter her alone is more embarrassing, but now that things are the way they are, I simply have to face them.

'Gustav thought you were taking a long time,' she says, 'he went in to look for you.'

'Gustav,' she says. Just the fact that she uses his name. I do it myself right afterwards, and it feels like an impropriety, 'Gustav's room' in Visby is what I say something about, and it feels like an inappropriate intimacy that we're saying his name.

We talk about accommodations – she tells me what a good flat she's been able to rent in Visby and repeats an offer she's previously made through him, that we can stay there when I come; as for her, she'll be on tour those days.

'It's not so central, but you can borrow my bike,' she adds, and the coals burn on my head (everything mine is yours, please just take it).

'I think it would be interesting to see a little of Gotland,' I remark, 'otherwise that graduation party isn't really something that interests me.'

'Gustav really wants to show you off.'

'Oh, I see, well, of course.'

We see him approaching, so we stand quietly until he reaches us. A moment of small talk, then the regional train comes in and Eva waves goodbye.

Gustav and I walk out to Vasagatan.

'Why did you look so surprised when you saw us?' he asks. 'You knew she was going to be with me.'

'Did I look surprised? In that case it was unconscious positioning, reflexive positioning because of confusion. I don't have a lot of practice in this situation, if you'll excuse me. No, I came here for the purpose of seeing her.'

'Well?'

'Well yourself,' I say, 'what did she say about me?' (Because I can assume that they talked about me in the minutes I was away.)

'That you seemed so small and delicate, and that she felt guilty.'

'Did she? Well, likewise in that case. Likewise.'

I felt guilty about what I had thought before I left home – foolishness about clothing, the need to assert myself. In our confrontation, I felt I was the stronger, not least of all because of the very concrete circumstance that she was the one dropping him off and I was the one taking over – I would not have been so eager to meet them on the way *to* Visby.

I wouldn't have wanted to be in her position – and that's why I'm ashamed.

'Why didn't you tell me she was a country bumpkin before?'

'Haven't I?'

'You've presented her as a woman of the world. I've been imagining a demi-monde, an actress of the femme-fatale type. And then she speaks a dialect from the north?'

'Western Bothnian. Isn't it pretty?'

'Of course. It sounds so soft.'

'But not dangerous, you mean?'

'Maybe that too, but in a different way in that case.'

We walk through the Old Town to Gustav's. The open doors of the small cellar restaurants release special continental scents in the mild night.

Jealous? All of a sudden it becomes crystal clear to me that I'm jealous of him, not of her. I know Gustav, I 'have' Gustav, but I don't share his experience of her, and that's what I would like to have – I would like to have her.

What do I mean, have? Devour. Like the troll in the story who wants to eat up the little princess, every last bit. I realize that the idea of me as the troll in this situation must be difficult to explain to an outsider – to be honest, it's a feeling that's untranslatable.

'What are you thinking about?' he asks.

'I'm wondering if I could become a lesbian,' I say (not that it's anywhere near an approximation, mostly to shake him up a bit).

As planned, he stops in his tracks, stares at me and imitates unmitigated terror:

'Oh no, I don't think I'm ever going to bring you and Eva together again!'

★

Gustav's high-school students are taking their so-called A-level exams and are inviting the teachers, along with their wives and husbands, to dinner in the banquet room at the Stadshotellet. I'm there so that they can get a look at me, and so they do.

A giggly girl confides in me that she never understood a

word of his philosophy class. A short-shorn boy tells me that he understood that Lindgren was one of those FNL-ers as soon as he saw him – not so hard to guess, I think, since he wears an FNL lapel pin.

I'm shocked by the youth of today. To be sure, people were drunk at their student parties in my day as well, but not generally already upon arrival. Here, they're staggering in to the first course.

At the table, I make conversation with the teacher who's been Gustav's supervisor. He's nice, but then there's dancing and general break-up. Several teachers think I'm a student and make shameful proposals (pupils who've graduated are clearly considered fair game), and finally I see no other way out than to sit and hold Gustav's hand to demonstrate that I'm here as his wife. Mrs Student Teacher – what a role.

Gustav doesn't drink – it just makes him sad, and that's naturally no fun. As for me, after my initial tipsy kindness, I just become sleepy – that's no fun, either. Once we've got tired of the crowd and the amplified music, we disappear without formal farewells and ride home to Eva's flat.

We can't stay in Gustav's rented room and the hotel is expensive and boring, so why shouldn't we stay at Eva's? Yes, why not? I have a sense that there ought to be a few good reasons against it – that there were some but that I've forgotten them – in any event, Eva suggested it, Gustav thinks it's practical, and here we are, lying in Eva's bed – an excellent, comfortable, fashionable square bed.

Commingling? Did someone say something about commingling? It wasn't me, was it?

The two-room flat is in a modern building a bit outside Österport, and it isn't particularly Gotland-ish. It's rented as partially furnished and doesn't say much about her. A few posters from theatre performances on the walls, an Oriental dance mask. No bookshelves? No books at all? Only a small pile on the windowsill; she probably has more where she actually lives. I recognize Jersild's *Pig Hunt* from a distance, and a Tito Colliander – Gustav's the one who's loaned it to her, of course.

And there: a cast photo, Eva in action. Oh yes, she can apparently be beautiful when she wants to. I don't know what role she's playing, but she looks remarkable; here she matches, better than in reality, the mythic proportions she had assumed in my imagination.

Gustav falls asleep before me, contrary to our usual routine; I lie a while longer and take in the smells of the foreign room. So it's here. In this building. In this bed.

There's a pair of red sandals lying under a chair on the floor. Lady's sandals, with high cork heels. My own are lying in the entryway, my flat, round-nosed boy-sandals. I've worn this kind since I was a child since they're the most comfortable thing you can walk in.

Do I have to grow up? Do I have to become a lady?

The morning is foggy and rain hangs in the air, but we get on our bikes to go look at the city. It's undeniably worth seeing with its cobblestone streets and old, low houses, and the ruins with picturesque restaurants in them and gardens with apple trees and lilacs in bloom – it's almost good that the weather is grey; if the sun were shining, it would be a caricature of an idyll. Gustav is also showing me around a bit distractedly – the exoticness has worn off for him and he's happy to be moving home. For the autumn, he's looking for a job in Stockholm.

When it starts to rain, we withdraw indoors, lie on the bed and read. I stay until Eva returns because Gustav says she'll be sad otherwise. Around three, a taxi stops outside, Eva rings the doorbell, I go and open and Gustav shouts a welcome from within the cloud of kitchen steam.

And thus we can devote ourselves to <u>no hard feelings</u> more thoroughly. She talks about her tour – four days on the road at different schools, different audiences, different kinds of youth influenced by different kinds of teachers. In some places, there was some hesitation about letting them perform since the press had claimed the play was left-wing, and there the audience was clearly more curious: the lure of the forbidden must be enormous.

'Best of all would be to perform in secret,' she asserts, 'in dim cellars at unannounced times. We would probably get more of the youth that way than we get when they see us during mandatory class time.'

They tell me more about the city, about those political phobias that affect both theatre groups and deviating teachers. Gustav wonders if there's anything in his file saying he's conducted political propaganda during his teaching – Eva's certain there is.

She's left-wing but sensible: another one. She's from a genuine working-class background, besides; Gustav, born a member of the petit-bourgeoisie just like me, doesn't hide the fact that this has contributed to his fascination with her. And nice – she's just as nice as he promised. Friendly in a quiet way – you'd probably say 'sweet'. She sets out coffee cups while I pack up my overnight things and then we drink coffee, too, before they both follow me to the harbour. It's no more difficult to talk to her than to anyone else you've just met – she's like anyone else, and everything feels unnaturally natural.

20

It's raining. June is usually the loveliest month at the Island, but this year none of the old rules seem to apply. The green looks grey through the filter of rain.

Gustav has gone out to fetch more wood – I hear him whistling by the outbuilding. Off-key, but not so off-key that I can't distinguish the melody and know the words.

It's Gustav's naughty wood-fetching song. In a moment he'll open the door with his elbow and slam it shut behind him with his foot (his hands occupied with his load – why doesn't he use the excellent basket I presented him on his last birthday?) and, with a crash, dump the whole armload into the wood box (why doesn't he pile it more neatly? There'd be room for a lot more then).

I'm reading the morning paper from yesterday when he comes in, and, without looking up, I ask him:

'What's a good lover like? One that's always willing, of course, but what more? What else is good?'

'You mean, what does Eva have that you don't have?'

'For example, yes.'

'It's not so easy to describe. But you could say a little initiative. A little improvisation. For example she nibbles on my ear when we're sitting in the bus, or things like that. You never do that sort of thing.'

'No. What's that supposed to be good for?'

'Try it,' he says.

'Listen. I broached this subject from a purely scientific stand-point, not to learn any tricks from your mistresses.'

'Tricks? Those aren't tricks. On the contrary. It's that she's spontaneous – she does what she feels like.'

'That's what I do. Like when I feel like listening to the Daily Chronicle to find out what time it is while we're having sex – speaking of which, can't you put the radio on the nightstand?'

He shakes his head. 'Don't make yourself sillier than you are.'

'By all means. The day I feel like tasting your ears, I'll do it. But I'll never become spontaneous, and if there's something worse than a lack of spontaneity, I think it's feigned spontaneity.'

He's quiet – perhaps it's an admission. Or maybe he's just thinking.

'Another thing about Eva is that it's so much fun to cook for her. She really enjoys good food.'

I can't compete with that. I've never accorded Gustav's cooking the praise it deserves, or even cared about what he's served. But I can't help it if I'm not interested in food, can I? If I were, I would have learned to deal with it myself. I'm just not the kind of person who thinks that food and sex are the most fascinating things there are, and who sees culinary and erotic dimensions everywhere I look, this latest trend with love feasts on apartment-house roofs that's become a national scourge – I prefer having everything in its place, shoes on the doormat and food on the table and erotica in bed, and that you don't need to make such a fuss about it. That's the kind of person I am, and I don't intend to develop any complexes about it.

I'll have to be happy until he finds a woman who cooks for him so he discovers how nice *that* is.

★

Punctually at the end of every term, my existential anxiety comes to haunt me. One fine day it's standing there beside my bed, hissing, 'What are we doing with our lives?'

The fact that a dissertation takes at least four years to write isn't much to throw in its maw. I recollect that a job counsellor once said something about libraries and I grasp at it just to shut it up: 'I can always get a job at some kind of library, someday.' I only half-believe it, but for now it'll have to be enough to tame the existential anxiety – not get rid of it entirely, of course, but to keep it on the rug. 'What are we doing . . .' – it starts when I wake up, and I quickly answer: 'Oh bother, I can always get a job at some library someday.'

Since I don't really believe that, it constantly skips my mind and I have to look for it over and over again – what was it, wasn't there something . . . oh right, library, something at some library!

This is obviously no answer to the question, 'What are we doing with our lives?', but it's at least one answer that works passably well to tame my anxiety about what I'll do in the future. The question 'What should we do with our lives?' I've despaired of finding an answer for. I don't know how to go about losing my life in order to find it.

For the summer, I've provided myself with portable work, language checking of an English translation of someone's dissertation in history. There's no pleasure in it, but the main thing is that it can be transported to the Island and dispatched in a rock cranny.

Gustav wants to go sailing. I don't say anything, either about coming along or about keeping him at home. The morning he had planned to leave, there's a downpour and the sea report provides no hope, so he postpones his journey.

We stay indoors all day, and I put on my raincoat just to take a walk to the postbox. It's empty. I sniff around in the forest but it doesn't smell like anything – nature seems completely washed out.

Dusk falls. He's lit the kerosene lamp in there and the window shines so invitingly when I return: a small square of golden light between the dark trees. Inside the room, the tobacco smoke is dense and I open the window wide. Gustav pulls on his big sweater.

'It stinks,' I explain.

'I can smoke your tobacco if you think it stinks less.'

For lack of argument, I simply glare at him.

'What are you sulking for?'

'I'm not sulking.'

'You bite if I do so much as look at you.'

'My stomach hurts.'

'Was there something in our dinner?'

'No, it's just nature's wonderful order,' I sneer.

'Well that's not my fault, is it?'

'It's completely and utterly your fault. Come and put your warm hands on me. That's the least you can do.'

Gustav loves to come lay his hands on my stomach. He agrees with the idea that if women have to put up with menstruation, it's not too much to ask that men have to put up with women who have it and at least contribute with a laying on of hands.

'Everything's my fault, I know that, but besides that, it's not particularly my fault that you have a stomach ache, is it?'

'Of course it is, since you're a man.'

'I may have an advantage because of that injustice, but I'm not the one who's invented it, am I?'

'It's because you're a man that I'm here, and if you weren't, you wouldn't stay here in a little cottage with me. Since you're a man, I'm here and since I'm a woman, I have a stomach ache. Thus it's your fault that I'm here and have a stomach ache. Doesn't that follow?'

He furrows his brow.

'If P then Q, and if R then S . . . and if not P or not R . . .'

'Then not Q, now P, thus Q and S: it's your fault, that's what I'm saying. By the way, your hands are completely cold. I want a hot water bottle instead.'

He spreads a blanket over me and leans his head against my stomach. It's not as good as a hot water bottle, but it's something.

'My hands get cold when you ask me to lay them on you because I get so nervous because I love you so much that I want to warm you so badly that I get completely cold.'

'There's nature's wonderful order,' I sigh.

Towards dawn, the rain stops spattering against the roof. I wake up because he's starting to pack.

'Now you can have peace and quiet for a few days.'

I grunt into my pillow to let him know I've understood.

'Will you still be here when I get back?'

I grunt again but realize that this requires a precise response and, with a supreme effort, push myself up out of the warmth of my bed.

'Yes, I suppose I will. This job will take a while, and I can just as well do it here. But you can call me.'

'If I find a telephone I will. It's difficult to dock when you don't have a mate.'

He carries his bags down to the boat and I watch as he sets sail and guides the boat out. I wave from the dock and feel like a seaman's wife on a mural.

Although only as long as I'm standing on the dock. Once I'm back in the cottage, I only feel how good it is to be alone. Well, and the nagging guilt of course, which is inseparable from that feeling: its shadow, its reverse. You're not supposed to like being alone – it's wrong. Especially when you're not in your own home but sitting like one of Strindberg's termagants in a house that's been emptied of its rightful owners.

I carry my manuscript down to the beach, sit in a cranny, read and moan: I'll never get this text in shape. I'll have to limit myself to correcting pure errors – the Swedish is going to shine through anyway.

The waterway is roaring like a highway, for now is when the Swedish people have their holidays. 'Like', by the way – it is a highway; the boats are almost lined up in a queue along the channel. The window panes in the cottage rattle, and it's just as noisy as at home in the city. It must be difficult for Gustav to find any free bays as a night port.

I follow his journey on the sea chart on the wall as the post-cards with Elliord Mattsson's familiar marine motifs drop in. I spend evenings in the large cottage since the phone is there. I sit practising saying 'I miss you'. By now it's starting to be true – I've spent time alone with my guilt for so many days now that I'm determined to be a tender and welcoming wife.

There's no trick to thinking that, or to writing it, but saying it – it feels so strange in my mouth: 'I miss you'.

On Tuesday evening, the phone rings, but it's only Mother-in-Law, who's wondering if I've heard anything from Gustav. I report on when and where his latest sign of life was sent from, and I wonder quietly if she also has a sea chart she follows him on: she doesn't like him going out on long journeys alone.

Then Gustav calls.

'Are you ever coming home?' I say.

'Yes, I think tomorrow. I'm not so far away, less than twenty nautical miles.'

'What does that mean, in terms of time?'

'It completely depends. But I'll be home for dinner.'

'OK, then I'll have it ready on the table.'

In my thoughts I prepare the welcome dinner, sit on the porch in the morning with a pad and pen and plan what to buy at the country grocer: beer and bread and fresh fish, and maybe a cake mix to put in the oven; once in a while, yes, about every hundred years, it can actually be fun to make dinner.

First I'll ride my bike to the grocer and then dig up some potatoes from the garden and fetch wood and water, and then pick flowers, I think. Of course there isn't much left of the fair meadow, mostly those blue whatchamacallits (Midsummer flowers?) that don't last more than a day, but the main thing is that they stand there when he comes in so he feels welcome. And then I'll be so good, so good, and I won't complain at all about having sex with him.

I've got to that point in my planning when a signal horn honks out in the water. I shade my eyes and see the StarBoat making a turn a bit beyond the dock. I make it down there in time to take the rope he tosses me.

'Already? I thought you were coming at dinnertime.'

'That's what I thought too, but the wind shifted overnight, you know, so I didn't have to tack.'

You know – the fact that the wind had shifted; anyone at all who cared would have noticed.

'That's what sailors are like, unreliable no matter what the weather. They say they're coming to dinner and then they arrive at lunch, before you've had a chance to go shopping or anything.'

'I didn't say when I was coming, did I? I said I'd be home by dinner, and I am. If you don't want me here, then I'll just have to stay on board.'

I reach out my hand to take his bags and he passes them onshore one by one. When he's also climbed over onto the dock I lift up two suitcases to carry them in. He takes them from me and sets them down, and then he hugs me.

<u>I keep forgetting</u>.

We put together a kind of lunch with the leftovers at home, kefir and cold potatoes to slice on hard-bread, then I ride to the country grocer while he takes a nap. He's still sleeping, tired from so much sea air, when I return; I put the groceries in the cellar and go down to the dock for a swim.

All day I wait for him to seduce me and I'm prepared to be so good, so good, but he doesn't, not even after a dinner of fish and newly harvested potatoes. He lies on the bed with a pipe and instead of starting to seduce me, he complains that I'm not seducing him.

'Be a man,' I plead. 'I think it's nice that you're above gender roles and cook and let me chop wood and all that, but do you have to be so soft and vulnerable because of it? It doesn't help that I make an effort – no matter what I do, you get sad.'

'I wouldn't be sad if you seduced me. Remember that Easter . . .'

'I remember,' I interrupt (the worst thing I can think of is when he starts on nostalgic memories). 'It was a special occasion. You know how lacking in spontaneity I am.'

'It's just that you're no longer horny for me.'

I can't think of a response. <u>Fathers and teachers, I ponder</u>: Can you be horny for your husband? Can you be attracted to, feel drawn to someone when there's no distance to navigate, no obstacles to overcome, when he's here? His body seems as familiar to me as my own, no more nor less exciting – how am I supposed to be drawn to that?

I sit next to him on the bed. He puts his arms around me and I let my clogs drop to the floor. His sun-bleached, summer-long hair rests prettily on the pillowcase, I think I could probably manage to nibble on his earlobe, but it wouldn't escape appearing to be an attempt at imitation, and he can't possibly want that.

Clumsily I fumble with his belt and zipper, until he starts to laugh and helps.

'You see how little is necessary? One little friendly gesture and you get my tail wagging immediately.'

I close my eyes and envy him his lust. Begrudge him it. Why does he when I don't.

'Say something nice,' he pleads. 'Say something beautiful.'

I think for a moment. Darling? Mostly we use that in cursive to express irritation. Beloved, dear? It feels so strange.

'Gustav,' I whisper. 'It's you. Isn't that beautiful?'

*

It's raining.

I stare out at the grey. Not a leaf is moving.

Gustav is sitting at the table reading Spinoza. He's cross because I pulled away from our morning embrace.

I've tired of proofreading the manuscript. I want something else to read, but I ploughed through all the old weeklies in the outhouse years ago. All that's left is a literary journal he brought with him from the city. I've tried to read several of the articles but just get angry because I don't understand them, and I get even more angry at what I do understand. How on earth can you write about literature this way? Why are these authors constantly praised to the skies in *Aftonbladet*, which I otherwise usually understand?

I've asked Gustav to look at the journal to explain if I'm the one, or if it's someone else, who's crazy, but he doesn't have time – he's reading Spinoza.

'Do you have to sit twisting that lock of hair the whole time? I get nervous watching you.'

'Do you have to sit there biting your cuticles,' he answers without looking up.

I take my fingers out of my mouth and sigh.

'I'm hungry.'

'We just ate.'

'Just ate? That was three hours ago.'

'It hasn't been more than two. You're eating us out of house and home, my dear.'

'*I* am?'

How can he claim something like that when he's actually the one who eats an abnormal amount!

'What about yesterday? Who was the one who took three helpings when . . .'

I interrupt myself when I hear how ridiculous I am, and tears fill my eyes. Why can't I stop myself? Why do I allow myself to be drawn into this again and again?

Like playmates, I thought happily once upon a time about Gustav and me. Like little children who can't stop teasing, then small, demon-like children who can't be left alone without torturing each other to the point of tears.

My tears run slowly and tickle the tip of my chin. I stare out through the window.

Maybe it's mostly my fault, but to the extent it isn't, it's the fault of the situation. Ah, the filth of soul in the twain.

I stare out the window and cry quietly with my back turned towards the room. Gustav reads Spinoza.

★

I've become a better person since I got divorced, Harriet writes in a letter.

I know what she means.

I would also like to become a better person.

21

I'm sitting reading a handout from the department for the next seminar when the doorbell rings. As usual, I'm sitting in my robe reading since I don't see any point in getting dressed on those days when I don't show myself to other people anyway. If anyone comes, it's usually Gustav. But when I open the door, it's not Gustav standing there. It's a man with big, curly hair and a beard: reflexively I grasp together the edges of my buttonless robe over my chest and wait for him to explain his errand.

'Howdy, I just happened to be passing by. Want to go get a coffee?'

It's his voice that's familiar. When I hear the voice, his features emerge from behind his beard: Aron.

Is that the earth shaking? Is that the world tumbling? Is that a symphony orchestra in the background playing *Pathétique*? The only sound in the stairwell is the Hootenanny Singers from the neighbour's radio.

'I suppose. I'll just throw something on. Come on in while I do.'

My voice isn't quavering. My dealings with Aron helped me develop a masterful ability to hide internal earthquakes, and there's no time now to figure out if this is an earthquake or not: since he's chosen to pretend that we saw each other last week, I opt for playing along. It's the easiest course of action for the time being.

He walks straight down my hall without taking off his jacket, sits down on the couch and looks around.

'Groovy flat.'

I wait for him to say something else, ask something maybe, but he doesn't seem to want to expand on his comment.

'A beer while you wait?'

He laughs, as if to note that he can indeed survive five minutes without a beer. I'm not sure that I have any at home, but I manage to find a pilsner left from the last time Gustav ate dinner here.

While I get dressed in the bathroom and Aron waits on my couch, I count. Five years – was it five years ago? 'Happened to come by' – he must have at least looked me up in the phone book.

I pull out my ponytail and comb my hair, trying to bring some order to my thoughts. So he dared to look for me. He trusted that I wouldn't make a scene and ask what he thought he was doing after five years without a sign of life, after having stomped my love in the dirt and let me down five years ago. He assumes that I'm not too afraid of earthquakes to let him in.

Of course I'm afraid. I'm totally mobilized, armed to the teeth with reservations. I don't know this Aron. I don't know who he is now, if he's someone who can make a ruin of me again, if he's still my great love. But I really want to find out.

I walk into the room and sit across from him. He's opened the paper, the cinema announcements, and we exchange opinions about the repertoire. We divide the films into good and bad, the ones we've seen and the ones we've not seen, and the result of this categorization is a couple of possible good ones that have not been seen by either of us; we don't explore the matter further.

It was dark in the stairwell; here by the light of the window I discover how much silver there is in his tightly curled mop of hair. At thirty-five? Maybe nothing unusual. I don't speak the observation aloud since I assume that he's heard about the charm of grey temples ad nauseam. His haircut suits him in any event – during the time I knew him, his hair was short in the way men wore it back then, and he was clean-shaven. But more hair suits him.

He gets up and walks over to my bookcase, stands holding his beer bottle and reads the book spines with his head cocked. The type, I think, who judges a person by their library.

'Mostly books for classes,' I say apologetically.

'English? Second year, third?'

'Postgraduate.' (I don't say 'doctoral studies' – it sounds so prodigious.) 'Then I don't know what I'll do. I know just as little as I did back then what I ought to do.'

Now the words snuck out, the words 'back then', and I decide not to play that 'happened to stop by' game any longer.

'Have you moved back to Sweden?'

'A couple years ago. We lived in Gothenburg first, but now we've managed to borrow a pad in Älvsjö.'

We?

'We?'

'A chick came along from England.'

Came along, as if she were something that happened to stick to him.

'Kids?'

He turns around and laughs (at my inquisitiveness or at the fact that it's awkward to mention it?).

'Two. But she brought one into the nest. It's only the little one that I'm complicit in.'

He doesn't ask about my familial relations; he can clearly see that I'm the only one who lives here.

'It was for her sake we moved here,' he explains. 'She got a gig at the British Institute.'

And what about him? What does he *do*? I don't dare be more curious, but he adds without my asking:

'And then she needed a house husband, of course. And so that fell to me.'

Now the world is upside-down after all. *Umwertung aller Werte*: Aron a house husband!

This vexes me. Not in and of itself – the fact that he's married is good, it automatically reduces the destruction this reunion can cause in my life. But that Gustav was right! Once when I was talking about my past, Gustav claimed that that Aron would soon find himself in a row house with wife and children – and I defended him, hissing, 'You don't know what you're talking about!' He didn't say it was a row house, or if they're formally married, but those are only details: the fact is, in any event, that Aron is domesticated.

We leave without having decided where, just to walk, along Fleminggatan towards downtown. I'm walking on Fleminggatan next to Aron, I think: I feel as though people should turn around and gape at such a sight.

We wander on towards the centre, over the bridge to Kungsgatan. At an outdoor café under the tower, he lifts his hand in a questioning way. I nod, yes, why not. We sit at a table in the corner facing the pavement. Here the traffic isn't too loud to make yourself heard in a normal tone of voice, and he abruptly picks up the conversation:

'Why English precisely?'

I shrug my shoulders.

'I started with Nordic archaeology. And then I took a course in ethnology – besides, it was a much more pleasant department.'

'That's the most important thing when you pick a subject, isn't it? That you can dig the folks there?'

I smile at his language: I recognize it. The ironic way of using slang, preferably a little dated. It's not quite that he speaks in quotation marks, but something in that direction: so that you know that the meaning of the word is approximate. He seems to like slang words because, more clearly than standard prose, they indicate that they aren't exact – they have built-in quotation marks, you could say. A barrier – something he was always an expert at.

'If that was the only thing, I would have studied philosophy, but I didn't know if I had the brains for it.'

Aron twists his face into a grimace which probably expresses what he thinks about false modesty, so I quickly explain:

'I want to be the best at what I do. I would never have been able to be the best philosopher in the city. But to write the city's best dissertation about the *Edinburgh Review* is something I think I can take on. Pure arrogance – I've never claimed anything else.'

What he's been doing himself this whole time is something I don't venture to ask him. Art is such a sensitive subject, such a sensitive area to get into if it turns out he has failures behind him. From what he tells me, he seems to have got as far as working as a director's assistant during some filming, but if he's still working in film remains unknown.

I ask about acquaintances in common, more or less temporary contacts from more or less strange circumstances. I'd forgotten these people, but I remember more and more names as we talk: did Dick ever leave for Australia? And Jessica, did she overdose? How did things go with Paul, Patty and what's his name, that crazy Dane . . . Aron is able to tell me some news but doesn't know everyone I ask about – our circles in London merely grazed each other. The past becomes so tangible from this conversation that once we've exhausted the subject and there's a pause, I dare to express what I had naturally been thinking the entire time:

'You looked me up. I would have never dared.' (If I had been you, I mean, but I don't need to be so blatantly obvious.)

He makes a disparaging face as if to say that it's nothing remarkable at all:

'I've always considered our relationship to be ongoing this whole time.'

There's nothing I would rather hear. Aron's and my relationship belongs to the eternal ones, elevated above such earthly non-essentials as whether you happen to see each other or not, communicate in writing or speech or know where in the world the other is. I want so badly to swallow his words and drown in his eyes, there's nothing I'd rather do. It's just that the effect of what's being said is disturbed by another voice, a voice from the past, and it's also Aron's, and it's saying: 'You understand there isn't anything between us. We meet like this when we both want to, but don't expect that I'll start functioning as some kind of <u>boyfriend</u> . . .'

A voice from the past, one evening on Ossington Street, an evening when I had gone to see him of my own accord and my dependency on him had started to become all too obvious – oh, Aron, you have no idea how well I remember every word from your mouth.

I would gladly have forgotten it, but since I haven't, I can't avoid noticing that what he's saying now grates. His words are actually so grating that my ears shrink from embarrassment. 'Our relationship has been ongoing this whole time' – I see, when did it start in that case, you could ask. Was it as soon as I moved away from London, since it wasn't ongoing while I was there?

But I don't ask any such questions. I peek out from under my bangs to see whether it was his intention to kid me, but he seems completely serious and just looks at me with eyes you could drown in. Maybe he has a poorer memory and believes his own version of history. No matter what he thinks about it, the fact remains that he's looked me up. Running the risk that it would be awkward, he's found it worth taking that risk. He's remembered that I exist and has found me, and no matter what he thinks about it, that's a kind of redemption. At least I'm not someone you can easily forget. It's a bandage on wounds that, to be sure, had already healed, a redemption even though I had already picked myself up again.

We leave that topic and start to talk about politics instead. It turns out that's one of the things he worked with in Gothenburg – he's been working on materials for the parliamentary elections.

'For which party?'

'Guess,' he says drily, as if it should be obvious.

I truly have no idea, and I don't want to embarrass myself by trying something stupid.

'You don't look like a right-winger.'

'I thank you for that.'

'But you must be some kind of extremist. Communists? You're too smart for that, anyway.'

'You'll have to revisit either your impression of me or of the Communists.'

'I have a hard time associating you with any kind of social engagement. Before, you were a living icon of everything asocial.'

'That's your private symbolism,' Aron says dismissively. 'I haven't changed.'

Here I'm uncertain about his version of history again. It's possible that he's right – that it was just me who was so blind to such things that I didn't see it even though it was already present. But it can't be completely without significance that the year 1968 happened in England as well as in Sweden.

The waitress cleared our cups away a long time ago, the guests at the table next to us have changed and our conversation has ground to a halt. I peer at the clock, twenty minutes to seven. He sees my glance.

'Say something.'

I think for three seconds and say:

'Jänken?'

He laughs and gets up.

'Right.'

He's still lost in the city; I shepherd him protectively, and with appropriate insults about people from Gothenburg, up to Sture Square where the film is showing.

It's dark as night when we come out again and I automatically head for home. He follows me through the intersections without deviating as if he intends to come with me, but when the subway comes into view, he stops.

I make no suggestions. In time we'll go home and to bed, no hurry. I want to digest this first.

'Do you have a phone?' I ask.

'Not yet.'

He pauses for effect, asks if it's a survey and if I want to know if he has a bathroom and a refrigerator – I laugh, recognizing it and nevertheless feeling impatient: do we really still need such posturing?

He puts his arms around me. My face at his neck and my heart skipping wildly: his smell! Aron's smell – I recognize it – and as everyone knows, there's nothing that pulls you down through the years as intensely as this, as everyone knows there's nothing that gets you to regress as quickly to a small, trembling child in a split second in the presence of the One Great Love.

'Call ya,' he says on his way down the stairs.

I nod. Do.

Eva moved from Gotland at the same time as Gustav, so now she's performing at schools in the Stockholm area and they stay in touch. Nobody can be happier about the way things are than I. If it weren't for Eva, I wouldn't be able to stand before Gustav with a clear conscience about this. As things are now, he has 'nothing to say', since 'he was the one who started'. In fact, I actually have two free passes, don't I?

Naturally I understand that infidelities can't be counted like this. The notion that they can even each other out is simply baroque. A higher understanding of justice wouldn't see that they have anything to do with each other. But in this case, I intend to keep myself to the usual low obnoxious insistence on equality; I will despicably repeat to Gustav his own words on the subject: that Eva created a new part of him that I wouldn't have been able to produce and so I didn't need to be jealous of it. Exactly so: Aron is a part of me that's been there the whole time but which has nothing to do with Gustav. I understand perfectly well that this precisely is the basis of jealousy, but I simply plan to quote him.

I've been the underdog for so long – morally superior, of course, but (are they two sides of the same thing?) inferior in the sense of a power balance. If I place Aron on the scales now, all of Gustav's small sins and affairs out in the sticks combined cannot maintain the balance. I don't like that things are this way – if someone has to be in the inferior position, I would prefer to be that person myself. But on the other hand, I feel so vulnerable in my relationship with Aron that it soothes my conscience.

I don't know how Gustav will react to this news, and prefer to let him know in writing. But what am I supposed to write? What's happened? Is this, or isn't this, the one great passion that once again has stepped into my life?

I'm not sure yet. Despite my complete mobilization, my resolution not to believe yet again in some ecstatic folly that will only leave me in ruins – and which in addition would ultimately make seeing Aron impossible – despite this, I have a fifth column within me. My self-destructive urge is so deep-seated, my longing for unconditional surrender, the great and lovely submission: to give myself up and perish. Without such urges, I don't know if there's any point in seeing Aron. Maybe it's necessary for me to fall down into a mindless crush again for there to be anything special about him, so that when we walk down Fleminggatan I am able to think *Aron and I are walking here* and that this is <u>it</u>. If that's what's necessary, what will I choose?

What does it mean actually, this wild desire in the primordial depths of my soul, to possess him? It's not a question of anything concrete: I would never be able to live with him, and the physical love act is only the most meagre of surrogates for the kind of possession I mean. Possession, or merging. I would like to melt together with him in a sense that has no meaning at all.

For now, I can do nothing besides tell Gustav what's happened, and what will happen.

'I'm glad I've got him back,' I write, 'as I would be about any lost friend at all. But whether we're friends is something I actually don't know – I don't know him. Aron belongs to my life in England, and that's a generation ago. Times have changed, and we with them, we're both married and neither of us has any plans to divorce. Nothing is as it was then, and we're reunited in a very peculiar way, since it isn't really "we".'

I emphasize that I hope that he won't consider this a reason to divorce either, but, on the other hand, I don't remind him that he doesn't have a leg to stand on since this has to be the first painful thought he himself will have.

I post it so it'll be there in the morning and spend the night regretting it. Letters are so dramatic – everything turned out so solemn and remarkable, and the fact that it's cowardly not to say things in person is something I've told him myself. I call as early as I dare to ask him to not read it, but he doesn't answer, and when I go over at lunch, he's already opened it.

The first thing he does is to argue against the parallel to

Eva – the parallel which, I admit, I didn't use as an excuse but as
an explanation. He claims that the comparison is lame.

'You're the one I love, and I've said that I can forgo her for
your sake. But you don't love me.'

'If you mean those movements of the soul, the racing heart
and all those other morbid conditions, then I don't love you. I
know how it feels, and it's possible I have a dash of that again.
My heart pounds when I see Aron, that's true. But I don't intend
to pay any attention to it. I'm convinced it'll pass.'

'My heart pounds every time I see you.'

'You can't go around with chronic tachycardia, can you? It'd
be unbearable.'

'It is.'

'Well, that's your business. In any event, I don't intend to
have any more passions. It's not so fun that it's worth the suffering. But I want to try to be friends with Aron if possible. The
fact that I want to sleep with him is mostly to reunite with the
person I was five years ago who slept with the person Aron was
back then, if you understand.'

'That metaphysical relationship is precisely what I have the
most against. I would mind it less if you slept with other people
if it wasn't anything like that, as long as you were metaphysically monogamous with me.'

'But you weren't the first man in my life. I have a Past, and it's
Aron. He has a mortgage on me. I was mortgaged to the teeth
before you'd ever laid eyes on me.' (Which isn't really true – I had
never counted on ever seeing Aron again; when I met Gustav I
believed it was a closed chapter. But a little simplification of the
past has to be permitted.)

'You are my better half,' I explain, 'but Aron is my worse one.'

'That doesn't seem very mathematical. Can you imagine Aristophanes' sphere divided in three as well? The next thing you
know, you'll be saying that he's your other twin soul.'

'That's what I used to think when I met him. It's true, we're not at all alike, not as alike as you and I are. I've never had an easy time talking to him. And by the way, he's so affected that there's nobody who can have an easy time of it.' (It's like playing ping pong, I think, with someone who not only catches the ball when you serve, but returns it with a vicious curve.) 'But it's true that there was a kind of spiritual kinship that made me recognize him the first time I saw him.'

'You can't have as many spiritual twins as you like.'

'Why not? Call it spiritual triplets then, or quints, or octuplets – I have no idea how many there are.'

'Does he make you horny?' he asks, abruptly, as if there'd been too much said about the metaphysical.

'Less than many others. That's not what this is about. Besides, I don't remember what it was like to sleep with him, I was so shy back then that I probably closed my eyes and didn't pay much attention to what he was doing.'

Gustav sits cleaning his pipe and looks around the room; I get up and fetch my tobacco, matches and an ashtray. He smirks at how eager to please I am.

'My slippers too, please. Then you can set the potatoes on the boil.'

'Darling, I'm so happy you're taking this like a man.'

'Actually,' he says, 'I'm more jealous of your relationship with Aron back then, five years ago.'

I turn quickly and look at him, almost surprised.

'You're absolutely right. You've understood me completely.'

*

The House of Film is the only place in town I know Aron frequents. I can't fool myself into believing it's for any other reason than to run into him that, time and again, I find myself there, especially since there isn't any film I want to see – I'm just using the café 'to get out for a bit'. But it would be even sillier to sit at home and fight internal battles about it, if this is where I want to be. I can just as well sit and read here as anywhere else, right?

After the seven o'clock showing of an old Buster Keaton with no acquaintances in the audience, I sit down with a cup of tea and *Aftonbladet*. Then I see him there, Aron, with a girl next to him. They're standing there reading the menu at the counter. I hide myself in my paper; I dismiss the idea of making a peephole in it and peer over the edge instead.

When they come over with their trays, they pass right by me. Aron slows his steps but I pretend not to see him. Why? I don't know – probably a reflex from ages past when we ran into each other at our pub in London and I pretended not to see him because to see him was the only reason I was there.

I hear snatches of their conversation and soon I'm sure that she can't be his wife – she speaks accent-free Swedish, but I can't tell what they're talking about.

I go get a refill so I have a reason to stay, and a short while afterwards I hear someone getting up behind me. I hear Aron say that he'll stay a bit longer. The next moment he comes over to my table. I pretend to be surprised and encourage him to sit down.

'It's been a while,' he says. I snort with laughter: it's been precisely one week and typical for Aron that it's now that he says it.

'Buster Keaton,' I say as if my presence needed justification.

He nods absently.

'I'm taking the night train. Do you think you could keep me company till then? I'm so tired that I'll probably fall asleep sitting if I'm left to my own devices tonight.'

'Wild night life?' I ask.

He grins:

'Baby screaming. Does that count?'

'I'll try to keep you awake if I can. Where are you going?'

'I have to go down and cultivate my contacts in G-burg.'

What does he mean, contacts? Work? Political connections?
Amorous?

'Listen,' he says suddenly (elbows on the table and chair
scraped closer), 'how about you and I be Ruthlessly Honest?'

'Sure,' I say and return his gaze (although my heart is sound-
ing an alarm: what does he mean by this?)

'Did you really not see me when I walked past your table
just now?"

I lower my eyes. Quick, let's find a justification for my
behaviour.

'Yes, I did, but I didn't know if it was appropriate to say anything since you had company.'

He laughs and leans back on his chair, takes out a cigarette
and explains between his teeth while he lights it.

'Ulla, she's married to a pal of mine. Tough marriage, needed
someone to talk to.'

'I don't know why I didn't say something myself,' he continues, 'I wanted to stop but my legs just kept on going – I
thought maybe you didn't want to see me and so I went completely weak.'

He says it as if it were something utterly strange he was
telling me, as if he were the first person in the history of the
world to whom something so strange had happened, as if I
would have a hard time understanding it – me! It's happened
to me on a daily basis in public places: the anxiety every time
he didn't or didn't want to see me, the panic that now it's over
for good – the fear of intruding where you're not wanted – my
legs carrying me away, shaking, from the only thing my insides
were crying for . . .

The thing that's difficult to comprehend is that Aron's the
one saying it. That Aron suddenly cares so much about me that
it makes him weak to think that I don't want anything to do
with him. It's not normal, it's not right. Or maybe he's always

done so but hidden it heroically so that we wouldn't develop a mutual dependency? No, I don't think he's consciously pretending, but I hold on to the suspicion that he's deluding himself.

He returns to the topic of 'pal with the tough marriage', begins to hold forth about how dangerous it is to get married.

'The need for the kind of loyalty that never fails, of course, we all have that. But to buy it with yourself as the payment – body and soul for an unlimited time – that's too high a cost. It's not worth it.'

I wonder when he's going to start saying mywife-doesn'tunderstandme, but he's smart enough to notice that it's hovering in the air, and when he does he quickly declares that there're no problems in their relationship, that Florence is a cool bird.

'Florence,' I giggle, 'what a name!' And I hurry to add, not only to keep from hurting anyone's feelings but above all to finally have it said, before he changes the subject again:

'I can't say anything, of course, with a husband named Gustav.'

Aron raises his eyebrows.

'You're married?'

'Not legally, but we live as married, as they say.'

'But you don't live together, do you?'

'Just intermittently, during holidays and such.'

'Gone on for a while?'

'Four years last summer. On and off a bit. But mostly on in any event.'

He peers through the cigarette smoke.

'I've always imagined you as the proverbial lone wolf.'

'Likewise,' I say with a sharp edge to my voice.

'Why don't you move in together, then?'

'Why should we?'

He shrugs his shoulders.

'Just because everyone else is doing it? I think we're married enough as we are.'

'And him?'

'Gustav isn't the type to follow the crowd, either.'

'Although a crowd of two is probably what he thinks is just right,' my conscience forces me to add. 'He's always wanted to live together, of course. And so there are conflicts,' I finish in the lightest of tones.

I lift his pack of cigarettes with a question on my face, he nods at me to take one.

'When we lived in Gothenburg and Florence didn't have a job, it was tough for a while. I was everything she had, and that wasn't what I wanted to be.'

He just left another train of thought incomplete now; was he comparing unequal relationships? But the fact that I am Gustav's everything – I didn't say that, did I?

'Purely objectively, she may have to be dependent on you,' I try, 'since you've torn her up by the roots and taken her to a foreign country, right?'

He looks at his watch as if he didn't hear my question.

'Are we going to spend our time here?'

'We can go to my place if you prefer.'

I have my bike outside. I don't offer him a ride, but he offers me one, if I'll promise to keep watch for black-and-white police cars. The physical exertion makes him more alert and he pedals off at a surprising speed, and I sit on the package carrier pressed up against him and remember how it was to be small and ride on my mother's package carrier, how I sang to myself because it sounded so funny when my voice jiggled.

He's out of breath when we get there and I fetch a cold beer from the kitchen.

'What's wrong with Gustav?' he asks suddenly while I remove glasses from the cupboard and hand them to him.

'Who claimed there was anything wrong with him?'

'His name.'

'That's the classic husband. All the jokes and cartoons, every-where, it's always a Gustav.'

He's standing with the glasses in his hands and looking at me, apparently making an attempt to imagine me with a car-toon Gustav, shakes his head and places them on the table.

Time's ticking. We sit on the couch and time's ticking so I'm starting to wonder if we'll have time. Aron sees me looking at the clock, he sees that I see that he sees me, we laugh and he starts to undress me. When he gets past my waist, I stretch out a free arm to pull down the shade.

And so it's like it was before in the world, although how it was then, I don't really remember that well. At this moment, the past is actually so immaterial that it could be something that happened to other people, something that someone told me about, but just now and just here, it's me and Aron, in this precise moment, we 'have' each other, and maybe, despite everything, that's not such a poor substitute for the metaphys-ical possession that one sometimes chases after.

But just for a moment, the work of a moment is what it is. A minute afterwards he has his clothes on, his jeans and his blou-son and his sandals, and has to go, muttering an excuse:

'It's not supposed to be like this of course . . .'

'Who says so?'

'All the experts in the area. You're supposed to take your time, they say, a rush job isn't erotic culture. Don't you follow the debate these days?'

'Fuck culture,' I say generously.

He sneers appreciatively, and I'm amazed at the pervasive feeling of well-being that comes from generosity.

'I'll be in touch when I get back,' he says at the door.

Strictly speaking, this is the most remarkable of all the

remarkable things Aron's said so far. He would have never said anything like it before, he never talked about where he disappeared to or when or why or if I'd ever see him again. Yes, he seems to have become civilized.

I can't help but open the shade a crack and watch him. He crosses the street and walks quickly down towards Fridhemsplan without turning around, and why should he?

'The splinter in the eye,' I think. Is that the locus of my infatuation? This thing that can't be explained rationally, nor be analysed in terms of friendship and the erotic? A distorting troll splinter that doesn't make me more clear-sighted. On the contrary, I'm dim-sighted and see what nobody else sees: an aura around Aron that makes him unique.

It's a glimmer that places my entire existence in a different light, but it has its price in the darkness that persists in his absence. When I wake up in the morning and there's no new meeting with Aron as far as the eye can see, I wonder seriously who on earth claimed that it's something desirable, this being in love.

22

Misgivings haunt me by Sunday afternoon. Who says that we won't have an election victory by the bourgeois parties? I mean, nothing says that we won't!

According to the Communist Party, it doesn't matter whether the government is bourgeois or social democratic. Their election posters say the government is riding the coattails of big finance. I took the opportunity to ask Aron when we were on the topic if he really shared the opinion that it didn't matter. He said no, a social-democratic government is worse since it simply serves the purpose of hiding class conflicts and luring society into corporate structures.

It's possible that he's right, it's even probable. I just can't stand to believe it. If that's the way things are, you can jump off a bridge sooner rather than later – if the Communist Party is the only thing you can place your hopes on.

It's true that I could also wish defeat on the current government, but when I think about Hedlund as prime minister, and Holmberg as foreign minister, the comments in the media here and abroad, the triumphal cry of the bourgeois parties – I don't wish it on them. I was conceived, born and raised in a country governed by workers, and though it be a workers' government in name only, the triumphal cries at its demise would proclaim it a defeat of social democracy itself, and the country I've lived in thus far would suddenly appear as a country that has always had everything wrong. My native land!

I don't want to experience that. The later in the day it gets, the more sentimental value social democracy acquires for me, these pitiful riders of big-finance coattails. And regret comes over me when I realize what a double standard it is, under such circumstances, to vote for the Socialists – in the safe knowledge that enough other people won't rise above voting for the Social Democrats and so save the government for me.

Towards evening I'm so worried that I call and ask Gustav to come hold my hand:

'I don't want to be alone if something happens!'

So he's with me when the election results start to arrive. We lie on the couch and listen to the radio. With every preliminary report, a few small stones fall from our hearts, and soon we break into smiles. After a couple of hours, it's already clear that the sitting government is safe, but only with the support of the Socialists' significant success. This time it wasn't irresponsible at all, on the contrary, it was unusually important to vote for them – politics is so full of surprises.

By eleven o'clock, we've heard enough.

'So I don't have to hold your hand any longer?'

'No, not at all. Now you can leave,' I say and turn off the radio. 'Now I can sleep soundly.'

*

I see Cilla less and less often, but when we do see each other alone, it doesn't take five minutes before we're on the same old topics: Women's Lib and vaginal orgasms, shameful diseases and the Pill (to have and have not), fidelity and jealousy: there's always new material. Cilla doesn't believe in bigamy. I don't either, I don't 'believe' in it at all – I'm simply living in it.

'But there's a difference between jealousy and jealousy,' I

clarify. 'There's a completely rational and reasonable kind that's based on the fear of losing each other. You can't repress it, nor should you. But if there's no basis for that fear – if the relationship is of such a nature that other relations don't pose a threat to it, then it's irrational to be jealous.'

'And you can reason your way out of it – is that what you're saying?'

'You should be able to.'

'Prove it,' says Cilla.

*

Gustav moves into a new flat at the end of the month. He's not allowed to stay in the student flat now that he's no longer studying, and moving in with me is even less an option than ever before: we wouldn't fit with all of our lovers and mistresses. He moves to Lindhagensgatan, towards Hornsberg, a dismal area dominated by factories and office buildings – not far from the Joy neighbourhood with its dismal café. So there isn't much of a view, but the flat is quite pleasant inside.

And so we're living in the same part of town again, on the same isle in the city. I often think about it just as I'm falling asleep at night – in particular on those days when we haven't seen each other but only spoken on the phone: We live on the same island in the world, I think.

But we wouldn't fit in the same flat. The first thing he does after he moves is to invite Eva, who needs somewhere to stay over the weekend since her husband wants the house to himself and his other woman. Gustav asks if I mind, but you can't really put yourself in the way of such an act of charity. 'Open your home to the poor rejected wife,' I answer.

I'm not the one standing in the way; Eva herself changes her mind. He keeps me continually informed on these developments:

'It started when she went and had a heart-to-heart with her rival. They fell into each other's arms and swore eternal

friendship, if I've understood correctly, and Eva gave up all claims
to John. "Just take him if you need him more", and the like.'

'Is it true? That the other woman needs him more?'

'Eva apparently realized that. But when John found out that
she had decided to do without him, he realized that she was the
one he wanted . . .'

'Aha. The pattern seems familiar somehow.'

'Doesn't it. You're not as original as you love to imagine.'

But I'm not the way I am in order to be original. On the
contrary: I think it's a relief to hear that other people have relationships as odd as ours. It's the same as when Cilla tells me
about her mother-in-law problems: her boyfriend's old mother
has such a hard time with the fact that they're not married that
when they come and stay overnight with her, she makes up
beds in separate rooms although they live together in Stockholm. This makes me feel relieved: my in-laws are perhaps no
stranger than other people's.

However, Gustav's new flat isn't occupied by either him or
anyone else for a while. He still hasn't got a permanent job.
He's been muddling along on so-called temporary subbing: the
agency calls him around dawn if they need him in Gubbängen
or Mörby. But now he's grown weary of running around and is
taking a longer temporary position at the closest place there is,
up north in Östersund.

On the eve of his departure, I buy a couple bottles of wine,
bring them home and get drunk methodically so I'll be nice.
True, I also become irresistibly sleepy, but as long as I can stay
awake, I'm nice. We make love enthusiastically and speak our
minds about this and that without fighting: isn't it amazing
what miracles a little alcohol can perform.

'How's it going to be with Aron?' he wants to know.

'Be? Not be?' I say (kindly and matter-of-factly). 'I guess it
won't be any different than it is, and it is the way it is. I haven't

heard from him for a long time. If I saw him more, I'd think about him less. Which would you prefer?'

'That you didn't see him and didn't think about him.'

'That's not possible. Besides, I'm not the one doing the choosing. It's possible he's disappeared again and won't show up for another five years. He comes and goes,' I sing (and what do I care, the cheap red wine inside me sings).

'So that's precisely what's so attractive, then, if I've understood you correctly?'

'Oh yes, men who just disappear – it's, what's the word – it's compelling. But,' I add quickly, 'that doesn't mean that I don't want a letter from Östersund every day.'

'Wouldn't you think about me more if I didn't write?'

'Uh-uh, because I'd know you were just sitting there not writing just so I would think about you.'

'You think you know me,' Gustav growls.

'Yeah,' I yawn happily and fall asleep with my nose in the crook of his elbow.

*

As soon as Gustav has left and the buzz has worn off – and with it my artificial obsequiousness – I start to get annoyed with myself retroactively over what was said during the night. What was he implying when he said something about being a 'pawn in some game', what did he mean by that?

I rip the dissertation out of my typewriter and knock out a letter.

> *Do you actually mean that you're walking around feeling like a pawn in a game? Whose game in that case? I'm not the one who's playing games. And who was the one who started pulling other people into our marital power play? Once you've started with that, the participants will naturally multiply so you become dependent on your relationship's relationship's relationship to the thirteenth degree.*

If this is a game we're playing, you, in any case, are more than a pawn for me – you're more like a rule of play, I mean a precondition. There's a line in this novel by Per Wästberg everyone's reading now that's become a standard phrase, something like 'I need you so badly but I can do without you'. A utopian relationship as you know. My case is a different one: I need you so badly but I can't stand you.

It's terribly difficult to be married . . . it's more difficult than everything! You have to be an angel, I think! (The Daughter in Strindberg's A Dream Play.) I've never pretended to be an angel, so don't blame me if it's hell.

But isn't there something about a Strindberg marriage after all? Would you really prefer a sugar-sweet idyll, or even a Wästberg marriage?

Gustav's letter begins with the usual report on his colleagues and teaching. There's one wise person at the school, he informs me – the cleaning lady. Sixty years old, grey-worn and with dentures, she says, 'I don't understand politics' and then talks about salary gaps, the educational system and aid to Third World countries with more sense than the entire faculty. Sometimes he stays in the faculty break room in the afternoon just so he can talk to her for a while.

After a panegyric about the cleaning lady lasting a page or two, he turns to the contents of my letter.

What's entertaining about a Strindberg marriage is probably the ingenuity of the parties in finding new models for torturing each other. But ours is the same old story almost all the time. Once in a while, when I play with the idea of taking us seriously, I realize how humiliating our relationship is. But I don't take it seriously; isn't that humiliating, too?

My colleague in Swedish Lit here is always talking about how important it is to take people seriously, that it's immoral not to do so.

A melancholy type who's probably read too much contemporary lit-
erature (or maybe too little?). In any case, I showed him Sandemose
instead – there's actually a point I found in your Sandemose: 'Why is
there something they call ethical seriousness but not ethical jest?'

By which I mean of course not an attitude of irresponsibility. As
you know, I've always claimed that you have to take responsibility
precisely for this: for how you perceive the world. What you usually
say about how you can see through your mood shifts and emotional
swings but can't do anything about them, seems to me therefore to be a
contradiction. Feelings are actions, something you choose – see Sartre.

Now I bristle again. Choose your feelings – how are you supposed to do that?

One has to be one of those over-intellectualizing professional thinkers
like you or Sartre to claim that modes of perception are something you
can choose like a hat model. By no means do I want to idealize acting
on one's feelings – 'it's good to put your passions into action' and the
like. I believe that you need to sit on your feelings if, upon intellectual
analysis, you find them inappropriate. If, for example, you find out (as
happens) that you are 'a socialist in my head but not in my heart', you
ought to sit on your heart; I thus claim the primacy of the head. But I
believe that feelings are real, as feelings, something distinct by nature
from the intellect. And if you can't understand that, then you've never
had any. In that case it's just a certain kind of intellectual phenom-
enon that you call feelings in the belief that you're talking about the
same thing as an 'emotional person'.

The fact that our relationship is humiliating is no news. But it's
when I start to doubt that humiliation is something worth striving
for – a notion that certain Christian doormat philosophers have tried
to submit to me – that I wonder if it isn't one's duty to end it.

And that you would prefer a sugar-sweet idyll is something I under-
stand, you know – who fucking wouldn't? Since I seem to have such

poor aptitude for the sugar-sweet, I'm truly sorry that I can't compensate for it with creative powers of Strindberg's class.

If our relationship isn't serious, is it then an ethical jest or an unethical one?

The following letters consist more of an exchange of information, but eventually he returns to the matter.

I've been thinking about why I believe that you shouldn't take yourself or anyone else seriously. It's probably simply that I believe that there are more positive consequences when you don't. Being with you may have transformed me into some kind of utilitarian – I realize how far I've come from doormats and potato-peeling.

Sartre's theory about emotions undeniably has its odd sides. It actually only analyses negative reactions such as fear. But I agree with him that we have responsibility for our feelings and that, in some sense, we're free to choose them. Therefore, for example, it's not an unreasonable (meaningless) command that we shall love our enemies.

I don't claim that it's possible to choose any feelings whatsoever, independent of external circumstances. But precisely because emotions are manifestations within us, we can manipulate them, in a different way than we can external circumstances. The fact that you're aware of your feelings and the reasons for them implies that you can affect them. For example, when I tell myself I'm jealous, I am thereby accepting a bunch of ideas and prejudices about what that means. Then I also see that I am neither jealous nor in love nor afraid inside: I'm the one that makes me those things.

You talk about sitting on your feelings, I about taking responsibility for them: maybe it's simply a semantic disagreement. In any case, my view doesn't at all mean that emotions should be reduced to purely intellectual phenomena. I am more in love with you than you are with me because I have decided to be that way.

'It's not just a question of saying "hallelujah"; you have to do it, too.'

This is no semantic disagreement. This is a disagreement in substance if there ever was one.

That you can sit on your feelings is one thing – you can choose to accept and cultivate or to deny and suppress your passions. But how can you positively choose feelings that you don't have? How can all the awareness in the world help in that? You can, of course, choose to ignore that and act as if you had them, but then you'll soon trip over the borderline to lies and pretence. And how do you do 'hallelujah'?

I'm brimming with eagerness to ask him, but Gustav's temporary teaching position is already over and thus our moral-philosophical correspondence. In the last letter he asks in passing if I have any objection to him visiting Eva on his way home and staying with her until Sunday.

That's when I get jealous, and I don't give a damn whether I could choose to not be and what it possibly may imply. My self-esteem is considerable, to be sure, but it doesn't prevent it from being sensitive – I won't put up with everything, and what I won't accept is being in second place. When Gustav comes home after an entire month in the north, it's into my arms he's to fall first, not any others along the way!

*

'You know very well that I would have come home directly if I'd believed you'd be standing on the platform at Central Station.'

Gustav plays surprised by my reaction, and maybe he is, in fact. I continue with my lunch, which was interrupted by the doorbell. He's standing next to the table still wearing his suede jacket.

'Why should I stand on the platform when there are others who do that so much better? I've understood that she's damned good at standing on platforms, both literally and in all other meanings.'

'That's why it's so nice with Eva – that you and she are so different.'

I munch my sandwich. He sits down on the free chair.

'But you know that you're the one I want, don't you?'

'Not at all. I know precisely how things are: what you want is a combination of her and me. You want me to be like Eva and always stand on platforms and kiss your ear and have orgies with your dinners, but I'm *not* like that, and using her as leverage won't work. Did you really think I'd be more prone to stand at Central Station when you come straight from her bed?'

'I didn't think anything in particular. I just wanted to see how she was since it seems like she's having a hard time again. And it was convenient since I was going that way anyway.'

'That way! It doesn't take more than half an hour to get there by regional train, and they go a hundred times a day. You can go anytime you like!'

'I didn't think you'd mind, and anyway, I asked you in my letter—'

'It was a rhetorical question – you weren't expecting an answer! When you called and I asked when you were coming home, you said "on Sunday, like I said in my letter", and you almost sounded annoyed that I hadn't understood it. Wouldn't you care if I did the same thing if the tables were turned?'

'That's precisely what you always do, and of course I get sad, but there's a difference because . . .'

'Because you *love* me, we've heard that before. I don't claim that it's anything but my pride that's hurt, but I claim that you should have been able to anticipate that.'

I get up to fetch my cigarettes from the bedroom. My fingers shake a bit with the match.

'Maybe I thought,' he says behind me, 'that it would only be fair if you got a taste of how it feels for once, too.'

I stand in the doorway.

'Which is it, then? Just a moment ago you thought that I wouldn't mind, and now it's because it served me right. Isn't that one explanation too many?'

'I do think my point of view is clearer than yours,' he answers calmly (oh God, his calm – if only he could get angry for once, but all he does is get sad, and I feel guilty and get more aggressive). 'I probably thought that you'd be a little annoyed, and I thought it was only right that you would, but if I had thought you'd take it so hard, I don't think I would have stayed at Eva's. Why are you all of a sudden?'

'I've accepted your relationship with Eva under the condition that you don't compare us – that's what I can't stand. You can't mix us up, you can't use her against me!'

'Do you think that you can always avoid comparing Aron and me? Don't you wish I was more like Aron in some ways? Don't you ever think, when you see him, that Gustav should be more like this?'

'Aron,' I sniff, 'I never see him.'

'Oh really,' says Gustav.

And it's an 'oh really' that makes me want to throw dishes at him, and I would if I didn't care about them.

*

Aron doesn't exactly make excuses for the long silence, but he mentions as if in passing that he stayed for a while in Gothenburg and that his kids have been sick. Since he doesn't exactly say it as an excuse, I don't have the chance to express my indulgence either, but I try to tell him without saying so that of course, you get in touch when you want to, don't think for one minute that I'm sitting by the phone pining away.

He's calling from a phone booth; there's traffic noise in the background.

'Where are you?'

'Hötorget.'

He says no more, leaving a pause for me to suggest a meeting? I think for a moment about how to say it, so I leave him every opportunity to refuse if this wasn't his reason for calling me.

'Do you need company to keep you awake?'

It works. He laughs and says 'yes please', and we agree to meet at Fridhemsplan.

I walk there; since Aron doesn't have a bicycle, it would only be in the way. I walk slowly, thinking that this is the first time in our history that we've made a date – that is, openly and mutually admitted that we wanted to see each other. Before, all we did was run into each other at different places – it could just as easily have been a for-lack-of-better relationship. I walk slowly and think that this may possibly be what I want most of all: to be on my way to a date with Aron.

At first glance, I don't see him standing at the stairs leading up from the underground – as if I had forgotten his new appearance and been caught off guard again. I don't notice him until he detaches himself from the background and walks towards me.

We wander aimlessly in the unusually mild evening, side by side with our hands in our pockets – as if we had our entire lives ahead of us. It looks relaxed, but actually it's continually tense: we have so much unsaid between us. We don't know what we are to each other, and our desperately upbeat conversational tone keeps us from finding out. Just as I'm walking along thinking about this, he declares:

'Seeing you makes me nervous.'

'Me too,' I say quickly. 'It's a pure adrenalin shock. Do you mind?'

'Maybe it's a good thing. That way you feel alert and don't get dull.'

'Quite right,' I agree (thus frittering away what could have been an introduction to some kind of clarification), 'so you stay awake.'

And so we discuss the results of the parliamentary elections instead as we wander around Kungsholmen, or rather, that part of the island where you can follow the shore: along Norr Mälarstrand with all of its old barges, over the small-boat jetties at Klara Sjö, past the huge brick complex of the city's Technical Services Office and back along Barnhusviken on walking paths under the naked willows, lit by lanterns.

Our walk ends at Alströmergatan.

Now we have more time, but not enough. He mumbles that he would like to spend the night, but the night traffic schedule sets the outer limit.

We haven't turned on the bedside lamp, but since I had turned on the ceiling light in the kitchen, there's enough to see him clearly if I don't close my eyes, and I don't – this time I keep my eyes open. I see his face on the pillow, boldly and hungrily I see how his face mirrors what he's feeling below. I see his eyes close and his mouth open, his forehead crease – expressions of pleasure and pain, so like each other. The idea that the act of lovemaking grows out of tenderness is not the whole truth. In this light falling in through the open door, I see that there's an entirely different element in it as well. Sadism is the wrong word, but it's like sadism though turned on its head: there's a joy in the thrill of control and the rush of power: to be able to do this to you!

You can talk to Gustav throughout the act – for Aron, the two pursuits seem to be mutually exclusive. In the silence afterwards, it seems that he's lying there listening, and the first thing he says is:

'Is that the underground you hear?'

It's almost not a sound, but simply a vibrating in the foundation of the building. I hardly notice it any longer since I've got used to it, but I've also wondered what it is. I don't really have a grasp of the underground's subterranean reach. It could also be the progress of a distant lorry that echoes throughout the neighbourhood. I'm listening, but I don't hear anything at this moment.

'It's just your guilty conscience,' I laugh.

'I thought your conscience was supposed to feel like a dagger to the chest, not such a muted and unarticulated grumbling.

'But I think I understand what you mean,' he says, starting to pick up his things. 'I too know how to behave myself, and I realize that hospitality has its limits.'

'Certainly in a bed of this size,' I admit. 'When it comes to sleeping, it's definitely a one-person bed.'

Since he has to go anyway, I can pretend it's just so I can get some sleep, too; I'm so strong that I can even help him to leave.

He puts on his clothes sitting on the edge of the bed, gets up and stands for a moment before the mirror, grimacing at what he sees. He walks by the dresser and helps himself to an apple from the bowl. I nod:

'Long journey ahead, best to take along provisions.'

I wrap my robe around me to follow him out into the hall. At the door he turns around, looks at me for a while and says, as if it were something that just occurred to him, and in his most teasing tone:

'One wouldn't believe it to look at you, that you're such a passionate type.'

I stand there in my hall. I stand directly across from him and feel like saying:

'I love you.'

Why do I feel like saying that just now? Is it that it would be contradicting him, shutting him up?

His statement irritates me, as such things always do. Ever since the beginning of our acquaintance, when it became apparent that he really wanted to see me as a mistress type, liberated to the point of promiscuity – me, someone who didn't know what lust was and had never had another lover besides him.

I've become more lustful, but not in general – only with him, Aron. And in any event, only half as lustful as he is: of course he's projecting himself onto me.

This is why I have the impulse to say something that would dumbfound him. Besides, I've always had a feeling that there's something nasty in those words, 'I love you'. An accusation even. I've always felt that when Gustav says it to me: something that insists, demands, gives rights. I love you (what do I get for it?). I love you (have you earned it?). I love you (do you love me just as much?).

Like that. Like an accusation, I want to throw it in his face. Of course, in affection as well – in the sense that I'm not listening to what you're saying, I don't care that it's a non sequitur because all I know in this moment is that I care so much for you.

But when I feel what else is in those words I have on my tongue, I don't say them.

'It takes two to tango,' I say. And: 'Hurry up or you'll miss your train.'

23

'I'm suffering from depression,' Cilla says.

'I'm suffering from rage,' I say.

Cilla's suffering from depression because her job is so boring. I'm suffering from rage because blokes are such jerks.

'Aron?'

'Who else.'

'No, when you say blokes, I mean. Because he's come back as if nothing happened?'

'No, not that exactly. I'm happy he did. As well he should have – imagine him moving back to Stockholm without looking me up.'

'You mean you've finally realized what a jerk he was before and you're getting upset retroactively?'

'Something like that. It was something he said when we happened to talk about our past recently. In his version of history, it seems that it was my fault that things ended in London. He claims that I was so quiet and dismissive that he thought I wanted to be left alone.'

'Isn't there some truth in that? I seem to remember that you yourself said you were reserved back then.'

'Thank God I was. I had to wrap up my feelings so that he wouldn't realize the extent of them and run for his life. It's obvious I couldn't talk to him when the only thing I could think of was how much I loved him, and that was the last thing he wanted to hear about.'

Cilla shrugs her shoulders. Doesn't she understand what I mean?

'Back then I would have humbly admitted that everything was my fault. But now, in my enlightened perspective after the fact, I realize what a formidable cad he was, since he must have understood what was going on with me.'

'If you mean that he was using you, I think that's a doubtful claim in principle. Using someone – that's never one-sided. Someone is allowing himself to be used, too. I've heard you explain that yourself in another context.'

'Of course. Back then, my only desire in life was to be used by Aron. But wouldn't it have been his duty not to accommodate it? He was big and strong and experienced, in any event bigger and stronger than I was, and no more in love with me than with anyone else. He could have done without me. It was simply convenient to have someone who volunteered wherever and however he wanted. But me? I had a fucking Passion. I was so in love with him that I was utterly insane – and don't you think it's immoral to sexually exploit a person who's mentally incompetent? Isn't that criminal?'

'In that case. If it's a question of using people who are prey to their emotions.'

It's not very hard to guess whom she's referring to.

'But Gustav is an adult,' I protest, 'I wasn't back then. He's much older and more mature, and you should be able to expect—'

'Do you mean that maturity has to do with calendar years?'

'Not exactly, but. Every person must be responsible for himself or herself – I mean – ough. What do you think I should do, then? Break up with Gustav?'

'What do you think Aron should have done?'

'Of course I don't think he should have married me or any-thing remotely like that, but he could have shown me the tiniest little bit of loyalty. He could have at least recognized me as a friend, just as valuable as a male friend – but it was never a ques-tion of that. I was just a chick to him. The fairest thing would be if he'd broken up with me long before it had got that far, as soon as he began to realize that I would screw myself up being in love with him.'

'Right.'

'What do you mean, "right"?'

'Precisely that.'

'Yeah, but it's too late for Gustav, a long time ago. And I want to have him, I've explained that a thousand times. Besides, if I broke up with Gustav, I couldn't stand having a relationship like this with Aron, either. To have a relationship like that, you have to have something to stand on.'

Cilla makes a display of coughing and choking on her coffee:

'And you,' she snorts, 'you're the one talking about being used!'

'No, right, I guess I shouldn't, then.'

I lift my feet onto the couch and cover my head with the pillow.

'Fucking Cilla. It was better to be enraged than depressed.'

'I'm sorry,' Cilla says.

*

Weeks pass between encounters. Sometimes he calls me just to talk. He asks what I'm doing and I answer that I'm reading *History of Criticism*, because I'm not really doing anything else. I ask what he's doing, and he says he's watching the kids. And so I tell him about a film I've seen and he tells me about a book he's read, and the whole time I'm wondering if he'll eventually say that he's coming into town, but this time he doesn't.

He's there anyway, I think. It's a joy simply to know this: Aron exists in this world, there's a person who's Aron, and even if I don't see him, it's a joy to think about it.

By all means, it's a qualified intellectualized joy, and you have to be able to appreciate that, but to the extent I don't, I'll just have to practise: I'll train my ability to make the most of intellectualized joys.

He's clearly eager to keep up our re-established contact in any case. He shows me more openly than ever that he cares about me. It's clearly not anything that will complicate his relationship to his family, but I shouldn't wish for that anyway, since I'm not ready to leave mine either.

Strictly speaking it's an ideal relationship, I think. Mature and balanced, capable of lasting indefinitely.

The same afternoon, Gustav calls, and we too speak in a friendly manner about neutral things. He complains that he's unemployed again and I complain about what a boring seminar I attended yesterday. We discuss our plans for the Christmas holiday and other uninfected topics, and since our conversation is going so well I take the opportunity to ask if he's heard from Eva since the last time – in blithe hubris I ask, believing that he couldn't have again.

'Oh yes, she was in town last Monday.'

'I see. And?'

'And we went out for lunch.'

'And then?'

'Then I showed her my new apartment.'

'And there . . . ?'

'Yes, there, since you ask.'

My cheerful tone catches in my throat. I feel that strange exhaustion again, and I just want to hang up and pull a blanket over my head and – nothing.

The truth, of course, is that I thought their relationship would dwindle away once he moved back to Stockholm. But that's when she moved, too, and apparently this is the way it's going to be.

I have 'nothing to say'. No: but I can feel. And it's worse to feel it when I can't say it. I feel disgust about this commingling and it's inexplicable that you can feel such deep and genuine disgust about the polygamy you're involuntarily part of, as if it ran against all of your innermost natural instincts, when the polygamy you're practising intentionally isn't unnatural at all. Gustav is Gustav and Aron is Aron, there's never a question of commingling, I know who's who and what I do with the one and with the other. But what Gustav and Eva do with each other is something I don't know. That's where I'm drawn into something I have no control over, and I can't help it that deep inside me there's a completely authentic feeling of being violated. To betray and to be betrayed – they're not the same thing!

My innermost instincts tell me to shout, 'No, now there must be an end, I won't go along with this any longer' – toss my head and once again declare the end of our sexual relationship until he breaks things off with Eva. But I have no right, not now that Aron's in the picture! Before he showed up, their relationship existed at my mercy (a fragile thread), but as things are now, I'm forced to accept it – oh, what a trap!

I have nothing to say – I simply have to chirp along on the phone as if nothing's happened. But I can't. I fall silent and allow my silence to say what I'm not allowed to say. Then he gets anxious, sad, nostalgic as usual, starts to assure me of his love and 'I didn't think'. He starts to talk on his own initiative about breaking up with her, as usual, and I bring out my martyr's halo, 'not for my sake', as usual. 'I don't want to be moralistic and disgusting,' I say, 'I want to be broad-minded and generous, and I'm not criticizing anyone, I'm not. But you know that it hurts me and you do it anyway, and I don't want to be moralistic, but you wouldn't do it if you loved me, I'm just saying, that things were different back when you loved me.'

I hate myself for being false and my anger gets turned on him. He ought to be able to hear that it's my sick conscience talking, but his own must be so sick that it deafens him. He just gets sad – he gets so sad that he swears he'll call Eva and break off his friendship with her on the spot if I don't come over and sleep with him. Then my innermost instincts command me to do so.

In the morning, there's a letter from her in the post. He says I can read it, but I decline. I'm in my generous mood. Gustav is mine and the world is secure. I'm lying in his bed in his blue-striped pyjamas reading the newspaper with the breakfast tray on my knees, and outside the December morning is as dark as night. I've slept well, I'm full and warm, and I really don't care about my husband's correspondence.

'She's having a rough time,' Gustav explains. 'John has found someone else again.'

Of course Eva's having a rough time. A husband who cheats on her and a lover who prefers his wife – I imagine myself in the situation and think she's truly not to be envied.

When I catch myself thinking this, I burst out laughing. Magnanimous Martina in action again, self-forgetful as ever: that's exactly the situation I'm in myself!

'What's so funny?' Gustav asks from the bathroom.

'It just occurred to me that Eva and I ought to have good reason to understand each other.'

*

For a long time, we've wanted to celebrate a real Christmas in the cottage: a crackling fire and the scent of fir and snow-heavy trees outside a window pane bedecked with ice crystals. But we never have a white Christmas any more – if it ever looks like a Christmas card at the Island, then it's at Easter; at Christmas it looks like shit: mud, and clouds hovering as low as the telephone wires.

Nevertheless, it's worse in the city. Once we've come out a bit by bus, something you could, with a little imagination, call a covering of snow appears, although it's as thin as a worn blanket, and not conducive to sledding even for the most creative of people. But the main thing is that we have the right feeling inside, we tell ourselves, and since we're equipped with as much Christmas food as we were able to carry and varied for every taste – prepared lutfisk and ham as well as gingerbread cookies and marzipan pigs – we live a carefree life for several days.

All of those firs we saw in the forest and imagined as Christmas trees are impossible to find now that we need them, naturally. They're either too tall or too bushy or too small or crooked. Finally we agree on one that admittedly has a hole in the back, but if we put it in the corner it won't show, and you can at least smell it – unlike the ones you buy in the city.

After dinner we exchange Christmas books and unwrap them and borrow each other's. And the fire crackles and the tree gives off its scent and the candles burn quietly, and we keep the peace with each other and, for the sake of the holy eve, with the little mice who are nibbling in the pantry.

On Christmas Day, the ground is so frozen that we can bike to church. But when we get there at eleven, it's locked and dark – there won't be any high mass. The demand is too low, of course: there aren't so many that are so pious that they don't go to the early service, I explain to an angry Gustav.

We light a votive candle for his ancestors resting in the cemetery; the flame flickers pale in the white daylight. We sit down to rest before the trip back, Gustav on our mittens spread on the ground and I on his lap, and we share a marzipan pig that I've been forethoughtful enough to stuff in my pocket.

'This is also a good old ritual,' I note, 'sitting and having a meal with the dead on a holiday.'

He laughs:

'When you're dead you're certain to prefer that people come to your grave with marzipan pigs than with votive candles and flowers.'

'I prefer to have them while living. And by the way, I don't intend to die before you, so don't worry about that.'

*

A better human? I don't think I'll ever be one. Quite the opposite. At the moment, I'm considering writing a contribution to *True Confessions*, with those blaring headlines about complicated adulteries and shocking discoveries ('I was seduced by my mother-in-law' etc.). The headline I'm imagining is, 'I didn't know how cruel I was until my husband cheated on me'.

I had been warned that Eva would be with Gustav for the weekend so I could stay out of the way. At first it didn't bother me any more than usual. I planned to go to the cinema in the evening, and I have nothing against going alone. It was when I spied Erik and Anna-Karin in front of a wallpaper shop on the way there that the first demon crept into me. Instead of pretending not to see them, as I usually do so that I don't have to stand there making small talk, I walk up to them and say hello.

I find out that they're on their way to the Lindgrens on Bragevägen and tell them that I'm going to the cinema so that they have a reason to ask if Gustav is also coming, so I have a reason to answer, with an appropriately inscrutable expression on my face, that no, he's up to something else. And so that they'll naturally mention to his parents that they ran into Martina, who was alone and looked so forlorn . . .

This insignificant little wickedness heartens me so much that later, when I'm sitting in the darkness of the cinema, I continue to play with the idea: the vision of Gustav exposed to his family and myself lifted by a wave of sympathy (obviously I don't consider the vision of myself exposed). I could go confide in Anna-Karin, <u>woman to woman</u> and in strict confidence, and she would pass it along as surely as if I had asked her to – oh yes, what delicious visions for my inner eyes while, for the hundredth time, my outer ones dully register the ads for Sanisept and Zingo soda, 'goes down good'.

This of course is only a mind game – I'm not yet mad enough to actually do anything of the kind. But thinking about it puts me in an infernally good mood, and the movie that follows, Pasolini's *Medea*, is hardly captivating, but doesn't exactly inspire kindness.

I need fresh air and take an extra loop on my bicycle, one that takes me to Hornsberg. I decide to ride past and see whether the lights are on in his windows. Three flights up, facing the street: the curtains are drawn and the lights are on. It looks so cosy and inviting, the windows illuminated. But these windows are not inviting. They shine exclusion. Inside: my husband and his mistress.

I hadn't planned this in advance, but as I stand there on the street, I get the impulse to go up and ring the doorbell. An utterly irresistible desire to make myself Unpleasant simply comes over me.

I don't want to play along any more and pretend that everything is natural and in order and between mature human beings, or to continue to keep myself at a discreet distance when required – I intend to remind them of my existence at an inappropriate moment, out of pure spite.

The front door is open.

I have the time to regret my decision and turn around many times on my way up the stairs, but I also work up my aggression step-by-step and go back up again, and with two steps up and one down, I finally arrive at his door and press the bell with my heart pounding wildly.

No reaction. I ring once again, wait, nothing happens, and I walk back down. I'm almost on the ground floor when I hear a door open and steps on the stairs. Suddenly a coward, I rush out into the street, but I fumble with my bicycle lock and don't get away before Gustav comes out of the front door.

'My book,' I say quickly, 'I needed that book I left here.'

He doesn't know what to think. He comes up and grasps my shoulders, his breath smelling of wine.

'But don't you know . . . ? What do you think Eva . . . ? What are you trying . . . ?'

He stands there helpless, saying meaningless things. I repeat that I just want the book. Finally he goes up to fetch it. My stomach hurts and my whole body is shaking. I pace the pavement. It takes several minutes before he comes back.

'Now she's sad and says she's going home. Can't you come up?'

'Absolutely not.'

I slap the book onto my luggage rack and pedal off.

'Your brother says hi,' I shout over my shoulder from a good distance.

Too upset to go home, I ride around the streets for a while – rain-wet streets, shining asphalt, snow in the air. I'm incredibly pleased with myself. I feel really, truly, properly evil: good at being evil, successful. Making myself unpleasant was my intention, and I succeeded beyond my wildest expectations. Now they're feeling awful up there – their evening ruined!

Above all I'm astonished at my initiative. I never believed I would dare to put something like that into action – exalted by energy: it was good, I tell myself in admiration. Truly, properly evil.

Then I ride home and drink a cup of hot milk to calm my stomach.

Early the next morning, Gustav comes over. Now he's angry. Yesterday he was just sad, but now he's angry and I retreat into a defensive position: What do you mean evil? Didn't I have the right to fetch my book?

'It was terribly awkward. We didn't know who was at the door. I was sitting there reading, Eva was tired and had gone to bed, and I didn't know if I should open the door. When she found out it was you, she got up and rushed to pack. She felt terrible, and you have to understand that with her guilt complex . . .'

'I can't help it if she has a guilt complex! We've met before without it bothering her. How am I supposed to know when it's permitted to show myself and when I have to pretend that I don't exist?'

'In any case, now she's gone home and decided that we won't see each other again.'

'I didn't ask her to go, I don't care about what the two of you do. I couldn't know that she'd be so upset. If I had known that, I wouldn't have come.' (There's at least one grain of truth in what I'm saying: if I had known what extreme consequences this would have, I would have reconsidered one more time.)

'But you know how sensitive she is! You can well imagine!'

'If people are so tender-hearted that they can't stand hurting other people, then maybe they should avoid getting involved in other people's relationships. It takes some nerve to expect me to be sensitive so that your mistress can tolerate your cheating on me with her.'

He leaves me dejected, my high spirits completely spoiled. Of course it was my intention to hurt them, but I didn't want my intent to be obvious.

I try to find comfort in the traditional moral belief that it's fantastical to demand that I not only accept his having other relationships but also considerately withdraw in order to facilitate them – I, the wronged one, the spouse whose rights have been violated!

Not much to comfort me – that rotten structure is creaky. And it can't speak alone, that moral. It's drowned out by others that say it's not one bit fantastical, it's simply reasonable: This isn't a question of rights – he sees and sleeps with whomever he wants, and the only healthy thing is to stay away when you're not wanted.

So I'm apparently not that healthy. The problem is that I didn't see it from the beginning. That I believed I could live up to this new generosity but only managed to go halfway – that is, not at all, but landing in pure, detestable hypocrisy: accepting their relationship in theory but in practice doing all I can to make it impossible.

If you're jealous, you have to at least admit it.

I feel like a walking failure. And not even like a great, magnificent Defeat but only the most ignoble little shortcoming.

24

At the beginning, I believed the odds of Gustav and Eva no longer seeing each other were 50/50, but it seems to be over. Of course, he hopes I'll break up with Aron in return. But for the moment, I don't know if there's anything to break up; it's been so long since I heard from him. And you can't call people just to say you don't want to see them any longer.

Particularly if you do.

We avoid the topic for now.

On one dark morning, we're awakened by the telephone – it's the substitute teacher line. Norra Latin needs a few hours of Swedish Lit. Half awake, Gustav promises to be there at nine o'clock, but he doesn't want to send me out into the mid-winter dark for that. So I stay in bed as, with a chaste kiss on my forehead, he ventures out to earn our supper.

I wake up gradually, get dressed and look for a piece of paper to write a note on, that I'm going home to work. I pull out a desk drawer and find the letter from Eva he was going to let me read a couple weeks ago. Since he offered, it's not sneaking, is it, even though it was on another occasion?

I skim through it. And I regret that I've declined to read such things before: maybe it would have been helpful. Her tone, when she mentions me, has an aggression that she's never shown in person. I realize that she's been jealous too, of course, and that I haven't been the only one to make myself out to be better than I am.

What upsets me more is that she's so well-informed about my private life: she mentions Aron. She asks whether he hasn't got in touch lately – it sounds as if he's been an excuse for them, in any case for Gustav; maybe it's something she teases him about since the whole thing is the basis for an accusation that Gustav is neglecting her. In any event, it shocks me to see Aron's name on her stationery. I know how loose Gustav's lips are and how he always keeps me up-to-date about Eva's relationships – of course he's said just as much about me to her. It's simply never occurred to me to extract a vow of silence from him. But if Eva wanted to hurt me – or Aron – suddenly all that seems possible to me, and it makes me uneasy that she knows some of his acquaintances from theatre circles.

No truly I say, once you become enmeshed in the relationships of others, it shall be avenged unto the thirteenth degree.

*

The seminars are still such that I'm dying of boredom. Indeed, I have died one thousand deaths. Every other week, one evening every other week: I enter the classroom hopeful and leave it howling in misery. This time it's a novel by Henry James on the docket. I've read it properly in advance, with pure enjoyment since it's a splendid novel.

Oh no, this is a misconception, as it turns out. For today, it's the lefties who take the floor in the discussion and explain that the art of illusion and the omniscient narrator are authoritarian tricks of a clearly fascistoid nature. And then no one dares to raise a hand and stupidly claim that they thought it was a joy to read that dangerous monstrosity.

I ride to Gustav's flat and hurl Henry James against the wall. 'You can't ever have any fun!'

'Is someone saying you can't like James?'

'Not at all. They just let you know that you're a fascist pig if you do.'

'I can't believe everyone was in agreement about that.'

'In any event they succeeded in persuading the group that he has a fascist narrative structure, and then you have to be a fascist sympathizer if you like him. You may as well shut your mouth and agree, and not try to imagine anything else.'

Gustav continues to write red numbers in the margins of a test he's grading, unmoved.

'There's nothing more annoying than lefty students!'

'Unless it's right-wing students.'

'You're not listening to what I'm saying.'

'Of course I am,' he says without looking up. 'You like James; stupid classmate says James fascist; you come home angry. Have I missed anything?'

'No, you've summarized it well. Aren't I right?'

'You're always right, aren't you?' Gustav says, flipping to the next test in the pile.

I pick up Henry James and put him in the bookshelf.

*

Just as I've ploughed through the literature course and started to prepare to call the professor to get an appointment for my test, the newspapers arrive with headlines about the strike of the academic employees' union. I enquire at the department, and it's true: my professor is out of service.

What am I supposed to do now? Starting to write feels uncomfortable – my brain can't hold a limitless amount of stuff at one time, and now it feels as if what I've already read will start to tumble out if I try to put anything else in. I'll have to play solitaire until the conflict is resolved.

When Aron calls, I take the opportunity to ask him about

this strike, because I don't understand it – I understand that high earners want higher salaries, but not why the left-leaning parties are supporting them. Aron explains, but I still don't understand. Strikes aren't ends in and of themselves, are they? Wage-earner power? 'Yes, but these are state employees, we're the ones who are their employers, you and I, Aron. It's our money they want!'

But it's not Aron's money, because he's never had a taxable income, and besides, he says that this is Social-Democratic propaganda.

I go see Gustav – he's landed at Norra Latin for the spring and it's not a regular position; he's not a union member. So he's working despite the strike, but ought to know about it since he has it on his doorstep. I ask if he's for or against it; he answers on the one hand this, on the other hand that.

Then I go out and buy *New Day* to get clarification on this issue. I return shaken.

'The Socialists aren't in favour of the strike at all!'

'No, who said they were?'

'*Aftonbladet*!'

'Do you believe everything you read in the evening papers?'

'I just didn't think they'd print bald-face lies about things that are so easy to check.'

I don't understand that tactic at all. Just as little as I understand Aron's communists.

*

The Island's peaceful days are over. The neighbouring house that's stood empty since the old woman died has now been invaded by a family with a horse-age girl and a moped-age boy. They mill around at the edges of my field of vision and transform the view from the window: it bothers me.

What's even worse is that the municipality is constructing a recreational village just five miles away: the roads will be paved, the country grocer will become a grocery chain store and the entire Island will vibrate with the rattle of mopeds.

If you want more countryside peace, you have to go there when it's not a weekend or a school holiday. But Gustav only has time off when it's a weekend or a school holiday. I chide him for having become something as useless as a teacher – there are jobs that don't prevent you from getting away. Why doesn't he have one?

'Like what?'

'Well the ones they call the free professions – author, artist, critic, whichever you like.'

'If I could get away, you'd never have any peace. Be glad that I'm out of the way when I'm at work.'

In reality, that's not what I'm complaining about but rather that I'm envious – envious that he has a job that he enjoys. A place to go to, colleagues, a context to which he belongs. My studies feel so meaningless.

I go out for a few days on my own to seek solace in nature, and find, as I do every time to my surprise, that it *is* a solace. We didn't have a winter worth its name this year, but even during this monotonously grey season, the landscape is so unexpectedly full of nuances. There are no kinds of weather that aren't preferable in the country. Even the night sky is eventful when you dash over the hill to the outhouse – clouds chasing each other and many more stars than back home. Or if you wake up before dawn since the room is too warm and smells of kerosene, you can open the window and get to see the moon rise yellow above the forest before slowly paling in the blue and pink of dawn – nothing like that happens in the city. It isn't until noon that it grows grey again, but the clouds are still a spectacle. You can lie watching them for an eternity.

You lie on your back on the dock and look up at the clouds and hear the ice melting.

*

'Am I bothering you?' Per-Erik asks on the phone.

'Not at all. I'm just sitting here playing solitaire, waiting for my professor to stop striking.'

He's clearly not prepared his next remark. There's a little pause and I make helpful conversation:

'It's been a while.'

It has, in fact: he's quit studying and has been working for a newspaper for six months. Now he's on his way to eat dinner, he manages to say, and was suddenly struck by such a need for company. He wonders if it's a possibility.

It's an excellent possibility. Gustav will be working on an old stack of tests he has to finish by Monday so he doesn't get lynched by his pupils.

We decide on a Chinese restaurant on Rörstrandsgatan, eat deep-fried shrimp and gossip about classmates. I tell him that the seminars are just as hopeless as before, which he doesn't understand. He thought they were so stimulating. What he really wanted to do was to continue and get his doctorate. Now he's going to have an academic complex – everyone at his workplace does.

I delight to hear this since I have a paid-work complex; I'd love to hear him expand on the topic.

'Isn't it rather scary to be involved in journalism?' I prompt him.

'There's a difference between journalism and journalism,' he answers quickly (so quickly that I get the impression that he's answered this question many times before). 'I could never stand to work for an evening paper, never mind a weekly. But working for a trade newspaper is something completely different.'

'Is it fulfilling?'

'That's probably not exactly what it's about – are graduate studies fulfilling, do you think?'

'The reading courses have been rather boring to get through, but writing will be a little more fulfilling, I hope. At least it's a creative activity. The biggest drawback to being a student, I think, is that you're so isolated socially. You never see people in normal ways.'

He looks as though he's wondering if I think that conversation at a table in a Chinese restaurant is an abnormal form (which is precisely what I mean), then he says that he's going to a conference next week which will end with a gala dinner at the Opera Cellar, and he can bring a Date along. And he wonders if it's a possibility.

'The Opera Cellar,' I say dreamily, 'I've never been there. But I should probably ask Gustav first.'

'Gustav?'

'My boyfriend.'

He doesn't even make an attempt to hide his astonishment, his opinion about how inappropriate it is that I'm sitting here if I have a boyfriend. You hear about girls who go out dancing and are scolded by disappointed partners when it turns out that they're not at all free for the night but are simply there because it's fun to dance – but I never imagined there were any false promises in having dinner with a former classmate. Per-Erik, however, does.

'And what do you think he's up to tonight, then?' he asks coldly. 'On a Saturday night.'

What does he mean, Saturday night? I become confused – I hadn't imagined there was something special about Saturdays. It's this social isolation, of course, in which weekdays and holidays flow into each other. Maybe it truly is stranger to see another person on a Saturday in particular? But Gustav's conception of all this must be just as poor as mine, despite his honest work, because he didn't have any reservations about it.

'He's home grading tests.'

'And you believe that?'

He laughs so loudly that the next table turns around to look, but now I'm angry too. 'Yes, I do,' I say, and don't continue the discussion.

Per-Erik beckons to the waitress and asks for the check, and the Opera Cellar isn't mentioned again.

I go over to Gustav's because I'm so angry that I have to tell him this stupid story, and to make sure that I'm not the crazy one. He's happily surprised to see me since I hadn't said I was coming, and he snorts reassuringly at Per-Erik's reaction: people have so many strange ideas, and you never know who has which ones.

We go to bed on the best of terms, and suddenly I start to giggle.

'You know what? If Per-Erik knew that I was here now, he'd believe that it was because I wanted to check to see whether you really were sitting home grading tests after he'd succeeded in sowing doubts in my mind. Do you think I came because of that?'

'No, but maybe it was!'

'I didn't think about that until just now. No, my darling, I trust you unconditionally. I trust you unconditionally that you'll let me know when you're cheating on me.'

★

Sometimes I suspect that I only function as a safety valve for Aron: when his bourgeois family life becomes too suffocating for him, he comes to me so he can breathe for a while.

This could be considered humiliating if my hunch weren't based on a close parallel. This is exactly how Aron functions for me: it's true that the old prescription of a lover to renew one's marriage functions precisely this way. It's not because of any technical discoveries in the erotic field, but simply because I no longer have to feel so captive and forced together with Gustav. Even if I don't see Aron more than now and again with months in between, the mere thought of him is a breathing hole. And as it turns out, that's all I need. I have too weak a libido to live with one man, but with two it seems to work.

Thus if Gustav is contributing to my ability to handle my entirely too insecure relationship with Aron, and, on the other hand, Aron is just as actively contributing to the reverse, then you could believe that they even each other out. From my perspective in any event. For a while it seems to me as if our marriage has experienced a second life: now that it's gone through these most recent crises and convulsions, and survived them, it seems we'll be able to continue for ever.

But this peace turns out to be deceptive. It requires that we not talk about it.

One afternoon I help Gustav repaint his kitchen. I take the dishes out of the cupboards and catch sight of a set of drinking glasses Eva gave him for his birthday. At the same time it occurs to me that he's wearing the jumper Barbro made him a long time ago, and I can't resist a cheerfully teasing comment about 'all of your mistresses'.

'Thus far, there are fewer than most,' he says dismissively – and my ears perk up and my mouth asks before I have time to consider:

'What do you mean, are there more than before? Have you . . . now again?'

And once the question's been asked, it's answered. Oh yes, a girl who was standing in for the secretary at school.

I have to set down the paint can I had just picked up. I haven't the strength to hold it in my hand.

'Was that necessary?'

'You can't expect me to be faithful when you're not.'

'I don't expect anything. It's just that I didn't think . . . Why did you break up with Eva, then? Wouldn't it have been better to just continue with that?'

'For you, maybe. Do you choose your lovers with what's best for me in mind?'

I take my coat and leave. I simply cannot. Gustav thinks I'm unreasonable and can't understand why I'm taking it so hard. I can't explain.

I don't expect anything. I just can't be in the same room with a man who cheats on me with women from his workplace.

I thought that the main seat of the feelings was the stomach, but jealousy seems to sit in the arms too: such a weakness that my arms just want to hang limply and I have to go home and lie on my bed.

The phone rings; I unplug it.

I read, I don't eat, I sleep. I plug the phone back in the next morning and call Gustav.

'I was just starting to wonder,' he says. 'How long you'd keep licking your wounds.'

'I never want to see you again.'

'I see. Shall I come up so we can discuss things?'

'I'm not joking.'

'I'm not either, but there are a few practical matters associated with a divorce, aren't there?'

I sigh. 'OK, come over, then.'

Before we've had time to start settling our matters, while we're still standing glaring at each other, the doorbell rings: Cilla wants company for lunch and is happily surprised to find the two of us.

I fumble in my pocket for a cigarette (what do non-smokers do when things are awkward?), Gustav makes the same motion at the exact same time, we look at each other and a certain effort is required not to burst out laughing.

We can't stand there explaining that we were just about to divorce – you could lose your appetite for less. And I would spare my friends any family arguments. We go out and have a Sunday dinner at Hörnan with untroubled conversation since Cilla has no idea that there's anything to be troubled about.

25

It's so lovely to be free and easy. It's lovely to have complete disregard for pretence and prestige, to not pretend you're any better than you are, and instead to allow yourself to appear exactly as you do when you're alone.

It's lovely, but it's not healthy. It's as if you were so free and easy that you went around farting at will out in public – that doesn't create a healthy atmosphere. The phrase is 'ruthlessly honest' when papers report on celebrities speaking out – it's a good phrase. Indiscriminate honesty is ruthless and it depends on the need of the speaker to be open, but it doesn't take into consideration how those hearing it will receive it.

I actually don't know how it came about that Gustav and I, from the very beginning, had such a lack of modesty between us that we could discuss things I'd never talked to anyone about before – from our masturbation habits and our digestive processes to intimacy with respect to our inner lives. When we later began to acquire erotic experiences with other people, it was just the same, and it's been quite interesting to be able to make comparisons.

But as a matter of fact, we've always hurt each other with our candour. The fact that this binds people to each other is no new discovery, of course. Neither of us holds a grudge really, not in the sense that we go around dwelling on offences once they've grown old. But the general feeling of hurt lasts, the feeling of having been injured – and the fixation on it that makes you not want to let go.

This is, as we know, how Strindbergian marriages always develop. Just less inspiring in reality than those of the literary titan.

I thought that our agreement to answer questions but not talk about other relationships without being asked to would be the ideal solution. So that doesn't work, either. No, it would have been a momentous discovery if it had been that simple: if a solution to the problem of infidelity existed, someone in the entire history of the world would probably have thought it up before us.

It doesn't work because it's impossible to keep from asking about even those things we don't want to know. And worse: because those things that sometimes don't seem too difficult to handle can suddenly, at other times, become intolerable.

There's so much we've been able to talk about with joyful and even arrogant delight in being able to Talk To Each Other About Everything. But something that's been said isn't 'gone'. It lies and festers at the bottom of your soul, and if your relationship later becomes poisoned by something else, it can bubble up like swamp gas. What were once intimate confessions that I was happy to get to hear, and happy I could handle hearing, I suddenly begin to turn and twist, full of suspicion: Did you say seven times one night? How do you count them, then – the *times*?

Or what he said about how my pussy is more backwards than others – was that a *criticism*? Is it better if your pussy *isn't* so backwards?

Boys worrying about their organs is a classic theme, of course (easy to read in advice columns as never before: Is it too small? Is it too crooked? Can I ever make a woman happy?). Girls probably worry just as much about not being the way one should be. In any case, it must be easier for males to find material to compare with – they just have to go to the city pool. But how am I supposed to get any perspective on my anatomy unless I ask a man with some experience? And who can I turn to who won't laugh at me? Gustav, of course, laughs at me, but it doesn't matter. It didn't matter, at that time, back when we compared our experiences in confidence and in trust.

Nowadays, I have the feeling that everything I say will be used against me.

*

Aron wants someone to go to the cinema with and I cancel a date with Cilla to be available. This of course goes against my principles – ever since I was twelve, I've been irritated by how girls drop whatever they're doing, including plans with friends, when a man expresses interest – but I excuse myself with the thought that if I saw Cilla as rarely as I do Aron, and she was the one who popped up unexpectedly, I'd cancel plans with Aron.

We see the film about the miners' strike, *Comrades, the Enemy is Well-Organized*. It makes him happy; it makes me despondent. Seeing that people can't handle power, not even the small amount of power needed to be elected representative for your striking comrades: within a few moments, they've been corrupted by the view from above and start to believe that the notion of trustees is that those elected should be able to trust their voters.

I feel distraught, anarchistic and distraught. I don't understand how Aron can feel uplifted by the same film, full of trust in the deepest ranks of the common man. That optimism – I don't understand where it comes from.

It may be that he has better prior knowledge than I do about the events in the iron ore fields. He has a book on the topic at home and invites me to come home with him and borrow it.

'Are there etchings in it?'

'Unfortunately not, but it has photographs at least.'

'Your family?'

'Coast is clear.'

The explanation comes later that Florence is in England for a week or two. She's taken the youngest with her, but he has to go home to take care of the other one.

Älvsjö is quite far away – regional train and bus – and I start to wonder how I'm going to get home again, or if he's planned to have me sleep over.

It's a standard flat in a standardly boring block of flats. It's furnished with rattan armchairs and large foam rubber sofas; at least we won't have to invade the marital bed. That's a relief. The boy isn't sleeping yet, but he's in his pyjamas, and Aron puts him to bed once he's said hello to me and said goodbye to the babysitter.

I look at the strike book. I look at the pictures for a long time and I'm surprised.

'The people don't look glamorous at all here. Why's that?'

'Did you think they did in the film?'

'Oh yes, it was the mythical Worker. Here they just look like your average Joe. Is it the seductive power of film that makes the difference?'

'It can be the mood of the observer as well,' Aron says and pours a splash of coffee that the babysitter's left in the thermos bottle.

Well, I guess it can be the observer's ideologically split personality: Power to the people, but screw the grey masses.

'Speaking of strikes, what do you say about the resolution of the academic workers' strike now, and Parliament forcing everyone back to work?'

'That was well done.'

'You don't mean that that's what the government wanted from the start, do you?'

'Can you explain the agency's conduct in any other way?'

I can't. But his world view makes me cold with fear. Was everything simply staged through sly calculation?

'Do you really still have any illusions about the Social Democrats?'

'I don't know about illusions. Basically, they have a good pro-gramme, don't they?'

He smiles gently.

'No, it's true,' I admit, 'they've essentially waived all the principles there are.'

'The only principle they don't seem to be prepared to waive is staying in power.'

I still can't refute him. I just don't understand how he can be an optimist about the future with the world view he has. Even Gustav's laughing pessimism seems less contradictory to me.

I'm not very happy about sleeping under his roof, either, but it's clearly what he has in mind.

'And the kid?' I have to ask as he starts to remove my clothes.

'Which kid?'

'The boy, if he gets up and wants a glass of water.' (That's what children in comics always do, the only ones I know.)

'He's eight. He can get his own water.'

'You know what I mean. If he asks his mother why you were lying on the sofa with some lady?'

'Pooh,' Aron says.

That can cover everything from the kid doesn't usually wake up to that his wife doesn't care if ladies lie on the sofas, or that he doesn't care if his wife cares. In any event, he doesn't elabor-ate, and then I drop it – it's none of my business.

In any event, I make sure to leave before the boy wakes up in the morning. I won't meddle in how Aron and his wife arrange matters, but all I know is that if I were eight years old, I would hate waking up with strange ladies in the house when my mother was gone.

*

Is it just growing older that makes the world go faster and faster, or is there actually something about the rotation of the earth that astronomers haven't yet discovered? Another summer is on its way. Gustav is going sailing, of course, but I hesitantly introduce the idea of something else – why not a bike tour?

Once he's had the chance to get used to the idea for a few weeks, he becomes enthusiastic about it. We spend several of these blissful evenings in May studying maps and catalogues from youth hostels, and finally decide on Öland.

We also peruse old photo albums from the family library. One of the nice things about a bike tour is that you feel such community throughout the millennia, with your parents' generation out pedalling in the thirties, on tall, robust bicycles with number plates. In the pictures, they pose before them wearing wonderfully unflattering clothing. We imagine how our descendants will sit looking at us in yellowing photographs in forty years and become mildly nostalgic.

We bring our bicycles to the shop for greasing, buy panniers and baskets and rain gear. As soon as school is out, we want to be on our way, but Gustav has to get the boat into the water first, since this is his only chance to get any help with it. My meagre bodily strength would be a poor contribution here, so I stay home, pack our bags and read up on Öland in the guide book.

Just before nine o'clock in the evening, Gustav calls from the hospital. The boat slipped off its trailer halfway into the water, and in the attempt to keep it from tipping, he slipped and sprained his foot, or maybe it's broken – he hasn't been seen yet. In any case there apparently won't be any bicycling, at least not this year.

I sit down and burst into tears.

'How can you be so fucking clumsy?'

'I didn't do it on purpose,' he answers patiently. 'I think it's awful too.'

'Couldn't that fucking boat have stayed on land until we got back?'

'I've already explained that I can't launch it alone. Now it's in the water anyway, and I can sail with one leg, too. We'll see, in a week or so maybe we can have a sail.'

'I don't want to sail! I want to bike!'

'Then you'll have to bike alone.'

'When are you planning on getting examined?'

'When they come for me. I imagine I'll have to stay here overnight at least, since it's so late. Come and place your cool hands on my brow.'

'What fucking hospital is it?'

'Danderyd.'

'That's so *far*!'

'Never mind. If you're in that kind of mood, there's no need.'

'Does it hurt?' I ask angrily (even more angry when I realize that this is what I should have asked in the first place).

'Oh yes.'

'OK, I may as well go for a bike tour if that's the only one I'm going to get.'

It takes quite a while to find him in the huge complex although he told me where he was as well as he could. I find him in a rather sparsely occupied waiting room with a pile of the hospital's dog-eared magazines. He doesn't look like he's dying, but his ankle is very swollen.

'You didn't bring anything to eat, did you?'

'You didn't say anything about that.'

'Can you go downstairs and buy something, then? There must be a refreshment stand at the entrance, or at least a vending machine.'

Finding it, and finding my way back, takes about half an hour, but the situation is unchanged when I return. Gustav eats the apple and biscuits while I pace and grumble about how inadequate the healthcare system is here in Sweden. I can't stand seeing him sitting there, patient as a lamb.

'Now how about those cool hands?' he wonders, wiping biscuit crumbs from the corners of his mouth.

'There aren't any – I'm a sweaty mess.'

'From running back and forth taking care of me, you mean.'

'From exasperation. How can you be so meek? It makes me mad. Can't you swear a little? Just a little?'

'Will that make things any better?'

'It would make me feel better. Didn't you even swear when it happened?'

He laughs. 'I think I started to say some naughty word when the trailer slipped, but then I didn't have a chance to say much at all.'

'OH DICK, right? That's the worst expletive you know!'

A grey-haired lady with her arm in a sling looks up at me. I sink down on the bench and snatch up the closest magazine.

'Well, I'm just quoting,' I mumble and hide my face behind a naked woman.

After almost another hour, Gustav is called. He tells me I should go home. I've hardly got through my door when he calls again: They're sending him home with a support bandage and some painkillers. They'll help him to the taxi, but from the taxi up the stairs to his flat, he needs me so he doesn't have to trouble the driver.

'Aren't they even giving you any crutches?'

'I think you can rent them – I'll have to check tomorrow.'

I take a deep breath, but he pre-empts me. 'I don't need any more opinions about the Swedish healthcare system just now. I need someone who will help me get home. Are you coming or should I call and frighten my old parents?'

'Of course I'm coming,' I hiss.

*

Early summer, intense blue sky, the sun pours down – my mood is at the freezing point. Firstly, I'm grieving the cancelled trip. Secondly, I'm suffering from guilt because I'm such an execrable egotist that I'm thinking about myself first. Somewhere in third place is my sympathy for Gustav, not so much about the accident – which he continues to bear with philosophical equanimity – but rather because he has to put up with me, too.

He, if anyone, deserves a gentle wife who sits at his bedside and reads aloud – well, he can read himself, that's about all he can do, but who sits embroidering, then, and cheers him up with her bright chirping, darts in and out with delightful little snacks on trays, puffs up his pillows and arranges flowers in vases. What he doesn't deserve is someone biting her nails out of impatience at being shut inside in the city during the summer's most beautiful weather and who paces the room swearing about the fact that military expenditures are allowed to swallow up tax money that would be better used for the healthcare system.

'Why don't you go to a real doctor and have X-rays taken?'

'The one I had was so nice, and it only cost seven crowns. Well organized, don't you think?'

'But you can afford to go to a private physician!'

'I can, yes. But what about others?'

'Loyal unto death, right? You could get gangrene or whatever, or it might heal wrong and you'll be an invalid!'

'There's no shame in that. Can't you love a man with a peg leg?'

'Don't joke about such things. I think health is important. Your stoicism gives me a rash.'

'Why don't you go to the Island so I can have a little peace and quiet here?'

'Oh that would look great. What do you think your family would say if I went out and lounged about at your summer place while you lie here helpless?'

'No, I understand that this is the only thing keeping you from doing that.'

'What else am I supposed to do? Since your mother comes over twice a day with her cool hands and meat casseroles, you can't claim that you need me.'

'Then go, I've said. Go take a bike tour if you don't dare go to the Island. You can invite someone else along.'

'You mean it?'

'I can't understand why you wouldn't do it.'

'Two fingers on the Bible and you promise to repeat that if others ask?'

He laughs.

'You're detestable. But you can go tomorrow if you sleep here tonight.'

'Fornication in a sickbed! Have you no sense of decency? Don't you know that suffering ennobles you so that you don't think about such things?'

'On the contrary – I have nothing else to do. The critical parts of my body are actually intact. It's my foot that hurts.'

'What do you mean, critical? Aren't feet critical?'

'I know you would have liked it better if it had been . . .'

'Darling. I think all of you is critical. But now I'm going to go call Harriet and ask if she wants to come along and ride.'

Harriet wants to come along, but it takes a while before she can arrange for her ex to take care of their child; bringing a two-year-old along is something neither she nor I finds desirable. We leave at the last minute, the final week before industrial holidays break out and all the ferries will burst at the seams with tourists. We ride around Gotland instead – all the energy I'd spent on grieving the trip to Öland would have been wasted otherwise, and everything I had planned together with Gustav so sad.

Gotland smells like seaweed and sheep and roses, is completely flat and made for riding a bicycle. But Fårö is such that you almost don't dare to talk about it – otherwise it'll disappear. Cliffs. Grass. Here and there a wind-tortured pine tree. Sheep and grey boulders impossible to distinguish. And the sea. And the horizon. And the occasional wind-tortured cyclist.

Harriet refuses to talk about it. In Sudersand she simply slumps down in a wind-protected hollow in a sand dune with a view of the sea, and I can't get her up again. I keep biking alone on paths that are ever more crooked, ever stonier, ever more private. When I've got lost, I knock on a door and an old man with snus in his beard stubble gets up from his sofa and says something that may as well have been a foreign tongue. But he follows me out behind his house and points. I ride in that direction and after a couple of hours, I get back to the main road and find Harriet's sand dune.

I write metres of letters. Harriet teases me when she sees me with paper and pen: 'Your guilty conscience in action again?'

'Isn't that appropriate?' I ask. 'Don't I have reason to feel guilty?'

'Well,' says Harriet, 'what would you think if you were the one lying in bed and he had left on a trip?'

I think about it. But I swallow my answer.

He wouldn't have.

★

When I get back to the city, Gustav is hopping around on crutches with his plastered foot. The Swedish healthcare system has no plans for it for a couple of weeks, so we decide to make our way to the Island and succeed in begging transport by car from the steamboat with a summer neighbour.

As long as Gustav is disabled, it falls to me to take care of practical matters. I fetch water and wood, I bike to the country grocer, I bail the boat, run back and forth to the food cellar, set the table, clear the table, pick up. It's less of a burden than it may sound since it's offset by the relief of avoiding discussions about who's doing what – not least of all the never-verbalized discussion, the silent struggle. He can handle cooking and doing the dishes, but we take turns without any problems in normal cases anyway – that's easy to handle. It's all the other stuff, the irregular and what's too minor to even talk about but has to be done anyway at some point stuff. Borderline cases: Does the task of doing the dishes include wiping the crumbs off the table (something we both tend to skip since it's so monumentally boring)? Is it the task of the person making the beds to hang up clothing that's been strewn about, or is that to be assigned to the private sector? Not doing something can be a rebuke: that's your business, not mine. Doing it can also be one: I'll have to since you never.

Now I perform all of these chores as something self-evident, and I realize that there were advantages to the old gender roles.

Perhaps I'm the one who's been struggling in silence since Gustav, as the sloppier of the two of us, doesn't see what I see. Things not being in their place doesn't irritate a person for whom things have no special place, and if they don't, you can't put them away, either.

But he sees the difference now that I've allowed my sense for order completely free rein and determine places for his things as well (I realize that it's simply tact or face-saving that's kept me from doing it before). He kids me, but he's forced to acknowledge how rational it is. Every time there's something he needs – the light metre for the camera, for example, a thing that he'd normally spend fifteen minutes looking for all through the whole house – instead he has to ask me. 'On the upper shelf in the hall closet, far left,' I answer quickly: and that's where it is.

It's beautiful revenge for all the times he's teased me about my pathological neatness, my habit of not simply kicking off my shoes any which way and then having to crawl under the bed to find one that's disappeared, but rather placing them side by side under my chair with my clothes over the back of it (undeniably like an illustration from an ABC book), or my way of stowing trash systematically in paper bags instead of simply dropping it – so I minimize my trips to the trash cans.

I'm pedantic as a result of impatience: I think life is too short to spend time looking for things you've misplaced or wasting more time than absolutely necessary on routine, life-sustaining tasks.

Everything in its place and Gustav in his armchair: that's very time-saving.

26

I'm not getting a grant for the coming year – there are far too many people competing for one. Student loans are available, but I already have as much debt as I want, and I'm faced with the need to find some way to make a living.

After my experiences with the publisher, I know that I don't like jobs in general. Things being the way they are, I may as well choose one that doesn't pretend to be meaningful or pleasant so that I don't fall prey to self-reproach over not being able to appreciate it. Besides, an intellectual occupation wouldn't work well with writing my dissertation. I think it would be nice to rake in a cemetery or deliver the post: I could be outdoors and think as I worked.

But the employment agency naturally has no such jobs on offer. When I mention the post office, the employment agent suggests the Postal Savings Bank. But that's more of a bank than a post office, isn't it? I know nothing about accounting, but the agent laughs: it's pure routine work – checking deposits and withdrawals, ticking off lines in columns.

It seems guaranteed to be soulless and unpleasant.

When I see the premises where I'll work, I'm almost ready to back out nevertheless: an office landscape, devoid of vegetation, row on row bathed in fluorescent light. I have to supplement my reasoning with a touch of ideology as well: the idea that it's good to take on crappy jobs in order to understand those who always live with them, and the idea that it's educational to try out something that's completely foreign – contradictory ideas to be sure, but I suppose I'll have to fall back on them alternatingly as needed.

The first day is exciting: learning how everything works, getting to know the girls around me (only girls) during the coffee breaks, running out for lunch and feeling at one with humanity, with all the others who are out during the lunch rush downtown. The second day is like the first although it's no longer exciting. The third day is like the second. After a week of working I realize that I haven't done anything besides work for the whole week and I'm struck by terror: is this what life is supposed to be like?

Gustav reminds me about how educational it is to have practical experience. 'Really,' I say. 'It's so educational that if I continued there I'd stay at the level of a twenty-five-year-old my entire life.'

But in other respects it works: I understand the common wage worker better. I understand, for example, that Saturday is something special. Saturdays are something very, very special, and I not only feel at one with the people for whom Saturday is a day off – I feel a violent need to make something of these weekends in freedom, live all the life I didn't live during the week.

Gustav still has the sailboat in the water and has recovered enough to be able to use it. Admittedly, there's a north wind and it's cold on Saturday morning, but that's all the better: I want the raging elements around me, cold and deprivations and terrors, anything, as long as I know that I'm alive.

*

Getting up at seven o'clock every morning and dashing off. Back home at half-five and crying because the day is over. The daily routine.

I used to look askance at people who had jobs – now it's those who don't who stand out to me: schoolchildren and students I see walking around on the street. They don't know how privileged they are, they don't have the sense to appreciate it – they haven't earned it! I look at them with hateful envy, these reminders of a past existence – remove them from my sight!

I've stopped going to seminars, since I don't have the time to prepare for them anyway, and then it's meaningless to attend. After a month the professor calls to find out what the status of my doctorate is.

First I'm flattered in the belief that I've been missed and answer as if he were an admirer I needed to keep on the line – that oh yes, it's true that I haven't produced much in the way of tangible results, I don't have any new drafts to present, but I have my plans, naturally I'm going around thinking about my dissertation the whole time (a Jesuitical lie, because I am not thinking of it other than to think sometimes about how I never think about it).

Then I finally realize that he only needs to know for the purpose of statistics, for departmental planning of advisers and teaching resources. That's when I tell him how it is: at the present time I'm completely preoccupied with earning a living, but I plan to return to the academy next term, dead or alive.

How do people who work full-time have time for anything else? For having a family life, for example. A child? Incomprehensible.

I don't even have time for a lover. Aron – when am I supposed to see him? Before I could easily see him during working hours, but he's almost never free in the evenings, in any event not when I am. On this point it's actually never happened that his and Gustav's wishes for my company have ever collided, and now that they do, I have no idea how to handle it.

This week I had told Gustav that Tuesday evening maybe, we could be in touch. I'd just got home, cried a little cry, washed up and put the kettle on the hob when the phone rang and I lifted the receiver to argue: I've asked you not to call right when I get home, before I've had a chance to recover from work. But it was Aron. He happened to have the evening free and wondered if I . . .

What do you do then? If I tell Gustav something's come up, he'll ask what, and if I answer, he'll be intolerably upset (so upset that I can't tolerate it, that is); my husband does know that I'm cheating on him, but not exactly when and how. Every bit of concrete information about it hurts him, and I can't demand that he accept being set aside point-blank. If I say no to Aron for his sake, on the other hand, I'll be so cross at Gustav forcing me to do so that I won't be able to see him, either.

I'm too soft-hearted for a double life. I could prioritize Aron in the same way as I was when I was choosing him over Cilla, but this is so much more sensitive. It's not just Gustav who would perceive it as a rank ordering – I would do so myself. I blankly refuse to compare or choose between them, a principle that isn't one of theoretical justice for the sake of principle, but a spontaneous need. It's a requirement if I'm to put up with bigamy.

But the result, in practice, ends up being celibacy. The only way out is to impartially and without fear or favour say no to both of them: 'Listen, I'm so tired tonight, can't we say another day, Friday?' or 'Saturday?' and then make sure that Aron doesn't call when Gustav is here, because then he'll get so upset . . .

Administering my private life takes up all the time left to me after work. It isn't enough for *having* a private life, only sitting on the phone administering it.

★

'So you think this is a way to work towards the revolution?' I tease Mikael when I find out he's returned to Stockholm and is now working at a day-care centre. He answers calmly 'yes', and of course it's one of the most constructive ways imaginable. It's just that I have to tease everyone who has a sensible job.

'How about you? Are you working towards it yourself these days?'

'I actually spent an entire Saturday last week with the *Women's Bulletin*, if you can count that,' I answer, exuberant with false modesty.

'What did you write about?'

'I didn't write anything, good heavens. I worked with my hands. Running dittos, collating, stapling. Volunteer work is stimulating now and again, although your back gets tired.

'Otherwise,' I admit, 'I usually think that I can't do anything about world problems until I've got my own private life in order. But it's strange that the more time I spend on that, the messier it gets.'

Mikael tells me that he's in the process of putting his own in order by forming a commune and wonders if I want to join. I'm happy that he's asked me, that he's had the idea of asking me, but I'm surprised that he can think it's a good idea. If a family of two is already too much for me, how would I manage one of seven or eight? Would it make anything less messy?

'The point is that two is too small,' he explains. 'You wear less on each other if there are more of you.'

'Do you get your own room?'

'There are two rooms for couples and three perfect for singles, and a common living room and kitchen and so on.'

So if Gustav came along, we'd get a room together. But we need one for him and one for me and one to have our domestic fights in – how would we find enough room in a commune? And if he stayed in his flat so we could continue to have our

sex lives and our fights there, I would only be living in the commune half the time, and that probably wouldn't work.

'Are you planning to share the running of the household?'

'Of course. That's almost the best part of the arrangement.
We take turns cooking dinner. You only have to think about
food once a week.'

Thinking of food once a week – as if that were an improvement. And for seven people! My shoulders slump when I try to
imagine it.

'And a bunch of horrible little kids, too?'

'One so far, there may be more. Don't you like children?'

'Not really. When they start to become human, five-six years
old or so. I admit, one-year-olds can be adorable to look at, but
I prefer to look at them from a distance.'

We agree that I'm probably not suited to commune life, but
he invites me to come visit sometime.

*

Is the autumn always this beautiful? I must have never looked
so carefully. The supernatural clarity of the air and leaf-gold in
careless abundance – I breathe it in greedily, as if each day were
my last.

And it is, for the most part: every day I can be outside and
breathe it in is the last one, because the next day is a work day.
Having a job thus has at least one advantage: you learn to pay
better attention and to take advantage of every minute. It's an
enhanced feeling of life, as among people who lived waiting for
the Black Death. Revels – that's what I want, revels with nature.
Before, I almost never made it to the Island in the fall when we
were able to go anytime we wanted to. Now that we're only
free on weekends, we go almost every week.

And there's no end to how much you feel at one with humanity when you're sitting in a traffic jam.

So that I don't become utterly stultified, I try to make my

everyday life mentally snug with literature. I get up at six in the morning so I have the time to read a short story or a chapter before I leave. In the evening I dive in again: novels, thick novels, novel series in eight volumes is what I want to gird myself with. I've even discovered an application for poetry, something I've never used before: during coffee breaks you only have time to read a page or two at most, and reading narrative text in this manner is too fragmented. But a poem is just right. I keep a small booklet of Baudelaire at work and consume food for the mind with my coffee without paying any attention to the derision of my peers; I'm not going to stay at this job very long anyway.

Like waiting for the Black Death, or like sitting in jail: you learn to make better use of those sources of joy that are available, and a small flower outside the cell window or a patch of sky can move me to tears.

There are no flowers at window-height on Drottninggatan, but one day my eyes catch sight of something sky-blue. It's a suit. A corduroy suit of Nehru cut. It's worn by a boy who has his office in a corridor outside the large office premises where I work but who sometimes walks through the room – something blue flashes in my field of vision. I learn to register it with my peripheral vision as soon as he walks through the door, and I can follow his entire path. I become accustomed to waiting for it and already smiling as I wait, anticipating.

A Nehru-clad, long-haired boy – a deviation in this environment.

When I carefully enquire of my colleagues – laying aside Baudelaire and joining the gang in the break room to learn about the subject – it turns out, quite rightly, that he's generally considered to be an oddball. 'Philosophical,' says one girl, 'daft,' says another. Then they tease me about him, as it says in those girls' books. I turn red and they're delighted: Martina is showing some human qualities!

Is this the most effective means for combating mental death? My existence seems full of meaning. I hum on my way to work in the morning darkness and only come home satisfied if the day has not been without its sky-blue streak.

I'm ashamed. I'm an adult! And I'm one who not only has a functioning weekend marriage but also an extra relationship for my free time. Do I really need to look for a crush at my workplace as well?

'It's probably a sign that you're alive,' Harriet says casually when I complain about how ashamed I am of my propensities.

Well, I wonder if it isn't quite the opposite: the very expression of mental death. It feels rather revenant-like.

'It seems as if I'm a child all over again. Why do I keep *looking* when I already have what I need? I thought people grew out of such things when they became sensible adults.'

'The question,' says Harriet, 'is when you'll grow out of the belief that you're going to grow out of anything.'

*

You see more of your girlfriends when they're without a man. Cilla is having such a period again. Sometimes she calls me or stops by in the evening to talk about our jobs and affairs.

'It was smart of you to pick that kind of obviously boring job,' she thinks. 'Mine sounded like it would be fun, but that means my disillusion is that much worse. I have too little to do all the time. It breaks you down to be underemployed.'

'I guess I have enough to do, but that's also the only positive aspect of it. To be honest, I believed it would be so grossly, supernaturally boring that it would transcend and take on a kind of boredom-glamour. But it didn't. It's just boring, just booooooring.'

'Well, you've learned something, haven't you? About the conditions of wage earners at least, like you said.'

'That's true. I've come to the conclusion that one should have more affairs.'

'Ough, no. I've just come to the realization that I've had too many. I sat down and thought about it the other day, but when I got to twenty I didn't dare count any further.'

Twenty! It's going to take me sixty years if I continue at this pace. And who will want me then?

'The worst thing is that so many of them were one-night stands, pure and simple. Or the kind that wilt and die within a week.'

'I have the opposite problem – that they're so abnormally perennial. I'll have to do some pruning if I want room for any new ones.'

Not that I think quantity is anything to aspire to – hunting for scalps has always seemed neurotic to me. But I start to wonder if what I'm doing isn't just as unhealthy: a stable double life, spiced up with a dozen half-physical crushes. I wonder if it isn't both healthier and more appropriate to simply have affairs with the people you want to have affairs with instead of refraining from doing so and spending the rest of your life regretting it. For example, maybe I should seduce Mikael while I still can.

I don't think I would have got to twenty even if I'd taken advantage of the opportunities – there aren't an adequate number of men that I like enough. But it's precisely because I'm starting to realize how few there are that I would really like to have an affair with that it seems all the more urgent to make the best of them.

Cilla is wandering restlessly in my room, from the couch to the window and back again, back and forth. She stops with her back towards me and, facing the window, as if she were talking to the passers-by on the street, she says:

'I want to get married now. It's time. Sowing wild oats isn't any fun.'

'It's no fun having it gathered into your barn, either,' I point out quietly. 'And if life is supposed to be this boring, you need some kind of compensation.'

'I think wild oats is a stage you have to get through, but it's probably best to have it behind you before you settle down, not the other way around.'

She leans against the windowsill and looks at me; I stare back.

'You don't have to fan the flames of my guilty conscience, thank you. Gustav does such a good job of that himself.'

'Oh, does he really? I thought he was determined to blame himself.'

'Not at all. That is, there's a contradiction to it. Sometimes he plays the role of victim of an incurable love, with whom I'm supposed to have empathy, but other times he talks about duties that he's taken on voluntarily, and which should thus be met with an effort from my side. In either case, the sum total is that it's my fault that he's unhappy.'

She shakes her head – an impatient little twist: that's not what she meant, of course, she's always claimed that you have responsibility for your own life. I think so too, but when he presents it like that it's hard to know where his responsibility ends and mine begins.

'Recently he's developed the bad habit of making me responsible for everything, and I don't know how much he means it seriously.'

'What do you mean, everything?'

'That his life has become the way it is. All the changes he's gone through since he met me, that he's changed his moral philosophy and that he dresses differently – do you remember what he looked like back then, wearing a tie and a hat! But it's fashion that's changed. Now he'd be wearing jeans and clogs anyway, even if I hadn't supported such a development. But he experiences it as being my influence, or he pretends to do so. To tie me to the crime.'

'The problem is simply that you were too young when you met, I think.'

'Wonderful!' I cry. 'Wonderful to have such clear-sighted friends who can tell you what the problem is! Can you also enlighten me as to what we can do about it now? We can't meet for the first time again, at a mature age, as if we'd never seen each other before.'

She admits that her ability to solve problems is weaker than her analytical acumen, and we part ways without having solved our respective situations. We've simply illuminated each other's by contrast, but we probably both feel we wouldn't want to trade places with each other.

★

'You shouldn't leave your diary lying around like that,' Gustav says.

I'm standing at the kitchen counter washing the dinner dishes. I turn around slowly and feel like I'm in a film, a bad Swedish film about relationship problems where the director's instructions say that the wife turns around slowly with a close-up of her face. I don't want to be in that kind of film.

'What do you mean? Have you read it in secret? When?'

'A while ago. Well, it was a couple of times.'

'Why did you do that? *Why?*'

'You never tell me anything. I wanted to know what you were thinking.'

'Nothing was in there that you don't already know!'

There can't be. Nowadays, my diary is nothing more than a pocket calendar that truly doesn't hold anything more than the most basic of information. I use it both as a calendar for reminders ahead of time and for an accounting of what's already taken place, and I only reveal my inner life in a very abbreviated manner. Such as 'Isl w G. Boat in rain. Period' or 'Dent. 2:30. C here, w to w. Read Kristin Lavr.' Or 'Disc w M abt comm – should I? Sem 7:15'. The most common entry is 'A didn't call', but that's no secret for Gustav either.

'You can ask if there's something you want to know. I'll answer, but if you don't ask, I'm not going to say anything that I'm not sure you want to hear. I thought we had that agreement, didn't we?'

He shrugs his shoulders. I hang up the towel I was using as an apron, sit down and light a cigarette (the whole time with the dreadful feeling of following a hopelessly untalented screen-writer's stage directions).

'What did you expect to find? "Oh how I love Gustav" on every page? I stopped writing that kind of diary when I became an adult.'

This hurts him, and of course it was an unnecessary comment. I get mean because I'm scared. What shocks me isn't so much what he may have read in my diary, it's that he's done so at all – that he's stooped this low.

It never occurred to me that he'd look at my calendar, because it's sitting out in the open – I know other people who would have done so out of pure curiosity, and in that kind of company I would have naturally put it away. People who have healthy self-respect don't do things like that. It's a question of their own integrity. It would never even occur to Aron, for example, to even think of . . .

No, don't compare him to Aron.

Would I do it? It's happened – in vulnerable and desperate situations, in my younger days, I've snuck a peek at other people's papers – but I didn't know that Gustav was so vulnerable and desperate. A crime of passion is what it's called, and it scares me silly. Who knows what he's capable of then?

And what can I do about it, other than carry my calendar everywhere I go from now on?

'You're not in love with me,' he complains.

'No, but it doesn't bother me. It wouldn't bother me if you didn't nag me about it all the time.'

'Why aren't you?'

'I can't fall in love on command. You're the one who claims that a passion is something you decide on. Go ahead and do it since you can: decide to stop being in love with me, and then we can have the world's best marriage of convenience afterwards.'

'I'm trying, but I can't. You're the one I love. That's simply the way it is. There are others who make me just as randy, but there's nobody I like having sex with more, because it's you.'

'That's simply infantile imprinting,' I say helpfully. 'Like the duckling and the shoebox. I'm simply your shoebox, because I was your first woman. You have to get over such things.'

He snorts. 'Speak for yourself. If anyone's a shoebox for someone, then Aron is for you.'

'Maybe so. He was my first man: that's a completely correct parallel. We all have our infantile behaviours.'

'And he's the one you're in love with.'

'Not at all. No more than with anyone else.'

'Why can't you stop seeing him, then?'

'I probably could, purely theoretically. It's just that it would be intolerable in the final analysis, since I'd never forgive you for it.'

'I stopped seeing Eva for your sake.'

'And you've never forgiven me for it.'

'You're using me,' he complains. 'You use my inferior position the whole time.'

'I don't know how to avoid it as long as you allow yourself to be used. But I've never wanted you to become dependent on me. On the contrary: I appeal to you to get up and stand on your own two feet!'

He's on his knees by my chair with his arms around my waist and his head in my lap, repeating like a charm:

'I love you.'

'That's not my fault.'

27

The day is clear and cold; when I go out to the street during my lunch break, I stop in my tracks and see a piece of sky in an opening between the buildings, and I burst out laughing when I realize what it is I'm seeing: I'm looking at a suit-blue sky.

So easily conditioned then, that I'm already reacting with joy like a good little Pavlovian dog when I see the colour itself, and the world is so topsy-turvy that it's the sky that's as blue as a corduroy suit. I would love to tell him about it.

While I'm still standing there on the pavement, he comes out the front door. It looks silly to be standing there laughing out loud, so I tell him that I'm laughing because the sky is as blue as his suit, convinced that he won't believe me.

He listens, peers up into the clear fall sky, and says, 'It's as blue as longing. Are you going to eat lunch?'

I am indeed, so we go together to Tempo's lunch bar.

The girls were right that he's a strange fellow. He speaks fluently but with jumps in association that I can't follow – about faces on the street, a book he's read, being a vegetarian, which he apparently is – all of it in quick chunks. Now and then he looks deep into my eyes. I look deep into his eyes, not knowing what else to do, and quietly wonder if he is truly insane.

He has beautiful eyes in any case, grey-blue in colour and with turned-down corners that give him a strangely melancholy aspect. When he pauses, I try to make conversation about work, and I wonder clumsily if he likes his job.

'I'm only a high-school graduate,' he answers.

So what? Do you have to just take what's offered? Is the luxury of hating your job one that only academics can indulge in? Or does he mean that he likes it because he's never had any higher ambitions? An answer worthy of an oracle.

When we pass the Look Cinema on our way back to work, he asks if I've seen *Carnal Knowledge*. He pronounces it wrong, <u>knowledge</u> as in <u>know</u>. I can't bring myself to correct him and get embarrassed, as if he's said something dirty, and angry at myself, this bashfulness in displaying one's education. In any case, I have seen it, and he has too (so it was clearly not an overture to inviting me to the movies). That is, when he starts to recap the plot, I become uncertain about whether we've seen the same movie. In his version, the point of the film was 'which is worse – to love or to be loved'.

I sit and think about it all afternoon among my piles of forms and columns of numbers, but no matter how I reconstruct it for myself and how I imagine what experiences can lie behind such an interpretation, I can't comprehend what he means. I can't come up with any other film about it, either. They're about love, the films and the books, about loving – but I can't call to mind any art whatsoever that deals with being loved.

And which is worse?

*

Harriet has a new apartment and invites us to a house-warming.

'Shall I bring my husband?' I ask.

'Of course. Oh yes – which of them, by the way?'

'What does it matter?' Cilla laughs, 'bring them all!'

And Harriet goofs around, 'Help! Where will I find that many dishes?'

Of course. Just because you're such an uncommonly faithful

type, you're immediately portrayed as some kind of Messalina. It's not that I've had any more men than anyone else – I've had a shorter list than my friends can imagine. It's just that those I have attain such sentimental value that I can never get rid of any, and so here I am.

'You pull your past behind you like a toy train on a string,' Harriet says, 'one coach after another. It's bound to get cumbersome after a while.'

'I like knowing where I have them. Rather than leaving a pile of discarded wrecks along the roadways.'

'It's bad form not to break up with one lover when you take on a new one,' says man-eater Cilla, who disapproves of bigamy.

'Why? If I choose them with some care, they'll keep for several seasons. As far as I know, by the way, the one-night-stand model isn't considered all that well-mannered either.'

'As usual, you have to insist on your own model,' Harriet seconds. 'Oligogamy?'

When I talk about my husband I mean Gustav of course, but as it happens, he's busy – he's taking his class to the City Theatre. So when Aron turns out to be available, I take him along instead as a demonstration. In several senses, literal as well: they're curious about him after hearing me talk about him for years, and he's not the worst person to show off.

He's a gifted interlocutor – he instantly starts to talk to a workmate of Harriet's, sitting closest to us at the table and unknown to us, with an ease that I envy. He relates stories from an institution where he worked temporarily as a guard: tragicomic anecdotes about conflicts of loyalty.

New sides of him appear, social sides that I had entirely forgotten he possessed since we virtually never socialize with other people. It's enjoyable to do so. It's enjoyable to be in company 'together with Aron', to almost be a couple with him. They say 'you two' to us, as you do with those who belong together: 'so nice that the two of you came', 'do you two want to ride with us – we're going in that direction anyway'.

That direction is only mine, to be sure, but Aron has time to come back to my flat for a bit before he has to go home. That's also lovely: being alone with him and hearing him express satisfaction with the evening: 'damned nice buddies you have'.

I'm as proud as if I had invented them myself. The fact that the feeling was mutual is something I had already heard from Harriet as we carried the dishes into the kitchen. I'm proud and happy to be able to offer them to each other.

But I wonder: why is it that being a part of a couple around others – one of the things I can tolerate the least with Gustav – is so fun with Aron? Is it simply because we're not really a couple, because it's just make-believe?

★

After a couple of hours of sleep, I'm awakened by the phone and Gustav's morning-cheerful voice.

'I came close yesterday.'

'Came close to what?' I ask, sleepily disoriented.

'To cheating on you. One of the girls lived in the same direction as me. She was so lonely and depressed, she said, and when we had walked around the block a few times, I felt I may as well go upstairs with her when she asked me to.'

'I see. And did she have shameful intentions?'

'I suppose she did. She lives with her mother, but she brought me into her bedroom and offered me a glass of wine . . .'

'Oh yes, you can definitely assume so, then. I don't understand young people these days. Her own teacher!'

'But I didn't give in.'

'I certainly hope not. You have to have some sense of decency if they don't. School girls – I think that's the limit.'

'It's the evening high school – she's not much younger than you are. And by the way, I've already assigned grades, so she wouldn't have got anything for it. But I thought since you haven't cheated on me lately, then I shouldn't either. Or have you?'

I just can't. His peppy morning mood, his casual tone – if I answered truthfully, he'd become quiet and unhappy. All he knows is that I was at Harriet's last night and thinks it's been a long time since I last saw Aron. He knows that I see him some-times, but he naturally hopes that each time is the last, and each time he's confronted by it anew, it hurts him just as badly – I know myself, of course I know how it feels! It would destroy his day, and it would destroy my own happy sense of well-being from yesterday. I simply cannot.

'Not since last time with Aron,' I answer.

It's a Jesuit lie, and he comprehends it as I intend: not since last time he heard that I had seen him. It's a lie, it's a false answer to his question, and I've thus broken the only agreement we have.

Another time, I excuse myself. I'll confess another time when it's not so fresh and not in such an awkward context.

But this is no solution. There is no solution. When he was the only unfaithful one, I wasn't generous enough to handle it in the long run. When we were mutually unfaithful, the depend-encies became unbearably complicated. Marital monogamy almost made me impotent. And being unilaterally unfaithful: this is something I cannot take responsibility for. What's left?

*

A notice in the paper says that Mikael has died in an avalanche in the mountains.

My first reaction is irritation. What the hell was he doing in the mountains this time of year? To go and die like that, before you've even reached the age of thirty – was that really necessary?

Then slowly the realization of what that means. That Mikael is gone. That I'll never see him again.

And a corrosive grief: that I didn't make the most of our

friendship, I didn't stay in touch with him while he was around –
I never even went to see him in his new home. And I never had
an affair with him. That's ridiculous, of course, but it seems I
would mourn him less if I didn't also have to mourn the lover I
never had in him. Mikael: one of the finest, most direct people
I've ever met. Even his death seems to be fitting in a macabre
way: The Mountain took him.

'I could stand at his grave and say that it was an honour to
have known him,' I explain to Gustav, sobbing.

He observes me sobbing for Mikael silently. Maybe he
believes that I'm idolizing him because he's dead, but I've always
done so. Maybe he perceives my crying as a reproach: that he
was the one standing in the way of our socializing. That's not
how it was, I know. It was the other way around: the time when
Gustav wasn't standing in my way was when I began to withdraw from Mikael. But I'm not claiming it's his fault, either. I'm
just lamenting.

★

The second month is like the first, and the third will surely be
no different. Getting up in the dark, sitting for eight hours at a
desk by fluorescent light, home in the dark, and small glimpses
of blue the only interruption in the monotony. I'm earning a
living, but nothing more.

I can't avoid becoming dull. My relationship with Gustav
has always been based on our ability to talk to each other – but
what happens when you have nothing to talk about? I refrain
from sharing the details of my crushes with him uninvited, and
what's left when we're not dwelling on ourselves and our relationship? Do we have anything at all in common any longer? I
make an attempt to look at what he's reading, but all he has is
a *Journal of Philosophy* and a book on sailing, and I get nothing
from either of them. His second subject, Swedish literature, is
something he actually despises. Teaching that course these days

involves everything on heaven and earth, but no literature to any noteworthy extent. Besides, as far as literature goes, he only finds it worthwhile to read Dostoevsky and a couple of others.

I loan him a novel by Saul Bellow that I liked; he reads it but has only criticisms as commentary, and I'm hurt, entirely unreasonably hurt. I'm gripped by a panic of loneliness when I can't count on his sharing my opinions, and so in pure desperation I argue my own points *in absurdum* and start to disagree with him in a kind of lust for revenge.

One fine day I catch myself defending the Marxist-structuralists who are ruling the roost in a literary journal solely because Gustav dismisses them as lunatics – there's no one else who could drive me to do something like that – and my arguments become hopelessly weak since they're only based on the principle of opposition. Having discussions with him is also irritating because of the pedantic tone he uses – is this an occupational deformity beginning to appear, or has he in fact always sounded this way?

'Don't you have any nice colleagues you can invite home sometime?' I ask. 'I never meet any new people – the world has grown so small.' The thought seems to have never occurred to him, and he can't think of anyone. He's lost contact with his friend from high school, and besides his term at the teaching college, he's actually never had any circle of acquaintances except for his love affairs. He's not really reclusive, maybe two-clusive: if he has just one other person around, he seems completely satisfied, and he usually makes sure he does.

Gustav's love for the human race is beginning to seem extremely theoretical to me – I start to surprise myself using such words as 'cynicism' and 'arrogance' in connection with him. There's a sense of superiority in him based more on distance than indulgence. Has he always been this way? Or am I discovering it just now, feeling that his contempt is also focused on me?

My need for new acquaintances and exterior stimulation,

my restlessness and my habit of gaining contacts by exploiting erotic tension – he doesn't understand it, and no matter how frivolously we joke about it, I suddenly find his lack of understanding hurtful.

My self-esteem and his have balanced out against each other, but I'm starting to think that mine's the one that's losing. He's tortured by the fact that I don't love him the way he loves me, but it tortures him as something incomprehensible: not for one moment does his conviction waiver that he justifiably ought to be the object of my passion. That he would be if only I wanted him to be. That the fault lies with me. He's so adamantly convinced of it that it undermines me.

He himself notes that he's become mean and started to say things intended to hurt me. He notices it, but he explains that it's because he's unhappy. And that's my fault: I'm also guilty of Gustav's faults. Everything is my fault.

And my guilt naturally makes me even more unbalanced. I'm not only hurt by his cruelty towards me but also by every word he says, and I defend myself by opposing everything. I even go to the bookstore and buy a pile of recently published books to see if there isn't something worth reading, but I can't find anything that I dare bring to him as an argument. There are books that you can read, but none that I dare claim he would have more joy from than reading *The Brothers Karamazov* for the seventeenth time. I have to resort to the other escape route and maintain that the comparison is ridiculous – contemporary literature has its own value – but I fail to explain how a worse book can be better than the best ones, and become angry that I've allowed myself to be tricked into the discussion again. Why am I supposed to defend modern writers? It can't be my fault that Dostoevsky is unsurpassed, can it?

That, anyway, cannot be my fault.

★

Just as I'm about to drag myself to a seminar, Aron calls. He suggests that we go to the cinema instead, and if he hadn't suggested it himself, I might have gone. But when he takes on the tempter role, my work ethic digs in its heels. Or my sense of self-preservation: I have to make a good impression on the professor if I'm to have any chance of getting the grant I need, and the bare minimum required is showing up for class now and again – even if I can't help reading the newspaper under the table.

I ask him to call later if he's still in town, and he says maybe, if it doesn't go too late.

The seminar goes on half an hour longer than normal. Every time I believe the discussion has ended and get up from my chair, another person raises their hand again. Finally, I decide that I may as well go on the dole and get up, followed to the door by the stares of my classmates.

I throw myself on my bike and pedal home against all the red lights, worried that he'll already have given up, believing that I preferred going out with my classmates for a post-seminar: a possibility that I couldn't resist mentioning to him. But Aron calls, and ten minutes later he's at my door.

He sinks down on my couch and asks if I have anything to drink. I have a bottle of wine, not because he usually asks for some, but because it's my own conditioning, given how much of that substance socializing with Aron required back then. It's a contact association when I see a liquor-store sign: Aron, I think, and go in to buy a bottle.

'I've got troubles,' he says.

I settle down expectantly into the pose of Tell me, can I do anything for you.

'The youngest is sick again,' he tells me, 'violent attacks of fever. No one understands why.'

'Children always have fevers – people know that much about children if they know nothing else.'

'Nice to hear,' he grimaces. 'And we've been given notice on our flat. We have a second-hand contract and now the guy wants to move back in.'

'The Housing Association has a special queue for urgent cases. Something will turn up – they can't just throw people out on the street.'

But he's taken the problems in reverse order of importance, as if he's getting through my reasons not to worry before he comes to the main issue:

'And we're pregnant again.'

Before I can respond, he lays out the catastrophe in all its breadth:

'Florence is losing her job since she's a temporary employee. No job, no home, and a population explosion. We'll probably have to set up a tent on the outskirts of town and send the kids out to beg.'

'What are we paying taxes for if not to allow people like you to live off public welfare?'

I pour him another glass of wine and fill my pipe thoughtfully. If I've ever envied his woman, I don't now. If there's something mixed in with my sympathy, it's *schadenfreude*. The thought that this will have to be too much for him, too great a burden, and once she's borne him ten children and is old and worn out prematurely, then he'll leave her and come to me, as I'll still be young and free . . .

That he won't do, of course. Their problems will probably simply bind them more tightly together, and the fact that she's a foreigner makes his responsibility weigh even more heavily: he can't simply abandon a woman with a whole flock of children in a strange land. Precisely this aspect of our rivalry, her handicap I mean, has sometimes annoyed me as unfair, I wish less than ever to be in her place.

Young and free: this is how I feel sitting on my couch. Without

a baby in my belly, I can draw deep puffs from my pipe. I'm satisfied being the person I am for Aron: a breathing hole, someone he
can come to and tell his woes. Not attached to any requirements
or duties, simply to enjoyment, films and books, conversation
and sex, free and carefree contact – the pure pleasure principle
personified. (I'm more accustomed to feeling like the displeas-
ure principle personified for Gustav: it's a much more dismal
sensation.)

He's lying stretched out with his head in my lap, his eyes
closed. The alarm clock on my dresser ticks through our silence.
We slowly empty our glasses.

When he leaves, he asks me for a subway ticket, broke as he
is. He leaves without our having had sex, and I'm happy: that
this isn't the only thing that draws him here, that it can be like
this, too.

Then I'm even happier when he changes his mind: a goodbye
embrace in the door, a goodbye kiss, he starts to laugh and asks
if we can't after all . . .

Happy that he can imagine not having sex with me, and
happy that he can't resist.

It's only three steps to the bed. I don't reject Aron without
a valid reason. As seldom as I see him, I almost always want
him. It can never be a duty with him, nor prostitution, because
I don't gain anything from it.

*

*When it comes to her, I believe neither in the desire of the flesh nor
in the incurable loneliness of the soul. When she strokes your hair
and caresses the hands of all the interesting men she meets, both at
home and in public, she's not driven by any true sensuality, but only by
the flirtatious need of her soul for company. She was born a hetaera,
without desire, but with a sentimental disposition, and in charming
mourning apparel, she will place white lilies on the coffins of all her
lovers.*

Otto von Zweigbergk about the main character in Hjalmar Söderberg's play *Gertrud*. I don't show it to Gustav.

*

Is it New Year's Eve again? The passing of time is less cause to celebrate than ever before. Quite the opposite: it's beginning to seriously bother me. I'll be having my midlife crisis any day now.

'What will you cook up when you're thirty?' Gustav asks. 'Will you have your menopausal crisis then?'

'It's not the future that tortures me. It's the fact that time passes so quickly now that it's New Year's Eve once a week. And that you collect so much past to fret about – ever more wasted opportunities.'

'Is there something special you regret in your life?'

I think about it.

'I regret a number of affairs I never had.'

Since I've quit the bank as of the holiday and Gustav's sadness can no longer spoil my joy about the blue Nehru boy, I tell him about it, simply to make concrete what I mean: it's not that I was in love with him, but it's an example of someone I could have had an affair with under different circumstances.

Gustav becomes just as jealous as if it were an actual infidelity I was confessing and not a missed one. And now that he already is, I use the opportunity to tell him I've seen Aron too, so that it's said.

I know how it feels, I know it's a reflex to start talking about divorce. Even so, I become impatient when he does.

'It's not possible for us to divorce. Haven't you given up hope on that account yet?'

'Of course we can if we're in agreement. We'll have to develop a strategy.'

All right, if he insists, I won't stand in the way. We try to agree on a method – not too abrupt to begin with. We've learned this – that just leads to nostalgia and immediate regret. We'll have to try to glide away from each other slowly and carefully. See each other now and again, but without commitments.

The season is right: a spring divorce ought to have better conditions for lasting (as it would have been best to enter into marriage in the autumn, if that had been what we'd decided to do). If we get through the spring and summer without a relapse, then there may be prospects for success.

We return each other's front-door keys as a first step. It feels empty not having his on my keychain any longer, but it's a relief to have mine back: he's never misused it by coming uninvited, but it's happened that he's threatened to do so, and a man who misappropriates the diaries of others could be capable of anything imaginable.

We don't talk about divorcing as friends. We don't believe in it. It could work if you already *were* friends, without being in love and without aggression. But you can't *become* friends by divorcing. It's something you may be able to start doing later, after a long-term quarantine.

What we're hoping is that we can divorce at all.

And in a renewed decision to glide apart, we fall asleep in each other's arms while the New Year's Eve fireworks echo off the building walls outside, sometimes at a distance, sometimes nearby in the neighbourhood, culminating at midnight and then at ever-increasing intervals.

28

In reports on graduate studies, the degree of study activity as of the 15th day of February shall be indicated. With respect to the calculation of the degree of activity, the Swedish Higher Education Authority states the following in its instructions: the degree of activity for students at the doctoral level who are not full-time students shall be the relationship between the standard time and the expected study time, both for the remaining portion of the doctoral studies, expressed as a percentage.

Each doctoral candidate shall be allocated a tutorial account. The total balance of this account is 100% x 3 during the entire study period. The calculation shall be made on the basis of the SHEA's frame rate. At the beginning of each academic year, the doctoral candidate shall make a withdrawal. This nominal withdrawal shall be charged against the doctoral candidate's account as a deduction. Should the actual withdrawal deviate from the nominal withdrawal, we must ignore this for the sake of record keeping.

Oh free studies! Oh spacious heights of the halls of knowledge!

This is what I encounter when I reunite with my alma mater, burning with research zeal, in the triumphant belief that I would escape further involvement with accounts, withdrawals and credit balances.

I make my way down into the very cellar of knowledge, to the stuffy vault of Sumlen Café, and settle in its deepest corner with a cup of coffee and a magazine.

★

'You again,' Gustav says when I call.

'Well yes, it's me. Were you expecting someone else?'

'We're supposed to be divorcing.'

'I thought we were going to drift away from each other, not shoot off immediately.'

'Of course. I'm just trying to note that we're drifting. Have you begun to take advantage of all your opportunities now?'

'What opportunities?'

'The ones I forced you to miss out on. Are you having any new affairs?'

'I don't have time for that. I have to take care of my affairs with the department so that my account at one hundred per cent times three doesn't melt away through nominal withdrawals so I'm left with empty pockets.'

'What are you babbling about? Has that bank job taken over your brain?'

'Not mine. It's FUB 69: doctoral studies according to the 1969 regulations for graduate studies, with the degree of activity indicated as a percentage. Any day now they'll be installing a punch clock. Do you?'

'Do I what?'

'Have any new affairs.'

'Are you interested?'

This is the warning signal: Stop and enter this area at your own risk. You might hear things that you'd rather not. Or it could also be a diversion to arouse my curiosity. I never know. So I always have to ask.

Indeed, he does have a new affair, and when he's told me about it, I have to improve my status by saying I don't need any new ones because I'm so happy with Aron (I'm not missing you any more than you're missing me); And So On. We goad each other on through curiosity and jealousy and status, and there is no question of parting as friends. We'll wind up bitter enemies before we've drifted far enough from each other that we can let go.

★

Finally something that looks like winter: a delightful snow-storm towards evening, the streets impassable (for cars; people could ski on them). I pull my hood over my head and stride out into the blizzard, the willow trees along the Karlberg Canal disappearing in white smoke.

I love this climate: the absurdity that humans live in it, build cities in it. It's such an unlovable country, and you can feel so generous and magnanimous when you love it all the same. You can walk the streets with the snow whipping your face and smile at it: 'Haha, don't try anything with me – I love this place on earth all the same!'

I fret about my life when I think of it as 'my life', with its lost opportunities, but on a day-to-day level, I like it. Of the forms of existence that I've tried, this is the one that feels closest to ideal: go outdoors and walk, inside and write, outdoors and walk, inside and write.

I can sense that there will come a day when I get stuck and suddenly not one more word will come out of my pen – not to mention the horrific day when I've finished writing, and I'm standing there having to figure out something to do again. But that's far away and the future doesn't bother me. I'm still just working on drafts; I don't know if it'll be a beginning or an end or a middle, or perhaps nothing more than working material. For the time being, I'm simply writing to get the flow going. And to have something to show the professor so I can apply for a scholarship.

★

The phone. I fumble for my watch, quarter past eight already? No, the face is upside down; it's quarter to two. Who's calling at this hour? There's either been an accident or it's Aron, I have time to think as I try to find a voice to answer with.

It's Aron. He's been clipping film together with a few buddies all evening, and they hit the pub afterwards, and then he just didn't feel like going home – he explains and leaves it to me to make a suggestion. I take the hint and ask, 'How long will it take you to get here?'

'Maybe ten minutes.'

'Then I'll go down and unlock the door at five minutes to two.'

I sit in bed and smile in the darkness. Aron, that error (a bad joke I can permit myself when nobody is listening.) Stumbling in from the pub in the middle of the night – oh yes, now I recognize him.

When I think about it, I don't believe that my enjoyment of this kind of caddish behaviour is a function of masochism. The nice thing is rather that it puts me in a position of moral superiority: Aron doesn't do anything for my sake, and when he sees me it's out of pure egoism, because he wants to, and that's nice to know. If I don't want to, I can simply say no; if I want to, I'll say yes and get to feel generous and great-hearted and pleasant.

There's probably no point in getting dressed, so I stick my feet in my clogs and put my jacket on over my nightgown. I still feel cold as I stand there with bare legs in the draughty stairway. He takes ten minutes longer than he was supposed to, and a neighbour passing by looks at me with an expression that doesn't exactly warm me either.

'If this becomes a habit, I'll have to give you a key to the front door,' I mutter when he finally emerges from the night in a burst of winter chill. (An extra key that I don't need.)

He doesn't seem particularly enamoured of the thought.

'There's so much symbolism in keys. It's so awkward the day you have to give them back.'

'Why give it back?' I say. 'Throw it in the sea when we're through.'

Maybe he means other symbols as well – that he doesn't want any implication at all that it's habitual. I didn't think he attached that much importance to symbols as such; as for me, I try to avoid it. I try to deny that this is a kind of manifestation of a rank order that I refuse to acknowledge: I only give keys to people I trust, and Gustav is someone I can no longer trust. Aron may be a cad from the perspective of common etiquette, but he would never misuse a key, never want to create awkward situations, never even think of it.

'No,' says an inner voice: 'because he doesn't Love me.'

'That's true,' I answer it: 'because it's only the Love of Your Life that inspires you to evil deeds, the only one that drives people to desperation and makes them impossible to have anything to do with.'

'You again,' I say when Gustav calls.

'Am I calling at a bad time?'

'Not at all. I was just thinking of calling you.'

'Oh really? What about?'

'A place in this text I don't know what to do with in my classification system. I need some good advice. What did you want?'

'I also need good advice. Shall we trade?'

'Well, no. My advice is better, of course, so you'll have to add something. A dinner, for example?'

'I see. You've not eaten since last time, I suppose.'

'There are hot-dog stands.'

'Strange that you don't get any fatter since you live on hot dogs and chocolate.'

'You have no idea how fat I am nowadays.'

He doesn't, but he'd like to see. I'm the same as always, and he is too, and once we've eaten dinner in Gustav's kitchen and discussed my text problems, we go to bed, just the same as we always are.

It's not until afterwards that I remember that he needed advice as well. When I ask him, he mumbles something into the pillow, something that sounds to me like 'it doesn't matter'.

'You've lured me here under false pretences,' I say and turn to face him with my chin in my hand, 'so now you'll have to speak up.'

He sighs and pushes the blanket down to shoulder height, turning his face towards me.

'I think I may be pregnant.'

'With whom?'

'Susanne, the one at the evening high school I told you about before.'

'But *Gustav*! Didn't I tell you – that's bloody *immoral*! Your own pupil!'

'She was the one who,' he moans. 'I didn't want to at all, but she just showed up here, came in the door and started taking off her clothes. What was I supposed to do?'

'Apparently you're the one who's always being seduced, huh?'

'It's not as easy to avoid as you might think. You can't just say "no thank you, I don't feel like it".'

'You can say that you have syphilis, then. Don't you have any imagination at all?'

'I don't lie as well as you do.'

'Couldn't you at least have used a candy wrapper?'

'She said she was on the Pill.'

Laugh or cry? My *schadenfreude* isn't straightforward. I'm happy to wish him all the shame, the scandal it would cause – I would love to see the eyes of his family members widen with horror.

But I don't wish the baby on him. If anyone is going to bear Gustav's children, it'll be me. I don't want this to happen.

'How sure is she? Has she had a test done?'

'Yes, it was negative, but apparently it's too soon. Now she's several weeks late. And she admitted that she hadn't been careful with her pills.'

'Young man, were you born yesterday? Timing and missing periods are nothing to count on if you've taken the Pill, and even less so if you've been careless with it.'

'But what if she is? What am I going to do?'

'Does she want a baby?'

'If I marry her.'

'And if you don't?'

'She wants to get an abortion because she can't deal with it alone, she says.'

'Does she know what you think about abortion?'

He moans.

'We've discussed it in class, and I don't hide what I think about it personally if someone asks.'

'I see. Now all that's missing is for you to say that she's an ugly and neurotic little girl who has problems communicating and an inferiority complex who doesn't know what she wants to be when she grows up, and the picture is complete.'

'She's not exactly ugly, but the rest is basically true. Why? You probably think it's all a smart trap to get me to marry her. You assume that everyone else is just as cunning as you are. I don't believe it. I've never seen such desperation as when she was here telling me about it.'

'Who wouldn't be desperate if they had to play such games?'

'But if it's true. What am I going to do?'

'I guess you'll have to marry her in order to save the life of your child. Then you can get divorced, because nobody can kill it then.'

He chuckles into his pillow:

'You're so good at cunning, darling.'

'I don't think what she said is at all true, and you're not to do anything at all until she has proof. But I think it serves you right to have to go around worrying for a little while, I really do.'

'Do you think it's a sin?'

'Yes. Having relationships with people who are so dependent on you, I think it's inexcusable if you aren't at least in love with them. By the way, I think it's a sin in any case if you're not in love, if you don't at least like each other, if you don't at least *want* it. If there's any sin against nature, then it's having sex with someone who you don't really want to have sex with.'

'So you wanted to have sex with me this time?' He lifts his head to execute a clown face with hopefully twinkling eyes.

'This time, yes. Nowadays I only do what I want in that area.'

'If only you wanted to a little more often. If we hadn't drifted away from each other, this would have never happened . . .'

'Oh really! So it's my fault that you run around getting your pupils pregnant! In actual fact, I'm the one who should marry her!'

'We could get married and adopt it.'

'Don't pull me into this! I'm here as an impartial counsellor, don't forget it, solely in the role of a private tutor. I'm happy I'm the one you're asking for advice, but don't try to involve me in any other way.'

'Who else would I ask for advice? There's nobody else I can talk to. You're so wise.'

'Indispensable,' I sneer. 'Can I get some sleep now?'

'Sleep. Sleep if you can.'

It doesn't take many more days before Gustav informs me that he's received word it was a false alarm; maybe my suspicions were baseless. I'm relieved. It was too macabre a story, but it also leaves me dejected in its wake. It's sad that Gustav is so changed. 'You're not the same person I once knew.'

'How was I back then?' he wonders with interest.

'You were soft and childish and believed you'd keep your virginity until you got married.'

'Who was the one who changed my mind then?'

'I couldn't imagine that you'd move on to depredation so abruptly. And by the way, you'd have changed by now even without me.'

'Without you I'd have married and settled down a long time ago.'

'Don't let me stand in your way any longer, then.'

★

I've got to the second section of the daily paper when the door-bell rings: Gustav wants to return that fifty-crown note he had borrowed the other day when he was too late to the bank. Oh right, of course. Nothing else? No, that was all.

He's standing on the hall rug looking at me. I'm still holding the newspaper in my hand.

'The *Red Top* column was a good one today,' he remembers.

I laugh. 'That's what I thought when I read it – that it was just the kind of *Top* you'd like. But I didn't want to call you just to point that out.'

He puts his hand on the doorknob.

'I see that *Virginia Woolf* is playing again,' I say.

'Right, I was thinking I'd go see it.'

'Exactly my thought.'

'It's so edifying to see that there are relationships worse than ours.'

'Isn't it? At least we don't beat each other up.'

I keep turning the pages.

'Grand Cinema, right?'

He smiles.

'The seven or nine o'clock?'

'The seven, then we can eat dinner afterwards.'

And so we go and see *Virginia Woolf* again. And Gustav treats me to dinner again and we sleep together again.

We can't get into the habit of doing this, we tell ourselves.

But we have such a good time together.

*

The winterlike conditions don't last for more than two weeks, then it's the usual grey mush for a couple of months. As soon as the clouds break apart, I grab the closest book, dash head over heels for the closest park and sit down to gorge myself on sun. Not bask – that sounds as if I can take my time; greedily and unhealthily, excessively: I gorge myself.

It's getting close to Easter. If I'm ever going to find out whether I want Gustav or just his place in the countryside, now is the time for me to not go to the Island.

Gustav's going to be there. And I'll be missing it terribly. But then I still won't know which one I'm longing for most, so I'll have to celebrate Easter in the country to figure out whether I'm still longing.

'Definitive conclusion,' Cilla agrees and invites me along to Småland. It's just Cilla and her new fellow who'll be spending the holiday there, none of her other family members, but even so I feel a bit in the way and wish she had invited me before I invited myself. A little like a fifth wheel, as they say, when you're the third and it's the fourth that's missing.

To be sure, the house is big enough for them to withdraw when they wish, and Cilla reassures me that it's lovely that I'm there. But I'm probably more uncomfortable than they are. Their love is in that first tiresome introductory phase, that stage of jolly banter. It's as if Cilla's actually talking to him even when she turns to me. It's unpleasant.

Gustav and I have never been like this around other people, have we?

Oh yes – he tried to in the beginning. That's when I kicked

him in the metaphorical shin. (We don't fight, but psychological violence is also violence. Although I do think it's advantageous if you can keep from throwing things at each other.)

I spend as much time as possible outdoors. The forest is a picture from a John Bauer fairy tale. The ground is mossy-soft and sinks under your feet; there's snow on the northern slopes and under the trees. There's a little pond you can swim in during the summer with water that smells of humus.

But it's not the sea.

Naturally: I miss the Island anyway because it's that place in the country that I'm used to. And I miss Gustav because he's the human I'm used to.

It's such a simple problem that I ought to be able to solve it in my head without exposing myself to travails in experimental psychology.

I pad around softly before the others wake on Easter Eve, walk the two miles into town through the forest, change a five-crown note into coins at the country grocer and grasp the handle to the phone booth. I release it, turn around and walk back with the one-crown coins jingling in my pocket.

I don't want to run the risk that someone else in the family will answer the phone. They live in the belief that we're happily divorced. And I don't want to admit how much I miss him.

The afternoon of Easter Monday, we drive back to Stockholm in a snowstorm and get home late. Gustav calls and says, 'Beloved, will you marry me?'

'It's so sudden,' I say.

'I got so sentimental being on the Island without you.'

'Me too. I mean, the opposite, not being there with you. I would have called if I hadn't been afraid to look one of your parents in the eye, even on the telephone.'

'I've had an insight. That I can't be happy without you, either.'

I laugh contentedly.

'There. If you're unhappy both with and without me, then it doesn't matter. I can think about my own happiness for once.'

'But I'm most unhappy about it being like this. I want to marry you!'

'Calm down. It's the wrong time of year for a wedding. If the emotions haven't run off us by the autumn, we can take up the issue again. But rushing into things like this can't turn out well. We haven't even known each other six years yet.'

'Six more months,' Gustav states. 'I'll give you six more months and not one day more. On – what will the date be? On the third of October you'll have to make a decision. Whether it's me you want or someone else.'

'Fine, fine,' I say.

It's a long way off.

*

After the Easter break, it's high time for me to get something done on the *Edinburgh Review*, but I haven't had time to do more than try to figure out where I was when Aron calls and suggests that I accompany him to Gothenburg for a couple of days. Neither my work ethic nor my sense of self-preservation helps this time. It's an opportunity I can't resist – particularly if I'll be forced to break things off with him later. I have to take advantage while I still can.

I love trains and I love Aron: the combination is miraculous. And when it's combined with sitting in a café, which I also love! Admittedly, the restaurant cars aren't what they used to be – just a snack bar and plastic utensils and sandwiches made of the same material. But it's still a café, and one that rolls on rails with a moving view of the country outside the window, and Aron's the one sitting across the table from me.

We talk about the war. The imminent one: the US has become

definitely crazy and the newspaper headlines are shouting about
world war. In my fear and wrath I also register something like
relief: It simply can't continue this way, it's not right that only
Indochina be affected year after year.

'Puritan,' Aron says, shaking his head. 'Puritan reasoning.'

'What do you mean? Is justice a puritanical invention?'

'No, but a guilt complex is.'

'It shouldn't be called a complex if the guilt is a fact. What
have we done to earn a life of peace and prosperity? What have
the Vietnamese done? It's clear that it would be more pleasant
if everyone had as good a life as we do, but if some people have
to be maimed and killed, you can't deny that it would be fairer
if it were a little more evenly distributed.'

'It's logical. It's too logical – you can't argue that way. And
the Vietnamese haven't given up yet; you shouldn't be doing it
for them.'

'I don't mean that we're all supposed to sit here waiting to be
bombed back to the Stone Age. Obviously you have to act *as if*
world-wide peace were possible, and justice. But believing in it
is another thing.'

'You have a soft spot for final solutions,' Aron says.

Do I?

We refill our coffee cups now and then and buy new plastic
sandwiches so we can keep sitting there, but around Skövde,
the staff start to look at us so strangely that we return to our
reserved seats.

Sitting closest to us is a grizzled old gent who reminds me of
the man on Fårö. It doesn't take Aron more than two minutes
to involve him in a conversation about the state of the world.
And not more than two and one-half for me to realize that this
grizzled gent is actually a fairy in disguise.

'What the hell do the Yankees think they're doing there?' he
says gruffly. He says 'Indonesia' when he means 'Indochina',

but his mistake needn't mean that he doesn't know what he's talking about, because this is the essential question. And the Yankees are, as we all know, everywhere, from Greece to the moon: What the hell do they think they're doing there?

The old man is getting off in Alingsås, and we help him busily with his bags. Then we sit there smiling.

'See?' Aron says. 'Folks ain't dumb.'

'Surely you don't believe that a fairy disguised as a snus-man represents the entire Swedish people, do you?'

'There are a lot of people who think the way he does, nowadays.'

'Think maybe, but they don't do anything about it.'

'Do you?'

I peel an orange.

Gothenburg is a place I've never visited. Aron's the one at home here and gets to lead me by the hand, laughing at how lost I am. We've never walked down a street hand in hand before and everything is so strange. A city that's entirely foreign and nevertheless very familiar, so Swedish: a large Swedish city that's not Stockholm, a piece of Sweden that's always existed here and lived its life without me. And a man who's walking beside me and looks as if he belongs to me, but who in reality belongs to someone entirely different.

'What will your buddies say now that you have the wrong woman along?'

'They don't get involved.'

That's what he believes. They may be open-minded, but no less curious than anyone else. He's made a date with two mates at a pizzeria on Avenyn ('Avenyn': well-known street in Gothenburg). To be sure, I can't see them raising any eyebrows when they catch a glimpse of me, but they're probably raising them internally, and the questions hang there unspoken in the air (did Aron leave Florence – knocked up and everything? Or is this chick just a fling?). Finally I go to the loo so that they can discuss the matter in my absence so the air is clear, and I am completely wrong if it isn't precisely what they've done by the time I return. Their eyebrows are in place, the chick is a fling.

Aron's business here is to discuss a documentary that a few of his acquaintances have made about a strike. They want to produce it through the Film Centre and Aron, who has contacts there, will take care of it – I'm not very knowledgeable about it – and that will be tomorrow; this evening they've organized a party at a commune where we're going to spend the night, and where they've invited everyone from the old gang in Aron's honour.

It's interesting to meet his friends, but I don't like them as well as he likes mine. Most of them seem to be revolutionary communists and so crazy that they make Aron look like a miracle of balance and common sense by comparison. Some are so revolutionary that they have close-cropped hair, but Aron informs me that their appearance is a part of their infiltration strategy: they sacrifice their curls in order to be able to speak to the common folk.

Mostly I sit quietly and look around. I watch the girls who come and hug Aron and wonder how many of them share my experience of him. I don't want to share it with anyone. I don't want to be here at all – I don't belong here. It doesn't help that I'm sitting next to Aron so that I can avoid questions about who I am from newly arrived guests, that Aron is sitting with his arm around my shoulders so that you can see who I am: Aron's bird. I don't want to be, since in reality I'm not!

It's a loneliness of that arrogant and unhappy type that one can experience under the influence of cannabis: you believe that you see me but you have no idea who I am In Reality. I don't belong here and I have nothing to do with you!

I've never had reason to observe the relationship between Aron and me from the outside, to label it. Aron is simply 'Aron', he's been Aron since I was nineteen years old and it cost me a great deal to learn that there are nameless relationships, those not covered by words such as 'friendship' or 'love' or 'marriage' or 'affair', which only exist in their own right.

But I can't begin to explain this to those observing us. You can't even start to excuse yourself by saying 'it's true, Aron is married, but I actually knew him *first*' – I don't get a chance to explain anything. I can only see in the eyes of the observers what it looks like.

And I don't like that vision.

The hours pass slowly, the bottles empty quickly, Aron gets drunk. At two o'clock he's lying with his head in my lap discussing the applicability of the Chinese experience, and I'm simply longing to be home with the *Edinburgh Review* and my typewriter. It feels like the bad old days when I sat in merry company such as this and waited for Aron to turn his gaze towards me and decide that it was time for us to go home and to bed.

But in this city, there's nowhere to go home to. We're going to be staying in this room, and when the guests begin to fall asleep, I realize that we're not going to be alone in it. Does Aron think I intend to have sex with him in the presence of others? I don't, not even if the others are deeply sunk in their drunken stupors. If this is an inhibition, it's one I prefer to maintain.

The problem ends up not mattering. Aron himself falls asleep after having discussed the final opponent under the table. I find a blanket to spread over us and awkwardly crawl in next to him on the uncomfortable couch. It feels like desertion to be the only one awake, abandoned for sleep – I'm not used to it. I lie there listening to the alien snoring in a room that's foggy with cigarette smoke while the morning light grows to full day and the spring sunshine outside the window shouts about a different life.

I'll take a walk in the harbour, I think.

29

What gives Gustav the right to pose such an ultimatum: <u>it's me or him</u>? Nothing at all. But he's doing it anyway, and he's serious now. There are only five months left already, and I don't know what I'm going to say to him. One day it seems obvious that I have to choose Gustav: it's worth giving up the rest of male humanity for a life of social security. The next day it's just as obvious that it's impossible and I'll choose Aron – but he's not on offer for me, so I'm choosing 'freedom', the right to see anyone I wish. The third day I become furious at such idiotic choices and declare once again that I refuse to accept them, I refuse to compare and move weights on the scales, I will not tolerate it!

It's an eternally running discussion in my tired mind. After a while, the thought paths become so worn that the rounds go faster and faster, I waffle back and forth and once again return to the starting point innumerable times in the same day: Gustav, I think when I wake up, he's the only one I can talk to. Aron, I think while putting the water on the hob, I can have a sex life with him. And while the water is still running through the Melitta filter, I have time to complete the entire round trip: no, I refuse to compare, I want both of them! But I can't have both of them, so a new round starts while I spread butter on my bread . . .

And so I see Gustav and think about Aron, and see Aron and

think about Gustav, and all the comparisons I refuse to make compare themselves and the scales tilt up and down to the point of seasickness.

A child, I think.

If I could only get pregnant and avoid having to choose. A final solution – yes. I would even accept it in the shape of a catastrophe.

With which one of them, then? It would certainly be more practical with Gustav, though it would probably be a more beautiful baby with Aron (this comparison makes itself). In any case, it would take up my time so that, for the next fifteen years, I wouldn't have to worry any further about what to do with my life.

I haven't done more than begin to play with this thought when my normally regular period is late, and it immediately becomes clear to me that even if it would be a final solution, who the father is wouldn't be entirely without significance – and as things stand just now, I cannot, to my undying shame, say which of them would be more likely.

Living in polygamy in and of itself no longer seems so degenerate to me – so many other people do it. But having a baby without knowing who the father is – this seems utterly, hair-raisingly immoral. I don't know why, since it's simply a natural consequence of this condition, but in the general consciousness of which I am a part, it seems to be the lowest depth to which a woman can sink. The least worthy of mothers.

New comparisons follow on: I start to examine their earlobes and toe formations discreetly, and I ponder how I can start talking about blood groups without arousing suspicion.

It's four days late, and it's obvious to me that this is the worst thing that could possibly happen. It robs me of the ability to choose, but I don't escape the need to do so as a result. Quite the opposite: it only extends it. For eight months I'll be weighing

arguments for and against, and just as I've finally decided that
it has to be Gustav (or Aron) I want to have a baby with, it will
come into the world and turn out to be Aron's (or Gustav's),
and then I'll be seized by disgust for his offspring and the kid
will be neurotic for life.

Eight days late, my period finally arrives and I rush over to
Harriet's and borrow pills, two packs that will last until I can get
my own prescription.

Or until Aron goes away for the summer – then I'll know
that it's Gustav if I get pregnant, then I'll know and won't have
to choose . . .

But I have to choose to stop taking the Pill then. I can't fool
myself into 'forgetting' it – what a shame that I live in a time
when it's no longer possible to get pregnant by mistake. You
even have to choose that!

Should I do it now? Build a family together with Gustav?
You have to have children at some point in your life. I've always
thought that it would happen another time, in a faraway future,
but I'll soon have passed all of the recommended ages for giving
birth. Why not now?

Anytime at all except for now. Because it would be an act of
panic, and if there's anything you shouldn't do in a panic, it's
to make babies. You shouldn't imagine that it's a way out, not
exploit innocent lives to bring some order into your own chaos.
If you're going to make babies, then it should be <u>in cold blood</u>,
because babies are what you want, not for obscure reasons, as
an act of panic or infatuation or depression.

Reluctantly and grimacing, I force myself to take the little
pill every evening and raise my toothbrush glass to the mirror:
Here's to the little innocent baby.

*

Harriet rolls her eyes and Cilla slaps her forehead when I tell
them I'm going to Paris with Gustav. 'Why not?' I ask irritably.

'We've never gone on a real trip abroad, and now that he finally has a little money and I'm still a student, we can travel cheaply with my student discount.'

'But you've said you're divorced.'

'So what? Now that we have the opportunity, wouldn't it be narrow-minded to miss out just because of that?'

Harriet and Cilla exchange a look that says there's no sense in arguing with me.

It's odd. If you're not properly married, that doesn't bother this liberated generation, but if you're not properly divorced either, then they become as indignant as old biddies.

What old biddies and peers think about the matter is something we avoid finding out. We don't tell our families that we're travelling together and sneak our separate ways to the bus terminal on Vasagatan. We pretend that we don't know each other until we've got on the plane without having run into anyone we know.

We've agreed on one more thing, right from the beginning of our travel plans: So that the entire week won't be full of discussions about our future, our past, our relationships with other people and with each other, these are forbidden topics for discussion until we set our feet on our native soil again.

The trip offers so much more and keeps us constantly supplied with new conversational material that it's much easier to keep to our resolution than I had imagined. Now and then one of us has something on the tip of our tongue – associations to the past come up rather easily – but when he tries to bend the rule a little I protest, and vice versa: if it's to be, then it's to be, and it's nice to be torn away from time and space and simply be the people we are, here and now, and with each other.

We go to the Louvre, of course, and Gustav shows me his Athena in the metope relief from Olympia, and I really want to quote his lines in that *Pimpernel Smith* letter, the first one he wrote to me; however, I see in his eyes that he remembers it himself. It doesn't need to be said aloud.

Or we're sitting in pavement cafés drinking Pernod and writing postcards, peering across the table in our attempts to see what the other is writing and to whom. When Gustav goes to the loo and is careless enough to leave his pile of cards on the table, I take the opportunity (our agreement said nothing about peeking, and he owes me one!): there's one to his parents and one to Erik, and yes indeed, there's one addressed to one Ingegerd Fredriksson in Stockholm whom I've heard nothing about. He writes about how hot it is and how fun it is to once again see cities where he's been before and about the Louvre, but he doesn't mention Athena. At least he's not starting up with that again.

On the last day, we browse through shops to buy presents for each other (the concept of 'souvenir' cannot exist in the world we've constructed for ourselves, but presents fall outside any concept of time). The touristy salt shakers with the Eiffel Tower on them don't tempt us, nor do we find anything at Bon Marché, and the prices in the more exclusive shops are dizzying. But in a tobacco shop where we wanted to buy pipe cleaners, we find ourselves stopping in front of a Meerschaum pipe: an original piece with enticing curves and a squiggly little lid on the bowl. We both look closely at it, and we look at each other, and we ask the clerk if there's another like it, but *non monsieur*, there isn't, and, besides, it turns out to be so expensive that we don't have enough money for more than one. We buy it for each other and sit down on a park bench down near the dock to try it out. Passers-by who see us handing it back and forth to each other suspect that we're smoking hashish, of course.

After we get home, we'll have to take turns with it; the details about how we'll do so is something we can't discuss since it's part of the forbidden future.

But at Arlanda we crash helplessly into reality again, captured in time and space and forced to make a decision about how we'll spend the rest of the summer. The weather is too beautiful for sitting in a library – I won't be able to concentrate. And if this is going to be my last summer with Gustav, it's best to take advantage – indeed, there's no limit to how much you can justify by saying you ought to take advantage, I discover.

We head out in the boat. Gustav allows me to set our course, and since I prefer to sail downwind and escape sitting like a fly with my feet on the ceiling (bracing myself against the edge and wondering what will happen when he falls overboard and I'm left alone), the winds bring us slowly but surely to the Island. This wasn't what was supposed to happen, but once we're in our home waters, we may as well continue the whole way.

It's almost evening and the wind is starting to abate completely when we round the final point and prepare to take the buoy. I stand on the foredeck and look towards land as we glide at an infinitely slow pace into the bay and, like a great sadness, it occurs to me what a fine little bay it is: here, I think, you should sidle in and make your night harbour on a gentle summer evening.

Thereafter, of course, I think of Per Gunnar Evander, just as every cultured person in a similar situation would do (as if he had a patent on the discovery that you can long to do something you're already doing at that precise moment – the experience is probably familiar to most people in these neurotic times. It's just because he happened to have become famous for describing it that you have to associate it with him if you're a cultured person).

In any event, I don't have any more time to think about either longing or Per Gunnar Evander since Gustav screams that I've almost missed the buoy. As usual, there are a few moments of bustling and panic until we have the landing behind us. When the ropes are hung where they belong and the sails are stowed for now in the cockpit, I climb over onto the dock, stand completely still for a moment and simply breathe and see.

The meadow hasn't been cut yet – the grass reaches almost up to the cottage window. Near the rock with the lovely reading spot, a duck family is splashing in the water and swimming out behind the reedy bush. My fishing rod is leaning against the wall of the cottage where I left it last summer.

It would be good to be at home here, I think.

*

While Gustav takes off for a long sail, I go into the city to work. There's a postcard in my postbox signed 'A', and I stand for a moment, staring stupidly at it, before I realize that it's Aron. Have I never seen his handwriting before? It's a rather common one, slanted forwards as we learned in school – not the backwards-striving type I have. As does Gustav.

The view is from the west coast, where he's on holiday with his family. What's above the A is a laconic message: 'Coming home the 20th. Will call the Sunday after if I can, hope you'll be there.'

I sit at home and read and don't leave the phone all day Sunday. At one-thirty it finally rings, but it's someone who's dialled a wrong number. Then Gustav calls. He's just come into harbour and suggests that I invite him to a pub to help him re-adapt to city life.

'Tonight?' I say. 'That won't work. Can you wait until tomorrow?'

'Are you busy today?'

'I don't know. Probably.'

'Aron?'

He must blame himself since he's asking. But it's the same old story. He gets so sad that it ruins my joy over seeing Aron,

and although I know how it feels out there on the other end of
the phone line, I can't help that it sucks away my energy.

'Do you have to be so jealous? Can you truly not allow me to
see Aron now and again, too?'

'My heart turns into a dishrag in my chest, it simply does. A
wrung-out dishrag. You know what I mean, don't you?'

'Yes, I know!' I shout, 'and my heart also turns into a dishrag
when you sound like this!'

The receiver is silent. This is even worse.

'I'm afraid of you,' I say quietly. 'You love me too much, it's
too easy to hurt you, I can't deal with your demands.'

'Aron, doesn't he make any demands?'

'No. How could he? Neither of us can have any claims on
the other. And it's fucking nice, I tell you, to be free of guilt
feelings.'

'Guilt feelings,' he snorts, 'you can handle that. But I get diar-
rhoea from loving you, I'll have chronic ulcers if this continues.
I can't stand it any longer.'

'But we decided that we'll talk through the whole shitty thing
this fall. Can't we wait until then? Although I don't know how it
will be possible when we can't say a word without hurting each
other and both walk away like dishrags.'

'We'll apparently have to stop seeing each other until then.
Maybe it's better for thinking about it, too, if we're divorced
from bed and board.'

'Since we just drift together the whole time, I guess it's the
only solution, isn't it?' I agree, without conviction.

'OK, see you in October.'

He hangs up the phone, and my heart is a wrung-out dishrag
in my chest.

★

Gustav doesn't call me any more, but a greeting by letter arrives
at the beginning of August. It's with a Bible verse like before,

but now he's taking them from Lamentations. Lam. 3:17 goes like this: *And thou hast removed my soul far off from peace: I forgat prosperity.*

The rest is copied from Spinoza's geometrical ethics – a contribution to the understanding of jealousy:

Qui enim imaginatur mulierem, quem amat, alteri sese prostituere, non solum ex eo, quod ipsius appetitus coercitur, contristabitur, sed etiam quia rei amatae imaginem pudendis et excrementis alterius iungere cogitur, eandem aversatur. Ad quod denique accedit, quod zelotypus non eodem vultu, quem res amata ei praebere solebat, ab eadem excipiatur, qua etiam de causa amans contristatur.

'For the one who sees how the woman he loves gives herself to another becomes not only dispirited because his own desire is forced back, but also acquires a distaste for her since he is forced to connect his perception of the beloved with another's genitals and excretions' (so that's *pudendis et excrementis*). 'In addition, the jealous one is not met by the beloved with the same facial expression as she showed him before – another reason why the lover becomes dispirited.'

Throughout the centuries.

Contristatur.

*

'You can't have everything,' Cilla says. 'You're not the first person to try, but you'll be the first one to succeed if you do. You have to choose.'

'But it's not a choice when the alternatives aren't actually interchangeable. We're not talking about commensurable units at all. How am I supposed to choose between them when they can't be compared?'

'You can at least handle things a bit more neatly so that Gustav doesn't have to know that you're cheating on him.'

'How you can call it "neat" is beyond me. Honesty is the whole point of our relationship, and without it I don't see any reason to continue it at all.'

'But you can't go around treating him like this your whole life, can you? Like a yo-yo: you let him go time and time again, but when he gets too far away you jerk the string . . .'

'How could you . . . aren't you my friend? Shouldn't you be on my side?'

'I'm not on anyone's side.'

'Exactly. You just sit there telling me like it is, brutally!'

She smiles a little (tired of the issue?).

'You know yourself how it is. You can say it as well as I can.'

'Anyone can, but what am I supposed to do? I don't know if I can live without Gustav any more. Maybe I've forgotten how to do it.'

'To me it seems that you've been divorced most of the time. In any case, you've mostly been complaining the past few years.'

'The complaints are all you get to hear. When things are going well, he's the one who's my confidant. Besides, it's probably easier to describe the things that pull you apart. Than the other things.'

The other things: what holds us together. That notion that *it's Gustav*, that he's the one I belong to – that's the sort of thing that's difficult to explain. It just sounds overstrung, as if you've read too many romance novels about the Right One. You can't say 'he's my human in the world'.

This naturally has to do with the simple fact that he's the person who's been closest to me, but it's not simply a practical issue of habits and opinions in common – there's something else as well. The idea that Gustav has seen me as nobody else has, he's even perceived my personality without underestimating it, overestimating it or looking past something – a half-mystical experience of Gustav as *the one who has seen me*. Such things cannot be explained.

We're sitting on the sofa in the new red level of the Theatre Café, furthest in. There's only a group of dark-skinned men speaking French a few tables away. A young couple hesitates at the door to Drottninggatan and we observe them distractedly, sipping cool beer from our mugs.

Maybe we're not as alike as we've wanted to believe, I think. I'm much moodier, less stable. But when I'm in my brightest mood, the one that harmonizes with his, then there's a communion like no other. We can lie in bed in the morning reading *Dagens Nyheter** and, from the front page to the radio guide, we giggle and snort at the same places. Strife breaks out unfailingly only when we begin to talk about our relationship. As long as we're lying reading the paper, communion of the souls and concord reign, but only as long as that.

I really don't know which of those is more important in bed.

'It's not that I have anything against choices as such,' I begin again (incapable of changing the subject). 'Well yes, I do, but I realize that I have to choose, that it's important to choose and to stand by one's choice. I'm actually not an egotist interested only in my own happiness.

'Believe it or not,' I say and grip my mug, 'I am Inspired by an Honest Desire to Do The Right Thing.'

I keep holding on to my beer mug and speak with the largest capital letters I can muster to excuse the gravity of the subject.

'*But what is The Right Thing?*' I ask in italics and with an apologetic smile.

Cilla laughs. 'Are you asking me? I don't know, but I suppose one should always try to avoid hurting other people.'

'That's your categorical imperative: never treat a person like a yo-yo? But how do you avoid it? It's obvious that I could stop seeing Aron, but it would be a meaningless gesture. Our

* Sweden's other major daily newspaper.

relationship would not become significantly different as a result. It's just something Gustav believes.'

'Can it become significantly different at all?'

'Not unless I do. And I really don't know if you can change your nature. I'd probably make myself unhappy to boot, and that can't possibly be my duty, can it?'

'How many other girls has Gustav managed to make unhappy during the periods when you've let him go?'

I have no idea. I've never thought of it. I push my mug away from me across the table and sigh.

'Do you mean that I should sit down and count those involved and decide that the right thing is what gives the most possible happiness to the largest number possible?'

'There may be no right alternative at all. Why do you assume the whole time that there is? You can put yourself in situations where all the options are wrong but you have to choose anyway.'

'But that can't be, can it? If the action is wrong no matter what you do, then you'll be forced to implement some kind of religious concept of mercy!'

'Hm,' says Cilla.

But does she implement it on me? No. She leaves me to my choices, where all solutions are wrong.

*

Florist delivery: a bouquet of red asters and Job 9:27–28. I look it up:

If I say, I will forget my complaint, I will leave off my heaviness, and comfort myself: I am afraid of all my sorrows, I know that thou wilt not hold me innocent.

I walk around the flat three times, twice around the block, three times around the phone, and call him.

'I've had a new idea. Can't we have a telephone relationship?'

'What do you mean telephone relationship? You mean like in Wästberg's *The Air Cage*?'

'No no, nothing dirty. We might as well see each other in that case. No, I mean so we don't have to be present with each other. It just complicates things the whole time. We can see each other over the phone instead. Since there's always so much to talk about, and we're the only people we can talk to.

'Isn't that an excellent idea?' I say proudly.

Oh no, not at all, because Gustav becomes so upset just by hearing my voice that he can't get anything useful done for the rest of the day. 'How about by correspondence?' I nag him. The same result: an envelope in the post with my handwriting on it is enough to give him a stomach ache.

*

That won't work, either. But there has to be some way out, some alternative to this unreasonable all-or-nothing. Something. Somewhere. Where, where?

*

I don't get a doctoral grant this year either; on the other hand, I'm given a secretarial position in the department. Office work isn't precisely what I'm longing for the most, but it's just a matter of a few hours per week, and seeing everyone else who wanted the job with their long faces is entirely too satisfying for me to turn it down. And there's the money, too.

Besides, from the standpoint of mental hygiene, it's precisely what I need: a job that requires me to deal with something concrete and routine. Collecting my thoughts for something creative is in any event impossible as long as my personal life remains in this state. I feel that I haven't thought about anything else at all in months or years, nothing but what I refuse to think about: Gustav or Aron.

*

The linden trees in Humlegården sough autumnally. I stare out the window and try to count the yellow leaves as they fall. When I look down at my book, I've forgotten where I was, and I decide to call it a day. I fetch my duffle coat from the closet and fish up an evening paper that someone left on the bench in the vestibule.

The Great Dictator is showing at the Grand Cinema. Better that than riding home and not getting anything done anyway.

When I come out on Sveavägen afterwards, it's late and dark, and it's started to rain. I'm longing for my home and my bed, and I pedal away as fast as I can. I almost pass Gustav on St Eriksgatan when I recognize him.

'What are you doing here?'

'I'm out walking. I couldn't read.'

Is it my fault? I straddle my bike at the edge of the pavement, waiting quietly.

'How about you?'

'Just went to the movies, *The Dictator*.'

'Yes, all alone,' I add considerately, but he doesn't answer my smile. He's standing with his hands in his pockets, his shoulders hunched as you do when you're cold.

'I don't really believe in this,' he says.

'What's "this"?'

'The great passion.'

I sigh. So this is what he's taking out for a walk in the raw cold of the night.

'No,' I say, 'don't do it.'

Don't do it, I plead, and get up on my bike again: don't believe in it, refuse to participate in it, stop hurting yourself on me.

30

We meet as agreed on the third of October at Gustav's. We talk
about our jobs, about what we've been doing since the last time
we met. We walk like cats around hot porridge, and then we
agree to let the porridge sit there and go to bed: if we start to
talk about serious issues, there won't be any going to bed – best
to do that first.

So we lie together again in Gustav's big plywood bed. It feels
so familiar, as if the depressions my body has made are still
there in the mattress, although if there are any at all, they must
belong to someone else.

No declarations of love, no declarations at all. There's no
time or energy for that. We simply curl up together in our
usual sleeping positions after 'making love' wordlessly for safety's sake.

Being together again: he sighs that it's like pulling a dirty old
blanket over himself. Yes, that's what it's like. About that impassioned and glamorous, and so blessedly mundane.

In the morning, there's only time for coffee and the paper and a
kiss on the cheek at the front door, as in other marriages in this
country on a morning like this. All day we're each preoccupied
with our own matters, but in the evening he comes to me and
says, as though he'd braced himself:

'Well?'

'What do you mean, "well"?' (To 'win time', to win two seconds of a life.)

'How is it going to be?'

'Well yes,' I say. 'Yes, I want you.'

'But how? Under what conditions?'

'As before. As always. I want to be your best friend, unconditionally.'

'But that option isn't available to you. I know that I have no right to present ultimatums, I know it. But I just can't do this any longer. You have to choose now.'

'Him or you, you mean?'

'Me or something else.'

'But that's no choice. Nothing else is offered to me. It's not in my power to choose him. My only choice is to choose to give him up, and I won't. I'm not choosing to give you up, either. I refuse. I do not accept this arrangement.'

'But you have to realize that not choosing is also a choice. You'll get the same result as choosing to give me up.'

'I hear you saying that, and I believe you, but it's not the same as my choosing it. If I say that I want you and act so that I don't get you, it's not the same as if I say that I don't want you, is it? There's an enormous, fundamental difference there.'

We sit across from each other at the kitchen table as if we were in a seminar trying to convince each other, trying to win the argument. Or maybe even better: as if at a negotiation table, where we have to come to a consensus solution in order to survive, must reason our way to how to be at peace with each other.

He laughs at my comparison.

'In any event, you're in a stronger position for negotiation since it must be easier for you to replace me.'

'Why do you think that?'

'Interesting women are more uncommon.'

'All people are equally interesting according to your ideology, may I remind you.'

'They're equally valuable, but it doesn't mean that you get as much out of being with them. In any case it's easier to find gents who are fun to be with.'

I've never thought of this, but maybe it's a natural consequence of a male-dominated society. On the other hand, it's harder to find gents who aren't prone to the taxing habit of taking themselves seriously. Even Aron – no, don't bring him into this now.

'Even if this is true statistically, the conclusion is wrong. As unusual as I am, it will be even harder to find someone who suits me. I've said that you're the only person I would be able to live with, and if it's not you, then it won't be anyone. But you're so easy to get along with – you can marry anyone. You're such a good adapter.'

Arguing about this in a friendly way, we make tea and set cups on the table. He hasn't been here in my flat for a long time. He looks around and discovers the Beardsley poster I got from Aron – not a present actually; he simply happened to have two and gave me one of them. It's a wall decoration that you see in just about every other home these days anyway, as common as Picasso's bull in a Minerva reproduction ten years ago.

'I see, you've bought it too.'

'A gift,' I say.

I may as well have hit him. 'Aron?' he asks with his eyes, and, when I don't answer, he naturally takes it as confirmation, and the fact that there's a poster on my wall that another man has given me hurts him so badly that I would have rather hit him instead.

'Doesn't it go well with my wallpaper?'

He doesn't answer, doesn't meet my gaze, simply reaches for the matchbox on the table to light his pipe.

Among all possible paths forward, lying is not one of them. I simply cannot remember. I can't even improvise a small, idiotically insignificant lie such as I've bought a picture that I haven't bought.

He gets up from the couch, walks around the room, sits down again, and lays his pipe down with a jerky motion. He didn't smoke at all before he knew me: this is my fault, too, of course.

'You don't love me. It's as simple as that,' he says. (For the how-manieth time is he saying it?)

'I don't understand why you need to make things so simple. I want you, but not under just any conditions at all.'

I can no longer bear to see him so unhappy. Internally I shout to him not to accept my conditions: Get up and go, don't allow yourself to be tortured any longer! Go now and I'll allow you to go, this time I will truly let you go. If I have any duty at all in this world, this is it.

He takes several quick puffs on his pipe, but it's gone out. He knocks it against the edge of the ashtray and sits with his hands between his knees, his shoulders slumped.

I should go up to him and put my arms around him. I can't. Suffering is so repulsive, I can't bear it. I just want it out of my sight, away.

He gets up.

I follow him to the hallway. He hasn't made it out the door before he falters:

'You can let me know if you change your mind, all right? One week, can we say?'

I nod. One more week, yes, if you want it.

His clogs clatter heavily down the stairs. I clear the table.

It's not quite dawn. I don't usually wake up at this time, and I lie and listen for what could have awakened me. But it's completely

quiet in the building – just the even hissing of the heating pipes
and the hum of the refrigerator in the kitchen.

What was I dreaming? I was rowing across water, straight
over a narrow sound. On the beach I pulled up the boat to bail
it out and was then going to row back the same way, but one of
the oars had disappeared. I walked back and forth on the beach,
a long, sloping hill with a pine forest, but I couldn't find it.

Symbolic: no return? Or literary: Who can row without oars,
and who can part from his love without tears . . .

In any case, it's imagery so banal that I'm ashamed to have
come up with it, even in a dream. Banal to the point of blunt-
ness. I won't acknowledge it. I hardly dare go back to sleep.

*

Days pass. I have constant impulses to call Gustav, write him,
see him. I fight them back. I haven't changed; I have nothing
to say to him other than what I've already said, so what's the
point? 'To comfort him.' But I know that I'm the person least
equipped to do that. It would be best for Gustav if I didn't exist,
and the best thing I can do for him is to act as if I didn't. So, lie
down, play dead.

Maybe he's right that I've never shouldered my share of
responsibility for our relationship. Maybe the only way for me
to take responsibility for it is to end it. Condemn him to freedom. If he's now truly gathered his strength for a decision, I
have no right to sabotage it. I must come to heel. Keep my
hands to myself. Let him go his own way. Give him a chance.

And if he takes that chance? If he's comforted by someone else?

I'm so weary of his suffering that I'm even able to think that
thought fully and to wish it. It's as if he were made to have
a happy marriage. Why should he keep dragging around an
unhappy one with me? No: may he please find someone to
comfort himself with.

It's possible I'll regret this bitterly in the future. I'll probably damn myself for having destroyed my life. But that's not the issue here. It's his life we're talking about now.

Stay with it. Remember, no matter what happens, that this is my foremost duty: not to hurt anyone. Remember this, and keep your fingers away from the phone. To be honest, it's not a question of calling to comfort him at all – it's to comfort myself. It's a completely absurd desire to see him so I can grieve with him that we're divorced – it seems kind of dysfunctional that we're sitting alone and each grieving the same thing.

But I have no right to demand comfort from him.

Who can comfort me then? Meeting Aron is only a solace for all the days I don't see Aron. It can't also be a solace for not seeing Gustav.

*

Weeks pass. He doesn't get in touch and we don't run into each other. We live on the same island in the city, but our activities involve different parts of town – I'm mostly forced into exile out at Frescati, and our paths don't cross.

Not a sign of life: I don't know if he's dead or alive.

But this was precisely the point: we were supposed to be as if dead to each other. And I've sworn that I won't be the corpse that peeks first. 'For his sake' is what I put in my way every time I'm about to reach for the phone.

I don't actually think as much about him any longer. A thousand times a day, of course, but not as much each time – no more than I can stand. I fill all of my time with work. I sit in the department office or at the library, I work at home on both weekdays and weekends.

'Have you become a better person now, like Harriet?' Cilla asks.

'If I haven't, at least I don't have to be reminded about it all the time. With Aron, for example, I'm a civilized person, almost pleasant, if I may say so myself. Or with you – don't I act human?'

'Were you uncivilized with Gustav?'

'Not because it was Gustav precisely – well, maybe he invited it, but, above all, there must be something with marriage itself that brings out the worst in people.'

Cilla twists her wedding ring absent-mindedly. Newly married with that guy she's lived with since last summer. When she told me about it she blamed social pressure, and I have more understanding for that than ever. If the social pressure to have a family is less now than it was before, I wonder how it was before. As recently as on my way to Cilla this evening, I met two old classmates on the street and didn't have time to change pavements. The first thing you ask each other in such situations is what you're doing ('I'm getting my doctorate' is what I say then; that's when I say that I'm 'getting my doctorate'), but whether you're married or have children is the second question, just as inevitably. Social pressure is like a steamroller, and you have to be a superhero to resist it.

'The mistress function probably isn't ideal in the long run either, is it?'

'I've never said that's what I want – I don't like it at all. My ideal is a relationship between two independent people, and Aron isn't independent since he has a bunch of family.'

'Can you even call him, since he doesn't have a job? Do you call him at home?'

'Is the newly-wed interested in what an affair looks like?' I laugh. 'No, I don't call him myself unless there's an emergency. I have to take advantage when he happens to be free, and that's not that often. It was probably easier to be a mistress before, when the wife was responsible for the household. These modern men, all they want to do is run home and make dinner the whole time. Women's liberation has destroyed the market for our guild.'

'I guess you'll have to get a lover from a more old-fashioned generation.'

'I don't want to have anything to do with those oppressors of women.'

Cilla laughs and I drop my smoking implements in my purse to go home, since I hear her husband arriving in the hallway.

31

Not a single sign of life for two months. I thought I'd at least get one at Christmas: doesn't he usually send Christmas cards faithfully to other ex-mistresses? I happen to know that he does, and I take it as punishment pure and simple when nothing arrives.

Ah yes, Christmas. Suddenly it's the Christmas break: no duties to tend to at the department, and the Royal Library isn't even open during the holidays – all of a sudden there's an ominous silence all around me.

Holidays have never bothered me before. I'm prepared to read my way through Christmas and sleep through New Year's Eve, not giving a fig about celebrating and such. But if you need more than one person to celebrate, apparently the same is true for not giving a fig. There seems to be no effect when I do it alone. If I'm lying in my bed with a pillow over my ears when the New Year's bells begin to bong throughout the city, it only looks like a social failure if Gustav isn't doing the same.

Who knows how he's spending an evening like this now. With my inner eye I can see him chatting happily at merry parties, tossing serpentines to bare-armed, shiny-eyed, marriage-eager girls . . .Well, who knows.

*

At the first seminar after the New Year, we discuss a dissertation chapter. A debate arises about a terminological issue, the meaning of 'realism' in an epistemological context. No one succeeds in figuring it out, and Viveka, the author of the dissertation, gives me a friendly nudge in the side as we walk out: 'You have a philosopher in the family, can't you ask . . . ?'

I nod. Of course, I'll find out for you. I have no desire to explain then and there that I no longer have a philosopher in the family. I have even less desire to explain that the philosopher I had would be so upset if I got in touch with him that, for the sake of his peace of mind, I can't ask him a simple factual question. And I can be a philosopher myself. I mean, there must be books I can look it up in.

But no matter how I search on my shelves, I find nothing. I can go to the library, but before I get that far, I've lost my patience: spending so much time on such a trifle which he can probably take care of in the blink of an eye – no, there must be a limit to my consideration. It's enough that it's sad to be divorced; that it has to be all that impractical as well is something I won't tolerate.

I write a few lines and, for safety's sake, I stuff the letter in an envelope with university letterhead and a typewritten address so that he doesn't get stomach cramps before he even sees the contents.

The days go by without any answer, and I get annoyed: can't he even answer a polite enquiry? Well, perhaps it wasn't entirely polite – I couldn't help but introduce the topic with something spiteful about knowing that every reminder of my existence makes him incapable of working for a week – does he really have to pout because of that?

Viveka also works at the department, so I'll see her again soon. When she asks, I explain that I've forgotten about it but promise to find out by tomorrow.

I don't want to call, so I guess I'll have to go to the library after all. But first I want to get something in my stomach, so I ride home with exasperation grinding in my head as I skirt the naked Christmas tree corpses lining the streets.

His answer is lying on the hallway rug. He's used his school's stationery, with a stamp on the envelope. The 'Official matter', with an elaboration on realism and what philosophers have said about the subject since Antiquity, takes up a bit more than a page, which I skip over, to the heading 'Private Section'. There I'm informed that he can at present receive letters from me without suffering a stomach ache: 'My resilience has been improved since, as you probably know, I have remarried.'

So he has. Yes, of course. It's the first thing he's done every time we split up, found someone else, so why not this time? But 'as you probably know' – what does he mean by that? Does he think I'm researching the subject, that I'm going to my acquaintances asking if they've heard anything about Gustav and his success with the ladies?

'I know nothing,' I write in reply (in a normal envelope), 'and I would rather not know anything, but if it so happens that you get involved in something that I can't help but hear sooner or later in some way – that you move in together or have a baby together, for example – then I'd prefer to hear it sooner, from you, to getting it through rumours about town. I, too, have a stomach.'

I do, and if I didn't know it before, I do now. I don't think I'm jealous, I don't begrudge him, I don't begrudge either of them. It's probably not jealousy, but I feel nauseous when the earth moves beneath my feet.

*

Aron calls the department and wants to have lunch with me. It's not really my shift, it's Tomas who has office hours, but he hasn't come yet, and before I know whether he will, I can't leave. I ask Aron to call again in fifteen minutes.

Tomas arrives but he asks me to take his hour. He's not in the mood, he explains.

Mood? Who's in the mood to sit watch in the office?

'I feel so fragile after that flu I had.'

Fragile? If I came to work and said that I felt fragile, it would be female nonsense, of course.

'I have to make sure the dittos are ready for the afternoon,' he continues his tirade of excuses. I can't stand to hear any more. The last one is so transparent that it's embarrassing (dittos – all you have to do is make sure the assistant takes care of them), and I say, 'OK, OK, I'll take your hour, you can take mine another day.'

I have a work ethic, even if it's nothing more than self-preservation. If it goes so far that you're shoving your tasks on other people by invoking your mood, then you're underwater. Today I would have really liked to see Aron, but just because I need it more than usual, I'm careful not to insist on getting away.

I begin to organize the freshmen's registration cards while I watch the phones. I hear Tomas in the next module flirting with the secretary, trying to get her to go to lunch with him. I make a morally disgusted grimace and pick up the receiver with a martyr's halo over my head as it rings during Tomas' office hour.

At first I don't recognize Gustav's voice since it comes so unexpectedly. When I do, the earth begins to rock again: What does he want?

He just wants to have us agree about the information issue and suggests a mutual agreement to inform each other if we become pregnant or enter into new marriages in order to protect us from hearing it around town. 'Of course,' I say, 'that's fine.'

'Otherwise?' he asks.

'Nothing in particular. Everything's as usual. Just as usual.'

'Don't you have anything to say to me?'

'No. What would that be?'

'I don't know, anything at all. It just feels strange that we wouldn't have anything to say to each other. As if everything were over.'

'Isn't it?'

'Of course it is,' he says quickly.

'What?' I say (meaning: why this emphasis, to convince me or you?). But he simply repeats, louder and more clearly.

'Of course!'

The seconds tick by.

'Your letter,' I say carefully, 'you signed it "Yours eternally". You didn't mean anything in particular by that, did you?'

He laughs.

'No, not at all, nothing more than precisely what it says.'

In that case.

'We can see each other sometime,' I say ambiguously.

'Not for a long time.'

'But you know where I am. I probably won't move again until I have to go to a nursing home. I'll send an address change then.'

Gustav promises to do the same, and so I return to organizing the freshmen in the card registry.

*

Viveka from the department invites me to come with her to the country for the weekend: her husband is away and she doesn't want to go to her cottage alone. She's an odd one, I think: having your own cottage and then not being able to be there alone. But yes, it's been a long time since I breathed country air. I'm happy to offer myself as a companion.

But when it comes right down to it, I'm not much of one. I retreat into my memories and I'm absorbed in conversations with myself. The place is in the same direction as Gustav's Island – on the mainland and not as far from the city, but the first twenty kilometres or so we follow the same road, where the memories line up as tightly as the bushes outside the bus window. It's barren winter, misty weather, muted grey and brown tones: beautiful, that kind of beauty that nature always has every season although you forget it and are surprised every time you get to see it.

It's a road I've travelled so many times that I can close my eyes and feel where we are by how the bus turns. On my way to the Island. No, not on my way to the Island. Never again.

Fear stings me and suddenly swells up with a very clear contour: What about at Easter? And this summer? What'll I do if I won't be on the Island?

Stop now, I say, and grab my fright by the ear: What's this? Does this have to do with Gustav or is it, as usual, just the loss of his summer place you're afraid of?

I think about it while the bus rattles around the curves and the muted grey and brown colours glide past and Viveka reads a women's magazine for lack of conversation. I think, but it doesn't make me any wiser: one cannot be separated from the other.

Naturally, I tell myself sternly, it's just a question of nostalgia. The thought of the Island makes you sentimental because it's a part of your life, and it's the same with Gustav. You're grieving him as a part of your past, as a part of yourself, in an expanded form of self-love.

I know, I answer myself humbly. But not only that?

Oh, I see. You miss Gustav himself, too? Can you claim that you know this Gustav Lindgren at all? Can you describe him, for example? Can you?

Of course I can – but what's the use?

Let me hear.

Gustav – well, he's a wise person for example, I mean sensible and reasonable, except when he's got something particular into his head. He's not one bit tactful or empathetic, he's too honest for that, at least I've always believed that although maybe – we can skip that. In any case, I dare to claim that he's the most secure, harmonious person I've ever met, well, he's nervously hypersensitive, but even so he has the unusual ability to take most things lightly, at least it seems so – wait a minute, what is this nonsense? What are you trying to get at?

Can you place your finger on something and say: This is Gustav?

No – not now.

Quite right: no longer, because Gustav was 'the one who loves Martina', that's how he was defined.

He was the one who defined himself that way! It's not my fault. I would never perceive another person solely in relation to me if he didn't do it himself. Someone like Aron, for example, with a strong personality, he's Another, not defined through me, and that's just the point of him!

We weren't talking about Aron.

No, we were talking about Gustav, who's a part of me and whom I grieve for as I can only grieve for myself.

'Here it is,' Viveka says as the bus slows for a stop that's simply a post at the edge of the road and a path into the forest.

She takes the path in and I follow after. The air is moist and mild, and I'm weak-kneed with fear.

Viveka sleeps late in the mornings. There's only a tuft of hair visible above the blanket against the wall across the room. I also want to go back to sleep but I can't. The room is full of grey February light and I lie and remember that I had another dream.

I was on the Island. Gustav's brother and sister-in-law were also there and they reminded me disapprovingly that I shouldn't be there since Gustav himself was on his way with his new wife. I tried to excuse myself by saying I was just going to fetch a few belongings that I had left there, I wouldn't stay long or be any trouble. But before I got away, Gustav and his new woman arrived, and he was very irritated to find me there and the last train had gone (train, not a bus or boat) and I had to walk home, but I had so many bags full of things that I couldn't carry them all . . .

The symbolism is still not too complicated for any amateur at all to manage.

★

Harriet is going on vacation to the mountains and comes up to borrow my skis – mostly it's only such practical matters that give us an excuse to visit these days. I'm demonstrating the bindings for her when the phone interrupts us.

Gustav. He wants some advice.

'I see, of course,' I say and sit down, gesture to Harriet to toss me a cigarette. 'What's up, have you got someone pregnant again?'

'Not as far as I know. But it's about the other thing we were going to inform each other about, moving in with someone. Should I?'

I produce a deep guffaw. 'Are you asking *me* about this? If you need to ask me for advice about this issue, it's probably a pretty weighty argument against it, as far as I can tell.'

'Why not? You're a wise person, and you know me.'

'You, I know. If she were the one asking me for advice, I would without a doubt say yes. I would advise anyone to marry you. I've never doubted that you would be ideal to share a home with. But I don't know her.'

'Yes, but I mean in principle.'

'In principle . . . my answer is yes. Try everything, try moving in together and see how it is. I'm sure it'll be nice – a calm and bourgeois family life is what you've always wanted. It's obvious that you should take the chance, as long as she's a pleasant person.'

He doesn't interpret the final sentence as a question. In any event he doesn't answer. And I don't want to know if she is, either. I don't want to know anything. Otherwise, what I would be most interested in knowing is if they were already acquainted during my time, if it's one of those Susannas or Ingegerds who were in the picture then, or if it's a new acquaintance. But it's none of my business. It's none of my business and I don't want to know and I ask:

'Who is it?'

'A colleague at the school.'

'Of course. With a master's degree in Swedish and English, right?'

'How did you know?'

I laugh. 'They all are.'

'What do you mean all? There are many kinds of teachers.'

'All the nice gals that men get married to.'

'You and your prejudices,' Gustav says, but I hear, with inexpressible delight, that he's not unaffected by these prejudices of mine, that he would rather it be something other than precisely Swedish and English.

'It's a good match, then. Just don't get rid of your flat right away – get a second-hand tenant for now. And no babies,' I say sternly. 'No babies until you know what you both want.

'Is that enough good advice?' I add when he doesn't respond.

'What do you think about it yourself? Are you sad?'

I think for a moment. I hear Harriet behind me packing the skis in their case. I'm sitting on the floor next to my bed and see there are dust bunnies under it again – didn't I clean last Saturday?

Why is he asking? Is there hope in his voice?

'None of your fucking business,' I say kindly.

And so we hang up after renewed reassurances of eternal friendship at some point in the future.

'Gustav?' Harriet asks when I stand up.

I nod.

'He's thinking about moving in with his new wife and wanted my blessing.'

'Oh my. Is he hoping you'll change your mind and try to prevent it?'

'I don't know. It may also have simply been a way to <u>break the news</u>, a little gently, you know.'

I actually don't know which one it was. I don't know where I have Gustav any longer. I don't have him at all.

*

Not only does Aron now have the key to my front door, he's also deposited a pair of slippers in my flat. That is, it's not that straightforward – maybe he'd be surprised to hear it described as a 'deposit', a pledge. It can also be explained by the fact that he happened to be taken by surprise in a storm once when he was in town, bought a pair of boots and decided it was a good idea to leave his old, worn-out espadrilles at my place: 'Maybe someone can use them.' Always watching his back, that one.

Gustav's slippers are unequivocal. A pair of blue moccasins, size 44, whose purpose was never anything other than for Gustav's use when he was visiting. They're still resting in my shoe rack in the hallway: a deposit, but one that has passed its maturity date.

He'll have to come get them sometime if he wants them, I thought, when Aron's also landed there, and then he can return mine at the same time – my slipper deposit in his home. Although, on second thought, I think I may keep them instead: I can accumulate a nice little museum over time.

*

When Gustav talked about moving in together, I assumed he was intending to move in with the new woman. However, as it turns out, they're living at his place. In Gustav's little studio flat!

I think it would be tough enough just having the same workplace, running into each other in the faculty lounge constantly, maybe eating lunch together, but then going home and eating dinner together, and reading and sleeping in the same room, day and night in the same room, always! I never thought there was so much love, so much that it didn't need a larger space than that.

I've had my own room my entire life, the only exception being the maternity ward and a few months thereafter, as far as I know. For as long as I've been conscious, I've never even reflected on what it would be like to share a room with someone else permanently – male or female, dog or cat. Never even in my most senseless moments. A door you can close behind you: isn't that a basic human need?

Apparently not. Gustav bubbles with well-being when he tells me about his new existence.

'Doesn't it feel crowded?' I ask, since conversation requires that I say something.

'I don't really own that many things, but of course I've had to make room in drawers and bookshelves.'

I meant in his soul. I meant that even if the soul doesn't take up physical space, I don't understand how two beings, no matter how non-spatial, can fit within twenty-five square metres. However, I don't immerse myself in the subject, to avoid hearing him explain that theirs are as one.

I return to the actual reason he called: the possessions we still have at each other's homes.

'My slippers, for example,' I remind him.

He laughs:

'Oh right, we found them when we were cleaning out the closet. They must go!'

It's at this moment that panic hits me.

Not before this moment? How is that possible? How can you be so blindly lacking in imagination that you can't imagine what a divorce means until it's made tangible by a pair of slippers?

That's how it is, anyway. It's at this moment when he cheer-fully mentions this, in a sentence with a new 'we', that it occurs to me: Gustav is now cleaning me out of his life.

And anxiety surges towards me like a wave, just like it, closes over my head like a wave, and I have to fight to catch my breath.

'Of course. Bring them here and you can get yours at the same time. I don't want them standing around in my hallway – besides, Another Man's slippers are here now.'

A pitiful attempt to assert myself, as if it were anything to place in the scales. As if an entire museum, a whole shoe store with the slippers of old and new lovers were anything against the fact that Gustav and I will no longer have any place in each other's homes.

We agree to meet that afternoon and exchange belongings.

For the Inuit, Torsten once claimed, slippers are a symbol of sexual relations with greater significance than coital faithful-ness: you can have sex with as many people as you please, but if a woman gives someone a pair of slippers, it's a unique distinction.

Judging by what I've read about this in the literature, it must have been a distorted interpretation, but in the context in which Torsten told me about it, it simply served the purpose of illus-trating how relative 'faithfulness' is and how backwards it is to pay attention to precisely those perceptions that are prevalent in the culture where you happen to be.

In the culture where I happen to be, there is rather a light touch of ridiculousness surrounding this footwear, something contented, cosy and bourgeois.

I would have never believed that their to-be or not-to-be could have such significance. That one pair of slippers more or less could cause someone distress.

I sort Gustav's books from my shelves and his records from

the beer crate, I fold up a sweater and a pair of pyjamas I borrowed at the Island. I fetch a glass bowl from the kitchen cupboard that he brought supper in once (fish au gratin, or whatever it was) and I put everything in two paper sacks. Gustav comes to fetch them and hands me another.

He hesitates for a moment in the hall, looks at me and asks:

'How are you?'

'How are you?'

He laughs.

'You see how fat and content I've become.'

'No fatter than four months ago.'

'I'm not? Well, more content in any case, I can assure you. Can't you be happy for me?'

'Of course, I am. That means there was a point to splitting up.'

That was the point, that's what I've explained to myself month after month, it was for his sake that I let him go, so that he would have a better life.

BUT WHAT ABOUT ME?

'Are you sorry?'

I'm standing in my doorway, looking at the linoleum.

'I'm afraid.'

Now that he's invincible, now that he's the strong one, I don't have to put up a front and I don't have to protect anyone's stomach any longer. I can tell it like it is: I'm afraid, scared to death.

'Things will be calmer this way,' he says, 'you'll be sure to find that out as well.'

He's going to go in a moment, so I have to ask while he's still here.

'Are you going to get married? Are you going to have children? Are you going to live together for ever and ever?'

'We'll have to see how it goes,' he says calmly.

'You never said that before!' I exclaim (before: during my time).

'Before, you never talked about letting things take their course and seeing how it went. Before, there were supposed to be big decisions and sacred oaths and putting our entire effort into it!'

He laughs again.

'I guess I've become more reasonable with the years, under your influence. And I'm not dependent on her in the same way I was on you.'

A marriage of convenience, of course. He can have one with others – just not with me.

'We can see each other sometime,' he says and turns towards the door.

'Maybe. In ten years. As things are now, I just can't.'

He cocks his head and plays the eager one:

'In five?

'Otherwise we won't belong to each other any longer,' he adds. 'I mean so we can talk to each other about everything.'

I snort. It's been years since we've been able to talk with each other about everything – about anything at all except our bloody relationship.

He strokes my hair, as you comfort a child. Then he picks up the sacks, taking one in each hand, slams the door behind himself and clatters quickly down the stairs. Relieved that this is over, I see.

32

They talk about butterflies in your stomach. Butterflies?

There's something fluttering in my stomach, but it's certainly not like anything as light and poetic as butterfly wings. It's more like windmills: heavy, dark, flapping wildly.

Or a turbine. Sharp, shiny blades that rotate, around and around and around, cutting through defenceless internal organs, again and again.

I can think about it, analyse it, describe it and find similes for it – just not get it to stop. Hour after hour, day after day: an incessantly spinning anxiety-turbine in my stomach.

I _panic_, and it's remarkable that there's no verb for it in Swedish, because panic isn't simply something you're a victim of, just as little as depression is something you quietly 'have': just as being depressed is an activity, panicking is as well. It's an activity that claims all my attention and all my strength.

I remember with annoyance how I've joked around with the concept of anxiety before, called it 'existential anxiety' when I've been a bit off or troubled about what I'll be when I grow up. That was a salon anxiety, a plaything anxiety in comparison with this _what-have-I-done?_ variety.

But I knew what I was doing – why does it come as such a shock? Maybe I 'subconsciously' didn't believe in the divorce before now, although I thought that I did – oh yes, you can always rationalize your behaviour by bringing in a few 'subconscious' factors in order to force everything to make sense. But how are you ever supposed to take responsibility for your actions if, running parallel to your conscious motivations, you have a set of others that are just as unknown as those of a stranger? I believed I knew what I was doing, and that it was my responsibility, so I could do my small part in reducing the suffering in the world. I didn't think it would be easy – I anticipated that I could regret it. But that it would be so difficult: if I had known that, I would have never made an attempt.

If I'm now just as unhappy as Gustav was, or even unhappier, then it wasn't my duty after all, was it? Sacrificing yourself would be an *unnecessarily* good deed, an overflow good deed, the act of a saint: I hadn't intended to take on such a thing at all. But I couldn't imagine it would be like this, could I?

The jolts of panic come unannounced – it's impossible to confront them with arguments. In my greatest moments of defencelessness, on the boundary between sleeping and waking, that's when it shudders through my soul like an earthquake: *Gustav* – without him my life is meaningless!

I shudder so much that I sit up, wide awake, and continue to ponder my situation. I try to talk sense to myself: What do you mean, meaningless? Do you think the lives of all single people are meaningless? No, I don't want to believe that. There are different paths to self-fulfilment and making sense of your existence. These opportunities come in different ways to different people. But Gustav was mine, and now I've lost him. What would Gustav have brought to my life, then? The meaning of being another person's joy. But I was no joy to him – all he did was suffer because of his love for me, didn't he? Well, yes, but if I had wanted to (if I had been able to want to), if I had made the slightest effort – he was happy with so little, and the smallest gesture of affection yielded inordinate appreciation (inordinate: it made me tired). Simply by showing up I made him happy, simply by being near him, even when I was cross and unwilling – yes, simply by existing.

Isn't this what I've been saying the whole time: it ought to be forbidden to love like this. Or the one who does so should in any event be prohibited from no longer loving, once he's been crazy enough to start. Once he's committed himself to being the meaning of my life.

'What's worse: loving or being loved?' the blue Nehru-suit boy philosophized. Here's another riddle: Is it worse to never have been loved, or to no longer be?

*

Work, don't think. Read, write, don't feel. One day at a time, each day on its own, stop thinking about 'my life'. It's worst in the morning, waking up and regaining consciousness. Getting to work as quickly as possible and working until I can't go on. Then I go to bed and think it'll probably be better tomorrow.

You can't live with chronic panic, so it has to go away at some point.

Well, the acute panic subsides, but it doesn't recede far – it's waiting behind every corner.

A beautiful morning. March: soft, moist earth turns dry in the sun, things are growing.

The pain reflex: a morning for going to the country. On mornings like this, we used to meet up at the bus stop with food sacks and book bags and rattle along on the bus out of the city, out to the sea.

Today. Maybe they will. They: Gustav's new 'we'.

There should be different words in our language for the 'we' that includes a second person and the one that includes a third. Nothing Gustav has ever said hurts me as much as when he says 'we' and doesn't mean 'us'.

If it only weren't spring. The light hurts my eyes. I buy new, darker sunglasses but it's not enough. I wish I had a black umbrella to walk under. I wish I could live in a black tent, protected from the sun and all this lush awakening.

There's only one comforting thought: he is well, he's happy now, it's better this way. (And of course the side thought: ha, I'm a better person than you are, because I can be glad for the happiness of others.) This thought has to be enough.

I'm in no condition to see him – I'll have to continue to pretend he's dead. And to try to think about him as one does about those for whom death has come as a liberator: he's better off where he is now.

I can't let my thoughts stray in search of other reasons for comfort. 'When I said "in ten years" then he said "in five", then he must care for me after all, maybe it's not too late . . .' If you start reasoning like this, it will never end.

*

I'm making no headway on my dissertation. I've lost the main thread and my perspective, and I sit buried in details. I'm despairing of ever climbing out again. I ride off to the Royal Library and borrow a few books to give myself the illusion of getting something done, although the ones I already have lying around half-read are more than enough. I go out to buy a paper, I come home and make coffee. The phone is silent; nobody comes to the door.

Dagens Nyheter with my morning coffee, radio with my coffee for lunch, *Aftonbladet* at dinner. Maybe I should buy a television? So I can escape my thoughts.

Or think about Aron. Sometimes I think about Aron, as though that could fill my life with meaning. I try to cultivate unhappiness about him instead of what I feel about Gustav, but it's not strong enough. He's a kind of happiness, too, and it doesn't help. You have to fight fire with fire, and unhappiness is only vanquished by a greater unhappiness.

So I think about Gustav anyway – 'happen to think about him',

constantly, constantly. I tear off the scabs in my chains of association before they've had a chance to heal over.

Every time I talk to my mother on the phone, she asks if
I've bought those curtains I got money for as a Christmas gift.
It's true, I had said it was what I needed the absolute most, but
since then I've lost interest in decorating my flat. The only thing
I want for that is a set of blackout curtains.

I never have visitors I can have fun showing off something new
to, either. Aron is completely blind to such things – strangely
enough, since you might think that creating different kinds of
environments would interest people who work with images,
even though interior decoration may not have any direct connection with filming striking shipyard workers. However that
may be, he wouldn't even notice if I hung up red-checked
cotton curtains on my green Jugendstil walls.

But if I answer my mother's question evasively any more,
she'll come to the conclusion that I've drunk up the money
or gambled it away or something along those lines. I make an
effort to get involved in the matter and I find a tape measure
to find out how high the windows are before I go look in the
shops. One metre ninety, I measure.

One metre ninety? This is a measurement that I recognize
from another context. Gustav's passport, that is.

What does this remind me of? Naturally: Eeyore. 'My favourite size.' About as big as Piglet, he said to himself sadly. My
favourite size. Well, well.

This is ridiculous – it's ridiculous and insufferable. Just because
my balloon burst, I imagine that it was my favourite colour and
favourite size. To be honest, I still wouldn't claim that Gustav
was my favourite size. I've always thought that one metre ninety
was more man than I needed. (I've liked shorter fellows, maybe
because they like small girls – sometimes, tall boys prefer tall

girls; short ones never do – or maybe simply because they seem more manageable.) But if this continues, I'll probably start to believe that he was my favourite kind in every imaginable way.

Just because it burst. Just because of that, there isn't a damned anything I can imagine that doesn't have associations to him.

What a fate it is to be born an Eeyore.

I bunk off the curtains and don't answer the phone. Let me chew on my thistles and don't come to me bearing gifts.

*

'So why?' Aron asks when I tell him that my marriage has been dissolved. (I haven't told him until now. He never asks about my private life, and, before now, I haven't felt the need to tell him anything about it.)

'Why didn't it work any longer?'

'It was your fault' is something I don't say. Of course not, partly because I would have seen Aron for the last time if I did, and partly because it's not true. It's possible that my 'subconscious' looks at it this way, it may be that it's the explanation for the creeping irritation I feel towards Aron, the stinginess that, for example, made me not want to invite him home but only agree to meet him in town. How the hell can you comprehend what the subconscious is up to (because, as the name suggests, it's not conscious)? It's possible that in my heart of hearts, deepest down, I've actually counted on Aron marrying me and I'm disappointed that he's not making the slightest attempt in that direction – I'm keeping all possibilities open but don't consider such rot to be anything to devote any thinking to, never mind talking.

'Why do people always ask that?' I say instead. 'It's as if the natural thing is that relationships work, when it's quite the opposite, it's remarkable when they do.'

'You mean it's the relationships that continue you should ask about? "They're still married – why is that?"'

'Yes! Can you tell me that? The fact that you and Florence aren't getting a divorce – why is that?'

He just laughs.

I've never met Florence and know nothing about what their relationship is like. Now and then I've suggested that he introduce us to each other, not so much out of curiosity as from a kind of need to reassure myself that she doesn't feel any hostility towards me – just as Eva during her time insisted on meeting me. I understand it better now: it's unpleasant to think that a betrayed wife is going around thinking evil thoughts about you. You want to make sure that it isn't the case.

Aron has never taken my suggestions seriously. Why not, actually? Gustav himself was eager to have us come together – he thought it was fun. She does know about my existence, doesn't she?

I've always been so careful with Aron, afraid of irritating him. But what's the point of seeing someone as we do if we can't speak in confidence with each other? I'm tired of this cowardly tact. Things can't get any worse, and now I want a straight answer:

'Does she know that you see other women?'

He looks just as pained as one could have expected.

'She probably prefers not to know anything.'

Probably. He assumes that if she knew what she doesn't know, she'd prefer to live in ignorance – that's his guess.

The same old story, then – the ancient, completely banal story of infidelity in secret. This shakes me up: that Aron. At the time I got to know him, he certainly didn't hide the fact that he was living in promiscuity. I've assumed that this was the custom in his circles and that his woman was of the modern type who are above such things.

'I see,' I say, so quietly that he doesn't have to hear it if he doesn't want to, 'I see, so that's why.'

★

Think about something else. Join a club. Change the world, get interested in something.

Vietnam meeting in the People's House, speeches and theatre, announced on posters plastered on the wall of my building.

I'm in the middle of locking my bike at Norra Latin when Gustav swings up and parks next to me.

Was this why I came here? No. Or well, yes, how should I know? It doesn't surprise me to see him here. He waits to walk in with me.

'Are you alone here?' I ask.

'Yes, as you see. Why, would you turn around otherwise?'

Maybe. In any event, I didn't come here to see Them.

We take off our coats in the cloakroom, walk into the room, sit down next to each other. A girl in front of us turns around, whispers to her neighbour, who then also turns her head – they're from school, Gustav informs me, and he thinks it's funny: Now people will talk.

'Can't you even sit at a political meeting accompanied by another woman without it being inappropriate?'

'Not without it being gossiped about in any case.'

His laugh. His movements. His way of stretching out into a half-reclining position in his seat, his way of twisting a lock of pale-red hair between his fingers as he listens. Those small habits that always irritated me back then. So strange: to be foreign to someone you know so well. Sitting here next to him, like sitting next to my husband, and yet it isn't him, although he looks exactly like my husband did.

'You have new shoes,' he whispers when the speaker up front is interrupted by applause.

'Not so new. At least six months ago.'

'But a new kind – those are lady shoes.'

'I thought I had to try to look a little more adult.'

He laughs, I shush him.

So many times I've sat next to Gustav in an audience and shushed him.

After the speeches, there's a break. We agree that we won't stay for the theatre and walk home together. The air is misty, mild and damp; the cinema marquees are turned off. We ride single-file without exchanging many words. Over Kungsbron, down the length of Fleminggatan, almost all the way to my flat, we have the same way. He stops at the intersection where I'm turning off.

'You don't want to come up?'

'I had actually planned to be home by ten.'

I nod. He's told her that, is what he means. And he won't make her wait. It's lovely. Of course I can see that it's lovely. He stands there, probably waiting for me to look at him and say goodnight, but I can't, I just can't do anything else.

'You can't be as unhappy as you look, can you?'

'You don't know how unhappy I can be. I didn't know myself.'

'But it's nothing I can do anything about, is it?'

I don't answer.

Certainly I had some notion that it would be an entirely too great and heroic decision, this allowing Gustav to leave, but I guess I thought that people could grow into decisions that are too great after a time. I had forgotten that my nature is the opposite. To grow out of decisions, no: I shrink out of them.

I've shrunk and shrunk to near oblivion. Of my great resolution to think of his well-being, there's not a trace left. I want to do everything in my power to sow unrest in his soul, appeal to old feelings, pull on old strings, upset and undermine him – it's just that I'm not capable of anything any longer.

He shrugs his shoulders. 'It's just because you don't have me that you miss me.'

'Solely for that reason,' I say tiredly, 'as soon as I had you again, I would stop missing you.'

'Well, yes, but not just that – you'd stop wanting me.'

It's hard to deny that – he has long experience to build his claim on. I could say not *this* time, but I can't demand that he believe it. I can't know it myself.

'It's possible,' I answer quietly, 'but it doesn't make missing you any easier. You can be happy to be rid of me, but think about how I have to go around with me my entire life, with such a disposition.'

'I'm not particularly happy that you're unhappy.'

Not even that? If he were at least happy, with *schaden-freude*, then he'd at least still be involved with me. Such a normal, humane little sympathy: you can only feel that when you've recovered from love and everything meant by it – everything we, in this cultural tradition, understand by the word 'love'.

'No, I want to see fat and happy people around me.'

I don't have the energy to smile. He holds his bicycle with his left hand, places the other around my shoulder.

'"Get a hold of yourself now",' he says. He says it with quotation marks, aware that it's a meaningless phrase, maybe simply as a marker that there's nothing for him to say.

'Will you marry me?' he says then.

Another meaningless phrase.

He stands up straight and grasps the handlebars.

'Is she jealous?' I ask, not wanting to know, but just to continue the conversation for a moment longer.

'I'm not exactly sure. But it's obvious that you hang like a dark shadow over our relationship, you can imagine.'

I look up at him – oh yes, please let me at least be a shadow, let me be there if only as a little shadow up in the right-hand corner, as long as I can be there!

'She dreamed something about you a couple weeks ago, by the way . . .'

But why is he telling me this? I don't want to hear it, but I can't manage to interrupt him either . . .

'We were at the Island and you came along too, or maybe you were leaving, and she thought you'd been inside and stolen something that belonged to her . . .'

Isn't this my dream? Are we dreaming the same dreams, his women? – Or did she get it from me – I mentioned what I'd dreamed about being on the Island the last time we talked on the phone. Did he tell her as he's telling me now? Does he have to be so open, does he have to be like a sieve? It's not right to say everything, he doesn't have the right!

He's leaning against his bike, I'm looking at his feet.

'Please don't talk to her about me,' I plead.

'It doesn't happen that often, but sometimes it's hard to avoid. You sometimes get to talking about your past, you know.'

Water droplets are sparkling on the pavement and the moisture in the air has condensed into rain. He straightens his bike again, he's going home now.

I can't keep him here. Now he's going. Bye.

It feels like dying. A meaningless expression, because how does that feel? But what I feel as I walk up the stairs seems describable only in those terms: like dying. I am past, I no longer exist.

*

'Is something wrong?' Cilla asks, whom I've finally reached through the switchboard at Swedish Radio. 'Has something happened?'

No, nothing's happened. It's just that my anxiety is so bad that I can't be alone with it. I've never experienced anything like it before. She promises she'll try to get off after lunch and come over for a while.

I go into the kitchen and make a thermos of coffee, then sit down to wait.

Of all the things Cilla and I have seen each other go through, we've never seen each other cry. It frightens me just as much as her that I can't make my voice steady. It only quavers and sounds so awful that I whisper instead.

'Gustav?' she asks and lays her jacket over a chair. 'But why?'

'I don't know,' I whisper. 'I don't know why I all of a sudden feel so anxious about it when I didn't before. We'd been divorced several months without my feeling bad as a result.'

'Maybe it's existential anxiety, then?'

'Maybe that, my thirty-year crisis. Hormones, or brain chemistry, or it was written in the stars that I would be afflicted by a great life panic just this month.

'Maybe I'm just blaming him to make it more comprehensible,' I add. 'Or maybe he was the only thing standing between me and my existential anxiety before.'

'So it has to do with Gustav after all, then?'

'It has to do with a lack of Gustav. There's a hole in my life where he was. Can such a thing give you anything but anxiety? I'm so afraid when I wake up in the morning and that hole is gaping at me, every single morning.'

'So it's separation anxiety,' she suggests.

I try to smile so it doesn't horrify her that my tears are dripping into my coffee.

'Page 117 in the psychology book, top of the page on the left. It sounds familiar. You could also call it fear of mutilation. I don't want to live the rest of my life as an invalid.'

She shakes her head as you shake your head at people who've lost their sense of proportion in their love troubles, like someone who knows better that time will bring loves and troubles that are just as upsetting.

Cilla doesn't understand. She still doesn't understand.

'Obviously time heals all wounds, I know that too. I'm bound to have other relationships at some point. But the thing is that nobody can replace Gustav. Don't you understand that?'

Even if it stops hurting in a year or two, an amputated limb cannot grow again, and, without Gustav, I'll live the rest of my life crippled.

'Are you just saying that you regret that you divorced?'

'Not at all. I don't regret it at all. I'm just grieving to death over it.'

I toss paper tissues on the pile on the floor and she looks at me with raised eyebrows.

'The whole thing actually reminds me of when people try to commit suicide time and again until they succeed by mistake. You probably didn't think a divorce would succeed after all the times you had tried.'

'But it wasn't a mistake. I've seldom been so convinced about anything as I was that we ought to divorce. It's just that I hadn't understood what it meant until now. Besides, my reactions have always been delayed this way: when Gustav started to court me, it took months before I discovered anything interesting in him. Or when he cheated on me with Eva, I had six months' incubation time before my jealousy broke out.'

'And the same thing every bloody divorce: first it went fine, and then not so well?'

I smile apologetically – yes, I'm sorry I can't offer more than such monotony.

Cilla drinks her coffee, I smoke her cigarettes and wait for her to say something.

Does she, just like Gustav, think I'm capricious and unreasonable? But in fact I'm the one who, for all these years, has never changed my position: before, I used all my energy to keep him at a distance, to defend myself against his voracious, omnivorous love – now I mourn him for dead and miss him every minute. There's no contradiction there. I need him just as much as before, in precisely the same way. It's Gustav who's changed. Gustav, who recently couldn't live without me, and who now has no use for me whatsoever.

What's unreasonable is the one great love. He wanted to give me everything, everything. Except what I needed: something less than everything.

'I don't think it can ever work when people aren't equals. You shouldn't marry your great passion.'

'I think we also agreed on that eventually, although we drew different conclusions from it. I mean, he came to the conclusion that he shouldn't marry me, and I that I shouldn't be his great passion. That's what made a marriage of convenience impossible between us the whole time. If only he could have listened to reason.'

'It's not always that easy.'

'Aren't humans creatures of reason?' I ask, upset. 'Aren't we? AREN'T we?' I answer myself.

And Cilla says nothing.

'Why does marriage make people so mean?' I ask.

'I don't doubt that you were mean, but I wonder if Gustav was every bit as saintly as you portray him these days.'

'It's true, I've always idealized him most at a distance. But now I have to, so that I don't begrudge him his happiness as he is now – it's best that he keeps his distance, because, every time I see him, I discover how unsympathetic he is, and I dislike him so much that I start to regret that I let him go.'

'Unsympathetic in what way?'

'Like yesterday, when he suddenly asked if I wanted to marry him – what did he do that for, when he's not even available for marriage now? To mess with me because it amuses him to be longed for?'

'Perhaps he was simply wondering,' she suggests. 'Scientific interest, I mean, just wanting to obtain information about the situation?'

I sigh.

'Probably. It doesn't occur to him how the listener receives such things. Or he could have just been blathering. He's spoken those words so many times that they come as a reflex every time he sees me. They slip out without him even meaning anything by them at all.

'But he's always been loose-lipped,' I add – more upset the more I think about it – 'he simply <u>speaks his mind</u>, never thinks of filtering his impulses to verbalize. He must be missing some kind of control mechanism, something necessary for making interhuman communication tolerable.'

It doesn't seem as though she really understands what I'm babbling about, so I exemplify:

'Can you imagine that he had the nerve to tell me about his wife's nightmares about me – and told her mine as well!'

'My God, you can't be around such people.'

'That's right,' I say, satisfied. 'You get so angry that you just want to marry him.'

'So you can control what slips out of his mouth, you mean?'

'So that I can give him a kick to the gut in return.'

In my room, the afternoon darkness presses in and Cilla reaches for the desk lamp. The traffic noise down below sounds like it will soon be rush hour. I have a satisfied feeling of having made her 'answerless', although I don't really know what it is she hasn't answered.

'What about Aron?'

'Ough, that.'

'Ough? Are you saying ough about the great passion now?'

'There is no passion great enough to fill a hole left by a marriage. And besides, I've said that one person cannot replace another – they're not interchangeable. Aron is Aron, and I'm happy to have him to the extent I do, but it has nothing to do with this.

'That's what Gustav has never wanted to understand,' I continue. 'And for him, it doesn't seem to work that way. I mean it seems that he's found a replacement for me.'

'But Martina, wasn't that the reason you divorced? As you were describing it back then?'

'Of course. I let him abandon me so that he could be happy with someone else. And so he goes and does it, in no time flat! And he talks about passions! Disloyal is what it is, deceitful and disloyal.'

'It's nice to see you can laugh anyway,' Cilla says. She gets up and pulls her jacket over her shoulders, stops in the door and asks:

'Can you sleep? I have sleeping pills if you want some.'

'I do nothing else for the most part. Except last night, but that was an exception. I'm really going to avoid running into him again.

'It's not the sleeping that's difficult,' I aphorize, 'it's the being awake.'

Cilla pretends to jot it down and we part laughing. Then I can continue to cry without frightening anyone else.

33

If only I could reach bottom and then rise again with a great and beautiful resignation I can manage to live on. I can't sink any deeper than that evening at the intersection when I stood face to face with the fact that I no longer have any power over him. But what I rise again with – well, it's certainly no great and beautiful resignation. For a little while, I succeed in imagining it, for a period of twenty-four hours or so now and again. I just don't know how it happens, nothing in particular has to happen, it's just some internal landslide – suddenly my reason is out of order, leaving space for wild speculation and crazy plans, and that little voice is there whispering again:

She could die. Couldn't she? You read all the time in the paper about people who die, don't you? She could get tired of him. She could fall in love with someone else. He could get tired of her. There are innumerable possibilities, actually – and I could help fate along the way, too. What if I got pregnant by him: a baby could manifest what I no longer can. Voluntarily he wouldn't do it. I'd have to trick him, get him drunk and seduce him when he's pissed and incapable – no, that may not work, but get him drunk enough so he doesn't remember what happened then, and then get pregnant with anyone and say that it's his . . .

If I could suppress this once and for all and not have to hear about it ever again. But it just continues, round and round in

438

the same paths, until I want to scream for help and mercy: an incomprehensible self-torture.

I can't request any more pastoral care of Cilla, and, besides, she's entirely too delicate in her attempts to understand. What I really need is someone who'll deal more severely with me.

I call Harriet and ask her to reason with me. She does – she says what my own reason has already said to me ten thousand times:

'Gustav?' she says, surprised. 'Oh, cut it out! I really think it's time you stopped this Gustav business.'

And it's good to hear her say so. I know it's the voice of reason speaking.

But that other voice doesn't keep still as a result. It's whispering, Oh, Harriet, you don't know. What do you really know about Gustav and me . . .

That arrogantly squeaking little voice of insanity.

*

It's not so I could marry Aron that I let Gustav abandon me. It wasn't even so that I could see him more freely. It had nothing at all to do with Aron except that he happened to be a catalyst: if it hadn't been him, it would have been something else. But since I can't get my subconscious to understand that, my bitterness festers, inaccessible to substantive reason: 'It's Aron's fault'.

Isn't that the reason why he's suddenly changed shape? What's the reason an infatuation passes generally – that an aura that's existed around a person shrinks away and you stand there astonished and stare at what was inside it?

I still like seeing him and talking to him – and people to see and talk to are so few and far between for me that I can't afford to lose one of them. Cilla won't come over unless I sound suicidal on the phone (and I don't insist unless I feel suicidal). Harriet also has a job to do, working as a substitute teacher as Gustav once did. Besides, she's moved into a commune with her daughter and is at least as inaccessible there as in a normal family, has to 'get home to dinner' every day it seems. They live in Djursholm, so you can't exactly stop by and claim that you were in the neighbourhood.

I need Aron in order to have someone to have a word or two with. But sleep with him? When I touch him, it's like the feeling you get when you touch a part of your body that's gone to sleep: yes, you feel it, but it's a feeling without meaning, without pain or pleasure, simply a kind of registration, and it's hard to comprehend that the body part that feels without feeling belongs to you.

He's never been a particularly talented lover, and I've liked him for that reason too – such an amateur, I thought tenderly. It doesn't amuse me any longer. The determination with which he attempts to 'satisfy' me makes me freeze up. It's true, it does require firm resolve and focus, but it has to happen as if in passing in order to work. I try to get involved, but my body doesn't allow itself to be commanded to do such things. It's so uninvolved that it creaks.

In Gustav's time, it would sometimes get to the point that he'd go to the pharmacy to buy cream. (I ruled out doing it myself: if you're not randy, you're not, was my point of view, and using sexual aids would be to admit that your sex life has another purpose than satisfying urges. I let him take care of the cognac and creams and never admitted anything at all.)

With Aron, such unromantic solutions will never be on the table. There will never be anything on the table, since our intimacy isn't one that includes talking about it. Bedroom realism is only appropriate in a marriage.

What's the solution, then? What's the point at all of a lover you aren't horny for? A marital spouse has other functions, but what's left of a love affair when the aura has evaporated and the desire has dried up? A friendship, at best, but Aron has entirely too many hormones to tolerate just being my friend. He has so many hormones that he doesn't need to be in love to see the 'point' of the act of sexual intercourse. My perspective would probably seem nineteenth-century to him, and maybe it is. Maybe I'm the only one in the world who has it.

It's not worth talking about it, but it feels so lonely that I cry when we're having sex, quietly of course so he doesn't notice, and so I become even more bitter because he's such an insensitive dolt that he doesn't notice.

★

'May I speak to Harriet?'

'I don't know if she's home,' the unknown commune member's voice says, 'but just one moment and I'll see.'

'Well, it wasn't anything important,' I say quickly, 'don't disturb her if she's busy . . .'

But he's already bawling so that it can be heard through all seven rooms of the house: 'Harriet! Phoooone!'

After a while there are steps and a scratching, and then Harriet says, 'Yes, hello?'

'Hi, it's Martina. I was just wondering something.'

'Yes?'

'I was wondering, what does it mean to "repine"?'

'Don't you have a dictionary?'

'Not a good etymological one like you have. Just a thesaurus, and there's so much there. "Repine: fret, languish, mope, be/feel despondent, brood, grieve, regret." So which is it: is repining the same as regretting? Or can you repine something that you don't regret?'

'I think you can,' Harriet proposes. 'Things can make you repine even when you're not the cause of them.'

'That's true, but what interests me is if you can repine things that you *are* the cause of without regretting them?'

'That's got to be a hair-splitting distinction. How so?'

'Oh, I was just wondering.'

My subconscious isn't very good at hair-splitting distinctions.

*

What's the real reason I have this obsession with finding an explanation? Why do I go around mulling over the reason our relationship didn't succeed as if it could be exhaustively clarified in one sentence, a formula that would come to me with the certainty of a revelation and at one stroke release me from my past? 'We were basically too different,' I suddenly think: the thought simply stands there in my consciousness with the pretension of explaining everything. Or another time: 'We were basically too alike.' Or: 'It was just that he loved me too much.' And yet again: 'It was Aron's fault.' Or self-accusatory: 'I simply couldn't adapt.'

I know you can't make things that simple. Why, then, do I have such a need to find a single, definitive sentence I can nail up as an epitaph for our marriage?

In vain I try to reason with myself. I even try to float the broadminded opinion that a divorce in and of itself doesn't have to be a failure at all: the relationship can have been nice as long as it lasted and then ended at just the right time.

This may apply to others, but not us. It wasn't at all nice as long as it lasted, and if it was good that it ended, it would have been better if it had never started. I can't have one truth that applies right now and one that applied back then. I need one absolute, conclusive judgement, without reservations.

They say that grief is a kind of work that you have to perform, a struggle that you cannot shirk. Is it the same with regret work? Do you have to admit regret as you must admit grief in order to get through it? Must you stop trying to rationalize after the fact, to make rational something that perhaps was pure insanity?

Yes, I'll agree to anything at all these days. I'll sign anything

and everything all at once, that I've committed the greatest stupidity of my life and that it was the only right thing to do, that
he actually wasn't anyone worth having and that I'll probably
get him back, that everything was my fault and that I couldn't
have done any differently, that we were made for each other
and that we should have never had each other – anything at all
if it can make me capable of living again. Just like a sick person
who'll take any medicine at all in desperation, I'm prepared to
adopt whatever I need to – fatalism, stoicism, cynicism, femin-
ism, spontaneism – I'll pronounce any formulas at all if they'll
have an effect on my anxiety.

My good old morning cheerfulness – how I miss it. I've
always been tired in the evenings, but in the morning, I almost
always got up with pleasure. The day's beginning was so clear
with its rituals: wash myself, drink coffee, read the paper. And
it was such a joy, just this waking up, having slept and being
awake and looking forward to washing myself, drinking coffee
and reading the paper. In short, to exist.

If only I had known that this feeling would disappear with
Gustav. Never again a normal weekday to awaken to – every
morning it's My Life sneering in my face. I stay in bed with my
blanket over my head as if I could hide, sometimes for hours,
before I can get my feet over the edge of the bed. There are
only one or two mornings a week when I have to be at the
department; otherwise, I'm the one who has to keep myself
going.

I sleep. Ten to twelve hours a day, I sleep, and the rest of the
time I walk around sleep-poisoned, heavy-headed. I move slug-
gishly between my room and the kitchen, set out my curdled
milk and bread and sit down to eat in silence. But it's as if this
effort were too much. I can get stuck in the middle of a bite and
simply not manage to move my jaws any more.

★

I'm always the one who's supposed to be available at those times suitable to Aron. It's always the one without a family who has to adapt.

This doesn't suit me. I say 'no' when Aron calls, or rather I say 'well', sound vaguely dismissive without giving any special reason. I can't claim I'm busy – all I'm going to be doing that evening is lying on the couch counting my toes.

But why should I see Aron if it will only make me sad?

No more than a couple of such occasions are necessary for him to stop calling – he's not one to beg, I should have known.

It wasn't my intention, of course. What my intention was, was something I hadn't exactly understood myself (unless it was so that he'd beg). After a couple of weeks I decide to call him myself – if the wife answers, I'll just sound completely natural and ask for Aron as if it were my right to do so.

But neither Florence nor Aron answers. It's someone who hardly seems to have heard of them but who's gradually able to tell me that the family has gone to England.

'I see, for how long?'

'I don't know.' (Doesn't he know? But he's living in their flat while they're gone, right?)

'Not for good?'

'I don't know.'

So Aron's also gone.

It actually doesn't surprise me. Quite the opposite – it's as if it's a logical development, as if it simply confirmed something. What, I don't know, but it feels like a statement: This is the way it's supposed to be, of course.

*

You get used to everything, I'm pretty sure you do. Maybe you get used to your anxiety standing at the side of your bed and you start to say 'hello' to it like an acquaintance.

I'm lying with my arms under my head, planning to get up any minute now. I'm lying thinking about human consciousness and starting to feel really cocky. How finely it's constructed: that you can abstract and idealize everything so that when you're missing something, you think: absence, and it becomes something, emptiness becomes a concept, a lack as something positive in the sense of a fact, something to live with. Even this going around missing him, thinking his name in my loneliness: this eventually becomes a kind of company.

Maybe I'll get used to living with a hole, learn to call the hole 'Gustav', learn that this is how my existence looks now. Even my anxiety takes on the security of something familiar and my longing itself becomes a kind of company. And living without any man at all, you can call it 'celibacy' and then it immediately sounds more interesting: like an experience to try out.

I can always find a way – my ability to adapt is endless. And once I've got through a few hours and have even started to work again, already then I start to get cocky: Haha, I'm surviving! I'm filled with defiance and triumph: I'm not so easily defeated, ill weeds grow apace and all that.

Until the phone rings, at ten minutes to one. Gustav needs the address of a translator. 'What do you need it for?' I ask while I browse through my address book. 'For an article,' he answers, 'I'm in a rush, no time to explain, thanks, bye.'

It's over in fifteen seconds. His voice, and in the background the music – it sounded like Handel, and it was his new life I was hearing. Before he didn't have a sound system – it must be something he's acquired with her.

I don't want to know. I want to know nothing, nothing. Every new piece of information, even as meaningless as that, is a new full day's work to get over.

★

My life is entirely meaningless. When I observe its different periods, it seems my life is like the word 'Schnur' in the dictionary, for which the first definition is 'shoestring' and second 'daughter-in-law'. All that's missing is that its third definition were 'camel' and the fourth 'broomstick'.

I'm sitting at the City Library reading Kierkegaard (accompanied by mocking epithets from my inner observer: I see, the stage when you look for literature he liked, authors linked to him – that stage, oh yes indeed). I convinced myself that I ought to read something edifying and gave myself the day off from my dissertation on the basis of mental insufficiency.

Besides, I explain to myself (to demonstrate that I'm no more stupid than my inner observer), it can't only be considered an act of nostalgia, but with just as much right it can be called an aggressive act, targeting Aron. Namely, we had a discussion about Kierkegaard right before he disappeared – if you could call it a discussion. I had mentioned that my acquaintance with him was among the most productive things about the philosophy lectures I attended once upon a time; Aron couldn't understand it. He didn't comprehend at all what could be interesting about Kierkegaard. I asked if he had read him – of course he hadn't, and he asked me to explain why one should do so. I did not. If people can't find a reason themselves to read Kierkegaard, I refuse to take on the task of doing it for them.

'A few stylish formulas,' Aron said, 'but otherwise what's so fucking remarkable about Kierkegaard? He was probably a product of the society he lived in. And wasn't he out of his mind, besides?'

'He was absolutely out of his mind, completely daft and terribly funny, and his fire was the greatest in Denmark, but otherwise there probably wasn't anything special about him, no,' I answered and got even more annoyed that he didn't notice how angry I was and that, if he had noticed it, he wouldn't have been able to understand why. That it was because of unhappy love, I mean.

I look on my shelves for the *Concept of Anxiety*, but it isn't very edifying, I have to admit. It's more crazy than funny. It deals with the fall into sin – I realize that I don't have it clearly in mind and have to go get the library's reference Bible to look it up. I know where it is, since the first time Gustav sent me a Bible verse . . . well, that's not relevant. Cbc, 'religion', Reference Room 3, furthest in on the left side.

As I sit with the black book in my hands, a Bible of the real old-fashioned kind, I happen to think of the anecdote about people who open to a page at random in order to receive a sign from above. Almost like reading your horoscope in the paper, I think. I close my eyes and open haphazardly.

My finger is pointing to I Chron. 9:39: '*And Ner begat Kish; and Kish begat Saul; and Saul begat Jonathan, and Malchishua, and Abinadab, and Eshbaal.*'

Of course. One of those genealogies the Old Testament is full of; the newspaper horoscopes are much better edited. But there must be something more fun than this – just one more attempt, then I'll stop fooling around. I cheat a little and take a steady grip towards the New Testament, but the Old is thicker than I guessed. I only get to Hosea after all, and I read:

And she shall follow after her lovers, but she shall not overtake them; and she shall seek them, but shall not find them: then shall she say, I will go and return to my first husband; for then was it better with me than now.

I scan the page – what is this all about, anyway? 'Israel's faithlessness' is the chapter title. I set the book back in its place.

There's no reason to let myself be affected by it – it was simply a parable. No reason to become superstitious and let it make me start to think about hints from above.

But it's too hard to keep it to myself. I hadn't planned on sending any more verses to Gustav, but who else would appreciate this? I run down the stairs to the shop and buy a postcard, write his address and 'Hos. 2:7'.

I can't keep such a good laugh from him, to think that it serves me right.

That's what I think myself.

★

The pub visits after seminars have stopped since the department moved to the new, sterile Frescati, far from the centre. If there's to be any socializing, it has to take place there. Sometimes a post-seminar will be held in one of these windowless, plastic furniture modules – wine and cheese and bread and candles: under such circumstances, even a module here can assume something vaguely resembling humanity, I mean cosiness. It brings to mind a room actually intended for humans to spend time in.

Normally it's just the same old doctoral comrades, but this evening a fellow from a neighbouring department has found his way to us – an orientalist, which sounds interesting. He has an interesting appearance as well: his entire face is full of beard, and I become interested in seeing what he looks like underneath. Middle-aged, a well-preserved forty-seven-year-old I would guess. I don't know if he teaches or is some kind of older student. A mature man – that would be suitable. To be sure, he's wearing a ring on his left hand, but so what? Marriages are so easy to dissolve these days. All you have to do is blow on them and they fall apart.

I sit through the entire evening for the sake of the orientalist; my need for new acquaintances is one of pure desperation. We sit on each side of the table and don't fall into direct conversation, but he keeps his eyes on me. Maybe I look interesting, too, unhappy and interesting? If people only knew how boring unhappiness makes you.

There's quite a bit of talk about a theatre visit we had planned – a few classmates were going to go see Strindberg's *The Dance of Death* together, but it's apparently impossible to find a day that suits all of these busy modern people, and the project fails. It doesn't surprise me when the bearded one slows his steps out the door and suggests that we go to the theatre together, 'just the two of us'. I answer that I'd love to, and he promises to buy the tickets for Friday. (Mature men like paying for tickets themselves.)

My need for new people is desperate, but I lack the patience needed for them. He tries to make conversation when we meet in the lobby at the Klara Theatre; I get so tired that I can hardly answer: 'tell me about what you do', 'tell me about your dissertation' – oh please, let's talk about anything but that.

Then, adding insult to injury, he seems to be the kind of man who wants something in exchange for having treated me to the theatre by seeing the play *together* – he constantly turns his gaze from the stage to me as if he wants to share my experience, and the curtain hasn't even gone down before intermission when he asks my opinion about the actors' performances.

During Act II, I start to close my eyes in order to be left alone; he can use his own bloody eyes instead of trying to see the play mirrored in mine.

I decline an invitation to go out to eat afterwards. He follows me to my front door and kisses me and it doesn't taste like anything. It just tastes like 'man' – completely abstract.

I break away impatiently; he looks guilty, an idiotic look, and I tell him goodnight before he has the chance to say anything.

The day after when we run into each other in the hall, he apologizes for his lapse. That he kissed me? I smile a little, dismissively. I only become angry when later the same day, in an empty cloakroom, he tries to do it again. He has to make a decision at least – either persist in his advances or be forgiven and stop, but not on the one hand talk about it as a reproachable misstep and on the other do it again – I demand some kind of consistency.

*

'Throwing yourself into the unknown'? You imagine that it's throwing yourself into the unknown, getting divorced. Quite the opposite: it's closing yourself up in the most known of all: yourself and yourself and yourself.

'Standing on your own two feet'? I was able to do that before. I thought I could do it before Gustav, but all these years my legs must have atrophied since now I spend my days lying on my bed.

'Mature, grow up'? I'm in the midst of childhood! It feels like I've been tossed back into the same humiliating conditions as in my greenest, most tortured youth when I walked around looking for My Husband, saw a marriage candidate in every living creature of the male sex and lived with hopes that were constantly flaring up, a conflagration of small and large flames, constantly being extinguished in disappointment. Back then, I was still invisible to them – the disappointment lay in the fact that the one I was looking at never looked back. Now for the most part he does, and the illusion that he could be The One bursts even faster. Nobody wants me – that was the greatest despair of puberty. There's nobody I want – the greatest despair of maturity. Although this is a change, it's hardly an improvement.

'New contacts, stimulation'? Oh, this excessively familiar hunt for new contacts: running to parties and meetings, conversing, flirting, exchanging phone numbers, and then not caring enough to answer when the phone rings. It's too tiresome to start again from the beginning – it's too arduous with new people. They only irritate me with their questions, as if they ought to know already, as if they ought to be someone who knows. The new person I would like to meet must be someone I already know – one I've met in a former life just like my wallpaper, someone who – just as wordlessly, painlessly, and inconspicuously – would melt into my life and simply be there. Like in the novels where the couple only see each other and realize that they are the ones, as in a revelation. I can't stand new people coming close to me as if they imagined that they could ever replace Gustav or ever become as intimate with me as he was. I can't stand them because they aren't Gustav – no, there isn't a man in the world I will ever forgive because he's not Gustav.

'Free, independent'? Vulnerable is what I've become. This Easter, for example, I was supposed to go out to the country with Cilla like last year. We had agreed on our time of departure and I was counting the days till then, longing to get away and out of this brooding. At the last moment, her husband apparently had to stay in town to go to the dentist, and Cilla didn't want to go then, either.

If you don't have your own husband to be dependent on, then you become dependent on the husbands of others, dependent on completely tangential people's dentist appointments. You hang by threads held by other people. 'Some other time,' Cilla says apologetically. 'That's fine,' I say, 'of course you need to stay with your husband', and I hang up the phone and cry for twenty-four hours.

You can't live as a single person in this society – I discovered that the first time we divorced. How could I ever forget it? The only stable relationships that exist are family ties; things such as friendship don't count. Get married or be lonely. There's no third option.

I honestly believe this is wrong. I believe that those promoting other and new forms of community are right: marrying and crawling into the secure enclosure of the nuclear family is to abdicate your responsibility to all those left outside. The change must begin somewhere, I tell myself. But I cry, It doesn't have to begin with me, does it? I don't want to be a pioneer in independence at all, or a martyr for the future of other people's grandchildren – I want a husband I can crochet ties for!

'Dignity'. I remember I thought that time I sat at the window in the cottage at the Island and cried about the ridiculousness and humiliation our relationship had sunk me into. Human pride and dignity!

The only perspective from which this could be considered dignified is that nobody sees me. I can lie on my bed and weep with fear all day long without being disturbed. I can blow my nose and walk down to Metro and buy food for dinner and pay without saying a word and return without anyone noticing me. My inner turmoil and deranged emotional avalanche is somethings nobody need know about. No one besides me needs to look at me in contempt.

34

Easter. In the city, that is. I invite Harriet for dinner, but her daughter has a cold and can't go out, and, besides, they had already planned Easter dinner in their commune.

I go out to shop for food anyway, as if I had someone coming over. I buy salmon and potato salad and set the table in my room instead of standing eating at the kitchen counter. I light yellow candles and put on a Mozart record. I do this to take care of myself since nobody else will, because it's so horrible when you don't have the strength to care.

As if this were any less horrible.

Easter Monday. How long the days have become! How slowly life crawls! Day in and day out – how tedious it is.

I call Harriet again.

'What's the sense of writing a dissertation?'

'Ha,' Harriet says. 'Why should there be any sense in that of all things? Do you think it's any less meaningless to work as a substitute teacher?'

'What's the sense of living, then' I whine, 'if there's no point to anything?'

'If you're already living, there's no sense in killing yourself, either.'

'But I'm tired of it! Just living and living and living – it's so monotonous.'

'It's nothing compared to not living – *that's* monotonous.'

I suppose she's right, of course. Being dead is probably not less monotonous, but possibly less tiring.

'I want to die' – that's a thought I've never thought before. I've never been afraid to die or felt anything else about it; I've never thought about death at all. I've been fully preoccupied with living, thought it was exciting: being young was an adventure in and of itself, one in which everything was new, I was new myself, and discovering myself was something that provided daily surprises.

Now I know myself. Now I know myself backwards and forwards to the point of annoyance and anger. And my impatience overcomes me: I'm tired of this, I want to die!

'You'll die eventually,' Harriet says calmly. 'There's nothing you can be more certain of – you just have to bide your time.'

I sigh heavily in the receiver.

'Wouldn't it be too sad if you were to off yourself in the flower of your youth?'

'That's not really what I want to do – I want to be old enough to die a natural death, immediately. I wish I were ancient and enlightened and Stood Above Everything.'

'You don't know what you're talking about. Getting old is just having lots of pains and losing your mental faculties one after the other. As for me, I think I'm entirely old enough as I am.'

No no, that's probably not what I want to do either, then. I just wish that it were ten years from now, for example. That time would move quickly, the near future. That I could hibernate and wake up when it's Another Time. Like in a film – clip, clip – 'Ten Years Later'.

This excessive sleeping is one way to dispatch myself. If I sleep two extra hours per night, that's fourteen hours fewer per week of waking: it's also a way to shorten your life.

'I'm not used to being unhappy,' I complain. 'People who've suffered from anxiety their entire lives seem to handle it, but I'm standing here utterly helpless. For me, my natural state is happiness, and so I get extra unhappy that I'm unhappy.'

'It's obvious that in the whole world, you're the pitifullest. Much pitifuller than those who have always been just as unhappy. They probably like it, in their heart of hearts, otherwise they wouldn't be that way, I suppose?'

'I wouldn't say "like". Maybe it's simply natural for them, so they don't have to feel self-contempt as well. I don't want to go around having a crisis – crises are silly. I want to be big and strong and float above everything!'

'Pride goeth before a fall,' Harriet says gaily, and nobody disagrees with that.

I wish Gustav had abandoned me brutally and perfidiously: it would have been a simple, unequivocal situation, with classically pure contours, that would have evoked the undivided sympathy of my peers. But a messy and dark unhappiness like this? To be sure, nobody is telling me straight off that I should blame myself, but it says itself. Blame: place the fault on. Yes indeed, I blame myself, every waking minute and even asleep in my dreams, I blame myself, and since no one else has pity on me, I take care of that too. I feel sorry for myself, oh yes, I swim around in the thick syrup of my self-pity.

I blame myself, I pity myself, I hate myself.

*

I can't wall off the spring – it bursts in without asking anyone's opinion. I can't sit indoors and read when the sky is glowing blue outside my window and the crocuses are sprouting up through the grass so you can *see* it – I have to go out and look.

I smuggle Taine's *Histoire de la littérature anglaise* out past all the guards of the Royal Library and settle myself on the lawn – not on a bench, I want contact with the earth, but Humlegården is under strict surveillance and it's best to behave properly. I sit primly on my coat spread on the ground and read my book nicely, and I don't think of an autumn day when we walked here through the park to eat dinner at Promenade, I don't think about it at all but collect my thoughts around what's in the book – until a bicycle bell jingles on the path. Gustav. Is he ubiquitous?

He's on his way in to the library and parks in the bike rack, and I wave to lure him off the straight path.

'Come sit in the sun, this is no day for the library!'

'I'm just running in with a book,' he calls, 'I have class in fifteen minutes.'

'Come sit for fifteen minutes, then.'

'I have to be *there* in fifteen minutes. The teacher isn't allowed to be tardy.'

'Sit for five minutes, then. It can't take a whole fifteen minutes to Norra Latin.'

He comes and sits on the low fence after returning his book.

'How are you?'

'Fine thanks, and you?'

I'm afraid. My heart pounds when I see him: what will he say this time? What will the rest of my day look like after this?

'I was just thinking,' I tell him and close my book, 'that bloody everything reminds me of you. It gets on my nerves.'

'Don't you think everything reminds me of you, too? Every time I go to the Island, I'm forced to think of you when I see that wallpaper you helped put up.'

'What do you mean?' I say angrily. 'That doesn't matter to you at all, does it?' (My eyes shining with hope: does it matter? Does it, does it?)

'Your rain gear's still hanging there, by the way. Do you want it?'

I shake my head (don't change the subject): 'It seemed to me you had forgotten me completely.'

'How so? I didn't think you wanted to hear from me. You said it just makes you upset, right?'

'That doesn't mean you have to treat me as non-existent.'

'But you were the one who . . .'

So here we sit squabbling in our dear, familiar way again. Gustav believes that he's the one who's clingy, calling constantly and feeling like he's bothering me. I claim that I'm the one who's writing constantly and never getting any answer – and isn't it lovely to squabble like we used to do.

But I want to take the opportunity to hear his opinion on a number of new thoughts I've had since we last talked, and shading my hand over my eyes so I can see his backlit face, I ask:

'What do you think about death? Your own, I mean. Have you ever found a positive side to the fact that you'll eventually die?'

He doesn't make a surprised face and he answers without a pause to consider by quoting:

'"It's a scandal that I have to die. I've never had any other opinion on the matter."'

I snort.

'You and your spiritual apple cheeks. Your mental balance is pure insolence compared to all the suffering in the world.'

'You mean compared to you – do you wish for death?'

'Not exactly here on the spot, but I've realized that there's a comfort in the thought that, no matter what happens, I'll die sooner or later. No matter how difficult life gets, there'll be an end to it. It's never occurred to me before – I've never really thought about death.'

'I think you're actually a rather solid optimist – the first time you happen to think about death, it's as a source of joy!'

'There has to be some point to pessimism as well. "It's not

enough that life is so bloody awful – then you have to die to boot" – it doesn't make any sense that way.'

'That's what I'm saying. As long as you care about having it make sense, then you haven't really lost your mental balance. As long as you demand logic in the midst of your unhappiness.'

Gustav laughs, I laugh too, we laugh together. Everything is so different from that one dreadful night on Fleminggatan when it felt like I had ceased to exist – this morning in the sunshine on the lawn in Humlegården, everything is so different that I look him in the eyes gaily and boldly and say:

'I think we'll end up with each other *after all*! Every other week I believe it.'

Does suffering make you noble? Oh no. Suffering makes you more brutal, and after the agony of these months, I'm so shamelessly crude that I don't hesitate to say something like this to a man who has rejected invitations from me before and who is fully justified in saying: 'You're wrong, get that out of your head for your own sake, this time I've detached myself from you for good.'

That's not what Gustav says. He laughs and says:

'I do too. Every other week, that is.'

'What do you think every *other* other week, then?'

'I look around at home and tell myself that this is how it is, she's the one I'm living with now and I plan to continue to do so.'

'But you don't Love her,' I say crudely.

'Oh yes' (slowly as if he's looking for diplomatic wording), 'I do. In a different way.'

'But you love me more,' I shout, 'because I'm your "likest"!'

He stands up and grasps his briefcase.

'There can be an advantage to not being too similar. I've actually discovered that there's a point to other people being . . . well, other people. Before, I mean with Birgitta and Eivor and the rest, women seemed like strange beings of a completely different species. Well, and then there was you, but it was me too, if you understand what I mean.'

'I always understand what you mean. I'm of precisely the same opinion. The point of someone like Aron, for example, is precisely that he's Another, a human being but a foreign species who commands respect. You can't marry someone like that.'

'Although I actually don't really know what that feeling of identity with you depends on,' he objects. 'We don't precisely agree all the time.'

'Do you always agree with yourself? I don't. Identity must be something else. But it was probably because you considered me "yourself" that you couldn't accept it when I disagreed with you.'

'And the other way around,' he smiles. 'That's what I mean – that it's better to know who's who the whole time.'

He unlocks his bike, rings the bell and speeds off, and I sit on the lawn under the trees in Humlegården and the world is different.

' "On s'aime",' I think – as if we were singular: this strange French idiom – and picture once again the croquet ball of Aristophanes.

We'll end up together, oh yes, if even he believes it (even if it's only every other week), then nothing else is possible. We'll end up together and everything will have meaning, suffering as purification and divorce as purgatory, and then there will be the paradise that we've earned.

The life lie. I allow it to take root in me and it sprouts more quickly than the crocuses in the lawn. It's already blooming, tall as a man, in fever-flaming colours and I smile at it, I close my eyes in the sun and smile so that it feels like my happiness is spreading from my face and through my entire body, and I think, I'll bet he was late to class after all!

★

I want someone to talk to. About death or identity or Taine's literary history or anything at all. I call Gustav.

He himself answers, so far so good. But he's sitting just now with a pile of tests he has to grade and asks if there was something I wanted. There wasn't, so he suggests that he'll call me back another day when he's less stressed.

The life lie wilts and fades. That's the problem with life lies – they're so sensitive to climate. A sturdy resignation would be more stable to live with. This I know.

But the thing about life lies is that they're also as hard to dig out as weeds – they blossom up again as soon as you turn your back. You think you've got them under control, they feel as dead as if nothing in the world could ever grow in you again. But hope – it lives its subterranean life, and after no more than a good night's sleep, it sticks its head up again, and it's such a lovely sight anyway, that little head.

Didn't he say that he usually thinks about me when he goes out to the cottage, as if it were something that bothered him – then he's not completely unaffected by me after all, right?

And of course he's busy with his demanding job and doesn't have time to talk to me any time at all, but it doesn't mean that it isn't the thing he'd most like to do in the entire world, does it?

What's ineradicable is the feeling I have that this is all a mistake, absurd to the point of comedy – we belong together and eventually the only thing that can happen is that we're reunited. Let's stop fooling around, quit it, stop pretending you're with someone else!

This feeling is so strong that I could convince myself that she's just something he's invented to scare me, to tease me. She's never existed. He's living there on Lindhagensgatan alone as before and I can go there one of these days and fall into his arms, laughing with relief . . .

Naturally, it's not that I believe it, but that's how it feels. I don't know her name, and if you don't have a name, you don't really exist. By not learning anything more tangible about her, I keep her unreal, like something he can quit when he's tired of fooling around.

35

In order to put an end to this trepidation, which prevents me from being master of my own thoughts, and to dull my pounding heart, which has become entirely too upset by so many sorrowful images, I see no other remedy than a dissertation.

Yes, I wish to lay this piece of ice on my heart.

Yes, I wish to.

When I started this process of getting my doctorate, Gustav requested a thank-you in the foreword. At the time, it was reasonable in the entirely usual sense that he had helped me by discussing my ideas with me – but now such a thank-you would also justify its place in my dissertation: if anything is to come of it, it's because of him since it's as a piece of ice on my heart that I need it. I consider citing Xavier de Maistre as a motto instead. I consider what impression it would make on the academic community.

*

In the cellar of a university building on Drottninggatan, an author is giving a lecture about his new novel – an announcement in the student paper.

I'm not one iota interested in his old novel, but I have to force myself out among people now and again. I run the risk of becoming seriously demented by simply sitting by myself reading and writing, living in excerpts and footnote charts – a paper life.

The cellar is crowded and stuffy, and the author is probably better at writing than talking. I just sit waiting for him to stop talking so the general drinking and free socializing can begin. But once it happens, I sit in silence at the table, with hardly enough energy to answer when spoken to.

I'm looking at a fellow from the literary association who's conversing with the author. He was once a classmate of Gustav's. I don't remember his name, but the strange thing about him is that he's so like Gustav in terms of appearance. Not close up – he has darker hair, but his figure and posture are so similar that it happened that people mistook them for each other, believing he was Gustav and vice versa. He's talking to the author about a poetry collection he's written himself but hasn't been able to interest any publisher in. They're sitting so close to me that I can't help but hear them. He's describing his poems and they sound hopelessly uninteresting.

I watch him, looking for similarities, but the more I see, the more they seem to fly from my sight. I see that it isn't him, but I want it to be him, I want GUSTAV.

And when I think that, it's as if I see the word in front of me in the room in capital letters, hanging in the air between myself and the people on the other side.

So I've already become demented from my work, so occupationally demented that I'm thinking in writing, *feeling* in writing. If I'd thought I heard a voice shouting his name, that would have seemed more normal, wouldn't it? But it's really in text that my longing for him manifests itself in this moment: I see his name before me, and it's very clear that it's written in big letters.

A mute cry in the capital letters of despair.

On my way out, I'm stopped in the cloakroom by a rather inebriated young man who stares me right in the eyes – the association Casanova. I've danced with him at some point but hardly exchanged a word with him as far as I recall and I'm a bit surprised when he suggests that I come home with him. I answer him politely (it's the easiest):

'Thanks, but I think I'd rather be alone.'

He stares at me and blocks my way up the stairs to the front door.

'We'll end up in bed together sooner or later, you know that as well as I do.'

I stare at him.

'*Would I! Would you! The intimate!*'

He's sufficiently confused to let go of the banister.

'Huh?'

'Delblanc, *Åminne*, Stockholm 1970,' I inform him and hurry up the stairs to freedom.

★

Again and again. It's like when you've had a tooth pulled and you can't stop your tongue from exploring the hole left, although it hurts and you know that it hurts. Again and again I'm there, in my thoughts, exploring the hole in my life, the hole left by Gustav, and pain and fear tear through me.

Maybe it's the case – I'm starting to believe it – that you also cultivate your pain. That I'm suffering intentionally: because that's the only thing keeping us together, the fact that I'm unhappy. If I stop caring, nothing will be left, then there will simply be nothing. As long as I'm suffering, there's a relationship between us.

Maybe it's also a superstitious perception that if only I can suffer long enough and deeply enough, then I'll finally receive my reward – the perception of poetic justice in the mind of one poisoned by literature. But reality isn't constructed that way. If my suffering is to change something, then it can only happen through Gustav, through a resurrection of his feelings.

So that I don't suffer in vain, I must therefore notify him

that I'm doing so, continuously keep him informed, not let him believe that I've got over it.

I write letters. Many letters – not long and sad, oh no, short and funny. I try to make my unhappiness amusing to him. He's not to be sad for my sake; pity is only unconstructive and changes nothing. I want to make him laugh – that's the only emotional string I believe I can still tug on. If there's anything that can drive him into my arms, it's the desire to laugh.

(Or maybe it's only in my nonsensical fantasy world that laughter is magical, that you can not only laugh away a divorce but also a marriage – the new relationship that in reality he's been living in for six months.)

In any case, I do the best I can. I post him all my self-mockery, all my gallows humour, all the wittiness I can muster. Quotes and newspaper clippings and brief, small messages. Not only things that have to do with me – like Hosea and Xavier de Maistre – but in general everything I feel like communicating. But I search in vain through the Bible for funny, sorrowful verses – he's already used all the good parts in Lamentations and Job.

One Sunday at lunch I turn on the radio for the high mass (I kindly but firmly request my inner observer to shut up) and hear a pastor explaining that the Holy Spirit is just like petrol for an automotive motor; the human soul is the motor, which admittedly *exists* but cannot function without *petrol* . . . If it had been in a church, I would have been forced to shush Gustav for his irreverent giggling. Now, there's no church and no Gustav here, and I realize that without someone to laugh with, without someone with whom I can keep all the idiocy of the world at bay through laughter, I'll become a decrepit misanthrope. I can't stand to listen to this kind of blather.

So I write it down, giggling in my thoughts with him, and jot his work address on the envelope.

★

No answers come from Gustav, and I start to fear that he simply feels I'm a bother. But after my letter campaign has gone on a couple of weeks, he calls and explains that it's because he hasn't found any good quotes for me – he doesn't seem bothered at all. He clearly appreciates being sought after and my grimaces of suffering amuse him appropriately.

'I'm trying to refrain from being affected in any other way,' he adds.

<u>Hear hear</u>! 'Trying' – hope flares up: so he has to make an effort, that is, fight against it, or in other words, he has to exert his utmost strength!

'Well,' I giggle modestly, 'you've always said that my sense of humour is my only advantage, so I thought I'd have to use that.' (It's a poor tactician who reveals her tactics, but it's so transparent anyway.)

'Speaking of which, it occurred to me the other day that it's too bad I don't get to see Harriet any more.'

Too bad he doesn't get to see Harriet – here the flames of hope flicker even higher! Harriet, who he used to say was like me but even worse, that we were intolerable together and one of us the most you could stand – if he's missing Harriet, then it's me he's missing!

'How did that happen?'

'That I thought of it? There was a colleague who was talking about her divorce and how she had lost all of her old acquaintances because of it. I thought about whether we had any friends in common – I didn't meet that many of yours, actually.'

'No, you didn't like the same people I did, for some reason.'

'I never fell in love with the same people you did, for some reason. But I happened to think about something Harriet had said at some point, and it occurred to me that I could actually talk to her, unlike most other people.'

'That's so true,' I say seriously, '*aren't* most people impossible to talk to?' (Darling, let us take refuge in a tower, you and I, sit there together and look down on humanity!)

'It was your acquaintances I was talking about just now. Otherwise, most people are rather pleasant, aren't they?'

I sigh. Am I already too much of a misanthrope for Gustav? Alone in my tower.

*

Aron calls, presenting himself as if it wasn't certain I'd remember who he was; this was probably a masquerade intended to give me the opportunity to make it clear whether I wanted to hear from him or not, since a certain lack of clarity about that matter prevailed the last time we talked. But I'm happy and let him hear it, and then he explains the reason for his disappearance: Florence has been blessed with a house. She's inherited a little single-family dwelling in a London suburb from her mother, who died in the spring. She's still there with the two small children; he's come back alone with the oldest boy so that he can finish his term at school here. Whether they'll be able to keep the house in the future seems to be an open question; they'll stay there for the summer in any case.

But now he's in Stockholm, standing in a phone booth at Central Station and wondering if I think that's a good place to be standing.

'Not at all,' I answer, 'my home is always open to you.'

'Do you have a dinner?'

'No, why would I? But my kitchen is always open to you should you feel like making one. You can buy something at Åhléns, for example.'

I hardly imagined he'd go along with it, but when he arrives, he has a sack with steak and frozen potato fritters and even lettuce and tomatoes. I pull out the frying pan and a bowl for him before I snatch *Aftonbladet*, which is at the top of the sack, and I settle at the kitchen table while Aron begins to cook.

467

I'm starting to believe that as long as you insist on not cooking yourself, there will always be someone else who will. If you just keep from doing it long enough, someone else will get hungry. That's probably the method men have used since time immemorial, incidentally.

Aron at the stove: it's a remarkable sight. It's almost as if we were married. No, not at all.

After we eat, we go to the cinema and come home again and have a beer and talk happily and easily and go to bed, and it's fun because it was an eternity ago last time, both the one thing and the other. It's an ideally free and undemanding relationship, of course it is, and I wouldn't want to be married to him in the least. There's actually just one catch: if he moves, it's the one he's married to who will move with him. Other relationships don't count in such a situation. You can communicate with old friends by letter, but old lovers – well, they're relegated to metaphysics.

★

On Walpurgis Eve, Cilla calls me and invites me over.

Oh I see, are people starting to feel sorry for me now? They're thinking, That Martina, she's probably sitting home alone on an evening like this, shouldn't we ask her, too? I'm not a social butterfly – I don't really fit at parties under normal circumstances, either, and less than ever in my current state of mind. The fact that someone would invite me because they truly want to have me is something I don't pretend to myself. But you see, I don't intend to make myself the victim of charity.

'Thanks,' I say, 'but I'm not really feeling all that well. I'm probably coming down with a spring cold, so I think the best thing is if I stay home.'

'But just for a little while? I'm just sitting here – I'm a grass widow and I'm so bored.'

Oh so that's how it is. The lady is a grass widow and then it's time to turn to your old childhood friends.

'So where's your spouse?'

'He's doing his reserve service in Lapland, and I miss him so terribly.'

But I don't feel like being the one who practises charity, either. If Cilla doesn't value my company enough to see me otherwise, then I don't intend to volunteer as soon as her spouse happens to be away. She can sit alone for a while and have a taste of what it's like for those who have no spouse.

'Another time,' I say, 'tonight I'm going to take care of my cold.'

I go to bed with an old Dorothy Sayers, feel petty and depressed in the way you do from being petty. I'm on the verge of calling her several times, but I stop myself with the thought that she's sure to have found something else to do, and then it would just be inane.

I wake up with an unease which is either a nascent cold as punishment for the one I invented or perhaps my conscience. Now I have to stop digging myself in anyway, go out and demonstrate and behave myself.

The fact that I'm running the risk of encountering Gustav with his wife is a horrible thought, to be sure, but there are many different First of May parades this year, and I don't know what her political affiliation is. Besides, I still don't know which parade I'll choose myself as I ride downtown – what I'd really like to do, in protest against how divided the parties are, is set up my own route which would include all of them; according to the maps published in the papers, it ought to be possible.

But the Socialist parade is the first one I run into, so I wait for a Vietnam banner and squeeze in a bit behind it, on the edge so I can lead my bike.

Strange that all the people in this march seem to know each other. It's only the way it seems, since the ones who know each other are the ones you notice – they say hello and wave here and there and walk together in groups. Naturally, they have nothing against my joining their ranks, but when they walk along talking with each other, it feels impolite to walk next to them listening anyway when I myself am quiet. It's as if I'm 'keeping quiet', as if it's something I'm doing intentionally, although I simply happen to not be talking.

I'm trying to be like normal people but it feels like there's a membrane of silence around me.

*

I wish my shifts weren't planned for Fridays just now. The holiday mood breaks out, my colleagues who've done their shopping slide large bags and suitcases under their desks for the afternoon, when their wives and husbands will come fetch them with the car and they'll drive out to the country.

And those questions when they try to make conversation: What are you doing this weekend? 'Nothing,' I answer, 'nothing special. No, I'll be home. Here in town, of course, in town.'

Fridays in May.

Does everyone have a country place except for me? Next week it's the same: 'And what are you going to do, Martina?' 'Just stay home, probably go see a film, otherwise I'm not sure.' 'But didn't you have a place in the archipelago somewhere?' 'I didn't – it was my husband's. My ex-husband's.' 'Oh, I see, that's how it was' (embarrassed silence and change of subject).

Friday after Friday. Every single weekend, every fucking weekend an embarrassing reminder of my civil status, my status of _bereft_.

Not that I envy the others their marriages. Viveka often talks about hers. Every other week it sounds like they've decided to have children and every other that they'll split up, but from lack of conviction neither happens. Tomas is regularly fetched by an attractive blonde on Fridays – they, too, seem to stay together mostly because they can't be bothered to do anything else: you can see it in his eyes that he's open to all possibilities and that as soon as he finds something that appeals to him more, he'll abandon her with impunity.

Without fail, one of the teachers, after a few glasses of wine at the post-seminar, will begin to talk about how happily married he is – clearly as some kind of excuse, since nobody can help but notice that he's carrying on with a girl who works at the library. They are practically cohabiting in his office and seem to have done so for years. 'Everyone knows about it except his wife' – when she calls and he's going out with The Other, he asks us to tell her that he has an evening lecture or a meeting. If this is what he calls being happily married, then it's what I call stolen happiness; since he assumes that his wife wouldn't give it to him if she knew what he was up to, then that's theft.

I despise it, just as I despise Aron living with others behind his wife's back without the vaguest wisp of qualms (and myself because I'm contributing to it). And quite the opposite, I despise Gustav because he insists on faithfulness – such narrow-mindedness, only having space in his heart for one woman at a time. (And myself because I can't even discipline my emotional life to a minimum of logic.)

When I see how pitifully most people's relationships function, I simply don't understand why I made such demands on ours. It was, of course, pure arrogance as well. I wanted to be a Good Wife, I wanted to be *happily* married, and if I couldn't be, then I preferred to be without – have you ever heard of such arrogant madness? Imagining that you could be married without hurting each other – what puffed-up ambition, what an idealistic, unrealistic demand. What pretentiousness, to believe that you can go through life without hurting others at all, and what a neat little undertaking for the future.

In any case, I certainly don't envy my colleagues their marriages. But I do envy them their summer cottages.

I can close my eyes and my body remembers: stepping out

onto the porch in the clear, cold morning air, the stillness before the wind rises. Following the path down to the outhouse, a narrow string through the tall grass – no matter how carefully I walked, I got sopping wet all the way up to my waist. Just as well to walk naked. Or later, once the meadow grass had been cut: the path hard and warm beneath the soles of my feet, the cracks of dryness towards late summer. And the smell of the dock in the sun. And the scent of the forest in the rain. And the rock cranny where I had my favourite spot with its view of the bay, my feet cooled by the surge from the wakes of boats coming close. The rock scraped against my lower back but if I set a cushion behind me, it was a perfect reading chair.

There's no other place – none after the trees and boulders of my childhood – with which I've grown in such a way.

How inconsiderate of me.

★

Gustav's bicycle is standing next to the lamppost in front of the Royal Library. I hesitate on the steps for a moment, but I can't keep avoiding him.

I find him in the catalogue room – he's searching for something in the card catalogue.

'What are you doing here? Have you started doing research?'

'I'm working on an article. A fellow at Sida ordered it. I'm just looking up a few references.'

He's leaning over an open drawer full of cards, jotting something in his notebook and doesn't look up. I don't know if I should go or wait.

It's me! Don't you see? It's me, Martina, the one who makes your heart beat faster every time you see her!

Finally he straightens up, looks at me and asks how I'm doing. Poorly, of course, and thus we're in the midst of our usual topic. Not even the weather would be a neutral topic if Gustav tried to talk to me about it.

'But you can't be serious. You can't want us to start over again, can you?'

'Why not?'

He shakes his head.

'It would just be the same as it was before. Exactly the same as before: too little fucking and too much jealousy.'

Is that all he has to say as a summary – Gustav's version of an epitaph for our marriage?

'Do you have to continue to speak disparagingly about our relationship like that? It's like mocking the dead.'

We stand in the aisle between the cabinets with the card trays, speaking quietly so we don't bother the researchers.

'Don't tell me you remember it as some kind of paradise either, even if you're idealizing it because it's over.'

'It wasn't as crappy as you're making it out to be. Besides, conditions have changed – I've become a different person since then.'

'Me too in that case, I've become spoiled. It's so nice to have a wife who's so domestic.'

So now he tells me. After seven years: now he tells me.

Domestic. Would I be able to be domestic if my life depended on it? Why not, if even Aron can?

'I could take a cooking class,' I say softly.

It's not one of my attempts to be funny, and he doesn't seem amused, either.

'And I could take a sailing class?'

I follow him to the exit, and in the lobby we resume a normal tone of voice.

'You wouldn't enjoy a bourgeois family life,' he says impatiently. 'I do but you wouldn't take to it.'

'I can adapt.'

'It would have been nice if you could have figured that out before, but it's too late now.'

473

'One year ago,' I say accusingly, 'exactly one year ago you said that you had come to the realization that you couldn't be happy without me either – and then you go and do it anyway! <u>Just like that!</u>'

'Yes, one year ago – back then I didn't know there was an alternative.'

Now he's laughing, but at the same time I'm overcome by the meaninglessness of the whole thing and let it go. What am I doing? Trying to argue him into a reunion, trying to convince him that it could be pleasant – meaningless. If it didn't work to appeal to his sense of humour, it would never work using reason. It's not the humiliation of the situation that overwhelms me, I don't care about that, but the absurdity: it's like an absurd play where we've swapped roles. I'm standing here saying what were once his lines, and he's answering with those that were mine. It overwhelms me with disgust and I don't want to be a part of it any longer.

'Well then it was good that things went the way they did. What luck that you didn't get married to me simply because you didn't know any better.'

I sit on the bench to smoke a cigarette before I go into the reading room. He sets his briefcase down next to me, slides his notebook into it, pulls out his bicycle key.

I try to talk about something else. 'Did you see that there are people who still wear their student cap during the First of May parades? I always get so nostalgic – it's been so long since I graduated.'

'I thought about that last week – it was eight years ago for me. In two years I guess there'll be a reunion.'

'What are we doing with our lives, that's what I think every time. What have I done with my life all these years?'

'The last eight years I spent on my great passion. One year waiting for it, six years having it, one year to get over it.'

'That you spent one year waiting for it is at least something you can't blame me for.'

'Can't I?'

'Of course, how stupid of me: you waited a whole year and then I'm the one you met. I'm the one who destroyed your youth! Really time for you to get something else done, you know, don't let me bother you any longer.'

He laughs and takes off.

New feelings throb in my abdomen (how many kinds do you have to go through?): now it's rage. He never loved me! If it was so easy for him to get over me, then it wasn't a love worth its name. As cold as a fish is what he is, has always been. His love was a hypothesis that it amused him to test – now it's been discarded, as other failed theories. How was I able to put up with him for so long? It mortifies me to think about how much past we have together. I want to get it back from him, I want nothing at all to do with such a person!

It's probably the same thing with the rest of his engagement, I imagine – his so-called faith which one could never see any evidence of. That was probably also a working hypothesis to flush away when it was no longer convenient. And his political convictions? What more are they than the latest craze?

No, now I've gone a bit too far. Now I've gotten so unreasonable that I've lost the thread. If there's anything I've always appreciated about Gustav, then it's his ability to whisper ironic comments out of the side of his mouth during a demonstration in the same breath as he joins in chanting at the top of his lungs. If that's schizophrenic, then it's in any event less schizophrenic than speaking solemnly about politics, but doing no more than speaking.

I can't get at him that way. But how about this: politics is the only thing that's truly engaged him; he knows nothing of normal human feelings . . .

Perhaps that's also unfair. Perhaps it's not simply theoretical interest in the one great love as an idea that's helped Gustav to put up with it for so long as well. But I simply can't be fair just now. I'm not capable of a nuance such as the possibility that he once loved me if he no longer does. Love is eternal, Gustav's only been pretending, and how upset it makes me to have wasted years of my life on someone like him.

Besides, I assume it's meaningless to demand logic of one's feelings. In every single psychology book, you can read that a natural stage of grief is rage against the dead – 'abandoning me like this!' – with utter disregard for whether the person in question has been snatched away by illness or an accident or suicide. In that case it's no stranger if you hate your ex without paying attention to who it was who actually abandoned whom.

It's no stranger than this. If there's anything I believe my long life has taught me, it's not to expect sense of your emotions. What I haven't yet figured out is what I'm supposed to do in order to manage them.

I hate Gustav and I simply assume, with my racked and tired soul, that it's one of the stages I have to get through.

36

'And what about you? What are you doing this summer?'

They ask politely and more or less interested, and they don't know that they're tightening the thumbscrews.

What do other people do? Travel? That would be nice, 'get away from it all'. But where? I don't want to go abroad alone – being in a foreign country without a context makes me depressed. Cilla? She's going to Yugoslavia with her husband. Harriet? When I ask, she replies that she hardly has enough money to take the regional train into the city.

I go to a rental agency to ask about cottages in the Stockholm area. Of course it's entirely too late – all the attractive properties were booked months ago. The office has thick notebooks with descriptions of the rentals. All you can get out of them is how many lovely cottages you've missed out on.

I glance through the ads in the paper and try calling a few. Most places are entirely too large and expensive. When I finally settle on one that sounds just right and take the trouble to get out to it on the Värmdö bus, I find an outbuilding the size of a normal doghouse, located at the corner of a larger building already rented to a family with three small children. 'Undisturbed location' is what the owner had assured me, but maybe it depends on what you're disturbed by.

Another ad leads me to the forests north of Arlanda. It requires an hour's walk from the bus stop, but, in return, it ought to be

undisturbed. For the showing, the couple who're renting it fetch
me by car at the stop. They look so confused when I'm the only
one to get off the bus, so clearly expecting a male person to be
following behind me that I almost turn around myself, like in a
comedic film clip.

The woman can't even help asking once we're sitting in
the car:

'Are you the only one renting?'

'Yes, I'm the one who called.' (Don't I look solvent?)

'Just one person?'

I look around the back seat, counting (playing the comedy
for myself).

'Yes, I'm just one person.'

The cottage turns out to have six beds, so you have to admit
that it would be a waste. Eyes follow me from behind the curtain when I walk back into the forest, after having declined a
ride back. Maybe I *am* strange?

'Wouldn't you be afraid to live in this remote place alone?'
the woman asked. 'No.' 'Wouldn't it get a bit boring after a
while?' she asked. 'I suppose.'

It'll probably be boring no matter where I go, but what decided
the matter, apart from the fact that the couple gave me the feeling
that I simply wanted to get away from there as quickly as possible, was that I missed the sea. That there isn't any ocean north
of Arlanda is of course something I should have known ahead of
time, but I didn't miss it until I didn't see it.

I'm ready to give up the entire enterprise – it's too hard to get
around and look at places when you don't have your own car.
Public transportation only permits round trips (at best, there
and back the same day) but no sideways movement, which
means that each visit requires a full day's trip.

With no faith in it, I make one more attempt, with a place at Tynningö, and decide unenthusiastically to take it. It's unnecessarily

large and not exactly remote, nor is there much sea – it's just outside of Vaxholm. But there are proper boat connections, and at this point, that's begun to be the decisive factor. The possibility of getting home again quickly. The first thing I do after taking possession of the cottage is to make use of it.

⋆

The cottage is both furnished and supplied with the most elementary household items, but there's still much to be bought. I walk through the aisles stocked with recreational items at the department stores and make small purchases and bask in the feeling of finally being a normal and fully fledged citizen, with a place in the country to make purchases for. Finally they speak to me, all these seasonal offers that fill the newspapers and shop windows. Finally they speak to me, too. I walk around at Domus and buy plastic tubs and suntan lotion and disinfectant for the outhouse and waxed tablecloths for my garden table – status objects if there ever were any. Even if these are the simplest of practical items, the important thing is the status they confirm: normality items, the kind everyone else is buying. I never knew what an all-consuming need I have to be like everyone else.

I go out again on the Vaxholm boat, with my bike saddled like a pack mule, bowed under paper sacks. Allowing bicycles on the boat must be a temporary oversight on the part of the responsible agency, contrary to the entire spirit of public transportation policy otherwise.

I lead my wobbly cargo carefully up the hill from the dock, across the island and down to the opposite beach – the county road passes right by the cottage. I unload and carry in, beginning a bit listlessly to unpack. It feels a bit chilly in the room – I'd best make a fire in the stove. But first I have to think about food. I didn't bring any fresh provisions from the city since there's a grocer on the island.

I ride down to buy milk and bread, instant coffee (since I couldn't remember if there was a Melitta filter in the place) and tea bags (since I hadn't seen any teapot). At the butcher's, I hesitate in the shadow of other customers, succeed in deciding by the time it's my turn and ask for a small piece of falukorv sausage. The clerk measures a bit.

'N-no, not that big.'

He moves his knife; I waver.

'Even smaller?'

He's so surprised that I become uncertain again. How do other people buy falukorv sausage, by the metre?

This piece, in any case, is so large that it'll be enough for more than one meal for me, who's only one person.

Back in the cottage, I continue to unpack and notice to my unreasonable joy that I've forgotten one of my most important notebooks at home, so I'll have to go back to the city again.

*

Independence. It sounds good. Independence must be a good thing. You can't have too much of it.

Can you? Actually it's a form of dependence, like everything else: namely, to be dependent on independence. It's a need like other needs, just as difficult to satisfy, just as difficult to harmonize with other's interests and with your own interests of other kinds.

I seem to have an oversized – I mean greater than average – need for self-determination, for sovereignty. In the practical sense, bachelor habits, and in an emotional sense: for example, that I hate to represent anything but myself or to be represented by something else, that I don't want to appear with someone who is 'my husband' or 'my friend'. I even dislike signing business letters from the department with my name, even if it's a pure formality and something that's part of my job. I want to count for one, myself, no more and no less.

This is an absolute and impossible demand that I immediately have to compromise on. I don't want to be unemployed, or friendless, or husbandless. But how are you supposed to have work or friends under such conditions? Not to mention having a husband.

'You've chosen to live as a single person – so what are you complaining about?'

No, that's not what I've chosen. I've simply discarded all the options for living together that have been offered to me. I'm what's left.

But I've never said I wanted to be alone.

You might think that 'independent' people would have an easier time organizing their life according to their own taste. But as long as you're not completely independent, as long as you're not living happily as a hermit in the desert, the easiest thing is to be average: then there are more people who are like you, a maximum number of individuals who can wish to organize their lives in a corresponding way.

If your ideal life with a partner is one that's not yet been realized, if it's a utopia never before beheld in this world, then, of course, the chance of meeting a person with the same goals is smaller. And if you meet one, you become dependent on him, even more so the more difficult it was to find him: the entire balance is that much more delicate.

'No,' says Harriet, 'it's not easy to be a great spirit in this world of petty middleweights.'

'Oh yuck. I'm actually not placing any kind of moral judgement on it. It's a strictly statistical argument I'm trying to present, to show that an independent person is more dependent than others.'

'So you're not saying that you're more remarkable than others, then? But you're more interesting in any event, aren't you? You have to at least admit that it's an advantage to be equipped with such an unusual ability to see through people, such X-ray vision.'

'On the contrary – that's the greatest curse of all. It doesn't help to be a master at inventing life lies when I can see through them all the time, more rapidly than I can produce them.'

'But there must be a certain entertainment value to it anyway, right?'

'Then that's the only value I can attribute to myself for the moment. But at what cost!

'Why can't I be like people in novels?' I ask. 'So exemplary, I mean. Clean and consistent and an *illustration* of something or other. Every time I think I've figured out what I'm an illustration of, like corruption in the myth of the one great love or something like that, then I discover that it's actually the opposite. And the other way around. There's no *tendency* in my story. The tendency in my life is like a compass needle – it points in all possible directions. Shoestring and daughter-in-law and camel and broomstick.'

'Then I guess you'll have to decide that this is what you're an example of.'

I laugh, truly delighted at the idea. 'How practical you are! "Prey to conflicting emotions", of course!'

'That's one way of saying it, if you want to be in a pulp fiction novel. To be a wandering cliché, is that really something to strive for?'

'I just want my Fate to Illuminate something, to find some kind of order to what's happening. Reality is so messy.'

'I thought you meant that you feel less lonely if you're like someone in a novel.'

'Not exactly. But more real.'

'Is that truly something to strive for?'

*

'You should take care not to become sad – once you've started, it will never end,' the poet Harriet Löwenhjelm writes.

I understand this when I come out to Tynningö for the third time, after having fetched more books and a radio: the place is already imprinted by my sadness. The road up from the steam-boat dock is a heavy way. The garden around the cottage looks gloomy. The old wooden building has a special smell. I recognize it as I unlock the door, and I think it smells like unhappiness.

There's no point in searching for new environments if you're carrying the contagion with you, if you leave sadness behind you wherever you set your foot so that the smell of unhappiness attaches to the curtains and can't be aired out.

Once it starts, it will never end.

I sit down to read. A fine summer rain is falling and I sit at the window with a book, but I don't get anywhere. I end up looking around, mindless. I look at the ocean, the small bit of it I can see through the now fully leaved fruit trees. The branches move slightly in the wind, the clouds are gliding across the sky. I sit as you do at a train window and let life go past.

No, now a cup of coffee would taste good – I try to cheer myself – now we'll go to the kitchen and make us a cup of coffee on the camping stove. Then we'll ride down to the grocer's and buy an evening paper to sit and read on the porch at dusk, with a pipe, how does that sound, hm?

Pictures: I paint small pictures of comfort for myself to help me limp forwards hour by hour, small still lives to move into. Although I'm bad at pictures of meals – meals require several participants so that they don't simply look pathetic. Mostly there are pictures of porch scenes with coffee and a pipe.

For those, the only sad thing is that nobody sees them. Here I sit on the doorstep of the little cottage, Swedish summer is darkening towards evening, red enamel mug and a gold tobacco package, as happy a picture as I can ever create. And it's completely wasted.

★

I can't work in such an undisturbed state. I should have remembered that. I try to create the perfect disturbance, like that time on the Island, but this time allowing the radio to report the news in Finnish and Serbo-Croatian. But it's distracting despite the fact that I don't understand anything, because suddenly recognizable names pop up in an incomprehensible harangue – Papadopoulos, Le Duc Tho, Mururoa – and my ears perk up reflexively, duped into believing they'll understand what's to follow as well.

I can't settle down. I go into town without even inventing a reason, go out again and it's nobody's business. Nobody knows when I'm going or when I come back. I go from one home to the other, from my apartment in town to the cottage in the archipelago – between Me and Me.

Is this punishment for my sins? As in Dante's *Inferno*, adapted to the type of sin: the egotist left alone for eternity. Whosoever wishes to save their life ('*psyche* is the word used, which is closer rather to oneself') . . .

To be honest, I don't feel uncomfortable in my own company, I've never done so before. It's not being alone that's terrible, it's being without Gustav. And since Gustav could have been with me, without Gustav is what I am when I'm alone, every single day.

When I look at myself from the outside, I can do nothing but shudder: the image of myself as alone is such a pitiful image, and it can't be denied that it looks meaningless in a horrible way, all that I'm doing alone.

This travelling between me and me.

But if it's so hard for me – someone who likes being alone – how is it then for those who don't like it? They are many.

I begin to realize how many there are: in the papers, I've discovered that the letters from readers are echoing with cries for help. The woman who writes that she was married for twenty-six years, has been a widow for ten, and can't get used to the loneliness so she's reaching out for a 'life partner'. Ten years! Ten years *during which you don't get used to it!*

Or the newly divorced man who says that he simply can't go to the shops on Friday, seeing all the families making their weekend purchases and remembering . . .

I recognize this with growing rage. If there are so many, how can it be that it's considered an abnormality? Every third household in Sweden consists of only one person (I looked it up!) and there are three million households: one million singles. Where is this million? Are they hiding in their shame behind closed curtains, never raising their voices except in the contact notices through which they hope to become transformed into normal members of society?

They say that the seventh year of a marriage is the hardest. Which one is the worst in a divorce? How much worse can it get?

The fact that everything reminds me of him – I thought that would dissipate over time. But it's just the opposite: more and more things do, until everything, literally everything, leads me there. My own flat is full of chairs he's sat in, doorways he's walked through, words that were said here and there. Things he's given me, for example the Vietnamese ink drawing he gave me on my last birthday (I mean, on the last birthday before our divorce). It tortured me so much that I took it down. But it didn't help: whether I left the spot empty or put up something else, it only reminded me of what wasn't there, and why. The Meerschaum pipe from Paris remained in his possession, but it functions as a 'souvenir' just as relentlessly because of its absence.

All the places he's been to remind me of him. All the places where he hasn't been are 'places where he hasn't been'. This country place: I would like to show it to him. It's not particularly similar to the Island – the flora here in the interior archipelago is lusher – but the grass is green and the cottages red and the sea blue, just as over there, and it's enough for me to make the association with it constantly. I would like to show him the place, take him around and tell him about it. I talk to myself all the time, formulate and memorize as if it were a question of remembering it until I see him.

The other night I dreamed he was here. We lay together in the garden, in the grass that was so tall that it hid us from passers-by. It was hard to wake up.

Last night I dreamed that I told him that dream.

And tonight? This could continue ad infinitum.

Reading books is no escape, either. Either they're books he's talked about, or they're books I don't know if he's read and would like to know what he might have to say about them. I hardly dare turn on the radio any longer. It's not just the Swedish top-hits nagging about love that's insufferable; nowadays I can't even listen to the *weather report* without bursting into tears when Öland and Gotland are mentioned.

The last time I was in town, I caught a glimpse of Torsten at an outdoor café next to the city library. I had the urge to go up and talk to him, but I was put off my stride when I discovered why: what I was seeing in Torsten was a-person-that-Gustav-has-been-jealous-of. It was for the sake of this connection – this fragile connection: they've never met, they've only heard each other mentioned, and I never even had a true affair with him – Gustav was only half-betrayed. So the person with whom Gustav was half-betrayed interests me more than any other person on earth – it's like when you're newly in love and everything that has any connection to the object of your affections takes on a sort of numinous aura.

But I'm not looking for it, like you do when you're newly in love. I try to escape – it's just that the associations won't leave me in peace. The suntan lotion was about to ruin me. When I bought the bottle, it didn't occur to me that it was the same kind we usually had on the first boat tours of the year so that we wouldn't burn our spring-pale skin to a crisp. It isn't until I've rubbed it onto my shoulders and stretched out on my bathrobe that the scent of Delial on sun-warmed skin shocks me with such a physically intense feeling of being transported to the StarBoat on Grindafjärd that it's unbearable. I have to dash out into the water to wash it off and I toss the yellow bottle in the rubbish; I'll have to try another brand or do without.

But how am I ever supposed to keep from thinking about Gustav when my own person reminds me of him? I can't look in the mirror without seeing that it's Gustav's ex. I can't comb my hair without remembering the time I sat between his knees at Kastellholmen and he untangled my hair so patiently (and I angrily tug so that tufts waft down to the floor). I can't take off my trousers without thinking about how he declared his love for my stubby legs; I can't see them without being overcome with sympathy for these no-longer-beloved ones.

Time moves on, but the only change is that there's more and more that reminds me of him in the most excruciating way: by not reminding me of him.

*

The sun beats down all through July – it's a hot summer. The sound is full of sailboats.

It's idiotic, settling near the sea where every white sail is a stab to the heart (or rather, a cramp in my stomach although it sounds too naturalistic). I constantly have the impression that I'm seeing his boat out there, and I sit peering to make out the marks on the sail. I don't know where he is; after our most recent encounter, we once again agreed not to have any contact since I couldn't handle it. So now I'm sitting here wondering instead.

How idiotic. I move around on the porch and sit with my back towards the shore so I won't see. Why did I want to be near the water anyway? The peace of the great forests, I think, that's where I should have gone.

Fortunately I have my bicycle, and riding is the only activity cool enough in the heat, except for lying and splashing in the water, which becomes monotonous after a while. I can take the ferry both to Rindö and over to Värmdölandet. I go off on an excursion and ride all the way to a church.

I sit on a bench and drink cold juice from a thermos. I wander around the cemetery and stop at a tombstone with an unusual inscription. At the top it says 'Hilda Andersson' – without a year, someone still living? – and underneath:

Mina makar

Oskar • 1892 † 1931

Viktor • 1888 † 1959

My mates, I reflect. Spouses. Can you have more than one? Doesn't the word 'mate' imply that it's half of a pair, or does it simply mean that you belong to each other? You can belong to several people – of course you can.

This unconventional idea appeals to me. Having your husbands collected under the same monument, under your own name. All those whom I have called mine. Oh please, no mass grave for my sake, you wouldn't need an obelisk to have enough room for the names. Something in an appropriate <u>family size</u>, that's all, for my most dearly beloved. After death, they should all be able to get along. Wouldn't that be lovely? And I wouldn't have to run hither and thither with white lilies, either.

I squat next to the grave and think, and I don't have to think very long to find the fly in the ointment here: those to whom I have belonged have in turn belonged to others, who have just as much right to want to host them under their names. Someone could even propose forming a family grave with me instead of the other way around. The vision of a monument with the inscription 'My mates' and 'Martina' in a column of eighty concubines doesn't appeal to me one bit.

This is how all good unconventional ideas are defeated. A couple is a couple is a couple, there's only room for two. If this is what 'mate' means, I wouldn't want it set in stone that I believe a couple has room for three – an unmathematical monument.

There's a phone booth down by the road; I call Harriet.

'Get your etymological dictionary, but quickly. I've only got a few coins.'

She disappears to go get it, returns after quite a while and asks, 'What do you want me to look up? Where are you, anyway? What are you doing?'

The phone is already buzzing to say that the coins are used up.

'I'm out riding my bike and wondering what will be on my tombstone,' I explain but don't have time to say the whole sentence before our conversation is broken off.

*

There has to be an end to it at some point – all imaginable thoughts exhausted. But I can't see any development. My moods move in succession without any logical context.

There's one that smiles gently, maternally indulgent: Have you finally got what you wanted now, a fine and stable family life? Well, about time. God bless you, you deserve it.

And the other way around, the irritation: How the fuck was that necessary? The tone you use with a friend who's caused some trouble that you don't appreciate – light irritation, absurdly inadequate in proportion to the significance of what it's about. The same feeling of incomprehension as you can have when someone dies, at news that a friend's been in an accident: 'Was this really necessary?'

Now and again, moments when I realize: the great panic. Mostly at night, mostly when I wake up and at the edge of awakening, I have a momentary insight. The panicked cry, 'No! It can't be!' – the impulse to spring up and put things to rights, call on all the powers of heaven and hell to help correct the dreadful error that has occurred – 'Go back, it doesn't *count*' – and the anxiety that this help will not be given.

Followed by headlong aggressiveness. The feeling of being betrayed in the most egregious way: How can he allow himself to belong to someone else after belonging to me – it's unforgiveable! It must actually mean that he never was my mate. He was simply pretending. The feeling of alienation: Gustav, who is that, what does he have to do with me? The urge to deny, to dispute everything that's been, to take back every bit of myself that he's received, for the idea that it's in the hands of a complete stranger is insufferable . . .

And then the tedium. That when nobody else cares about you, you can't bring yourself to care about yourself, either. This paralysing tedium: nothing is worth doing when there isn't anyone to do it with. No book worth reading, no country worth seeing, without someone to talk to about it.

You might believe that once I've gone through all of these, that I'd be finished. But no: that's when the performance begins da capo.

37

'You had a phone call,' Tomas says when I get back from lunch, 'Gustav Lindberg or something like that.'

Lindgren. Gustav Lindgren.

'Did he say what he wanted?'

'No, but I said that you'd be going home after lunch, so he could call you there.'

Of course he couldn't say precisely what it was about. We've avoided each other since the spring, and if he's looking for me now, then either his relationship with The Other has ended, or it's news of the kind we previously agreed we wouldn't let each other find out about among the family notices in the newspaper.

How long is he going to let me swing between these two possibilities?

I take the elevator down, get my bike from the car park and pedal off towards downtown. There's a headwind but the air is clear and nice. After each weekend, more boats have been moved away from the docks along Brunnsviken to their wooden stands on land – soon there won't be any left in the water.

At Norrtull I cross over the Stallmästaregården area to reach the main road and almost collide with a truck full of park benches on their way in to winter storage. I brake at the last moment and have time to smile reassuringly at the terrified driver.

Finally summer is over. As late as October there have been

relapses, but now dead leaves whirl on the streets. Now it's definitely over, and may there never be another summer.

I think about what I was supposed to be getting done this afternoon – go to the Post Office and pay my rent, wash my hair, finish polishing the manuscript for the chapter that will be discussed at the seminar; the Post Office will have to wait, I'm riding directly home now. He must know that I'm waiting.

Apparently he does – the phone rings one minute after I've got through the door. My heart pounds after my dash up the stairs.

'Yes?'

'Martina? It's Gustav.'

'Clearly. Tell me quickly what it's about. Family news, apparently?'

'Yes, you said that you wanted to know . . .'

'No details, just answer my questions. Born or died, married or divorced?'

'None of those yet, but we've decided to legalize our relationship. And we're going to have a baby. I don't suppose anyone will believe that we had decided to marry before we knew, but we had.'

'Martina? You're not saying anything.'

'I'm still here. But what do you want me to say?'

'What are you thinking?'

'I'm thinking about what I have to do this afternoon.'

I'm thinking that I want someone to talk to, or not talk to, because what is there to say? But I would like to have someone here.

'You don't think you could come over for a bit, do you?'

He hesitates, and I add quickly:

'I'm not going to make things difficult, if that's what you're afraid of. I don't intend to present any obstacles to your marriage or make a scene or anything like that. I think I just want to see you one last time as a free man, if you understand.'

'By all means, I'm pretty sure I dare to look you in the eye. But I'm going to eat lunch here first, so it'll take an hour or so. Why don't you make us some coffee?'

An hour or so. I put on my duffle coat and walk down to the Post Office, admiring my composure.

The wind is blowing. The leaves are falling. It's over now. Now nothing can become any more difficult than it is.

'So I wasn't the one who would bear his children.' No, have I ever believed it? Never seriously, I'm not the child-bearing type.

But Gustav's going to be a father. That snatches him away – that makes him so alien that it's almost beyond the pain threshold. That he's going to have a baby without me.

I remember a passage from Vonnegut's *Slaughterhouse-Five*, a fantasy about a planet on which it took seven different genders to create a baby. I think that what I would wish for is something like that: that more genders than theirs had been needed, that I would also have been needed. That I was part of it. Now I'm not even there as a small shadow in the right corner any more.

On the way back, I buy bread and milk. I make coffee and set out the cups before I sit down to read. When I hear his clogs in the stairway, I put in a pipe cleaner to mark my spot and go to open the door. Don't make it hard on him – I've promised that. And as it happens, it's not needed, since it turns out that it's *not* easy for him, either. He fumbles for a handkerchief and blows his nose standing there in my room. I look at him, distrustful – is it a cold? But apparently it's not.

'Oh I see,' I exclaim, 'am I the one who's to comfort you perhaps?'

'Yes please.'

I think for a moment and say, 'Your old parents will be happy. That you're finally going to be properly married.'

He mumbles, 'Yes, yes, they will.'

'If it won't make you happy yourself, then I don't think you should do it,' I say matter-of-factly. 'You shouldn't marry just for the child's sake if you weren't going to do it anyway.'

'We were going to do it anyway, I told you.'

'All right then, but then you must put your heart into it too. Whatever you do, do it with fervour . . .'

I burst out laughing. 'Damn, now we're in the middle of this absurd play again. I'm standing here saying your lines. I don't know why I should have to pluck up your old values and preach them to you. Sit down now and I'll get you some coffee.'

He sits down and looks around the room for a little while before saying anything.

'I'm happy about it – both about getting married and about becoming a father. It was just that I got so nostalgic on my way here. I must have been suffering from that vice you've always had, idealizing at a distance – you've got such an aura around you. It's so strange not to have seen you for so long, as if you didn't exist.'

'I exist,' I say calmly, 'and I intend to keep doing so, if that's any comfort to you.'

The fact that he is emotional makes me so calm. Confidence and strength stream into me from his weakness – a temporary weakness to be sure, and a strength just as temporary, but it makes these minutes easier.

'It occurred to me that if *you* went and got married, I would naturally react like Kierkegaard when Regine Olsen married Schlegel,' he muses.

'What did Kierkegaard do?'

'First he saw to it that their engagement was broken off and then he was incredibly upset that she married someone else, wrote a lot of bitter books about the faithlessness of women. When he died fifteen years later, by the way, he bequeathed his entire fortune to her, but it turned out to be just a few bottles of wine.'

'If I leave any wine bottles, I'll be happy to bequeath them to you, but I'll probably never be that wealthy. They'll be empties, possibly. And I don't think I'll be writing any bitter books.'

'Aren't you bitter?'

'Not at you. I'm bitter at life, which created us for each other but did it so poorly that we didn't fit together.

'Although it's obvious,' I add hastily, 'I think most of the fault lay with you.'

'Do you mean that it didn't have to end like this?'

'I can say whatever you want in order to comfort you except for this: that you wouldn't have been able to have me. This past year I've had so many insights that you could have called me and got me to City Hall with ten minutes' notice.'

'You shouldn't marry your passion. And you can't treat other people that way, as tools to get slow-witted people like you to understand what it's all about. And besides, ten minutes would have been enough time for you to change your mind. We wouldn't even have got as far as Fridhemsplan.'

'Oh so many good reasons. Do you need that many?'

'Isn't it true? Wouldn't you have changed your mind?'

'By all means. Whether I had married or not, I would have repined to death. But that it couldn't have been the two of us – I don't intend to ever say that to comfort you. Anything but that.'

'Say something else, then. What would it be?'

'Well, I can say that we can see each other anyway, or that we cannot see each other, I can give you my blessing, or my curse, precisely as you wish. I can say that we'll have each other in heaven. Or what do you think, maybe there won't be any of that in heaven?'

He sits playing with his spoon, trying to get it to balance on the handle.

'I'd always imagined that we'd spend our old age together.'

'But there's a thousand years till then, or in any event thirty. A lot can happen in a thousand years, or thirty.'

'You mean that some day when our children are grown and my wife has left me and your lovers have all died off, then we can move in together at the old folks' home?'

'Then we can devote our final days to a nostalgic depiction of all the years together that we've missed out on. And to arguing about whose fault it was.'

He laughs. 'So nice to hear that you haven't changed.'

'Likewise.'

We drink our coffee and talk about other things – about the cinema repertoire and books we've read, about what we did last summer and about the demonstrations on Wednesday against the Norwegian parliament's decision to award the Peace Prize to Kissinger.

'It's really the joke of the year.'

'It wouldn't even succeed as a joke – it's too sick.'

'Marching to the Norwegian Embassy will be a new experience in any event, even for habitual demonstrators.'

'Yes, there's been no reason to go there before, as far as I can remember.'

He goes over to the window and looks out – it's started to rain, a sudden and heavy shower. He waits as it passes. I sit peering at him: I realize I'm looking for physical signs that he's pregnant.

'I'll expect a cigar from you.'

It takes a moment before he gets it, and then he laughs, 'Of course.'

'When will it be?'

'The doctor says the beginning of April.'

When he leaves, I make an errand to the newsstand simply so I don't have to sit alone when he goes. I'd rather part on the street.

'Does it feel less nostalgic now?' I ask on our way down the stairs. 'Did my aura disappear when you saw me?'

'Oh yes, it feels much better. You exist in any event, that's the main thing.'

I nod, yes, I promise you.

'I'll exist as long as I live.'

The light changes at the crossing and I step down from the pavement. He raises both hands – a strange gesture, a cross between a wave and a blessing, or as if he were opening his arms in surrender. He says nothing – his entire face expresses that this is a farewell for which there are no words, his entire person a resigned manifestation of it.

He heads home; I cross the street to buy an evening paper.